READ WHAT FANS AC
ARE SAYING

VOL. 1: PROLOGUE.

"An amazing book. . . . The whole story was great, but the ending gave me goose-bumps and the best feeling inside. Can't wait for the next volume."

—Hila Hopkins

"Thought-provoking and compelling. . . . I love the way it has caused me to think differently about my mission on earth and to look at my husband and children in a different light."

—Hillary Johnson

"It feels so real. . . . It is so intriguing, readers will keep turning the pages until the very end."

—Brenda Ramsbacher, President, Reviewers International, Scribblers

VOL. 2: WHERE ANGELS FALL

"This book is incredible! It broadens the spectrum from just our mortal scope and makes readers contemplate our place on the eternal battlefield. The plot is suspenseful, the characters are believable, and the setting is one of the most changing and oftentimes contentious areas of our world: the Middle East."

—Kaleb Valdez

"An edge-of-your-seat thriller. . . . I can't wait for volume 3 to be published. . . . I have read the *Left Behind* series and this series is shaping up to be far better."

—Mike Heiner

"It's a rare author who can spin a heart-gripping, page-turning story while at the same time filling it with truths about the things that really matter from an eternal perspective. Chris Stewart has done a masterful job. . . . I stayed up all night to finish it and then was mad that it was over!"

—Emily Watts

PRAISE FOR CHRIS STEWART

Shattered Bone

"Stewart writes with . . . Clancy's knack for spinning a thrilling global techno yarn."

—*CNN Sunday Morning*, Off The Shelf

"A new techno-thriller star has been launched. If you enjoy books where the action starts with a bang on the first page and ends with a bang on the last, you'll devour Shattered Bone."

—*Tulsa World*

The Kill Box

"A thriller writer who knows how to deliver."

—*Flint Michigan Journal*

"The plot builds to a page-flipping climax."

—*Booklist*

The Third Consequence

"His mix of fact and fiction explodes off the page with the immediacy of a live CNN war-zone video feed."

—*Publishers Weekly*

"Fast and furious. The author writes in a crisp style and tells the story with a certain authentic touch."

—*Stars and Stripes*

The Fourth War

"Stewart's experience as a fighter pilot comes into play in vivid flying scenes . . . but the scope of his ambitious fourth thriller is much larger. . . . Many of the novel's surprising details feel entirely authentic. . . . Stewart is impressively skilled at presenting the entire tapestry of his war—the many threads of the terrorist, allied and American forces—and should hold his readers' interest."

—*Publishers Weekly*

THE SECOND SUN

THE GREAT AND TERRIBLE SERIES

by
Chris Stewart

VOLUME 1
Prologue: The Brothers

VOLUME 2
Where Angels Fall

VOLUME 3
The Second Sun

VOLUME 4
Fury and Light

VOLUME 5
From the End of Heaven

VOLUME 6
Clear as the Moon

THE GREAT AND TERRIBLE
VOLUME 3

THE SECOND SUN

CHRIS STEWART

First printing in hardbound 2005.
First printing in paperbound 2010.

Visit us at DeseretBook.com

Library of Congress Cataloging-in-Publication Data

Stewart, Chris, 1960–
The second sun / Chris Stewart.
p. cm. — (The great and terrible ; v. 3)
ISBN-10: 1-59038-486-5 (hardbound: alk. paper)
ISBN-13: 978-1-59038-486-2 (hardbound: alk. paper)
ISBN-13: 978-1-60641-684-6 (paperbound)
1. Terrorism—Fiction. I. Title. II. Series: Stewart, Chris, 1960– .
Great and terrible ; v. 3.
PS3569.T4593S43 2005
813'.54—dc22 2005021136

Printed in the United States of America 72076
R. R. Donnelley, Harrisonburg, VA

15 14 13

To my brothers—
the truest friends a man could ever have.

is born Azadeh Ishbel Pahlavi, only child of Rassa Ali Pahlavi, grandson of the last Shah of Persia. Her mother, Sashajan, dies within twenty-four hours of her birth, but she lives a happy childhood, raised by a loving father. Everyone who knows her recognizes a special quality that she possesses, a sort of radiance or spiritual maturity that sets her apart. Lucifer's followers find her, and the adversary sends one of his mortal servants to murder her, but she is protected by Teancum, a heavenly messenger sent by the Father to preserve her life so she can fulfill her mission on earth.

Crown Prince Saud, heir to the throne of Saudi Arabia, also finds the Pahlavi family. Recognizing how precarious his own situation has become, he forms a desperate plan to seek help from them if the need should arise. He also contacts his friend in the United States, Major General Neil S. Brighton, asking to meet him during his upcoming trip to Saudi Arabia.

General Brighton, newly appointed as military liaison to the National Security Advisor, feels the weight of his assignment and the price it exacts from his wife, Sara, and their twin sons, Ammon and Luke. The boys are doing all right, basically on course with mission preparations despite a lively lifestyle. Neil wishes he could say the same for Sam, the foster son he and Sara have adopted as their own. Sam's abusive birth parents have made his road difficult, and even the love of the Brightons is not sufficient to give him a testimony of God's love for him. Instead of going on a mission, he chose to join the army, and now he serves in an elite Delta unit specializing in covert missions in the most dangerous regions of the world.

Neil Brighton travels to Saudi Arabia, and during his meeting with Prince Saud, a servant comes running to raise an alarm. A "Firefall" has been called—code for an assault on the royal family. Too late to help, Prince Saud learns that his wife and children have been assassinated, the first step in Prince

Abdullah's plan to take over the leadership of his country. Prince Saud flees with his second wife and his only remaining son, a boy of four, taking them by helicopter to Iran and consigning them secretly to the care of his distant cousin Rassa Ali Pahlavi, Azadeh's father. On the way back, his helicopter is fired upon, and he barely has time to get a Mayday message out, pleading for Neil Brighton to rescue his son, before missiles destroy the chopper. Abdullah's spies intercept the message, and the race is on to find the last son of Prince Saud. What no one knows is that Rassa has persuaded his powerful friend, Omar, to smuggle the princess and her child out of the region.

Soon the mercenaries of Prince Abdullah flood into the valley of Agha Jari Deh, seeking the young prince and the man Rassa. When Rassa refuses to surrender the boy, they burn him to death before Azadeh's eyes and begin the grim task of killing all the young boys in the village, as well as any of the villagers who oppose them. Their work is interrupted by the sudden arrival of American soldiers—Sam's unit—dispatched to help Prince Saud's son. The Deltas frighten off the remaining enemy soldiers, but they are too late to do much good. Destruction and carnage are everywhere, and they hold out no real hope of finding the royal child they have come to rescue. After a quick assessment of the situation, the captain orders them back to the choppers, but on his way, Sam feels an impression that someone needs his help. He turns back to see Azadeh and feels instantly that he knows her somehow. As his platoon leader pulls him away, he calls to her to find her way to Khorramshahr, a refugee camp on the Iran/Iraq border, where he promises to have someone find her.

Prince Abdullah, spurred on by Lucifer himself, continues his plan for the destruction of all his enemies, beginning with his father and expanding to include the United States. The

*"All the people upon the face of the land
were shedding blood,
and there was none to restrain them."*
—Ether 13:31

*"The blood-dimmed tide is loosed
and everywhere the ceremony of innocence is drowned."*
—W. B. Yeats

chapter one

AGHA JARI DEH VALLEY
EASTERN IRAN

Azadeh Ishbel Pahlavi sat on the cracked stone and cement steps of her father's house and looked west. The smell of acidic smoke still drifted in the air. Behind her, she heard one of the villagers, a stranger, rummaging through what remained of their kitchen, scavenging for any pots and pans that may have been left behind. Azadeh knew the thin woman wouldn't find anything worth keeping; too many others had already picked their way through what remained of her father's house.

Some of the scavengers had been people she knew, even a few family friends, but most had been people from the other side of the village whom she did not know well. Each had done the same thing: approach her devastated house and pass her on the steps, ignoring her altogether, as if she weren't there, then rummage through her belongings and haul away a few possessions without so much as a word.

There was a small crash as the stranger in the kitchen picked up a piece of pottery and dropped it, the sound of broken clay scattering across the wooden floor. Azadeh heard another crash and more broken clay, but she didn't react, her face remaining passionless and calm. She leaned back against the cold brick, listening to the final looting that was taking place in her house. It was nearly all gone, everything they had owned, every piece of furniture, every item of food, the kitchen table and utensils, the coal-fired heater, small television, blankets, mattresses, her clothes, all of it had been taken. She had nothing now.

Her father was gone. All her family. She was nothing. She had nothing. She was the same thing as dead.

Looking west, she had a clear view to the sea, the afternoon sun high, the terrain falling gently before her, the gradual slope of the valley dropping toward the salty waters of the Gulf. Behind the village, the mountains rose, gray granite, white snow. The trees were green in the valley, and the orchards along the river were covered in heavy blossoms, some of the early varieties close to bearing fruit. The sky was clear, and all the remaining villagers were out and working: preparing for the burials, tending the young bodies, cleaning up the debris, patching the bullet holes in the walls, sweeping up broken glass. Some had even started the work of rebuilding or repairing the damage done to their homes.

Hundreds of people worked around her.

But Azadeh sat alone.

DHAHRAN ROYAL PALACE
DHAHRAN, SAUDI ARABIA

Six hundred miles to the east, Crown Prince Abdullah al-Rahman leaned over his father's deathbed. A small mirror had been placed on the gold-draped nightstand, and, uncomfortable with touching a body that was so near to death, he took the mirror and placed it near his father's mouth. It misted, but barely, and he set it back in place. Standing upright, he looked around the enormous bedroom, with all of its leather, jewel-studded ornaments, fine art, and gold. To his right the *kafan,* a perfect cotton shroud, had been neatly folded and placed at the foot of the bed, waiting to cover the king's body once he was dead. A beautiful mahogany box had been placed on the shroud, and Abdullah could smell the fragrance and incense that were waiting inside. The funeral, or *Janazah,* would take place later in the day, before the sun had gone down. After being washed, his father's body would be wrapped in the shroud, his face turned toward Mecca, and the final prayers said.

Abdullah thought it ironic, and he couldn't help but smile, a dreadful twist of his lips at the corners of his mouth. Martyrs were to be buried as they had died: in their clothes, their bodies bloody and unwashed, their faces covered with the dirt of their battle, their open wounds bearing testimony to their martyrdom, and, if they had been so lucky as to die while defending the faith, their weapons placed in their hands. The king would not be given such an honor.

The new crown prince glanced again at the box of incense and the washcloths that had been placed near the bed, knowing that his father's body would be cleansed when he was finally dead, then wrapped in the white cloth and placed in the grave.

There would be no martyr's honor for his father, no bloody hands or dirty clothes, no open wounds or heavy weapons placed inside his cold hands. There would be no glory or salvation in his death.

But the truth was, his father *would* die a martyr, though no one would ever know. His father's wounds would never testify of his martyrdom, for they were internal and unseen, like the blackness and corruption that had cankered his soul.

That was what happened when one died for the wrong cause.

The crown prince scoffed, an angry huff of his breath. *Democracy and equality.* What had gone through his father's mind? Were these the tools Allah had intended for his kings? Were these the concepts the Great Prophet had taught? No. Not a one. And surely his father knew that. Which made him a heretic. No, he was much worse than that, for a heretic could sin in ignorance, a heretic could be foolish or blind. His father had not been deceived; he had knowingly chosen his path. He might have been a traitor, but he was no fool.

Abdullah thought back on what the old man, his true mentor, had told him the first time they had met, that day long ago on the beach in southern France. It had been a long time before, but it still seemed so near that even now he could feel the heat of the afternoon sun. He could still smell the seaweed and hear the soft lap of the sea. And he could hear the words of the old man as if he were still standing there: *"You might as well say the sun comes up in the west as to call your father a fool. The king is a visionary. And the most dangerous kind."*

The old man had been right. His father had been a visionary, and yes, the most dangerous kind. He had poisoned his family with his visions of democracy, which left Prince Abdullah no choice.

So Abdullah had killed him. But there was no sin in that. Not after what his father and his brother had set out to do. Abdullah thought of the poison surging through his father's veins, turning his organs black. As he stared into his father's face, watching him die, he felt not a twinge of uncertainty nor a hint of doubt or remorse. He felt no sadness or guilt.

But then Abdullah had never felt a moment of guilt in his life.

He stared at his father, watching his lips turn from blue to gray. "What did it get you, my father?" he mumbled in a low voice. "What did your riches buy you? What your power, what your fame? In the end it brought you nothing; it could not even protect you. It brought you nothing but shame. But I will not squander it, my father. I will not squander our ancestors' great power or their wealth. I will use it; I will build it; I will see my will done. I will pick up the battle of our fathers and build upon the legacy of the last thousand years."

The king of Saudi Arabia took a deep breath and struggled to move, his hand lifting half an inch off the bed.

Abdullah's smile turned into a deep frown, and he lowered his head. He knew that a dying man's hearing was the last sense to go, so he leaned toward his father and whispered. "Can you hear me, Father?" he asked him. "I know that you can."

The old king struggled, lifting his hand again. The prince smiled at the motion and placed his mouth right up to the old man's ear, feeling the heat of his skin on his lips. As he spoke his voice changed, as if another man were there. "It has started, my father," he whispered in a soft, evil hiss. "There is no turning back. You might as well lift your hand to stop the sunrise as to bring an end to this plan. Like your own death, it is inevitable. The endgame is set, and there's nothing you could do now, even were you to live. The age of the West is fading, giving way to a dark power again. A new day is dawning, a day of deep secrets and powerful men, an age of dark miracles, dreadful rumors, and a red, sinking moon, a day of a bright flash on the horizon that does not come from the sun. It will be an age of power and oppression far greater than has ever fallen on the earth. Even as I whisper to you, Father, even as my breath touches your ears, the final battle has begun. The sun is setting on the frail world you have known. It is passing, and with its passing, the greater kingdom shall come.

"You have lost this war, Father. You have failed in your plan. And your dreams are fading along with your breath. But

I will pick up the blade for you, Father, and I will fight for the right cause. I will pick up the battle that you were too weak to fight, and I will build up the kingdom that you sought to destroy.

"So go now, my father. Go to my brother. Go to your wife and your children as well. Go to those who are waiting, be they in paradise or hell. Go and tell them you have failed, but I will not fail them too."

The crown prince, soon to be king, paused and lifted his head. He was finished. It was all he had to say. So he straightened himself and stared at his father's gray face, then heard a soft movement behind him and turned to see the mullah standing there. "Say your best *Janazah* for him," Abdullah commanded the religious leader, his voice normal now. "My father has much to be forgiven for, and he will need your most compelling prayers."

FALCON 53
OVER NORTHERN IRAQ

Army Special Forces Sergeant Samuel Brighton sat on the chopper floor near the door, his feet pulled up, elbows on his knees, his chin resting wearily on his folded arms. He was surrounded by his men, but most of them were asleep, their heads and shoulders slumped in exhaustion. He turned to look out the open cargo door of the chopper, feeling the cool air raise the hairs on his neck. Behind him and to his right, three other choppers followed their leader through the night, their navigation lights set to dim, the faces of the pilots reflecting the green and yellow lights of their cockpit displays. The night was dark—the moon had gone down, and dawn was still another forty minutes away—but the air was clear, a cold front having moved through and blown the dust from the sky. The starlight was enough for him to see by, his eyes having had hours to adjust to the dark.

Sam watched the landscape speed below him. The desert was barren, with clumps of Joshua trees and dry grass clinging desperately to the banks of the dry wadi walls, the same ancient rivers that had run through Iraq since the days of Babylon. The *Wadi at Tubal* passed directly below, erratic trenches that had been scratched into the earth as if by enormous fingernails, and he could see occasional pools of shallow water reflecting the starlight along the bends and narrow turns in the sandy streambed. The landscape continued to pass: rock, sand, a few trees here and there.

Staring at the desolation, he wondered again. *This* place was the cradle of civilization. *This* was where it had all begun. Four thousand years had come and gone, and *this* was the place men had chosen to fight and die for again and again. *This* was the place that had produced so much bloodshed and so many wars.

"Let them have it," he muttered to himself. "There is nothing here worth fighting for. Certainly nothing worth dying for." But even as he grumbled, he felt a quick twinge of guilt. The people here were as desperate as the landscape: bone dead and dry, struggling like the desert as they clung to life, hoping for rain, hoping for time, hoping the next day would be better than the day that had passed.

He hated it here. It was so desperate and lonely. It caused a blackness in his heart.

But the people were trying—at least a majority of them were. And he was doing some good, so he would try not to complain.

The lead chopper turned thirty degrees, making the final turn to Camp Freedom, the base camp that was his home now and for the next several months. As the chopper leveled out,

Sam was left to face the eastern horizon and he gazed through the darkness, looking across the barren terrain.

It was out there, far away, the little village in the mountains, south and east now, a few degrees off his right. Across the *Sara al Hijarah* and the northern tip of the Gulf. All the massacred children, the fires, the destroyed houses and the burned tree.

All of it was out there.

And she was out there as well.

He thought of her face, dirty and streaked with tears. He thought of her eyes and her trembling shoulders. He thought of her hands, clasped so tightly at her chest. She was so young. So small. And so beautiful.

But that wasn't the reason he couldn't get her out of his mind.

"I knew you," he whispered again to himself. "I knew you . . . somewhere. I know that I did." He rubbed his hand across his eyes, keeping his eyes looking east. "This veil . . . this veil my mother spoke of . . . "

Was it possible that in the last days it would grow thin?

It was crazy, and he knew it. It was impossible. She was just another girl, another victim, another casualty that would be forgotten when the next battle began.

But there was *something* about her. . . .

So Sam stared through the darkness, thinking of the mountains of Iran, knowing that she was out there and knowing just as surely that he would never see her again.

Somewhere in the desert of western Iraq

He stood alone as the sun rose, clinging to the last of the dark. He was a tall figure, his shoulders broad, his arms powerful. He closed his eyes as he waited, facing where the sun would soon rise, the last of the moonlight casting a pale glimmer on his face and forming a shadow under his heavy brow.

He stood unmoving, a great form in the dark, a shimmering statue against the coming sun.

He was the Son of the Morning, the Prince of this World. And he was incredibly powerful.

Balaam and the others waited behind him. From where they stood, with his cloak and hood hiding his pale skin and sick eyes, the Master still looked majestic, perhaps even beautiful. But Balaam had seen him up close, and he knew it wasn't true. The Master could be handsome, yes; he could show a face of beauty and great splendor when he was forced to. Balaam cursed, almost laughing, knowing that when the Master showed himself to mortals he could even still force a smile. But like a reflection on shallow water, there was no substance to his beauty, no heart and no soul. Up close, the Master's skin had grown pale, dead and yellow and cold. And it had turned soft and supple, as if it might slough off, like a costume of skin that was no longer attached to his soul. Even his eyes shimmered yellow, like those of a sick animal.

His master was miserable. Balaam knew that. And his fellow demons knew it as well.

Yes, he could work miracles to deceive or appear as an angel of light; he could cite scripture to make the mortals think they were on the right course while he soothed and manipulated and cursed and controlled. He could stir secret combinations and murder and sinister works in the dark.

But he could never be happy. It was impossible. He was a dismal wretch, dark and ugly and perfectly miserable. And he was condemned to his misery for the rest of all time, condemned to a body of spirit, incomplete, not whole.

He was the Prince of Darkness, the Accuser, standing to watch a warm sun rise that he would never feel. The day would dawn bright and sunny, but he would remain in the dark, his day as cold and dismal as the death of a child.

Standing on the edge of the desert, the Great Master glanced over his shoulder to see the last of the moon disappear, then cursed and growled, an unnatural sound in his throat. Another day had passed. Another night gone. The eastern sky was turning pink now. Another day had come.

Another day closer to *His* coming. Another day closer to the end. Time was growing short! And there was still so much to do!

He snarled again, half from rage, half from fear. A sudden panic set in.

The Enemy was shortening the days, stealing his precious time! The Enemy was quickening time. Everyone felt it. Even the mortals, in their ignorance, sensed the quickening of time that was robbing him of the opportunity to destroy the souls of all men, robbing him of the time he needed to wreak havoc and despair, robbing him of the pleasure of his famines and heartaches and wars.

He needed more time, much more time. Time to find the good ones and drag them to him.

But *He* was stealing it from him.

How he hated Him!

* * *

Behind the Great Master, his servants cowered in the shadows of the coming morn. Master Mayhem was foul now, and it scared them to be near him when he was in such a bad mood. Each day he grew more bitter, more quick to attack. So they stood as far away as they dared, out of sight, in the shadows, but always within the sound of his voice, knowing that he might call them and that they had to be ready to move.

How many spirits stood behind the Master, even he didn't

know. So many had chosen to follow him that they had never been numbered, but this much was clear: There were far more dark angels at his beckon than there were souls in the world. This meant every man, woman, and child could be tempted one-on-one, all of them receiving the personal assaults they deserved. And his angels weren't all men . . . no, there were many women on his side. The bitter female tempters had proven incredibly powerful, able to speak to the mortals in ways that even the Master didn't know, able to whisper especially dark thoughts into their mortal sisters' ears.

So behind him, in the morning, an untold number of fallen angels waited, all of them ready to move at his voice. They all felt his power. But they felt his anxiety too.

The sun finally peeked over the horizon, sending a great shaft of light across the gray sand. He stood and watched the day break, then took a long, angry breath.

Yes, he *was* the Son of the Morning. He was *so* powerful. There was much to fear from him as his majesty grew.

He smirked and turned away, turning his back on the sun.

If his enemy was shortening time, then he could work harder too. He would accelerate the battle. He would drive his angels in a fury of heat, sweat, and fear. His heart slammed like a hammer. "Go!" he hissed to his angels. "They are waking now in this part of the world. I want you waiting for them the moment they open their eyes. Do your work. Say your whispers. You all know what to do!"

WASHINGTON, D.C.

It was late in the evening when General Neil Brighton was driven home from the White House. He sat in the backseat, reading and tapping at his Blackberry, trying to respond to the insufferable amount of email he had received that day while his driver maneuvered expertly, using the HOV lane although the traffic wasn't so heavy as to slow them down anyway, it being almost midnight on the east coast. Brighton looked up occasionally to watch the passing cars as he thought, then returned to his work, thankful for a few minutes of quiet time. After receiving the third death threat in a month, he had recently been assigned a security detail, a decision that he had originally objected to but now was grateful for. It gave him time to work as he traveled to and from his office at the White House, and he had grown to be amazed at how much he could get done.

The driver pulled off 495 and turned inside the Beltway, varying his route through the side streets but generally heading south. He doubled back once, then made his way through a quiet neighborhood before coming to a stop in front of Brighton's house.

"Sir," he announced their arrival, and General Brighton looked up.

The general tapped at his PDA device, then slipped it inside his blue Air Force jacket.

"What time in the morning, sir?" the driver asked as Brighton pushed open his door.

"Plan on five," Brighton answered wearily.

"Going to sleep in, are we, sir?"

Brighton smiled. "You know, every once in a while."

The sergeant turned and rested his massive arm on the back of the passenger seat. He wasn't merely a driver, he was a security specialist, and Brighton figured the sergeant could have lifted the car and thrown it across the street, judging from the size of his arms. But he also understood that wasn't why he had been selected to the Pentagon's Special Security Detail. The sergeant had been picked for his brains, not for his muscles. It was his responsibility not just to fight his way out of trouble but to avoid getting into it, a task that demanded far more than a six-pack chest and thick arms.

Still, Brighton couldn't help but be impressed. He thought back on his and Sam's recent fight in the German bar. There wouldn't have been any trouble if this guy had been there.

His thoughts raced again, lighting on Sam, wondering where he was tonight. Then he patted the driver on the shoulder. "Thank you for the ride, Sergeant Hamilton," he said. "Sorry to keep you up so late again."

"Happy to help out, sir. But I won't be here in the morning; I've got small-arms training at the range. It will be Master Sergeant Dawson if that's okay with you, sir."

"That's fine," Brighton nodded, then stepped out of the car and made his way across the lawn. Hamilton started the engine, but the car didn't move.

The lamp on the street corner cast a weak, yellow light, and as he approached his front door, Brighton realized that he hadn't seen his house or his yard in the daylight for several weeks now. It had been going on—what?—seventeen days since he had had a day off, and his schedule was always the same: up before the day broke and home after dark.

Stepping onto the porch, he turned and nodded to Hamilton, who waved back before slowly pulling away from the curb.

Neil Brighton stood a moment, watching the car drive away. It was cool, fall was coming on, and the evening air was not as heavy and humid as it had been just a week before. A dozen tiny moths flirted with the porch light that Sara had left on for him, but the front door was locked and he reached into his pocket to pull out his keys. Unlocking the deadbolt, he slipped inside the house.

A single, small bulb burned over the range in the kitchen, casting a dim light down the hall and into the enormous living room, but the house was otherwise dark and quiet. He knew Sara would be reading upstairs on their bed. She generally waited up for him, no matter how late he got home—said she couldn't sleep without him anyway, so she no longer tried.

Standing in the hallway, Brighton realized that he wasn't alone.

He didn't move for a moment, letting his eyes adjust to the dark. Then he heard the breathing and saw a slow movement and he stepped toward the figure sitting in the wooden rocking chair.

"Luke, what's up?" he asked.

His son sat in the dim light with his eyes closed, his arms folded on his lap, his feet square on the floor. "Hey, Dad," he responded simply, but didn't say any more.

Brighton placed his briefcase on the steps (he would have to lock it in his security safe before he went to bed), pulled off his jacket with his medals, and dropped his flight cap on the steps next to the briefcase and coat. Loosening his tie, he walked into the warm living room. The house was peaceful and smelled of cinnamon and apples from the candle that Sara frequently kept burning near the kitchen sink.

Brighton didn't turn on the lights. He sat down on the couch and leaned back wearily.

"Long day, Dad?" Luke asked.

Brighton took a deep breath and considered the things he had been dealing with for the last couple of days: the assassination of the Saudi Royal Family, the assault in Iran, all the children who had been killed. And that was just the beginning. It got much worse than that. Prince Abdullah, the Crown Prince and heir apparent to the throne of Saudi Arabia, had become unpredictable. And now there were reports, very troubling, coming out of Pakistan. Too many meetings among the wrong men. Movements of al Qaeda soldiers. Rumors of something happening—something deadly, something big. It all had to fit together, but Brighton had no idea how. All he knew was that for the last week the hairs on his arms had seemed to stand constantly on end.

It was coming. And he knew it. He just didn't know when—

"Long day, Dad?" Luke repeated, his voice penetrating the dark.

Brighton realized that several minutes had passed and he hadn't answered. "Yeah. Kind of long. You know how it is."

Luke nodded slowly. He knew this job was killing his dad, sucking the life from him like the air from a balloon. But he knew he couldn't change that. It was just the way it was. His father would never even think about asking for another assignment. That would have been cowardly, weak. His father would die from exhaustion at this post if that was what he had to do. U.S. soldiers died every day, that was nothing new, and there was no way he would quit just because it was hard.

But Luke couldn't help worrying. He had seen a real change in his dad.

The two sat in silence for a long time, neither of them feeling much of a need to talk. It was enough just to share a moment together in the dark. It seemed the silence said more than words could express anyway. So they listened to the clock on the mantel as it ticked time away. A few cars passed outside, and the old house creaked as the wood cooled from the heat of the day.

Luke rocked, his eyes closed, a peaceful look on his face. "Hey, Dad?" he finally said as he rocked back and forth.

Brighton lifted his head. "Yes, son?"

"It's true, isn't it, Dad."

Brighton was silent a long moment before he finally said, "Yes, Luke. It's true."

"I know that now, Dad. I think I really know."

"I'm glad, Luke," Brighton said.

Luke let the rocking chair come slowly to a stop. "Thanks for teaching me, Dad. And thanks for knowing yourself."

"I love you, Luke," Brighton answered.

"I know you do, Dad."

"For we wrestle not against flesh and blood,
but against principalities, against powers,
against the rulers of the darkness of this world . . . "
—Ephesians 6:12

chapter two

AGHA JARI DEH VALLEY
EASTERN IRAN

Azadeh sat alone on her porch.

The afternoon had grown late, and though the sun was low it was still bright and yellow in the mountain air. Lifting her hand, she pulled her light *chador* around her neck and thin shoulders. The long cloak covered her head but not her face, and she pushed the light silk back, tucking it behind her ears, exposing her eyes to the afternoon sun.

The villagers worked quickly around her, solemn, quiet, a great depression hanging like a black mist in the air. The men and women kept their voices low and their backs bent as they concentrated on the cleanup and rebuilding. There was so much to do, such a mess to take care of, and that evening, before the sun would set, there would be a community funeral for all those who had been killed.

Azadeh shuddered suddenly as she looked at the devastated village around her.

So many dead children. So many shattered homes.

But the villagers had grown used to living with death, and the passing of their children was not the only thing they feared.

It could get worse. It would get worse. There was a dark brooding in the air.

Azadeh sat in a stupor. She didn't think, she didn't feel, she hardly even breathed. She occasionally sighed, her shoulders shuddering from a long night of tears, but otherwise she didn't react to the commotion around her. And no one stopped to talk or give her comfort; indeed, no one paid her any attention at all. The villagers, her neighbors, those who had previously been their friends, those who had known her father and her mother since before she was born, those men and women and their families who had shared the same food, the same holidays, the same mosque and prayers, acted as if they were blind to the young girl. They all looked by her or through her, around her or past her, but no one looked at her, for she was poison to them now.

The villagers had known it would happen. Some of the older ones had been saying it for years, especially those who had lived through the revolution that had thrown out the Shah. *No good could come from having a grandson of Shah Pahlavi living here.* How many times had they said that? Now they had been proven right. The army had returned to the village.

The Iranian Special Forces had come back. Black uniforms. Darkened faces. No mercy. Only fear. They had accomplished their tasks, always deadly and thorough. Then came the American choppers, terrifying as well, coming on the wings of black beasts with long stingers protruding from their noses and black guns spouting fire from their open chopper doors.

The armies had come, just as the old men had said that they would. Though they had come looking for Pahlavi, it was the village children who had been killed.

Oh, the children! Why the children? And why only sons?

It was madness! It was evil. But the villagers had seen evil before.

In the end it all came down to *Insha'allah*. It had to be Allah's will. Who were the villagers to presume they could understand his ways?

So the old men had been right. The name of Pahlavi was cursed. And now Azadeh was the last Pahlavi, which meant that she was cursed too.

She knew that she couldn't stay here. The soldiers would return. They would come looking for the young boy. They would come looking for her.

Two village men walked by her on their way up the road. Azadeh watched them hopefully as one of them caught her eye. The bearded man stared, then pointed at her, and the other man sneered. Making a slicing motion, he moved his hand across his face, drawing a line with his finger from his eye to his throat, indicating the scar of an outcast who had been banished from home. Then he pointed at her, making his message clear.

Azadeh glanced painfully toward the scorched tree that stood against the afternoon sun, its black limbs reaching upward like bony fingers for the sky. Someone she didn't know, an old man from the village council, had come and wrapped her father's body in a blanket and dragged it away. Had she had the courage to watch, she would have seen the shallow trenches in the soft dirt form under her father's burned and brittle legs, but instead she had kept her eyes on the black marks that had scorched the old tree, blankly staring at the singed leaves and blackened soil where fuel had been spilled.

Azadeh glanced again at the tree, then dropped her eyes to her lap.

No! This wasn't *Insha'allah!* This could *not* be Allah's will! No god could have wanted all this misery, death, and fear.

And if he did, she didn't love him. Not if *this* was his will.

The image of her father's murder flashed again in her mind and she passed a trembling hand in front of her eyes, trying to push the memory away. But the memory was so vivid it was all she saw now: the expression on his face as the flames grew around the base of the tree, his clothes growing dark and then bursting into flames, his hair curling back, and the final sound of his cries.

She shook her head and focused, trying to think of something else, some kind of happy thought, a pleasant memory. She tried to think of his face in a peaceful context: cooking breakfast in the morning, fishing in the small stream on the south side of the village, working in his fields. She tried to think of him shearing their lambs, one of his favorite things to do. She tried to think of his strong hands, his shy smile, his deep eyes. She tried to think of his rough cheeks, always stubbled, or the warmth of his arms as they wrapped around her shoulder when he kissed her good night. But she couldn't picture any of it. All of the details were gone. It was as if he had vanished—as if he had never been. All she could picture was his suffering, the pain in his eyes. All she could hear was the whoosh of fire and the sound of his cries.

She sighed in sadness, thinking of her father's words. *Zaman öekast dâdan hame delöekastegi*. Time defeats all heartbreaks. He had tried to believe it. She had tried to believe it too. But she knew it was a lie, for this was a heartbreak that would never heal. Not completely. Not in this lifetime. It was a part of her now.

She lifted her eyes and gazed again to the sea. Behind her, the mountains rose up to meet the blue sky, which was growing cloudy as the wind picked up. A storm was brooding in the mountains up north, along the border, and it was headed her way.

Azadeh took a last look around her, then pulled a deep breath.

No. This wasn't right. This could not be Allah's will.

So she sat, rebelling a moment, refusing to move. She knew what she had to do; she had known it all along. It wasn't as if she had to make a decision. The decision was made. There was nothing to think about, nothing to plan, no options to weigh. There was nothing left for her. She had no choice now.

The soldiers would return. She was an outcast. She had to leave.

Standing, she turned for the ramshackle house and made her way through the debris the soldiers and scavengers had left behind. Moving into the kitchen, she found a stranger still there, a few pieces of silverware protruding from the old woman's clenched fist. Azadeh stared at her defiantly and the old woman stepped back, then suddenly turned away. Azadeh watched in silence as she left the house.

Moving down the narrow hallway, Azadeh stepped over pieces of broken furniture and spent rifle shells, making her way into the back bedroom, where she quickly looked around. The floor was covered with the tattered remains of her mattress, broken pieces of plaster, torn curtains, and pieces of older clothes. She moved to the center of the room and fell to her knees, throwing aside the clutter, searching desperately through the rubble.

But she knew she wouldn't find them. Her only treasures, the brush and hand mirror, were gone.

She sat down near the window. Then she saw the old burlap sack where she had hidden the clothes. Crawling toward it, she picked it up and held it in her lap. The string around the opening of the sack had been pulled open, and it appeared to be stuffed with nothing but old, tattered rags. Pulling on the pieces of cloth, Azadeh emptied the contents onto the floor. Underneath the rags she had hidden her father's leather jacket and a pair of thick boots.

She pulled on the boots, then stuffed the coat back inside the burlap sack and tucked it under her arm. The rough burlap scratched her skin, but she hardly noticed as she stepped cautiously back down the hall.

Reaching the kitchen she paused a moment, then passed through the archway and onto the porch.

Azadeh walked away from her home, keeping her head low. Her neighbors ignored her as she made her way to the narrow road that dropped over the hill to the village below. At the base of the hill, the *suq* was completely deserted. All the stalls were empty, the movable kiosks out of sight. There would be no open market today. Azadeh walked around the three-foot-high brick wall that identified the market. For some reason she couldn't identify, she did not want to go in. Before her, to the west, she could see the rolling hills descending toward the waters that the Saudis had recently started calling the Arabian Gulf, but that everyone else still called Persian. Behind her, the *el Umma* rose in the afternoon sun, and Azadeh stopped and turned to look on it a moment, the old guard tower jutted out of the rich valley soil, the granite walls the same color as the mountains behind, the bulwark deep gray though spotted in places with black moss. Azadeh knew that it had been one of her father's favorite places to be. She squinted at the tower. "You did not warn him," she whispered, as if it could understand. "He was your friend. You didn't warn him. You failed in your task."

She stared at the tower as if expecting a reply. "It's okay," she then whispered. "I forgive you anyway."

Turning her back on the tower, Azadeh started walking,

leaving the village behind. The terrain sloped gradually toward the sea, and she picked up the winding road leading to the main highway that ran north and south along the foothills of the great Zagros Mountains. As she walked, she kept on the left side of the road, using the well-worn pathway, though she tended to stay closer to the protection of the tree line and bushes than the path sometimes ran.

She moved quickly, for the way was downhill, and the sun dipped toward the horizon, growing into a bloated red orb until the village and even the rising guard tower were left behind.

In the final turn in the road, Azadeh Ishbel Pahlavi glanced back at the village for the last time.

Though it would be many years, and though she didn't know it yet, one day she would return to her old house on the hill.

* * *

As Azadeh walked away from the village, a shadow stood unseen near the top of the hill. He watched her intently as she walked down the path, noting the slump of her shoulders and the slow drag of her feet. Eventually the road turned, and the young girl walked out of sight.

Balaam remained alone in the shadows for a very long time.

He had once been a great teacher. He had once held such control. *He had once sat with the Son of the Morning at his council of power!* But now he was nothing. Once his great voice had sounded through the bright hallways of God, but now it had turned coarse and scratchy, as if he were always out of breath. Pale-skinned and dull-eyed, he was shrunken and hopeless and completely miserable. Condemned to wander the endless expanse of this world, he clawed constantly at the ankles of those he had once loved, scratching and pawing to drag them into hell. It was a bitter work, dark and dejecting, completely devoid of any sense of satisfaction or worth. But it was all he had. It was what he had chosen to do.

As Balaam watched Azadeh leave the village, Lucifer emerged from the shadows and moved to his side. Balaam turned to face him, his head moving anxiously on his thin neck. Lucifer stared a long moment, looking down from the hill. "How many years have you been watching her?" he hissed sarcastically. "Yet you haven't stopped her. In fact, it would seem you've accomplished nothing at all."

"No," Balaam answered. "I've made her miserable. Sometimes that is all we can do."

Lucifer bit his lip. It was not enough. "Those we can't destroy, we can cause to suffer, but I want more for her. She stays true to her principles. She has not faltered at all. She doesn't have much, but she honors what truth she has."

Balaam shook his head. There was no answer for that.

The two spirits stood in silence as the coming storm gathered around them and darkened the light. Lucifer looked up at the weather and smiled testily. "I would churn it," he whispered. "I would sharpen the elements to hedge up her way."

Balaam nodded. Yes, he could do that, but it would not be enough. "Give me time," he muttered anxiously to his master. "I will get her."

The Dark Master shook his head. Frowning, he motioned. "Can you feel them?" he whispered, leaning closer to his slave.

Balaam barely nodded, a fearful move of his head.

"He is out there," Lucifer hissed. "He's out there. With her father. They will help her, I'm sure."

Balaam stood silent. The servants from the other side made their work so much more difficult. And they seemed to have grown even more powerful, or at least more willing to demonstrate the power they had.

Lucifer clenched his fist and cursed bitterly. "I hate her," he whispered, staring at the empty road.

Balaam didn't answer.

Didn't they hate them all?

chapter three

As the sun moved toward the horizon, a north wind picked up until it was blowing down from the mountains in cold gusts that snapped at Azadeh's clothes. The clouds were rolling in, and she stopped to study the darkening sky. The first layer of thin cirrus had already passed overhead, and heavy, darker clouds were beginning to droop along the tops of the highest mountain ridges. Turning, she saw that the snow-topped peaks behind her were already shrouded in heavy mist and fog. Even as she watched, the temperature dropped and the air grew heavy with mist. It would start raining soon, she thought, putting her father's coat on. Though thankful for its warmth, she also realized it wouldn't be enough to get her through the night. Not if it was raining. Not without some kind of shelter overhead. She looked quickly around, then heard a crash of thunder as the mist fell lower on the mountains, moving down through the canyons to roll along the foothills.

The road was empty, the sun had set, and the twilight was growing dim as the bloated clouds moved west, robbing the evening of its remaining light.

Pulling up her leather collar, Azadeh ducked her head and pulled her *chador* tightly around her neck. Having lived in the mountains, where the winters were long, the summers short and intense, Azadeh knew how dangerous a spring storm could be. She had seen them sweep in from the north, bitter and cold, and drop five inches of hail and frozen sleet before they blew out again, coming and going as quickly as summer rain. She knew the temperature on the mountain could drop 40 degrees in a matter of hours. It often snowed in her village during *No Ruz*, the Iranian New Year's celebration in the last week of March, and it wasn't unusual for it to freeze many weeks after that.

Looking around, she realized for the first time that she had absolutely no plan. She had no idea where she could go or what she should do. Her only objective up to this point had been to get away from the village.

She remembered briefly the man who had sneered at her while running a finger across his throat, and she shuddered, the overwhelming loneliness washing over her again.

She was ***durandâxte***. An outcast. She understood how it worked, for she had seen others cast out from the village before—a woman caught in adultery, a younger girl who'd been raped, a son who'd refused to marry the girl his father had chosen for him—the reasons for being ***durandâxte*** were many, but the results were the same. "Stay and we'll kill you. Go and you'll live. Where you go or how you live, we don't care anymore. You are ***durandâxte***, it matters not, but you must leave us now."

But what was she to do, out here all alone? A woman—any woman, but especially an underage girl—couldn't just trot around the countryside without an escort. She couldn't drive: she had no money and no way to get around. Worse, she had no friends or relatives she could turn to, no one who could help her at all.

For the first time since leaving the village—really for the first time since watching her father die—Azadeh started thinking, her mind clearing enough to recognize the danger she was in.

She needed help. Someone to turn to. She could not survive on her own.

But no one would help her . . .

She shuddered suddenly, but not from the cold.

* * *

Lucifer turned to Balaam. "What is the worst decision she could make now?" he asked in a patronizing tone. "What is the worst thing she could do, as far as we are concerned?" Lucifer already knew the answer, but did his pupil know? It was a test. He always tested. It made him feel good. It was part of how he controlled.

Balaam stood beside him, his weak shoulders slumping, his eyes burning with a pathetic desire to please. He stared down at Azadeh with a dark, hateful frown. "I don't know . . . " he muttered fearfully, terrified of disappointing his Master but more afraid of his punishment if he were to say the wrong thing.

The Dark One hovered over him, and Balaam felt his cold breath, like a chill of stale air escaping from an old grave.

Balaam looked away. He hated being with the Master. It almost hurt him inside. His eyes were so piercing, his power so complete, it was like falling into ice water—it sucked the very warmth out of him. The Master was never kind to his angels; he distrusted, even hated, all of his followers now. And Balaam was no different, he was hated as well.

If they had just won the war! If Jehovah had just been

destroyed! If . . . if . . . all these ifs. The regrets piled on Balaam like a robe of thick steel. He could have been a great leader! He could have ruled a world! But now . . .

His head fell in rage.

Then he tightened in panic as the Master drew near. He took a breath and held it to brace himself for the scorn.

"I asked a simple question!" Lucifer sneered. "What is the worst thing the mortal could do now? Where is the one place we don't want her to go!"

Balaam's fists clenched with tension as he suggested, "The American mentioned Khorramshahr. She would find safety there."

"Yes!" Lucifer shouted in a sarcastic reply. "Yes! He got the answer. Someone give this lad a reward!" He loomed over Balaam, a master over a child. "Now think, then," he continued with a hateful sneer. "We don't want her to go to Khorramshahr. Where could we tell her to go?"

Balaam thought, then shook his head. He simply didn't know.

"Where is the most immediate danger? Where would she almost certainly be killed!"

Balaam's face remained blank, and Lucifer swore. "Idiot!" he screamed. "How could you be such a fool! Who does the young girl trust now? Who is the only friend she has? Omar, you idiot. Isn't that clear! And where are the soldiers? They are at Omar's house! He isn't there. He is hiding. But they are waiting for him. They are searching and waiting; they know he was involved. So if we can lead Azadeh to Omar, the enemy soldiers will find her, for they are waiting there."

Balaam nodded eagerly. Yes, that was true.

"And you called yourself a teacher!" the Dark One laughed derisively. "I'm embarrassed for you, Balaam. I really am. Oh, the *Great Teacher*," he taunted, his voice dripping with sarcasm as his eyes flashed again. "Oh, the Great Teacher, the great Balaam. He used to be someone, but now he's just a fool!

"Stand back, Master Balaam," he then said, pushing Balaam aside. "Stand back and listen, my child, and if you listen, you will learn." He grew very serious and took a step toward Azadeh.

Walking beside her, Lucifer leaned toward her ear. His robes moved around him, blowing back as if from some unseen storm. His eyes glared as he watched her; then he started to speak. His voice was gentle and sweet. *"Omar is safe. He will help you. You must go to him, dear. You have no one else. Nowhere to go. It is the only safe place to be. Go there, and go quickly, do not think more on this, dear. You must go to Omar! What other choice do you have?!"*

The Dark Master spoke to her softly, keeping a constant drumbeat of lies in her ear.

* * *

Azadeh considered her situation, her heart heavy, her mind weak. But the only person she could think of was Omar, her father's best friend, the bear of a man who liked to meet with her father on the ancient guard tower, the mysterious companion who had occasionally visited their home. A gruff man, all business, a man who reeked of wealth and power, Omar had shown an occasional interest in her. He had been kind, had brought her books and items of clothing: a *chador* or small scarf, once even a new pair of shoes.

Might Omar help her? She didn't know. And she didn't know how to reach him anyway. She had no idea where he worked (it seemed as if her father didn't even know) and only the vaguest idea where he lived, for she had been there only once and that was four or five years before. She closed her eyes and concentrated, trying to picture Omar's home. It was somewhere north of the village, up along the foothills near where the river cut through the canyon; she remembered standing on the riverbank and looking down on her town. It was a sprawling brick, stucco, and mud house, far larger than anything Azadeh could ever hope to live in, with pastures for Omar's horses, rows of olive trees, and a natural orchard along the rolling foothills.

She turned toward the mountains and stared through the deepening gloom. Could she find it? She didn't know. But if she was to seek help from Omar she would have to walk north, toward the mountains and into the heart of the coming storm. And she would have to climb, which meant even more rain and deeper cold.

Azadeh looked around her, wondering where else she could go. Who was there to help her? Whom could she trust now?

* * *

"Omar!" Satan whispered, *"you must go to him. Go. You'll be safe there. Don't think now, just act. It's the only thing you can do!"*

* * *

The answer seemed apparent. Omar was the only person she could think of who might be willing to help.

Azadeh felt a soft drop on her cheek and looked up at the sky. The rain started falling in a light drizzle, and the wind turned very cold. But the rain didn't last long. It turned quickly to ice pellets and then heavy sleet. She heard more thunder in the distance as the hail and sleet blew against her neck.

She thought a final moment, then started walking. She had made up her mind.

Turning north, she left the road and began to make her way across the open terrain. Coming to an ancient rock fence, she climbed over and snagged her brown dress, tearing it up to the knee. She examined the torn material, then resumed walking. As she made her way up the mountain, a dark and gloomy dusk settled in. She heard movement around her and stopped to listen carefully, her imagination picturing horrible demons in the dark. She felt it, she sensed it. There was someone there.

* * *

Lucifer smiled with a horrible grin, a sick twist of his lips at the corners of his mouth. He didn't smile because he was happy—he hadn't been happy for more than ten thousand years—he smiled only because he had her, because she was doing what he said.

He turned quickly to Balaam. "Go ahead of us!" he said. "Go! Find the soldiers. Move them in this direction if you can. Rile them up. Make them angry. Prepare them to find Azadeh when she appears from the dark."

* * *

Azadeh stared through the darkness, certain she was not alone. A small herd of goats moved toward her, the matriarch bleating as she complained of the cold. Azadeh touched the goat's head, then trudged along again. The terrain started rising to form the foothills at the base of the mountains, which were completely shrouded now in dark, heavy clouds. She made her way to the forest, where the ground became spongy with old, rotten growth. The temperature continued dropping to a bone-chilling cold, and she started to slip on the wet ground.

It grew dark very quickly and within a half hour after sunset she could barely see, the heavy clouds sucking up any light from the moon and the stars. To her right, in the distance, there was the faintest white glow, nothing more than a thinning of the darkness and a tint of white. The village was down there, perhaps four or five kilometers to her right, and the low lights from the market shimmered miserably in the cold.

Azadeh stopped and looked at the soft glow that lightened the darkness. She was so homesick, so lonely, she thought she might die. But she pulled her scarf around her and kept walking.

* * *

Lucifer walked along with her. He was laughing now. Soon Balaam appeared at his side. "You were right," he said simply. "There are many soldiers there. Omar's house has been taken over with Iranian secret police. They are looking for him now, and they are very upset. If Azadeh goes much farther, they will find her. And if they find her . . . well, who knows what we could convince them to do? Many of these soldiers are our servants; many of them worship you, Lord. If we can lead Azadeh to them, they will take her and have her, I'm sure."

Lucifer snorted with pleasure. He had been proven right again. But that was no surprise. It was always so. Could he ever trust his servants? he wondered. Would they ever be worthy of him!

He looked over to Balaam, his eyes dead and lifeless, almost covered with film. "It may not matter," he muttered. "She may first die from the cold."

Balaam shook his head. Either way, they would win.

Lucifer leaned over to Azadeh. *"Keep walking,"* he hissed. *"Keep moving toward Omar's house. You will find safety there."*

* * *

Azadeh walked all night because there was nothing else she could do. She knew if she stopped she would die. It was as simple as that. The temperature was now midwinter cold, and the rain and sleet were intermingled with snow.

Snow. This far south. At this time of year!

It was an evil omen, an omen she could not understand.

But she tucked her head and kept walking, pulling her arms near her chest. She took one step, then another, traveling in a direction she thought (and then hoped) was northwest. She prayed as she walked, sometimes closing her eyes. "The rain comes from God. The cold comes from God. Death and life come from God. Please, God, I want to live."

To live she needed to find Omar. But which direction to go? The night was so dark, and she was so cold.

By ten P.M., her hair had frozen in long strands at her neck. By midnight, she could no longer feel her fingers or feet. By two o'clock, she was walking unsteadily, stumbling through the wet sleet, her teeth chattering so fiercely they seemed to rattle her brain. Everything started to look familiar. Had she been here before? The trees pulled closer around her as the forest thickened and the terrain grew more steep. Every few minutes she would stop and listen, trying to peer through the dark. Which was north? Which was south? She couldn't see more than a few feet ahead. Reaching an awkward turn in the path she tripped suddenly, falling into the brush and the wet forest floor. The decaying leaves that enveloped her felt surprisingly good. Soft. Like a blanket. The bushes were a pillow, and she almost felt warm.

It was time to sleep. She had done all she could. *I'll just lie here a minute,* she thought. *For a moment, I will rest. I feel so tired and cold.*

Closing her eyes, she felt a tear on her cheek. Rolling onto her side, she pulled herself into a tight ball.

Death and life come from God. Please, God, I want to live.

* * *

Lucifer stared at her as she fell into the brush. *"Sleep, little child,"* he hissed his most evil lies in her ear. *"Sleep now. It is over. There is nothing left in this life for you. You have nothing left to live for, nothing to look forward to. You are alone. No one cares. You don't have a friend in this world. You are worthless, you are miserable, there is nothing worth saving left inside of you. So lie there, my child, just lie there and die. You have nothing left to live for. It is the only thing you can do."*

Balaam stood beside the Dark One and listened, a cold chill on his spine. The master was *so* convincing, even at these most vile lies. He almost laughed in delight.

Then he heard a voice from behind him and felt a hot stab of fear. He saw the light, he felt the power, and he almost fell to his knees. Then his master felt it too, and he turned around and screamed.

* * *

Azadeh woke suddenly and looked quickly around. There was a fire . . . no, a light. And she felt peaceful and calm.

A lone figure stood over her, causing her to squint in the dark. Then he reached down and touched her, wiping the frozen tear from her eye. She felt his bare finger and shuddered, feeling instantly warm. "Azadeh," he said to her, and she pulled a deep breath.

"Father!" she whispered, excitement and relief in her voice. "Father, is that you?" She struggled to stand.

Rassa Ali Pahlavi stood over her, an expression of worry and deep concern on his face. But though he looked like any father would look staring down at his freezing child—his eyes were drawn with sick worry, compassion, and alarm—he appeared much younger and lighter, much happier and more pure, as if the cares of this world could not affect him so deeply now. It was as if, though he watched her, he knew there was something more. He was assured of the outcome, and the moment didn't seem to trouble him so.

He bent down and touched Azadeh's shoulders, helping her stand, then put his arms around her and held her close to his chest.

"Azadeh," he said simply, "you're going the wrong way."

He held her more tightly, and she sensed his deep warmth again.

"Father," she said, "I don't understand."

"You're going the wrong way, Azadeh. Omar isn't at his home tonight. Remember, he had to flee from the army. He left with the young princess and her child. And even if he was at his house, Azadeh, the soldiers are waiting. You would be in great danger if you were to go anywhere near."

"But Father, what do I do, then? Where am I to go?"

Rassa pulled away but kept his hands on her shoulders. "What did the American tell you?" he asked patiently.

Azadeh thought, her mind clearing. "Khorramshahr," she whispered.

"Yes, Azadeh, Khorramshahr. Do you know where that is?"

Azadeh pondered this. "West of the border, along the Persian coast," she finally said.

"Yes, that's right. You must turn around. You are in

danger. Stay away from the village. Do not try to find Omar. Do you understand, Azadeh? Will you do as I say?"

Azadeh didn't hesitate. "Of course I will, Father."

Rassa stepped back. "Azadeh, I can't stay here long."

She almost wept with disappointment. "Please, Father, you cannot leave me now!"

Rassa stepped back, and Azadeh saw another man standing there. Beside him, nestled between two huge juniper trees, a beautiful fire roared. Near the fire, dozens of soft pine tree boughs had been cut and piled to form a thick blanket on the ground, and the boughs from the lower branches had been pulled down and tied to form a roof overhead. A steaming cup of stew was being kept warm by the fire.

Rassa took her hand and led her forward. "This is John," he said.

The other man smiled at Azadeh. He was so beautiful, young and strong, with brown eyes and long hair. There was something about him that drew her to him. He bowed humbly in her direction, but he moved with such confidence that she felt instantly safe and secure. He smiled at her quickly, and she felt her knees quake.

Rassa helped her sit down, and she huddled up to the fire as John handed her the warm stew. She ate hungrily, growing instantly warm. Rassa moved away, near the outer ring of the fire, all the time looking out, as if he were on guard. When she finished eating, he moved quickly back to her side.

"Sleep now," he told her.

"But Father . . ."

"No, Azadeh, it is time that you rest."

She stared at him, exhausted, then started to plead.

He reached out and touched her lips, and she fell silent again. "I need you to remember something for me, Azadeh."

She nodded wearily.

"Remember my final words, for they may be the most important thing I can say. There are times in your life when you feel completely alone, times you feel abandoned, as if there is not a soul in this world who cares about you. But when you feel that way, Azadeh, remember there is *another* world. There are others watching over you from the other side of the veil. We watch. We listen. And we understand. We never leave your side, Azadeh. Someone is always near, someone who knows you and loves you and wants you to succeed. You are never alone. There is *always* someone there. Think of that, remember, and it will give you the strength that you need.

"Now there is nothing more I can tell you, nothing more I can do. It's time that you sleep now. Lie down. Close your eyes."

Azadeh wanted to answer, but she was so exhausted, her body so heavy, her eyelids great weights. Even staring at her father, she felt her mind drift away. Sleep. Yes, she would sleep. She felt peaceful and warm.

She lay on the soft pine boughs and curled into a tight ball. Rassa moved toward her and tucked his leather coat around her neck. Then John came forward and laid a thick blanket on her too. The boughs overhead kept the rain back, and the heat from the fire warmed the side of her face.

"Sleep now, my daughter," Rassa whispered in her ear. "Then rise in the morning and turn your feet west. Go down to the coastline; it will be warmer and safer there. There will be early vineyards and berries. Keep the sea on your left and stay away from the road." Rassa touched her eyes. "Sleep now," he whispered. "John will keep the fire going, and I will watch over you."

In seconds she was breathing very deeply and slowly.

Then the rain stopped falling and a warm south wind blew,

coming up from the waters of the Gulf, sweet with the smell of grass and honeysuckle from the valleys below.

John looked over and smiled, and Rassa nodded in gratitude.

* * *

Azadeh slept peacefully until midmorning. By then the sun was shining brightly and it was growing warm.

Waking, she looked around her and rubbed her eyes, completely confused. Where was she? What time was it? Why was she alone? Then the memory came crashing back and she drew a quick breath. Jumping to her feet, she looked around desperately.

"Father!" she cried. But there was no one there. "Father," she called again. But she knew that she was alone.

She looked at her bed. She had slept with her father's coat on top of a few broken pine boughs, but it was not as she had remembered from the night before; there was no thick bed of cut pine boughs. She turned and looked behind her, searching for evidence of a fire. The earth was clean and smooth. There had been no fire there. She rubbed her eyes, disbelieving, half in awe, half in dread.

Had she become delirious? Had she lost her mind?

She turned in a circle, holding her hands at her head. Had it all been a dream? Wasn't any of it real?

Then she saw something shining and looked down at her feet. Her silver brush and mirror had been carefully arranged on a large maple leaf, the bright silver handles catching the light of the sun.

She cried out, moving her hand to her mouth, then swallowed painfully, catching the lump in her throat. Her eyes welled with tears and her heart burst in her chest. Lifting her head, she looked up at the sky.

"Thank you," she whispered, though she didn't know to whom she spoke. But she couldn't help smile as she lifted her head.

Now *this* was *Insha'allah.*

This was God's will.

* * *

Azadeh followed her father's words, doing exactly as he said.

She turned west and started walking toward the lowlands that defined the coastline on the east side of the Persian Gulf. The going was much easier, for she was walking downhill, and the air had turned dry and warm. Making her way through the forest, she quickly realized that she had been walking in circles most of the night before, disoriented and lost in the dark. Breaking from the forest, she saw the green valley that spread down to her right, the green slopes gently bending toward her village, which was just a little more than five kilometers away. On the edge of the forest, she found a wild patch of berries and ate until she was full, drank from a small stream, then lay in the sun to feel its warmth. Moving quickly then, her heart feeling inexplicably bright, she turned for the main road that led from the Agha Jari Deh Valley to the lowlands along the Persian Gulf. Agha Jari Deh was tucked against the mountains at almost seven thousand feet, but the terrain to the west dropped evenly toward the sea, the landscape shifting from steep slopes and rocks to gentle hills covered in orchards and finally ending in the sandy bluffs that extended to the shore.

It would take her three days, maybe four, to make her way to the U.N. refugee camp on the southwest border of Iraq. Thinking of it, she felt peaceful inside. Before, she had heard stories of the camp, stories that had filled her with fear. And it was illegal for an Iranian to enter the camp, but she didn't care. She didn't fear Khorramshahr. Her father had told her to go.

Putting the mountain range behind her, she walked toward the shimmering waters.

* * *

By late afternoon, Azadeh had reached the descending terrain on the west side of the mountains. Though she stayed away from the road, afraid of being picked up by one of the many military convoys that patrolled the roads every day—or worse, by one of the *Mutawwa,* the religious police—she still made good time making her way down the trail.

Just as evening was coming on, a rickety bus loaded with migrant farm workers pulled up beside her. The bus—faded blue paint and rust from the front tires to the rear exit door—creaked and belched smoke as it slowly rolled to a stop. The front door swung open, and Azadeh peered in carefully. The inside of the bus was crammed with four or five destitute-looking Sunni families who were likely heading up north to help with the planting on the potato farms.

The driver, an old man with a faded gray turban, salt-and-pepper beard, and thick glasses, studied Azadeh for a very long time. "Where you going, child?" he finally asked her, just as she was stepping away.

Azadeh hesitated. What was she supposed to say? She clenched her teeth and answered defiantly, "Khorramshahr."

The old man studied her a little longer. "You in trouble?" he demanded.

Azadeh shook her head. "No, *Sayid,*" she replied.

"You running from the authorities? Are the *Mutawwa* after you?"

Azadeh shook her head again. "No, my *Sayid.*"

The old man stroked his long beard while two dozen sets

of eyeballs stared from the tattered seats of the bus. She heard the cries of several babies and smelled a propane griddle cooking flour cakes from somewhere at the back. She glanced hopefully toward the smell, her stomach growling so loudly she was sure that everyone heard. The old man cocked his head, then pointed to the back of the bus. "Get on," he told her.

Azadeh hesitated. "*Sayid,* are you sure?" she replied.

"Get on," the man repeated. Then, turning in his seat, he called over his shoulder. "Irshad, come up here. Get this poor girl something to eat."

* * *

The next day, as evening was coming on, Azadeh hid in the thick brush on a gentle hill that looked down on Khorramshahr. She studied the road along the border, which was guarded and narrow. She knew there were two guards in the guard shack, but they seemed uninterested. As she watched, the road remained empty, as it had been all day.

The Iranian position regarding Khorramshahr had changed over the past year or so. Though it was still illegal for an Iranian to enter or seek refuge in the compound, the Iranian leaders had decided they were more than happy to send their discontents and disgruntled into the U.N. refugee camp. Most of those who left were only troublemakers anyway, and it served no purpose to try to keep them in.

So, although the soldiers still manned the guard shack, it was pretty clear they didn't care one way or another if any of their countrymen tried to slip across the border. As night came on, the two guards settled in, getting comfortable for the night.

Azadeh waited until darkness. Then, before the moon rose, she slipped from the shadows of the brush and climbed down the hill. Moving quietly, she crawled through a small trench that defined the border between U.S.-occupied Iraq and Iran.

Twenty minutes later, she was inside Khorramshahr.

chapter four

IN THE HIGH MOUNTAINS ABOVE THE AGHA JARI DEH VALLEY
TWENTY KILOMETERS SOUTHWEST OF BEHBEHAN, IRAN

The rains came down in steady sheets, then turned to snow, which accumulated so quickly it completely covered his tracks. Omar was a huge man, and strong, and he climbed like a goat, steady and powerful and with very sure feet. But he was hungry and cold. And afraid for his life.

He paced himself carefully, keeping a constant gait. He knew if he stopped he would freeze. Stop and die. Walk and live. And it was the same for the child.

So he huffed and kept walking, his head bent, his legs sure but slow.

He glanced down at his chest. Using part of his robe, he had fashioned a tight pouch. The young prince slept near his body, his face pressed against his chest. His large coat wasn't buttoned, but tied around his middle now, leaving room for him to move more freely and for the young boy to breathe.

Omar climbed. His hands were nearly frozen, but his feet were still warm, the constant exertion keeping the blood circulating down to his legs and toes. He glanced at his watch; a little past two in the morning. Thirty-six hours now since the soldiers had first appeared, thirty-six hours since he had tried to save his good friend and ended up with the child.

Slipping on a rocky spot on the trail, Omar grabbed a branch to stop his fall, then paused and turned around, struggling to catch his breath. The snow had quit now, and the clouds parted suddenly, the strong winds of the mountains seeming to push them aside. The storms had come without warning, appearing out of nowhere, but they disappeared the same way, melting into nothing at the sweep of a hand. Behind him, the tops of the mountain were still capped in white clouds, but the moon was high now, the snow fresh and white. His eyes had adjusted to the night and he could see almost as clearly as if it were day. He saw the lights of the village, many thousand feet below, and farther in the distance, the starlit shimmer of the sea. To his left, he saw the treeline and the giant boulders that stood at the crest of the Agha Jari Deh Valley. In the moonlight, he could just make out the tiny, rutted road that followed the nearest canyon, running toward the top of the mountains before it sputtered out, becoming a narrow, rocky trail. For the past day and a half, he had stayed away from the main trails. He knew that was where the soldiers would be. As they were too lazy and too inexperienced to find their way through the mountains, he knew he would be safe if he stayed away from the roads. The trail he followed now was a game trail, and not used by men.

He stood there and breathed a long moment. He was thirsty. And hungry. But he was almost there.

Kilometers below and behind him, the young princess was hidden in a small cave, too frightened and weak to go on. She might be dead now, he knew that, but there was nothing he could do. She couldn't walk anymore, or chose not to, so he had left her hidden there. He would send someone back for her as soon as he could, but he didn't know what they would find. If she was strong, and if she wanted to, then she would be alive when they found her. If not, it didn't matter. Either way, he had done the right thing.

Turning, he started walking again, picking his way carefully.

Half an hour later he saw them. They had been waiting for him.

The smugglers, three men in long beards and dark clothes, had been following Omar for almost two kilometers. In addition, they had been watching him from a distance for almost the entire day. With all the soldiers searching along the lower trails and roads, with the fires in the village, the sounds of gunshots and helicopters, they had to be on their guard, willing to take no chance, their long-time friendship with Omar aside. Yes, they trusted him, and yes, he had helped make them rich. And yes, they had known him since they were little boys, but there was friendship and there was business, and this was business now.

So they had waited and watched until they were sure it was safe. Now they emerged from the trees and stepped onto the trail.

Omar knew they had been following him, but still, he was surprised to look up and see the three men standing there.

"Praise Allah, blessed be his Great Name," he said in a weary sigh of relief. "I need you, my brothers. Come! Help me here!"

The mountain men walked toward him, their huge coats flowing behind them like dark sheets in the night. Under their garments, blunt-nose machine guns protruded from their hips. Behind them, Omar could hear their horses and smell the animal sweat. As the men moved toward him, he undid the leather belt around his waist and lifted the sleeping boy.

"What is this!" the lead smuggler cried, causing the young boy to stir.

Omar shook his head to silence him. "You won't believe me," he whispered. "But trust me, my brothers, he is worth far more than gold. Far more than his weight in diamonds. Now, hurry, he is hungry. And I am so weary, I fear I might die."

chapter five

New York City, New York

The firm of Danbert, Lexel, Taylor and Driggs had their main lobby on the seventieth floor of the Iron Gate building in midtown Manhattan. The reception area was breathtaking, with wood panels, granite steps, marble pillars, and oak floors, all hand-crafted pieces of decorative architecture from Italy, Turkey, and Greece. A thin, sunlit shaft of an atrium extended five floors above the center of the lobby, and original pieces of fine art lined every wall: Rembrandts and Picassos, a single Renoir, two Rubens. Ancient (and illegal) pottery artifacts from Mexico and China were displayed in glass cases along the main hall. And though the décor hadn't been updated since the firm had moved into the building back in 1952 (how does one improve on perfection?) it still exuded an air of timelessness and beauty that rivaled most any building in the world.

Danbert, Lexel, Taylor and Driggs occupied the seventieth through seventy-sixth floors of the Iron Gate building, as well as two apartment suites underneath for visiting dignitaries, and a fine penthouse for the senior partner on the building's top floor. But the elevators from the main lobby didn't rise to the firm's office suites, at least not without the proper security code. The sixty-ninth floor was as high as the general public could go.

On the surface, it might have seemed odd that they did not make themselves more accessible. But the last thing the firm wanted was to be readily available.

Though certainly the wealthiest and most successful firm in the world, Danbert, Lexel, Taylor and Driggs was not registered with the city or state government. The firm's telephone number was unlisted—if you didn't already have their number, then the answer was no. If you didn't know whom to approach, then they didn't need you. They certainly didn't advertise, and few people outside of their sphere of influence knew who they were.

Their client list was short, perhaps fewer than five dozen governments and business organizations in all, but taken together their clients controlled a large percentage of the exploitable wealth in the world. The lawyers, former high government officials, and consultants at Danbert, Lexel, Taylor and Driggs specialized in creating commercial agreements between governments and industries, managing international public relations, influencing legislation, setting trade policy, and helping to determine international currency and exchange rates. The firm, with its eighty-nine partners and associates, was perhaps the most exclusive business organization in the world, and the partners were a veritable Who's Who of international CEOs and former government leaders. The board of partners included two former U.S. vice presidents, a former Secretary of Defense, and three former Secretaries of State. A twice-elected British Prime Minister was the newest member of the firm, and he was only one of sixteen former foreign presidents who sat on the executive board. The just-retired Chairman of the Joint Chiefs of Staff had recently been invited to join the firm as a junior associate. He would spend two or three years working seventy hours a week; then, if he had potential (generating $100 million in revenue was the first step in demonstrating he was worthy), he might be offered partner. If the senior members liked him. Maybe. One day.

Junior associates averaged somewhere in the low eight figures in salary; ten to twelve million was expected, though a few made more than that. The senior partners made so much money it didn't matter anymore. How much was enough? It was hard to put a figure on it exactly, but this much they knew: It was less than they made.

Somewhere along the journey, each of the partners realized it wasn't the money that they craved anymore. They had made so much already, and it was so easy to make more, that a few hundred million was basically meaningless. What motivated them now was not money but power—the ability to influence the events of the world. The ability to call virtually any man on earth, be he president or prime minister, CEO or head of an illegal cartel, and have him be willing not only to talk to them but then to do what they said. Power was their heroin. Power was their meth. It was 100 percent addictive, 100 percent pure. And over the years, each of the partners had learned one vital truth: Power could drive a man to do things he would not ordinarily do. It could change him. Distort him. It made him different inside, altered in subtle and yet irreversible ways until he was no longer comfortable in his old world.

After tasting such power, they could no more live like common men than a lizard could live in the sea.

As the years passed, the firm demonstrated another remarkable trend. No one had ever left the organization. No one had ever retired. No one had ever taken leave or resigned. They all died in place, most at a very old age, for once they had tasted the power that the firm could provide, the lust continued to drive them as nothing else could.

Despite the high profile of their previous jobs, the list of partners and associates who worked at Danbert, Lexel, Taylor and Driggs was a highly guarded secret. Just as one didn't take the elevators to their lobby without the security codes, one simply didn't apply to become a member of the firm. From the busboys in the corporate dining room to the secretaries who answered the phones, from the maintenance crews who cleaned the bathrooms to partners who worked on Partner Row, everyone came with a personal recommendation from someone inside the firm. Every employee, no matter what he or she did, had some kind of personal tie to another member of the firm, which was one of the keys to controlling their enormous influence and wealth.

And when the lowest level secretary made almost $200,000 a year, the firm didn't even know what the term *turnover* meant. Danbert, Lexel, Taylor and Driggs was one loyal army, faithful and trustworthy to the core.

* * *

The meeting took place very late on a Saturday night. A terrible storm had settled over the city, and the wind was fierce and howling, with lightning and hail beating down from the darkest core of the storm clouds. The powerful charges of electricity flashed constantly, illuminating the billowing storms from within. A fierce rain beat the windows, and the seventy-six-story building swayed perceptibly, an eerie movement underfoot, like an anchored ship that bobbed on a huge, swaying sea. And this wasn't the first violent storm to hit Manhattan in the last little while; New York City had been racked with severe weather for weeks. Thunderstorms, even tornadoes, had swept through lower New York state, flooding many townships and leaving the Hudson and East Rivers swollen and bloated with debris. The torrential rains were now more than the crowded city could take—too much water and nowhere left for it to go. The upper portions of the city had already been evacuated, with bacteria-spewing raw sewage and river rats taking up residence in the warehouses and brownstone flats that lined the two rivers on the north side of Manhattan.

In addition to the unbearable rains, the storms had brought unwelcome guests. Floating balls of poisonous spiders had been seen, black widows and brown recluses drifting across the water and infesting the upper parts of the city. Dozens of venomous snakes, no doubt washed down from upstate, had been killed in Central Park. Muskrats and other river vermin were now seen frequently. But more often they were heard, their padded feet scratching at the windows and walls, searching for shelter, searching for food. And the backed-up sewage had begun to spread diseases from cholera to dysentery.

* * *

The lightning flashed from the thunderstorms that hovered over the city, illuminating the narrow canyons of Manhattan with great strobes of light, but when the elevator opened and the three men emerged to the lobby, none of them seemed to take note. They had much more on their minds than the weather. They wouldn't be in the city long enough to feel its effects anyway.

An attractive, middle-aged assistant was waiting to meet the three men. She graciously shook their hands, lightly kissing the senior member of the delegation on both cheeks. The men were dressed immaculately and trimmed to perfection, and it was clear from their faces that the surroundings at

Danbert, Lexel, Taylor and Driggs were not particularly impressive to them. Their palaces were every bit as beautiful, and they had many more palaces than they would ever admit.

The men followed the assistant to another elevator, and she punched in the code to take them to the top office suite, but the Saudi prince entered the elevator alone. His assistants stood by, keeping watch on the lobby floor. The door closed, and when it opened three floors above the main lobby, the managing partner of Danbert, Lexel, Taylor and Driggs was waiting for the prince in a broad and dimly lit hall. The usual pleasantries were exchanged as the managing partner led the Saudi prince into his private den, a large room crowded with books and papers but as well appointed as any other room in the suite. The coffee was poured, but the two men held their cups, neither of them taking a sip. The lights of the world's greatest city glowed dimly through the huge windows that extended from the office ceiling to the floor. The prince moved to the window and watched the rain as it fell, imagining what it would feel like to tumble eight hundred feet and hit the rock-hard pavement below. He stared a long moment, thinking on great deeds in the past, then turned toward the other man, who was standing behind him. "It is time," he announced in a low voice.

The managing partner, Drexel Danbert, moved around his desk and sat down in his chair. "Are you certain?" he asked.

"Yes," the prince answered, then began to explain.

* * *

Twenty minutes later, the American studied the sheet of paper before him, his hands shaking as a tiny film of perspiration began to form on his lip. His eyebrows, neatly trimmed and white, rose as he read, then he looked up at the prince. The youngest brother of the new Saudi king met his dark eyes.

Drexel struggled to hide the incredulous look on his face. "You're not serious!" he said in a horrified voice.

The Saudi nodded slowly. "Yes, Mr. Danbert." He lowered his eyes, gesturing to the paper the American was holding in his trembling hand. "Those are the instructions I was sent to deliver to you." The prince raised his hand and pulled on his dark goatee, not saying any more.

Drexel watched him stroke his whiskered face, noting the thin tattoo on the prince's little finger, a crescent with two black stars, symbol of the royal House of al-Rahman, a powerful family that could trace back its roots almost three thousand years, back to the Fathers, those who had introduced so many evils into the world.

The Saudi hesitated, then sipped his hot coffee from an exquisite Spode cup, a single piece of china worth more than most Americans would make in a year. Though the coffee was black and sweetened with eight cubes of sugar, it certainly wasn't his *chai* that he loved so much, and he considered it so weak as to be barely drinkable.

Drexel stared at his own cup, seeing his image reflected on the smooth surface of the black coffee. He took a painful sip and lifted his eyes to the Arab again. "But what about—" he started questioning.

"I am but a messenger, Mr. Danbert," the Saudi interrupted, his voice impatient now. "I have told you all that I know."

The American hesitated, then huffed in frustration. "It can't be. It makes no sense. I don't understand!"

The Saudi swished the black drink around his teeth before answering, "Mr. Danbert, I don't know what more I could tell you. But were I you, I would anticipate the market and make adjustments now."

Danbert thought quickly. The firm held much of each

partner's wealth in a series of privately managed investment portfolios. These funds contained five, maybe six hundred million in properties along the east coast, and another quarter billion of assets between San Diego and Marin County on the north side of the San Francisco Bay. And that was just real estate. How much were the partners holding in U.S. stocks and securities? He didn't even know. It might be a billion. It was difficult to estimate.

And he had to dump it. Dump it now. Dump as much as he could.

"But we can' t . . . we can't just . . . " his voice stuttered and he paused, then started again. "Look, Imad, we can't dump it all. It is impossible! Not in two weeks. Not in secret. I'd have the SEC camped out in my office! Investigators! The press. We don't want that kind of attention. We don't want any attention at all. Think of what you are saying. We dump *a billion dollars'* worth of U.S. assets in the next fourteen days? You've got to be kidding! Talk about obvious!"

The Saudi swished another mouthful of coffee, then simply said, "The decision is yours. You can do what you will."

Drexel hesitated. "But the timing couldn't be worse. You *must* know that is true. The market has dropped eight or ten percent in the last month alone . . . "

The youngest prince almost smiled, his dark eyes beaming with deadly pride. Drexel watched him solemnly, then leaned back in his chair. "Oh," he stumbled, frowning. "Ohhh . . . " He held his breath, understanding. "You're doing it, aren't you, Imad? You're driving the market down."

"No, no, of course not."

"Don't lie to me, Imad!" Drexel jumped up from his chair. "The Saudis, your government, by which I mean your older brother, Prince Abdullah, is holding . . . what, fifteen or twenty billion in U.S. stock and other securities? And if you guys are suddenly in the market, if you are selling what you have . . ." Drexel glared at the prince. "It's you," he sneered in anger. "You're dumping on the market, aren't you, my friend?"

The prince sipped his coffee.

Drexel watched him carefully, his thin face turning pale.

The young prince, barely more than thirty, had the same snake eyes of his brother, hard and deep and cold as glacier ice. The prince watched the panicked American, then pushed himself up from his seat. "Yes, Drexel," he finally answered in an angry tone. "We are selling our U.S. assets while there is still something to sell. Now, you are a smart man, and I think you understand what we are going to do next. You know what is coming. So make your move while you can. Liquidate your assets and get into something else. Gold. Other markets. Chinese currency is a great deal right now. And since it is likely the Chinese will emerge as the most stable government over the next couple years, I would think it might be a good time to look at the yuan.

"But remember this, *Drexel.*" He dripped the American's name now. There was no pretense to their relationship anymore. He spoke for Prince Abdullah, which made him eminently powerful. "The finances of the situation are not our central concern. You know the plan. The objective. Don't lose sight of that now. It makes no difference to my brother what you choose to do. Stay in the market or jump. Move or sit tight, it's completely up to you. He is offering this warning as a professional courtesy, and that is all. But know this, my friend, either way, we will move."

"But what are you thinking? What could you do that would cause a meltdown over here?"

The snake eyes stared at him. The American hesitated, then caught a quick breath, his face falling like a mask into a horrible frown. He shuddered. "No," he mumbled feebly. "You *never* said over here!"

"We lied to you, Drexel. What more can we say?"

"That was *never* our agreement. That was not a part of the plan!"

"The plan has changed, Drexel. You will have to adapt. But let me ask you something, and I want you to think about this. Did you really believe your nation could just sit out this war? We think not, Drexel, we think not. The U.S. was *always* our target. And you can plead naivete or ignorance, but deep in your heart you *had* to know that was true!"

Drexel lifted a trembling hand, then fell back on his chair, his face turning as gray as the dark clouds outside. "You said . . . " he was mumbling, barely able to speak. "You said you were going to move against Israel. You would use the weapons in Gaza. You said nothing of this."

"Yes, we said all of that. And it was our original plan. But as I said, we realize now that we have to move against your country too. It has grown too bold, too ambitious, long-armed and powerful. Things have changed over the past few years, and we realize the U.S. is too strong. Democracies are rising, sprouting all over the world, and if there's one thing we can't endure, it's another democracy in the Arab world. We've got to act against these growing cancers before it's too late. In order to do that, we've got to take down your country. Once we have forced it to turn inward, to focus on its own problems, we can do what we want."

Drexel fell silent, his brow wet with sweat. "You lied to me," he stammered, repeating it over and over again.

The prince watched him a moment, then stood up to leave. He patted Drexel's bony shoulder as he passed. "You'll get over it," he said. "Now it's time to get back to work."

* * *

Drexel listened carefully. The elevator door down the hall slid open, then closed. The prince was gone now, leaving him alone in the huge office suite. The night slipped around him, the dim lights in the den illuminating his face in deep shadows, creating dark pits along the cheekbones that lined his deep eyes. Drexel stared at his aged hands, forcing himself to settle down, then leaned across his desk and picked up his cigarettes. He was at two packs a day. Had been for almost fifty years. They said he'd die of cancer before he was old enough to retire, yet he kept skipping along, feeling healthy and strong.

But this thing . . . this ugly thing . . . he suddenly felt *very* old.

He pulled a smoke from the thin package using only his lips, sat back and lit up, and drew in a long drag.

They were about to unleash a very evil genie indeed. Generations would pass before the final price would be paid. And it was his job to assist them, to give them advice, to help them anticipate and counter what the United States would do. It was his job to help them deal with the firestorm to come, a firestorm of their making, a firestorm *they* controlled.

He pulled another drag, feeling the bitter smoke fill his lungs. He got a sudden buzz and leaned forward on his desk.

The war was upon him.

But the U.S. was going to fight back. His people wouldn't just lie there and let the ashes of history be heaped on their graves. He knew that, he knew them, the Arab propaganda decrying their weakness and decadence aside. Yes, they had grown spoiled and immoral, but the entire world had! Who hadn't turned rotten? Who wasn't decadent? Was there a single nation on this earth that wasn't as weak as brown pulp!

No. They were all weak. There were no heroes anymore.

Still, the Saudi prince and his brothers were underestimating his countrymen. It didn't matter how much they paid him, he couldn't change that. The U.S. was going to fight them. They would fight for their lives.

And the U.S. could be a junkyard dog when it came time to fight. Dirty. Merciless. A nightmare that chased its enemies through every storm and dark night. Its people could be ruthless and efficient when they made up their minds.

They would not die lying down. Hadn't Afghanistan or Iraq taught his clients anything!

Sitting in the semidarkness, Drexel couldn't help but think of what one of his early partners had told him the first time they had plotted to bring a foreign government down. "If you go after the king, make sure that you have the weapons to kill him. Don't just take a knife, take an Uzi and a shotgun and an M-1A Abrams tank. Take every weapon you can assemble. And be ready to run."

Drexel shook his head, flicking a piece of brown tobacco from the tip of his tongue.

His clients were going after the king. But were they powerful enough to kill him before he came after them?

He wondered . . . yes, he wondered.

It could go either way.

WASHINGTON, D.C.

He dreamed it again.

It was a clear summer day. The air was clean, almost crisp, the sun bright and warm. He stood in the middle of a great field, the grass stretching for miles in every direction, a great ocean of green that didn't seem to end. There were no mountains, no trees, no hills, fences, roads, power lines, no nothing, just the endless grass and the blue sky. Two colors. One horizon. The two met perfectly. And it was quiet—oh, so quiet. It almost pounded in his ears.

The sun slipped behind a sudden shadow and he looked up to see a line of beautiful clouds, a billowing cluster of thunderstorms that seemed to appear from out of nowhere. They loomed before him, growing with incredible speed. A nearly perfect black anvil blew out in front of the storm, which was dark blue with white edges illuminated by the low sun. The backlighting tinted the clouds in deep purples and pinks and cast random shafts of sunlight on the green grass below.

The first time he'd seen the clouds, he thought they were beautiful. But now his stomach tightened and he took a quick breath, feeling his heart start to beat faster.

The fear was pushed away by the infinite nature of the scene. The sky was so huge, and he was so small. The grassy field rolled for miles, and the monster clouds billowed overhead.

Then the storms turned black, and lightning flashed from the sky. He knew that this would happen, and he covered his head. It was dark, the wind blew, and he felt a deep, sudden chill.

Then he heard it, a silent whistle. He lifted his eyes in time to see the white burst from the nuclear core. The flash grew into a white-hot mushroom with deep orange and black edges where the air had been vaporized. Another explosion, then another, on his right and his left. It seemed the whole world was exploding. He saw a blast wave move toward him from the closest mushroom cloud, a black wall of fire and heat that emitted from the mushroom core. It moved across the green grass, a wall of superheated air bloated with smoke and flying debris.

Then he saw a figure walking calmly into the coming storm. He was young and broad-shouldered. He didn't turn around, but he looked so familiar: the clothes, the brown hair. The dreamer knew that he knew him. But he couldn't quite see.

The stranger kept walking, slowly moving toward the advancing fireball. The wall of destruction screamed toward him, and the young man disappeared, swept up in the advancing debris.

* * *

Neil Brighton woke suddenly, his heart slamming in his chest. He sat up, his face sweating, his hands clenched against the sheets. His breathing was labored, and yet Sara remained sleeping on her side of the bed, her face in her pillow, her hair spread across the white sheets. He sat there in the moonlight that illuminated the room, staring straight ahead, trying to focus his eyes. He didn't move. He didn't dare. The terror had not gone away.

The mushroom clouds. The young man.

Who was he? Why so familiar? Why couldn't he see his face?

He swallowed the lump in his throat, then rolled to the side of the bed.

It was only a dream. But no, he knew there was more. A line from his patriarchal blessing seemed to roll again and again in his head: *God will always warn you of danger. He will provide a way. There will come a time in your life when you will have dreams, but from these dreams, you will be warned.*

That was the reason the nightmare had such a powerful impact on him. He had never suffered from dreams. He had always slept peacefully, waking with only thoughts of the coming day. But he'd had this dream several times now, and it was always the same.

He thought, his shoulders slumping as he sat on the side of his bed.

There will come a time in your life when you will have dreams, but from these dreams, you will be warned.

For a long time he sat motionless, resting his face on his palms, staring at the dark floor. Finally Sara rolled over, and he looked at the clock. Almost four in the morning. Time to get up anyway. He had a meeting with the National Security Staff, and he had things to prepare.

* * *

General Brighton got a call on his office desk phone a little after ten in the morning.

"Neil," a husky voice boomed through the nonclassified line. "Aaron Statskily. You got thirty seconds?"

Aaron Statskily. Chief of Staff of the army, thin, bespectacled, a marathon runner who had won more purple hearts out of the Gulf War than any other man. He and Neil had gotten to know each other at War College, the interservice advanced training school for up-and-coming officers, then lost touch for a few years before hooking up again in D.C. Not close, but professional, they respected each other and spoke frequently.

Neil glanced at his watch. He had a 10:15 meeting at the Pentagon, and it would be tight, but the good news was that when General Statskily said thirty seconds, that's about what you got. He, like General Brighton, was a man crunched for time, and he milked every second out of every minute he had.

Outranked by two stars, Brighton was deferential to his friend. "General Statskily, I always have time for you," he said in a friendly tone.

"Cut the crap, Neil, I know how busy you are. You're juggling more fur balls than a constipated cat."

Neil smiled. Aaron Statskily mutilated or created more awkward metaphors than anyone he had ever known. "Okay," he answered with a light laugh. "We both are busy, General. So what's going on?"

Statskily coughed. "Professional courtesy." His voice was not booming so much anymore.

Neil hesitated. Professional courtesy. He knew what that meant. Off the record. General to general. A private conversation among close friends. "Gotcha," Brighton answered, sitting on the edge of his desk.

Statskily went on. "I got a call from Colonel Dentworth, an old friend who runs our manpower shop, you know, the flesh peddlers down at the army's Military Personnel Center. He told me something interesting. Seems some of the Cherokee guys have been looking at your kid. They've been watching him. They like him." The general hesitated. "They like him a lot."

"Really," Brighton answered, feeling a sudden jab at his gut.

"Yeah. Sounds like they want to bring him into their group."

Brighton gritted his teeth. But he kept his voice even. "Well . . . " he started to say. "That's very . . . cool. Not surprising. Sam's a very good soldier."

"Apparently so. Now, I'm sure you know the reason I'm calling, but let me state the obvious. We want to know how you'd feel. You know the Cherokees. You know what they do. They fall directly under the National Command Authority, as you certainly know as well, since you're the guy at the White House who tasks them all the time. It seems to raise the question: Is that going to be a problem for you? Would it make it more difficult for you to do your job, knowing your son is going to be assigned to the most aggressive and high-risk unit in the army?

"So I'm asking straight up. Do you want me to kill this? If you do, everyone understands. One word from you, Neil, and we put this thing to bed. Your son will never be disappointed because he'll never know. Not so much as a whisper. You have my word."

The four-star general fell quiet. Brighton stood and paced back and forth, pulling the extension cord with his hand.

The truth was, he was proud. Scared. Terrified. But proud all the same. The Cherokees were the absolute best of the best. The tip of the sword. Nothing like them anywhere.

But what they did was so dangerous.

And Sara would have a fit if she knew.

Could he deny Sam the opportunity at the most coveted assignment in the army? Sara would be furious, and it would make his work more difficult, but Sam had joined the army to do something good, and there was no way in the world Brighton would deny him this.

chapter six

The Khorramshahr refugee camp was named after the Iranian city that was half a day's walk to the south. One of Persia's major ports, with a huge, smoking oil refinery sitting on a small island in the middle of the Karun River, Khorramshahr had been an early target when the Iraqi army advanced during the opening weeks of the Iran/Iraq war. Virtually the entire Iranian population had fled the city, leaving an empty shell behind for the Iraqi army to loot. Devastated during the fighting, the city remained a ghost town after the Iraqis withdrew until, in 1983, relatively confident they would not be overrun by the Iraqi army again, Iranian citizens slowly began to return.

Khorramshahr was a small camp set up along the Iraqi/Iranian border. Administered by the U.N., but overseen by the Iraqi government and protected by the U.S. military, the camp sat on a small plateau looking over the *Wawr al Hammar* marshes that fed on the brackish waters of the southern tip of the Tigris River. One hundred ten kilometers southeast, the Tigris dumped into the Persian Gulf. Behind the camp, the Zagros Mountains rose out of the rolling plains;

west and north were the salt flats and marshes that defined the border between Iran and Iraq. Built on a barren prairie, the camp was suitable—except when it rained (at which time it became a sucking mud hole), or when the wind blew from the mountains (at which time all of the tents would blow down), or during the annual locust infestations (there was no way to keep them out of the food), or during the freezing temperatures of winter or under the burning summer sun. All in all, Khorramshahr was a great location for a refugee camp—for about three weeks a year.

A "temporary" camp, which had already celebrated its twentieth birthday, Khorramshahr had originally been established to protect Iranian *Balgus* refugees, those who had taken the opportunity during the chaos created by the first Gulf War to flee religious persecution in their homeland. Ignorant and wildly optimistic, the *Balgus* refugees had hoped to enjoy a better life in a more-free Iraq once their neighbor was rid of Saddam Hussein.

Things didn't go as the refugees had planned. Saddam didn't fall. The Iraqi government didn't welcome them after the war. And they couldn't go back to Iran, not without fear of death. So they were left in the temporary camp until the geopolitical environment changed. Even after the U.S. liberation of Iraq, a fight in which, even after all these years, the outcome was still unsure, the refugees were left hanging in limbo—not welcome in Iraq until the national government was on much more firm ground and yet unable to return to Persia, even if they had wanted to.

International law guarantees refugees the fundamental right to safe asylum as well as the right of non-refoulement, meaning that refugees will not be forced to return to the country from which they had fled. But international law can't force a host nation to absorb the huddled hordes in their refugee camps. So the Iranian refugees were caught in no-man's land, left to live for years in the "temporary" camp.

During the early months of Khorramshahr's existence, Iranian insurgents infiltrated the camp with members of the Absolute Committee of the Islamic Revolution, a clandestine group controlled by militants in Iran bent on punishing those who rejected the true laws of God. As a result, the Iranian refugees lived in constant fear that they would be killed or abducted by members of the ACIR. They were forced to stand guard over the children and to carefully taste their food, terrified that it might have been poisoned. Many were randomly beaten in the middle of the night. Khorramshahr was also infiltrated (with the help of the ACIR) by common criminals and thugs from Iran—murderers, rapists, deserters, and thieves, as the Iranian government quickly learned it was cheaper to send their worst offenders across the border to Khorramshahr than to take the time to try them and then keep them in jail. Worse, Iraqi soldiers, backed by Saddam Hussein, regularly launched military attacks in the area, injuring and killing refugees in order to stir up the ethnic hostilities that already existed between Iran and Iraq.

In the early days, the Khorramshahr refugees also suffered from insufficient food, water, heat, sanitation, medicine, and doctors. The summer before Saddam Hussein was driven from power, a group of human rights activists from various European countries made an inspection of the camp. Their report described Khorramshahr as hardly more than a prison camp where children died regularly as a result of infectious diseases. The report stated that malaria, typhus, and dysentery were spreading among the refugees, while many were prohibited from attending the hospitals in the neighboring Iraqi city of Al Basrah. Three-quarters of the inhabitants of the camp were undernourished due to the insufficient rations, and the drinking water was contaminated. The ACIR had stolen what little the refugees had been given, and anyone who left the camp and was stopped at an Iraqi checkpoint risked prison and torture. Many disappeared without a trace.

Since the U.S. invasion of Iraq, after which the U.N. had taken responsibility for the camp, things had gotten immeasurably better. Able to provide safety and the basic necessities, Khorramshahr had become tolerable. But it was a very long way from paradise. And it would never be home.

* * *

The young woman lay on her cot. Her eyes were closed, but she was not asleep and, as the darkness gave way to the early morning light, she opened her eyes and stared up.

Lying quietly on her bed, when everything was silent and the shadows were full, when her mind was not yet occupied with all that she had to do, she was just beginning the battle over her emotions. The young woman realized it was a dangerous and unpredictable time of day.

If she let her mind wander, who knew where it would go, especially after she had spent another anxious night fighting through the dark dream. She felt the thin blanket around her legs, tightly wrapped and damp, and remembered the dreadful feeling of waking in sweat.

The dream didn't change much. Sometimes it was raining, sometimes it was dry, sometimes it took place in the mountains, sometimes down by the stream, but other than the setting, the basics were the same: the same tree, the same flames, her father, the smell.

So Azadeh guarded her thoughts carefully to keep the darkness at bay.

Over the past few weeks she had learned it was just around the corner, always lurking. The darkness. The anger. A depression so deep that if she ever fell in, she knew she would sink down forever and never come up for air. It was always there, always simmering just below her smile. It was the first thing she thought of in the morning and the last thing at night. It was the air that she breathed, a secret part of her now.

But she knew how to fight it. She had learned from her father how to keep the demons at bay. She had to keep the window closed and not let anything in. She couldn't consider her situation, or the sense of injustice would suck the life from her soul.

So she forced herself to be happy. It was all she could do.

She would keep on believing, keep on smiling, keep on trusting God.

But sometimes she wondered what she would do if she saw him again. What would she do if she met the soldier who had assassinated her father? She could picture his face, his flat nose, greasy mustache, and dull, deadly eyes.

Some mornings she prayed to forget him.

Some mornings she prayed she never would.

* * *

Three weeks later after arriving in Khorramshahr, Azadeh had fallen into a routine. The camp provided food and shelter but very little else, and her days had become very much the same: wake on her small cot with a thin, cotton blanket over her shoulders, stand in line to wash, stand in line to eat, stand in line for drinking water, stand in line to speak with a U.N. refugee worker, stand in line to write a letter or glimpse a newspaper, stand in line for lunch, stand in line for another drink of water, stand in line, stand in line. Looking at the back of some stranger's head pretty much defined her life now.

Soon after being admitted to the camp, Azadeh decided to write a brief letter to Omar, hoping against hope that he might be able to help her. As she stared at the single sheet of paper, her weekly allotment, she struggled to think of what she could say. Her mind drifted back to that horrible afternoon when the soldiers had appeared, then Omar at their back door, coming to warn them. She thought of her father's oldest friend, his hair wet with rain, the deep curls hanging in front of his eyes. He was sweating and panting heavily, his hot breath creating puffs of mist in the cold.

"Take them!" her father had commanded Omar, pointing to the young Saudi prince and his terrified mother.

Azadeh remembered Omar's huge shoulders and thick legs propelling his weight up the rocky trail, holding the Saudi prince like a piece of limp baggage, the young boy appearing weightless under his powerful arm. The princess clung to Omar's shoulder while holding one hand to her mouth. The mist gathered quickly around them, and for a moment they looked like gray spirits moving through the orchard and across the wet grass. Omar had stopped and looked back, then turned and pushed them along, herding the princess and her son toward the rocky trail that led up the mountain. The group was soon swallowed up in the mist, and the sound of their footsteps quickly faded away.

Sitting on her small cot, Azadeh wondered for the thousandth time if Omar had been able to keep safe his charge. If not, her letter didn't matter, for he was certainly dead.

But if he was all right, then where was he? Would he get her letter? Would it be safe to reply? She was just a young woman; she had no right to contact him in the first place. Such a great man as Omar, would he stoop so low as to answer her anyway?

Then a dark thought occurred to her, leaving a cold pit in her stomach. *Might the soldiers trace her letter to Khorramshahr and come looking for her?*

She thought a long moment, a cold shudder inside, then slid the pencil and blank sheet of paper into her small burlap sack and placed it under her cot.

She considered for three days, then finally made her decision. That evening, when the sun was about to set and mourning doves were calling to each other from the birch trees behind the last row of tents, she summoned her courage, feeling compelled to try. She took out the pencil and started writing, choosing her words carefully, the Persian script poetic and articulate from two thousand years of heritage.

Master Omar Pasni Zehedan:

It is difficult to consider the possibility that my words might not find you in good health nor even find you at all, but I remember with such deep emotion that night that you came to our home and I felt a need to thank you for your sacrifice and what you were willing to do.

My father, as you must know, has been called home to Our God. I think I knew my father as well as anyone on this earth and I can tell you without hesitation that he looked forward to your conversations on the old tower as much as anything in this life. It is my belief that he loved you, Master Zehedan, as he would have loved a brother had that gift been given to him, and I pray you will remember his soul in your prayers.

I find myself in a situation which, though not home, is safe and tolerable. I am here in Khorramshahr. There is no school, and few young people my age, but it is safe and we eat, and are generally provided for, so I will not complain. What am I to do, I have not yet formulated, but I maintain my faith that, over time, Allah will light the way. I take one step into the darkness, then wait for His light. Insha'allah. I trust in His will.

Were you to have opportunity, and were you to feel it

appropriate for one such as yourself to show kindness to one such as I, I would look forward to hearing of your good health and well being.

I pray, as always, that Allah our God, will place warmth in your soul and peace in your mind.

Respectfully. Humbly.

Azadeh Ishbel Pahlavi

Azadeh stared at the letter, reading it carefully, then folded it twice and placed it in the brown envelope. And though she had fantasies of Omar receiving her letter and sending some of his men to whisk her away, her main reason for writing was to establish some type of contact with the outside world. She was desperate to believe there was someone out there who cared.

Still, she almost smiled as she reviewed the brief note. She felt like a little girl writing to an imaginary friend.

After sealing the envelope, she realized she didn't know Master Zehedan's address. She struggled as she thought, then did the best that she could, using his full name and a guess of his home's location on the north side of the Agha Jari Deh Valley, five kilometers north of the village.

Two weeks later the letter was returned, *deficient address* stamped across the back flap. She stared at the unopened and tattered envelope, a discouraged look on her face, realizing that if she were to get out of Khorramshahr it would be on her own.

* * *

As the weeks passed, Azadeh had taken to reading her letter again and again. She always carried it with her, tucked inside the white sash around her waistline, for it served as a reminder that she could not lose hope.

Though she had no idea what the outcome would be or where she would end up, she knew she was far better off in

Khorramshahr than any alternative and she was grateful to be there, regardless of how bleak or hopeless it might seem.

She missed her father. She missed her village. She missed everything. Sometimes the homesickness washed upon her like a wall of cold water, leaving her shivering and lonely and cold. But she knew that God had something in store for her, for he had protected her until this very day. So she did not lose hope. There was reason to live.

And just as she had done since she was old enough to remember, she started each day with *sala'h,* or the first Morning Prayer. Turning toward Mecca, she joined with the true believers from all over the world who demonstrated their faith in Allah by falling to their knees.

* * *

Azadeh believed, because she had been taught by her father, that Allah was closer to humanity than a father was to a child, and that nothing in this world deserved an equal surrender of self.

As a united people, Muslims begin each day by prostrating themselves in worship of their God, whom they consider the creator of the universe and every being therein. Bowing to pray is a demonstration of their surrender to the Allah, for even the name of Islam means *submission* to His will.

Azadeh had also been taught that she must always face Mecca when she prayed, for that was where the great *Ka'bah* was.

The *Ka'bah,* a stone building shaped like a huge black cube, was far and away the most sacred structure on earth. Forbidden to non-Muslims, originally built by the Prophet Abraham and his son Ismai'l, the beautiful but simple structure was built for the purpose of worshipping Allah, and the ceremonies that were observed there had been performed by the Prophets for thousands of years.

Inside the *Ka'bah,* the Black Stone had been placed. Older than the creation of the earth, round and small enough to hold in two hands, the Black Stone was composed of several fragments of rock bound together by silver. According to Islamic tradition, God had given the Black Stone to Adam after plucking it from paradise.

Because the Stone came directly from Allah, it was revered by all Muslims as the most holy object on earth. It was His gift to man, evidence of His being, and every Holy Prophet from Adam to Mohammed had at one time touched the Stone.

As the centuries passed, the *Ka'bah,* which housed the Black Stone, was frequently damaged by calamities and war. In the early seventh century, a fire had ravaged the *Ka'bah,* and when it was rebuilt, the Arab tribes could not agree who should have the right to install the Black Stone back in its place on the wall inside. After many arguments, arguments that nearly escalated into war, the tribes finally agreed to let the next person who entered the courtyard decide who would be privileged to place the ancient stone in its place. As God had intended, the next person to come into the courtyard was Mohammed. A young man, not yet a Prophet, Mohammed placed a piece of cloth on the ground and set the Black Stone at the center. Then he asked each of the tribes to select a delegate to gather around the cloth. Together they lifted the cloth with the Black Stone off the ground and carried it to the *Ka'bah,* where Mohammed himself set it in place.

Azadeh had been taught that if one kissed the Stone, which was smooth and soothing and emitted a pleasant fragrance from Abraham's hands, it would bear witness to that person's worthiness on the Judgment Day.

Several feet in front of the Black Stone was the Zamzam

well, another reason why the *Ka'bah* was considered so sacred. Tradition told that while Abraham was away from Hagar and Ismai'l to visit Sarah at Mecca, the angel Gabriel had hit the ground with his wings on this spot to bring forth a flow of clear water from under Ismai'l's feet.

For these reasons it was essential for all Muslims to face the Most Holy Mosque of *Ka'bah* as they began their morning prayers, and Azadeh had never even considered breaking this command.

Once she had prostrated herself on her prayer rug and faced the city that contained the Black Stone, she closed her eyes and repeated the words her father had taught:

"Oh Allah,
I am the daughter of my father, Your Servant
And the daughter of my mother,
Your gift to me.
My soul is in Your palm
I receive light by Your finger.
Your judgment is perfect,
Now I ask you by every name given to you by the Prophet
That you keep my life in Your palm
That you touch me with Your finger
to remove my sadness
and give me joy today.
Prophet Muhammad,
Peace be upon him."

And though Azadeh had great faith in this prayer, she had come to believe that there had to be something more, for she had been comforted and lifted beyond the words of such prayers. She'd been wrapped in a blanket that she could not explain, and the blanket seemed to grow warmer when she whispered other words. So she closed her eyes again and boldly added other words to the prayer, words of her own, words that had not been taught to her.

"Allah, my God," she began in a quiet voice, "I don't deserve this. In my heart I realize I don't deserve what You have given to me.

"You have given me life. Yet I am a weak and unworthy child. You gave me a mother who wanted me, though I don't remember her face. You gave me a father who loved me so much that he put aside everything that he cared about in order to take care of me. You gave me health and a strong body, and the opportunity to be here in this life.

"And while You have given me disappointments and heartaches, I accept them as well. I accept all of your gifts, both the good and the ill.

"You've kept me safe, given comfort, and brought peace to my heart. So please show me someone I can help, for I would like to do something for You today. Show me someone I can comfort in order to thank You for what You have given me.

"Show me Your will, God, and I will follow Your way."

With those words, Azadeh took a deep breath. Standing, she moved to her tent flap to look out on the refugee camp, one of the most empty and lonely places in the world. Then she squared her shoulders and slipped into the harsh sunlight.

chapter seven

WASHINGTON, D.C.

Ammon and Luke Brighton met for breakfast at one of the little gut-food places that lined the Student Center building on the campus at George Washington University. It was midmorning. Ammon had just come from his first class. Luke had just come from the gym. They each bought a cinnamon roll, big as a saucer and with about a thousand grams of fat and sugar, then sat down at one of the small tables in the hall. Hundreds of rushing students passed by them, but they concentrated on their food. Five minutes later, no longer hungry, they sat back and relaxed.

"What you got going today?" Ammon asked.

"Not a lot. Econ quiz. Biology lab. Same old, same old. You think Dad is still planning on meeting us down at the harbor for . . . "

"No. He called me earlier. Said he couldn't make it. Said maybe sometime next week."

Luke scoffed. "Yeah, right. When pigs sprout wings and fly."

"Don't be angry at him, Luke. He's doing the best he can."

"I'm *way* more than angry, but I'm not angry at him. I'm angry at *them*. The ones who put him under so much pressure. They ride him like a bad horse. They keep whipping and whipping. One day he's going to fall down. You can only ride a horse so long, spur it so many times, before it blows out its lungs."

"Pretty graphic," Ammon smiled.

"I feel graphic," Luke replied.

"Still, don't be ticked off at Dad. And don't worry about him either. You and Mom worry too much. I can see that God sustains him. Can't you see it too? He's doing something very important, and God knows that. I think he'll be okay."

Luke nodded, took a last bite of his bun, then stood up quickly. "Got to go," he said. "Econ quiz. I'm not ready."

"So what else is new?"

"You need a ride this afternoon?"

"No. I'll take the Metro."

"Okay. See you later, dude."

"Good luck on your test."

* * *

Luke had seen her before—many times, in fact. They were in the same freshman economics class, but then so were a couple hundred other kids. Sometimes he would see her at the gym. He lifted weights. She always ran. They passed each other in the hall, but they never spoke, for it seemed whenever he saw her she was never alone. He didn't know where she was from, but it appeared that her entire high school class had followed her to college, for she was always surrounded by friends. But though they had never spoken, he had watched her. Icy blue eyes. Long, blonde hair. She was beautiful. And sophisticated. And where did she get that tan? She had a lot of money; he knew that from the way that she dressed. Those who had it, those who *really* had it—not just a few million but much more than that—had a thing about them that was hard to hide (assuming they wanted to hide it, which, of course, they never did). If money talks, then big money screams, and everything about her screamed like a high-pitched cry in the dark.

Luke was sitting on a bench outside the university library when she walked up to him. It was a brisk fall day and a cool breeze blew, taking the humidity and smog of the district and flinging it east. He was reading—cramming, really—for the upcoming quiz when her shadow fell over his textbook. He didn't look up. She waited for a while, then, apparently growing impatient, she took a step to the side, formed the silhouette of a pterodactyl with her fingers, and flew the shadow across his page. Luke looked up, his eyes growing large. "Hey there," he said, keeping the book open in his hands.

She smiled shyly. A pure act. "Hi. You look busy."

Luke flipped the book closed. "Not really," he lied. "Well, kind of," he admitted. "I've got a test in a couple minutes."

"Well, that's *very* important. I'll just leave you alone." Her voice was soft and deliberate. She oozed confidence.

"Are you kidding?" Luke jumped up. "I mean . . ." he stammered. "It's okay. I'll do fine. In fact, it's my economics class. We have it together."

"Really?" she answered.

Luke slumped just a little. Hadn't she ever noticed him?

He nodded to the bench beside him. She dropped her backpack and sat down. "Luke Brighton," he said.

"Alicia Debonei. Yes, it's French, which is a coincidence, because so is my father, but please don't ask."

An introduction like that raised a lot of questions, which was her point, of course, but Luke didn't bite. He shrugged his shoulders. "It's cool," he said.

Alicia crossed her arms in front of herself. Her forearms

were slender, but her legs were long and strong. She wore a light blue halter and a white skirt that was just a few inches too high. She had on leather shoes with an insignia he had never seen before, though he recognized it as Italian; a diamond ankle bracelet that was obviously real; no earrings, but a couple of diamond and sapphire rings on her fingers; and a soft fabric headband made out of something . . . shiny, he had no idea what it was. Turning toward him, she flipped a strand of blonde hair from in front of her eye. Her hair was a soft color, fine and silky. She was not a bleached blonde. He stared at the movement, mesmerized just a moment too long. She met his eyes and smiled. He looked away.

"Are you ready for the econ quiz?" he asked, the only thing he could think of to say.

"Are you kidding! I was completely lost in that class about five minutes after the professor introduced himself."

"It can be kind of tough."

"How are you doing?"

Luke hunched his shoulders. He had a 97 percent average, but if she had been struggling, that might not help him right now. "I'm doing all right," he answered carefully. "But I have to work really hard."

"All work and no play makes Jack a very bad boy," she teased.

Luke laughed. "I don't work *that* hard."

She crossed her legs and seemed about to say something when her cell phone rang. She was holding the silver phone inside her palm, and she glanced at it discreetly as she silenced the tone.

"You want to get that?" he asked her.

"No. It can wait."

"No big deal if you want to get it . . ."

"Really, it can wait."

She tucked the cell phone in her purse. Luke heard it ring again, but she ignored it and focused on him. Then a different ring-tone emanated from the purse. Embarrassed, she opened it and silenced a tiny, black phone.

"You're a busy girl," he said.

"So sorry," she sighed. There she went, tossing that pesky strand of hair once again. He really wished she wouldn't do that. It was completely distracting. But then, so was her smile. So was everything about her. He had trouble thinking of the most basic thing to say.

"So, Miss Debonei-whose-father-is-French-but-let's-not-talk-about-that-right-now, where you from?" he finally asked her.

"Okay, an average question. Not original, but safe. A casual icebreaker, good enough to get things started, but certainly not going to break any rules."

"Okay," Luke laughed, "I'll try again. So . . . tell me about your father. Is it true he's an American-hating French industrialist whose grandfather helped the Nazis during World War II?"

She stared at him, then started laughing. "Wow, I guess I was asking for that."

He only smiled in return. But it was a good smile. His face was dark, his eyes bright and friendly.

She bit on her lip. "I guess I'm a little bit like you. I come from all over, not from only one place."

Luke hesitated. "Your father was in the military?"

"Hardly!" she laughed.

"Then, I guess . . . "

"Let's not talk about that," she cut in. "What *I* want to know is, how many times have you met the president?"

He hesitated again, surprised. "A couple. How did you know?"

"Oh, I know about you, Luke Brighton. I guess lots of people do."

Luke was dumbfounded. "I didn't think you knew who I was."

"Of course I do," she laughed. "I did a little asking around. It wasn't hard to find out. In a school with a lot of famous people's kids, especially from the government and the international diplomatic corps, how many of their fathers had direct access *to . . . the . . . president.*" She paused and accented each of the last three words. It was clear from her emphasis that she understood.

Few people recognized what it *really* meant to work for the president, to actually have access to him, to talk to him every day. Few people really understood what kind of power that could bring. Very few had felt the rare pulse of muscle, the tingle of adrenaline, the incredible flush that came from being near *the man.*

Alicia understood it. He didn't know how, but somehow she understood.

She lowered her voice conspiratorially. "My father hates the president, I must tell you. I mean, he has such a deep-seated, visceral hatred for him, it almost makes him sick. Now, don't get me wrong, he's never met the man, so it's not personal. He's met the last three presidents, but he has never met this one. He's from the wrong circles, you understand, the wrong pack and all, but he would pay a million dollars to spend an evening with him. Not just to share a photograph opportunity at a fund-raiser; that's not how my father operates. He is much more intimate, much more . . . you know . . . friendly than that. But if he were to ever spend an evening with the president, heaven knows what he might say! He thinks the man is deranged. Thinks he's damaged the world. He considers him as evil as anything since Hitler, and on a bad day, maybe worse than even him."

Luke's defenses shot up. His shoulders squared and his jaw set. Then he looked at her smile, her blue eyes and soft hair. She watched, then leaned toward him. "Don't worry, Luke Brighton, I'm not like my father," she whispered.

Luke pulled his head away from the soft breath that had just touched his ear. "Who is your father?" he asked.

She punched him on the shoulder. "Why does he keep coming up?"

"Because you keep bringing him up," Luke answered with a grin.

"Well, yes, I suppose I did . . . "

"Debonei . . . Debonei," Luke thought out loud. "Duh! I know your father. He owns Capital Media Group. How could I be so stupid! It's only, what, the second largest—no, the largest media empire in the world."

Alicia nodded weakly, again, all an act.

Luke shook his head. "I'm sorry. I should have recognized you," he apologized.

"You're kidding!" she answered. "Like you should apologize for that?"

"Well, you know, I just suppose that you couldn't go many places in the world and not have people recognize your name."

She shrugged her shoulders, uninterested. "Enough about me," she said. "Unless you have a fascination with money, and I'm hoping you don't, then who my father is isn't any big deal."

Luke glanced at his watch. Class in three minutes. "Our econ quiz," he said.

Alicia didn't move. "We can make it up tomorrow. I've already talked to the professor. He said sure, no big deal."

Luke nodded happily. He figured Alicia asked a lot of

favors and wasn't disappointed very often. But that was fine by him. He could use another day to study anyway.

"So, are you going to be a hotshot pilot like your father?" Alicia asked. "Isn't that what he was before he became a hotshot presidential aide?"

"Don't know. Maybe. I love flying, but I haven't decided. I've got a little time to think about it, I figure."

"You act like a fighter pilot, did you know that? A little bit arrogant, but in a nice sort of way."

Luke faked an expression of hurt. She kept on smiling at him.

"So," she nodded to his textbook, "do you like our econ class?"

"Yeah, I actually like it a lot."

"I hate it. And I'm not stupid either. I'm not your typical empty-headed blonde, but there's just something about it that I don't understand. All the numbers. All the theories. I like things that are more tangible, you know, something I can really think about."

"Have you declared a major yet?"

"Oh, definitely."

"And that is . . . ?"

"Political science."

"Really!" Luke answered. "Why poly sci?"

"Because I *love* politics. All kinds of politics. And I'm *good* at it."

Luke laughed out loud. With her father's money and that smile, she could dazzle her way anywhere. "I can see that," he answered.

"Bet on it, baby, I am."

This time they both laughed.

The campus was quiet now. Most of the classes had started, so the sidewalks were almost empty; a couple of guys throwing Frisbees to their dogs on the quad were about all that was left. "You taking Econ II next semester?" Alicia asked as they watched the dogs jump in the air.

"I won't be here next semester."

"Had enough of school? Going to drop out and join the army? Hike around Europe for a while?"

"Probably not," Luke answered. This one was kind of tough to explain. "You see, I'm LDS . . . " She looked confused. "You know, The Church of Jesus Christ of Latter-day Saints . . . "

"You're a Mormon!" she exclaimed.

"Yeah."

"Oh, that's cool. I mean, I'm open. I've got a couple good friends who are Scientologists. I know a couple Mennonites. Lots of Jews. No Jehovah's Witnesses, but whatever, it's cool."

Luke shook his head at the comparisons. "I'm glad you're open," he said.

"I'm a Christian. Methodist. You know, we're kind of the church-of-everything's-cool. We go our own way, don't put a lot of pressure on others. The golden rule is what rules us. That's the way it should be, don't you think?"

"I can respect that," he answered.

"You're a Mormon . . . " she repeated, her voice trailing off. "Oh, my father would love that. My mom would freak." She thought in silence a moment. "But that means you don't party. No doobies. No smoking. No JD on the rocks."

Luke nodded. "Kind of grim, huh."

She looked at him, amazed. "That means you don't, you know . . . hook up or, you know, or anything, right?"

"No. But sometimes I watch TV on Sunday. And one Friday night, when I was fourteen and my parents weren't home, I snuck down to the 7–11 and drank a whole Big Gulp of Coke."

She looked at him, incredulous, until she saw his smile. She punched him again, sensing the sarcasm in his reply. "So . . . okay, I get it. You're a—" she lifted her fingers to form quote marks—"'Mormon,' but you don't, you know, really live all that clean."

Luke shook his head. "No. Actually, Alicia, I really do. At least I try."

She stared at him, astonished. "Really?"

"Really."

"I just think that's *so* cool."

"Thanks." He was glad.

One of the students with the dogs threw an errant Frisbee that landed at his feet. He stood and threw it back, tossing a perfect spiral that hit the other guy in the chest.

He returned to the bench and sat down.

"So, I still don't understand what your religion has to do with you not going to school next semester," Alicia asked.

Luke paused. How to explain it? "You've heard of missionaries, I suppose."

"Used to see them all the time in Europe. Young guys. Short hair. All dress the same: white shirts, black pants, with red ties."

"Yeah, well, they don't have to wear black pants and red ties, but that's not really the point. The point is, I'm going to go on a mission."

"You're going to be a preacher?"

"Kind of. Not exactly. But for two years, I will."

"Do you *have* to do this?" she asked him. "I mean, does your religion require it? If you don't go on a mission, will you go to hell?"

"I don't have to. I want to. We all have our agency; this is something I want to do."

"But you don't *have* to, right? You could stay here at George Washington if you wanted?"

"Yeah, sure I could."

Alicia smiled as if something were clicking inside her pretty head. She thought a moment, then seemed to make some kind of decision. Glancing at her watch, she said, "It's almost lunch. You want to go get something to eat?"

* * *

Luke and Alicia started seeing a lot of each other after that. Luke didn't know why he liked her so much, but he really did. He liked her friends. He liked her roommates. He certainly liked the Porsche she drove. They had a great time when they were together; they seemed to laugh all the time. But it was much more than that. She was interesting and sincere, and she listened to him. It seemed they could talk for hours. She would tease him. She would challenge him. Everything about them just clicked.

And there was that smile. And that hair. And everything else.

Both of them had been dating lots of different people when they first met, but that changed before too long. Being together every night, there was no time for anyone else.

chapter eight

Camp Freedom
North of Baghdad, Iraq

The HH-60s landed as a formation, four choppers in an echelon position, each maintaining a position five feet above and to the right to their leader as they descended through the semidarkness. The sand blew out before them as their enormous blades stirred the air, sending the dirt—fine as talcum powder—up and over the choppers in a vertical whirlpool of sand. The pilots landed quickly through the blowing dust, barely able to see. Because they had been flying through the night, when the choppers put weight on their wheels, the landing pistons hardly compressed, for the choppers had expended all of their fuel and most of their ammunition as well. Upon touching down, the pilots nosed their choppers over and taxied across the corrugated steel that had been placed over the uneven terrain, moving toward the load-up area.

Dawn was ready to break, and the sky was in the transition from deep black to dark gray. Pulling onto the loading tarmac, the choppers came to a stop. As they did, the soldiers opened the cargo doors and began to spill out, thankful as always to be on the ground. The men wore full battle gear: desert camouflage battle-dress uniforms (BDUs), flak jackets, Kevlar helmets, and brown leather boots. Each soldier also wore multiple web belts and a small pack containing ammunition, rations, water, smoke grenades, radios, miniature GPS receivers, grenades, smokes, lip balm, night vision goggles—all the essential elements of modern war.

A hot breeze blew up from the west desert, the air uncomfortable, brittle and dry. It had been a cold night but it would be a hot day.

As the soldiers, all Delta Special Forces with subdued unit patches on their shoulders, piled out of the choppers, it was clear from the way they walked that they were exhausted. Sweaty and covered with grime, most had spent the night on their bellies, crawling through the dirt, spiders' nests, and rat droppings that covered the cement floors of an old weapons storage complex that had recently been taken over by insurgents again. When the battle was over and the bodies identified, the Deltas hadn't been surprised to find Iranians, Syrians, Kuwaitis, and Chechens but not a single Iraqi among the dead.

Homegrown Iraqi insurgents were getting hard to find now, the glory of dying for their cause having lost some of its luster for those faced with the continual prospect of death and defeat. But there always seemed to be others who were willing to fight, imports from other nations who were determined that the Iraqi people would never have any more freedom than their own.

It was an irony, of course, and a bitter one too, that the Iraqis had to fight their own cousins as they faced the most important question in the last thousand years: Did they want their liberty as much as those who hated freedom wanted to keep it from them?

From the beginning of time the same question had been

demanded again and again. Did a nation truly value its freedom enough to fight for the cause?

* * *

The horizon turned quickly to a silvery hue from the dust and smoke that hung in the air. Sam Brighton, sitting on the right-hand door of the first chopper, dropped to the tarmac the moment his pilot brought the helicopter to a stop. He was dirty and tired, maybe more than any of his men, for he had spent almost six hours in a crouching position, hidden in a dark ditch, covering their movements as they crawled and shot their way through the old storage compound. The black camouflage on his face was smeared with perspiration. Combat was work, the hardest work in the world, and the cool night temperatures in Iraq weren't enough to have kept him from sweating like a pig.

Dropping from the open door of the army HH-60, Sam led his team away from the choppers, then circled his fingers, telling them to gather on him. The eleven-man squad assembled as he took off his helmet and pulled out the foam earplugs he had stuffed in his ears. A few of the other soldiers, the more experienced ones, took off their helmets to pull out their earplugs as well. The inside of the Blackhawks averaged 120 decibels, and Sam didn't intend to lose his hearing—not from flying, anyway. Maybe from shooting his weapon, the butt of his M-60 stuffed up near his ear; maybe from firing off rocket-propelled grenade (RPG) rounds; or maybe from being too close to incoming artillery shells; but not from sitting like a sardine in the back of a noisy flying machine.

As the men circled around him, the choppers lifted and turned toward the refueling area, flying away from the well-organized tents and portable buildings of Camp Freedom.

Sam waited until the sound of the chopper rotors and

turbine engines had faded away, then turned to his men. "It was a good night," he said, congratulating his team. "We killed a bunch of bad guys and didn't lose anyone. Thirteen to zero. Not a bad soccer score. More, though, it was important for us to take the safety of the compound away from them. But listen now, we've got another mission tonight. Brief at 2200. Get some sleep and be ready. We'll rally for team dinner at 2100. The cook promised steak and potatoes. That will give you something to dream about. Now go get some rest."

He paused, his men standing with stooped shoulders around him. "Any questions?" he concluded. The group was silent, tired but happy, and very ready for sleep. "All right. Thank you, gentlemen. I'll see you tonight."

Sam stuck out his hand, and his team gathered in a tight circle, placing their dirty hands upon his. "Wolfman!" they cried together, yelling their unit's call sign, then turned and split up, heading for the enlisted hooches and tents. Showers and chow could wait; they were too exhausted now. In five minutes, most of them would be asleep on their cots, their weapons carefully secured but their faces still dirty, some gloves still on their hands, their flak vests on the floor. Two hours from now, a few would wake and head for the showers (a base-camp luxury that had to be taken advantage of), get something to eat, then hit the sack again. But most would sleep straight until late afternoon, when the sun started dipping and the temperature started to fall.

Sam watched his men separate, wiping a stream of black sweat from his eyes, then turned to follow, head low, helmet under his arm, weapon slung across his shoulder, his flak vest open at the chest. The sun was just half an orb above the horizon, but it seemed he could already feel its heat. Amazing how quickly the desert transformed from cold night to hot day.

Sam had walked only ten steps when he saw his

commander moving toward him with a deliberate stride. The captain looked determined and stared directly at him. For a moment Sam pretended not to see him; he was tired and irritated and he didn't want to talk. He didn't like the captain. The two rarely saw eye to eye.

Then the image of the murdered children in the Iranian village flashed again through his mind. How many reports and affidavits had he been required to fill out, detailing the gruesome attack at Agha Jari Deh? He suspected his captain had another report or statement for him to sign. He turned away and kept walking.

The thought of the massacre churned the juices in his gut. He thought of it too often. He wanted to leave it behind. He wanted to never think of it again. But everything around him seemed to remind him somehow: a small hand, a buddy's letter from his son, a local girl in her white dress standing on a street corner and staring at him—too many things brought back the dark memory. And the continual rehashing of the mission, what went right, what went wrong, who were the killers, why had they done what they did, it all amounted to nothing but dark memories. He was growing more bitter at having to rehash it again and again.

He thought of the girl, her dark eyes and long hair, exquisitely beautiful, even in her grief. He thought of her reaching out to her father, a charred corpse. He wanted to forget her, wipe the memory away. But he knew that he wouldn't. It was the price he would pay. All soldiers paid a price for their service by the thoughts that remained in their heads. A few of the memories were good. Some were evil and dark and painful. They had to live with them all. That was just the way it was.

But this one . . . this one was different from anything before. Harder. More fierce. Why couldn't he keep her out of his mind?

Sam glanced at his commander, then lowered his eyes.

"Brighton," the captain called out, and Sam reluctantly turned to face him. The captain, long and lanky, a West Point graduate, walked quickly toward him, an uncomfortable look on his face.

"What's up, boss?" Sam asked after saluting wearily.

"You got a telephone call," the captain answered.

Sam looked surprised. "I hope it's not your little sister again," he said dryly. "I've told her a thousand times not to call me at work."

The captain didn't smile. His little sister, the new Miss Virginia, had become a hot topic among the men in his squad, and he was growing a little weary of their constant jokes. "In your dreams, Sammy boy." He slapped Sam on the back. "And over my dead body. Now come with me."

"Where are we going?"

"You have a phone call. Quick. He's been holding."

The two men started to walk. "Who is it?" Sam asked, though he suspected that he already knew.

"The White House," the captain answered.

Sam shook his head. His dad on the phone.

His father, an Air Force two-star general, was on special assignment from the Pentagon to the National Security Staff. He worked at the White House, directly for the president, acting as special counsel on National Security affairs. It was one of the most coveted jobs in the military, but Sam also knew that the weight of the assignment was crushing him down. His father had aged fifteen years in the past twenty-four months, the pressure squeezing the life out of him like the juice from an orange.

His mind raced, trying to think of a reason that his father might call. Would he call with good news? Probably not. His gut tightened up.

The captain quickened his step toward the Operations Center. "Pick it up," he said. "He's been on hold for five minutes already." Sam recognized the strain in the captain's voice. He had grown familiar with the sound, and he doubled his pace. But his boss deferred to him, walking at his side instead of leading the way. Sam knew it was unnerving to the captain whenever the White House called. Truth was, it was unnerving to the regiment and battalion commanders as well—it was unnerving to everyone from the chief of staff down. But there was nothing he could do about it. His father was who he was. Sam didn't say anything as the captain walked nervously at his side.

Though he had never talked about his father, never so much as mentioned his name, it was impossible for the men in his unit not to know, and Sam knew how stressful it was for the captain to have the son of a two-star general in his command, the son of the special counsel to the president, no less. Best case for the captain, it was a zero sum game: Everything went perfectly, Sam stayed healthy, and no one said anything. But if Sam got wounded or killed, or the unit didn't perform in an exceptional way, who would answer the hard questions that would come slamming down? Who was going to call the White House to tell the old man? Because of this, Sam knew the captain would happily ship him out, send the source of his problems to the next unit down the line. And Sam understood it. He would have felt the same way.

The irony was that Sam was the best soldier in the unit, courageous, faithful, always ready to go, always willing to put his neck on the line. Which was *exactly* the problem. Sam acted as if he had no fear. He acted like there were angels protecting him every day. He wasn't stupid, but he was brave, almost brazenly so, and his boss often scolded him for having to be in the middle of the fight.

"Geez, man, can't you ever stay out of the line of fire!" his captain had once screamed at him.

Sam looked up from examining a bullet hole in his shirt. The shell had shredded the loose material directly under his arm, leaving an entry and exit hole two inches from his chest.

"Do you *always* have to be in the very thick of the fight!" the captain cried again.

Sam had shaken his head, pushing his leather-gloved finger through the hole near his flak vest. "Wow, that was close." He looked up and smiled.

"Can't you just *once* stay at camp and take your turn guarding the perimeter like everyone else!"

"Hey, baby, that's not why I'm here," was all Sam had replied.

So it bothered Sam to have the captain walking at his side, almost half a step behind him, as if Sam should lead the way.

Moving into the Operations Center, the unit XO, a young major with a ridiculously thin mustache, was holding the satellite phone, which he thrust toward Sam as if it might explode. Then he turned away quickly, pretending to work through a pile of papers on his desk. Sam noticed his regiment commander, a thick lieutenant colonel, standing by his office door. The captain walked toward the colonel but neither one of them said anything, though they tried not to make it obvious that they wanted to hear.

Sam turned his back to his commanders. "Hey, Dad," he said.

"Hi, Sam, how are you?" his father's voice echoed through the satellite phone.

"Good, Dad. Fine. What's going on?"

There was a short pause, which Sam immediately noticed, and his chest tightened again. "Things okay, Dad? Mom okay? Luke and Ammon?"

"They're all good, Sam . . ."

Sam considered the other possibilities. He thought of his biological parents, two social misfits who constantly struggled along. "Did the old man get knifed in another bar fight?" he asked. "The ol' lady call for more money? Tell them to bite it, Dad, you don't owe them anything . . ."

"No, Sam, none of that. Really, everything is fine. I was just calling to, you know . . . say hello, see how you are."

Sam didn't believe it. He had already recognized the anger in his father's voice.

There was another moment of silence. "I understand you just got in from an operation?" the general then said.

"Yes sir," Sam replied. He knew this wasn't the reason the general had called, but he had no choice but to wait until his father got to the point.

"It went okay, I hope?"

"You know how it is over here, Dad. You take one step forward, you hit a land mine and get blown a couple steps back. But tonight was pretty good. We got a couple of the bad guys and took back some of their ground. And none of my guys were hurt, which is all I could ask."

"You're all right then . . ."

Sam was growing frustrated. "Dad, you really didn't call me to talk about the mission, did you?" he said. "I go out every night. You never call. Now, what's going on?"

Sam heard the sound of rustling paper, then the soft squeak of his father's office chair, indicating he had stood up. "Sammy, you had a mission a couple days ago," his father said in a quiet voice. "A mission into western Iran."

Sam bit his lip. "We probably ought not to talk about this right now."

"We need to, Sam."

"It was a coded mission, Dad. If you really want to discuss

it, I need to get to a secure telephone." An image of the massacre shot again through his head. "But Dad, I'd really rather not talk about it, unless we really have to."

"Sam, listen to me, okay. I know about the mission. I'm the guy who sent your unit there. And I don't need you to tell me about it. I already know everything. But there's something you need to know. Something you're not going to like."

Sam sighed bitterly. What could be worse than what he had seen? "Whatever it is, Dad, I think I can handle it," he said.

* * *

Major General Neil S. Brighton stood in his White House office, a cramped inner room stuffed with classified folders, locking file cabinets, a small desk, and two blue leather chairs. He ran a hand through his thick hair and paced, the phone at his ear, while staring angrily at the front page of the *Washington Post.*

The photograph was grainy and blurred, but heart-wrenchingly powerful. A picture may be worth a thousand words, yes, but not one of them had to be true, and this photograph was painfully deceiving. A dead child, a smear of blood on his chest, a dried trickle of red running from his shoulder and down the underside of his arm to drip peacefully off his fingertips and onto the ground. A woman crying in anguish while holding her son. Smoke and black vapor filled the entire background; it looked as if an entire village was in flames. Two U.S. soldiers stood side-by-side, looking past the carnage, one of them smoking a fresh cigarette. Their eyes were dull and deadly, as if there was no feeling at all. Sergeant Samuel Brighton was in the center of the photograph, rubbing his hands on the side of his face.

U.S. Soldiers Accused of Iranian Atrocities
Pentagon denies secret war in Iran

The general stared at the picture of his son and thought of his wife. She was going to be sick. He thought of Sam's brothers. They would turn white with rage. He read the byline on the story: Mr. Lawrence O'Neil. The reporter *had* to know the story was a lie! The photographs had been floating around radical Arabic newspapers, televisions, and web sites for a couple days now, but no one in the western press had bothered picking them up. No one believed the accusations. Until Mr. O' Neil.

Brighton thought of his position in the White House, knowing he might be forced to resign. If the press made the connection between him and his son, if they smelled the fresh blood, regardless of the absurdity of the allegations or what the truth was, he might be forced to withdraw in order to protect the president.

If he had to go, he didn't care. He would resign if they asked.

The only thing he cared about was protecting Sam, a young man whom, though adopted, he loved as much as his other sons.

Brighton slapped the paper on his palm and swore bitterly.

It was a lie. Everyone knew it. But that was how the game was played now. The U.S. had a lot of enemies who didn't care about the truth.

Inaccurate but true was an acceptable standard to them.

The general swore again, breathing into the phone. "I'm holding the *Post,*" he finally said to his son. "Your picture's on the front page."

"Really!"

"Before you get too excited, you better let me explain."

Sam remained silent while his father read him the first five paragraphs of the story. The telephone hummed when his father was through. Sam was clearly stunned. "Has Mom seen the picture?" he asked quietly.

"No. Not yet."

"Can you hide it? Hide the papers? Tell her friends not to say anything."

"I'm trying, Sam. But it's likely that—"

"It will kill her if she sees that. She'll go through the roof."

"Listen, Sam, let's not worry about your mother for right now. I'll try to keep it from her, but even if I do, that's not the main point. Worst case, she sees it and throws a couple pillows at the paper boy or maybe writes a nasty rebuttal, which would only muddy the air. Either way, she is strong, I'm not worried about her. It's you, my boy, that I'm worried about . . . "

"You're worried about me!" Sam exclaimed. "Over this! Come on, Dad, if this is the worst thing that happens to me, I can certainly handle it." His voice was light now and clearly relieved. "So some puke gets my picture from Al Jezzera and prints some lies in the press. So what! Think I care? Me and my buddies quit reading the newspapers a *long* time ago. This is no big deal, Dad. No big deal at all."

Brighton hesitated. "I was worried . . . " he continued.

"Who you better be worried about is that slime-ball reporter!" Sam said. "Who is this guy, anyway! Is he such a fool as to believe his own words?"

Brighton almost laughed. "You want his name? We could go meet him in a bar next time you're back in the States." Brighton laughed as he thought of the recent scene in a German pub, when he and Sam had been forced to fight.

"Go and get him, no way! I say you send his sorry butt over here. Let him spend a week with my unit, then see what he writes."

Brighton smiled in satisfaction. What a difference that would make.

"So I made the front page of the *Post?*" Sam muttered, then chuckled again.

Brighton could picture his son's face, the great smile and strong chin. "Yeah, pretty cool, huh," he answered. They were both laughing now.

"You know, Dad, my only regret is I've wasted my fifteen minutes of fame while I'm over here. What a bummer. I feel cheated! I don't get to savor my time in the sun." Sam laughed again. "Bummer," he repeated, then grew serious once more. "But listen, Dad, try to hide it from Mom, okay? That's all I care about. This slime-ball reporter, my image, my face in the press, that means nothing to me. And it will blow over long before I get home anyway. But it will hurt Mom. She'll get angry. So try to hide it, will you?"

"I will, son," Brighton answered, "but there's something else I want to talk to you about . . . "

Brighton fell silent as his mind raced through the past couple of days. He thought about his dead friend, the Crown Prince of Arabia. There was so much going on. So much uncertainty. He was truly frightened. He had a stone in his chest. What was going on in Saudi Arabia, one of the most vital and dangerous places on earth? Had Prince Abdullah come to power? Had Abdullah killed his brother? What had happened to the king? *Had he killed him too*?

The general huffed in frustration, then threw the newspaper on the desk. It landed face up, Sam's picture staring at him, and he flipped it over with the tip of his pen.

He thought of the Cherokees, the elite Deltas that were going to pull Sam into their midst. They went to the worst holes on the face of the earth and did the most rotten missions, taking care of the problems that no one else was willing to tackle, no one else could handle, and no one in the government wanted to acknowledge had to be done.

One in ten thousand soldiers was asked to join the Cherokees, and Brighton was proud of his son. But he was afraid for him too. The unit suffered horrible attrition. Theirs was a dangerous, hungry, exhausting, and blood-soaked world. They were also a group of the most dedicated soldiers in the military. Every one of them believed they were serving a cause that was worthy of their deaths. Though he knew Sam had the passion for the task, he was less certain that he himself would be willing for his son to make that sacrifice.

As he thought, the phone line fell quiet until he heard Sam's voice again. "Dad?" Sam was saying. "Is everything okay?"

Brighton clenched his jaw, then took a deep breath. "Sure, Sam, everything's fine. Really busy, you know. Sorry. I lost my train of thought for a moment . . ."

"That was more than a moment."

Brighton didn't reply.

"That's okay, Dad," Sam answered. "It just means you're getting old."

"You have no idea, Sammy, no idea. What was I saying then?"

"We were talking about my mug on the front page on the *Post*. But then you said there was something else you wanted to tell me."

Brighton hesitated. He shouldn't say anything, but he couldn't hold back. He would say only a few words. "Sam, I'm going to give you a heads up, okay? But this is just a private conversation between father and son. You understand me, Sammy. This is private, okay?"

"All right, Dad," Sam answered. "This is between you and me."

"You and me, Sam. You understand that . . ."

"Maybe it'd be better then, Dad, if you just—"

"No, Sam, I want you to know. I want you to know that I gave it my blessing, so that when they talk to you, you won't hesitate for me."

"What are you talking about, Dad?"

"Listen, Sam, just listen, all right? Some things are happening. Some good things, some bad. And some of them will affect you. So you've got to be ready." He paused again. "Sam, I know you expected to stay with your unit in Iraq for a year or more. But it might turn out differently. You might find yourself somewhere else."

Sam paused before asking, "Why would I have to leave my unit? What are you saying, Dad?"

Brighton was firm now. "Just keep yourself sharp. That's all I should say. Keep busy. Do your mission. But be prepared for something new, something that makes me very proud. It might be a week. Might be a few days. Either way, be ready for a call."

Sam thought a long moment. He knew from the sound of his father's voice that he wouldn't say any more. "All right then, Dad. I'll be ready. Now you take care of Mom."

"I will."

"And Luke and Ammon."

Brighton cleared his throat. "Sam, you know that Ammon and Luke will be leaving on their missions soon."

"How are they?" Sam wondered.

"All right."

"You don't sound too convincing."

"They are okay," Brighton answered. "But you know, sometimes I wonder about Luke. He seems so unfocused. So . . . I don't know, easygoing, like he's satisfied with whatever life gives him. He doesn't push himself like you and

Ammon do, and I worry sometimes. He's been seeing this girl. He really likes her. Sometimes I wonder what's going on in his head? Does he really see the big picture?"

"You know that I didn't see the picture either, at least not the same picture as you."

"You did what you did. And I'm always proud of you."

"Yeah, well, you tell Luke he better get himself prepared for his mission. Tell him that for me, Dad. Tell him he better go or I'll come home, pig-thump him, drag him to the bishop's office, and sign the papers for him. I mean it, Dad. I didn't do it. It was a mistake, I can see that, but I have another purpose now. He's got his own mission, a real mission, and I am counting on him."

Brighton hesitated. "I'll tell him," he said.

"I'm serious, Dad. Tell him to go on a mission or I'll come home and bust his head."

Brighton almost laughed. He knew Sam could do it, but it might be harder than he thought. Luke had grown two inches and thirty pounds since Sam had seen him last. "I wonder if it's a good idea to force someone to go on a mission by threatening to bust his head," he said.

"Okay, I'll rephrase that. Tell him to *please* get ready for his mission or I'll be very, *very* sad."

"Okay," Brighton laughed. "He won't want that, I'm sure."

"Okay then, Dad. Now, listen, I think I'd better go."

"All right. Keep your head down."

"I always do, Dad."

"That's not what I hear."

"Yeah, well, whatever. I'll see you sometime, okay? Tell Mom I love her. Tell her I might be able to come home for Christmas."

"I'll tell her, Sam."

The two men said good-bye, and Sam set down the receiver on the satellite phone. He stared at it a moment, unaware that his commander was watching him.

A few days, his father had warned him.

What was going on now?

* * *

Major General Neil Brighton sat on the corner of his desk, pondering what the future might hold for his son—for *all* his sons. Unbidden, the face of Prince Abdullah swam before his eyes. The general knew the prince; they had met many times. And there was something about him, something . . . cold. He was so cocky. So prideful. So full and arrogant. It was almost as if he knew something that no other man knew, as if he saw something coming that no one else could see.

Brighton reached over and picked up a red-bound report. Classified. Top-secret. White House National Security Staff. He flipped it open and looked at the photograph and the two-page memo inside.

The Pakistani general's face was gritty and grim. His mustache hung over his large lips, and his eyes were dark as wet coal. The Pakistani was in charge of his nation's nuclear program. And the photograph showed him talking to one of Abdullah's senior men.

Neil Brighton shivered, cold running down his spine.

His instincts were screaming. No, this was more than that. This wasn't just his instincts. The Spirit was shouting at him: *Danger. There is danger.* He shivered again.

The idea of danger led his thoughts again to Sam and the Cherokees who would be recruiting him within the week. The unit was so secret that even the code name was classified and changed every three months to keep Congress and the press at bay. They were a top-secret Special Forces unit that worked on the razor edge of the law. Some would argue that what they did was illegal (the U.N. would certainly say that it was), for they slipped across the borders of both friends and foes, operating in countries against which the U.S. was not at war. And they did things, they got to people, that no one ever talked about—no one in the military, no one in the administration or Congress, certainly no one in the press. They operated in Israel, Europe, and Pakistan. They operated in Tajikistan, southwestern China, and Saudi Arabia as well.

They were the best America had to offer, her most valiant sons, willing to sacrifice and suffer to take peace to the most dangerous parts of the world.

The general shook his head sadly.

Was it a good use of fine men? Sometimes he wondered. It wasn't clear anymore.

He frowned and looked up, staring through his bulletproof window at the deep White House lawn. What had brought them to this moment? Why had it come to this? Things had accelerated so quickly, and they were accelerating still.

The world was spinning. Would it ever regain control?

chapter nine

Camp Freedom
West of Baghdad, Iraq

The night after Sam Brighton had taken the call from his father, his team had been tasked to do a night recon on some suspect houses in Northern Baghdad, but the mission had been aborted due to lack of helicopter transports to infiltrate the team. As a result, Sam spent the night in his bed, under his covers when it was dark, quiet, and cool, instead of having to sleep in the middle of the day, with the light, heat, and noise. He got a good night's rest, something he hadn't enjoyed in more than two weeks.

Next morning he woke early, ate some breakfast, cleaned his gear, swept the tent floor (a completely pointless thing to do), waited in line for a nonclassified computer to send some emails (he mostly communicated with his other army buddies scattered around the world), then went down to the unit Operations Center to see what was going on.

Entering the enormous tent, Sam felt the cool air. Outside, the morning sun had already grown hot, and the air-conditioned tent was a welcome relief. The Ops Center was stuffed with loads of electronic and communications gear—satellite telephones, GPS receivers, more than two dozen portable computers, hand-held devices, UHF radios to talk with the unit's helicopter pilots and ground crews, FM radios to talk with the ground troops when they were in combat on the ground—and all of this equipment demanded cool, clean air. The desert was excruciatingly hard on men, equipment, and machines, and it was a constant effort to keep everything from choking on the sand and dust.

The Ops C. was quiet; only a few soldiers were there. None of the unit's combat teams had been tasked with combat excursions, so, except for a few standard security patrols in the small towns along the road between Camp Freedom and the airport, everyone had a little time to catch up on things. For a moment, Sam wondered what day it was. He glanced at his watch, a military issue black dial with the date and time: 9:36, Sunday morning. Now, wasn't that nice, he thought, the Sabbath was being honored, even in a war zone. Coincidence? Absolutely. But a nice one all the same.

He looked past the communications consoles in the middle of the room and spotted Joseph "Bono" Calton, a dark-skinned lieutenant who was one of his very best friends.

Bono was relatively old for a lieutenant. For one thing, he'd converted to the LDS Church as a senior in high school (despite the objections of his father, a devout believer in the Great Church of the Money and Having More than the Other Guy Down the Street), then served a mission, spending two years walking up and down hopeless apartment buildings in Germany, preaching the gospel in a country where it seemed that no one really cared. Then, despite the fact that his parents were wealthy, Bono had insisted on supporting himself through school. Fiercely independent of their money, he worked a series of menial jobs, seeming to take great pride in waiting tables and janitoring at a local school in order to pay his own way. The result of his independence was that he hadn't graduated until he was twenty-five, whereupon he had immediately joined the army. Many times Bono had wondered aloud which had disappointed his father more, when he had joined the army or the Mormon church? Now a Special Forces officer, he was a poster boy for the twenty-first-century soldiers fighting an unconventional war—fluent in Arabic and German, an expert marksman, equally good with a sophisticated GPS computer and in hand-to-hand combat with a knife. And he seemed to have the endurance of a mule—he could hike for twelve hours without stopping to rest. Most important, with his dark skin and dark eyes, he could blend in perfectly with the local populace. Sam had always wondered why his friend was so dark-skinned, but once he had seen a picture of Bono's mother, a beautiful Moroccan his father had met while spending a summer in Northern Africa, he understood.

Three and a half years out of college, the lieutenant had just celebrated his twenty-eighth birthday, though he looked a bit older, with his dark face and sharp eyes. Having grown up in L.A. and graduated from one of the rich-kid high schools they made prime-time soap operas about, if anyone had an excuse to be spoiled, Bono certainly did. Sam knew that his dad had made a zillion dollars in the dot-com craze, getting out when the getting was good and settling down to a life of tennis, margaritas, and investing his cash. But when it came to money, Bono seemed completely uninterested. The only thing he really ever talked about was his family, and sometimes Sam got tired of looking at pictures of the two beautiful blondes, one his daughter, one his wife. Maybe he was only jealous—it was painfully clear the lieutenant had something special that he did not have.

Like a lot of guys in the unit, the lieutenant had several nicknames: Sniper (for his shooting), Abu (his dark features), the Mule (his flat-foot plodding). But most called him Bono for his inexplicable attachment to a brand of cheap Korean running shoes. Still, he was such an imposing figure that none of the enlisted guys dared call him anything but lieutenant to his face. And in a formal setting or in combat everyone called him "sir."

It hadn't taken more than a few days for Brighton and the lieutenant to become very good friends. They were alike—dedicated, fearless, both with a bit of attitude. And both were in the army because they loved the fight and believed in the cause. Sam knew that Bono could have followed in his father's tracks, taken over his business affairs and spent Wednesdays mornings on the golf course and Friday nights at the club. He also knew that Bono would just as soon drive splinters of wood under his fingernails as spend his life behind a desk.

In this one thing the two men were the same. They were driven by ambition, but not by ambition for cash.

Bono hadn't yet noticed Sam standing near the doorway, so he kept his head down, concentrating on his work. In the quiet of the empty Operations Center, Sam's thoughts drifted back.

* * *

Sam's Delta unit had been bouncing in and out of Iraq, Pakistan, and Afghanistan (as well as several "non-host nations," where they had not been invited and were *definitely* not supposed to be) for more than three years. As one of the Army's most highly trained and versatile units, the Deltas went where they were called, which meant they spent a lot of their time on the road. While most army combat units were eventually assigned more-or-less permanent facilities for their living quarters, some of the more fortunate ones even ending up in former palaces of the ruling elites, the Deltas were not usually so lucky. Knowing they were far more mobile and in high demand, they didn't spend a lot of time worrying about their living conditions. That seemed fruitless and wasteful. They were Deltas, after all—they didn't need air conditioning or swimming pools. They needed clean weapons, lots of drinking water, and a mission every night.

Bono had been assigned to Sam's unit just five months before. Sam clearly remembered the day he had been tasked to pick up the new lieutenant at the airport in Baghdad, where he watched Bono climb down the makeshift ramp from the enormous 747, a contract carrier ferrying soldiers in and out of the country. Sam took him to Camp Freedom and showed him his tent (which had become suddenly available when the previous captain had been killed by a sniper while out on patrol), then helped him unpack his gear and showed him around.

On the afternoon of that first day, Sam sat in the corner of the Ops Center, watching the young lieutenant work.

Like any organization, the U.S. Army had its share of weak, cowardly, selfish, ignorant, and truly bad officers. But such men never made it into combat positions, or, if they did, they were quickly removed. Men's lives were on the line, the chain of command understood that, and no one suffered fools in a combat zone. Indeed, the men who volunteered for and achieved the status of combat officer were some of the best that the U.S. had to offer. But still, there were variations in their capacities to lead. There were good officers and great officers, brilliant leaders and others who were not as talented or creative. Sam was instantly curious which kind of officer the new lieutenant would be.

It generally took the enlisted men a few days, maybe even just a few hours, to evaluate their new platoon leaders, and their first impressions almost always proved to be uncannily accurate. Sam was better than most at evaluating his leaders, so, knowing he would be working with the lieutenant for the next eight months or so, he set about to watch him and learn what he could. He watched how Bono took care of his equipment, how he spoke to the men—both the senior officers around him and the men under him. He listened to the tone of his voice and the things that he said. He noted the things he carried around in his pockets and the optional equipment he had.

On the evening of Bono's first day, the regiment commander pulled Sam aside. "What do you think?" he asked in a whisper, nodding toward the newest lieutenant in his outfit.

Sam stared at the back of Bono's head. "He keeps a military-issued Bible in his chest pocket all the time. He collects knives and switchblades. Got more than a dozen in all. He's got a drop-dead gorgeous wife and he pulls out her picture every chance that he gets. And he's got a tiny, pearl-handled .22 strapped to the inside of his calf, a cheesy little thing that isn't going to kill anyone unless he shoots them point-blank. Looks like something he might have picked up in Harlem for thirty bucks and some crack. But it's only three inches long and real easy to conceal."

The commander waited, not knowing. "So . . . ?" he pressed.

"I like him," Sam answered. "In fact, I like him a lot. He's thorough. He's careful. But he's not afraid to act. He likes his family, and that keeps him from being too stupid, but it's pretty clear he's not afraid to get in a fight. So yeah, I like him. This is a guy I would go to battle with."

The lieutenant colonel nodded and smiled. "Good. You got him, then," he said. "Show him the ropes for a few days. I'm not reassigning you from Captain Rogers's unit, I just want you to work with him for a while, is all."

"Sure, sir. But then, if it turns out that he and I work well together, maybe you would consider assigning me to the lieutenant's squad permanently."

"Not bloody likely," the commander shot back. "I need you with Rogers. You are too important to him."

* * *

Three nights later, Bono had been sent on his first patrol. As the highest ranking enlisted man in the squad, Sam stayed close to his side.

It was just after sunset. There were four of them in a battle-hardened HUMVEE, the standard military personal transport that had, since the first year of the war in Iraq, been reinforced with thick armor walls and floor. Years before, when the U.S. had first invaded Iraq, the soldiers had been forced to compensate for the inadequate armor in the original HUMVEE design by piling sandbags on the floor and strapping scrap iron to the sides. It was the only way they could think of to protect themselves from the seemingly unstoppable roadside bomb attacks that occurred every day. The terrorists had proven ingenious, even brilliant, the U.S. generals had been forced to admit. Taking the path of least resistance, the terrorists (Sam refused to call them insurgents; anyone who primarily targeted innocent Iraqi civilians—women, school children, old men sweeping sand off the streets, young mothers carrying their babies while waiting for the bus—was clearly a terrorist and not worthy of any other name) had learned how to hide among the civilians, how to hit and then run. They had two primary weapons: suicide bombers and, for those not yet willing to have a face-to-face conversation with their Maker, what the U.S. press called IEDs, Improvised Explosive Devices, or simply roadside bombs. The local troops called them dead REDs, or Remotely Exploded Devices. These ingeniously improvised roadside bombs could be made of almost any explosive material, including old mortar shells, plastic explosives, grenades, and nails packed around TNT. Most of the detonators were activated through cell phones, and the battle tactics were simple: plant the device, hide, wait until a U.S. convoy or Iraqi government vehicle drove by, dial the cell number, and watch the enemy get blown to bits. On Sam's first tour to Iraq, at a time when the Iraqi government was fully functioning though still in its early days, the terrorist cells had been using dead REDs on an almost daily basis. In fact, on Sam's first day in the country, even while riding from the airport, his convoy had been attacked by a roadside bomb. No one had been hurt, but a lot of sand had been blown in the air. A quick investigation of his good fortune revealed that the terrorist had panicked and called the cell phone number too late, causing the powerful, double-packed mortar shell to explode after the convoy had passed. Phone records would indicate he had nervously dialed two wrong numbers before finally getting it right, allowing time for the convoy to pass. But still, the sound of the explosion had proven a lousy welcome to the country.

Though Sam and the others would laugh about it many times, each of them, inside their guts, hated to wonder.

Two wrong numbers, and they had lived. One good dialer, and they might have died. How many of their nine lives had been sucked up on that one?

It was all so unpredictable.

That first night with Bono, while driving away from Camp Freedom, Sam had slapped the side of his new HUMVEE as he drove. The HUMVEE was heavy with its extra armor and a full load of weapons and fuel, and it felt slow and cumbersome under his hand.

With the new lieutenant sitting at his side, Sam kept his eyes moving, his head constantly swiveling from one side to the other. The sun had set, and it became dark as only the desert can be, a sort of eerie, moonlit twilight that emphasized the shadows and created fleeting ghosts of gray and black that seemed to run across the road.

Earlier in the day, a couple of Apache attack helicopters had reported that a single anti-aircraft missile had been launched toward them from a small cluster of shacks and tin-roofed, cinder-block shanties on a tiny peninsula near the Tigris River. There had never been any reports of hostile action in the area—the small village was inhabited by dying fishermen and their old women, the younger generations having been taken either to serve in the army or to be servants in the city many years before—and none of the Apache's defensive systems had detected the presence of a radar-guided missile, but because one of the pilots had insisted he had seen a smoky trail coming toward him before falling out of range, Bono and his team had been sent to investigate.

The men approached the village along the winding, dirt road that followed the bends in the Tigris. The land was marshy here, with cattails and reeds growing higher than a man could see, and the water was slow and brackish and heavy with silt. The fishing had once been good here, but that was years before, and the small village, never more than an Iraqi *dinar* above the poverty line, had fallen into abject destitution over the past generation or so.

Approaching the village, Bono commanded Sam to bring the HUMVEE to a stop before venturing onto the marshy peninsula. It was maybe three thousand meters to the village, about two miles or so. Bono got out of the HUMVEE and stood near the front wheel, studying the village through his night vision goggles. Sam opened his door and followed until he was standing at his side. Staring through the goggles, Bono could see the common fire flickering between the shanties and a few old men standing near, but that was about all. He dropped his glasses and listened. The birds had fallen silent, but they never cried at night, and the only sound to be heard was the water lapping gently against the marshy shore.

Bono turned to Sam. "You realize, of course, there's no way to approach the village without announcing our coming."

Sam nodded as he studied the sandy road that led to the village. It was pitted with mud holes and deep ruts, with broken branches and dead palm leaves lying across the rough track. Years might have passed since a vehicle had been driven down this road, and it would take them some time, maybe five or ten minutes, to navigate across the marsh to the village. He glanced back at the HUMVEE. It was a great machine, powerful and heavy, but loud. Very loud. Built to carry men into combat, there was nothing stealthy about this vehicle. Its enormous diesel engine belched like a locomotive, maybe louder, and with sometimes more smoke.

"Think they've heard us already?" Sam asked the lieutenant.

Bono shook his head and nodded at the night air. "Wind is blowing towards us. They haven't heard anything."

"We could hoof it to the village."

Bono thought. "Don't think we should," he said. "We need the protection the HUMVEE has to offer. Especially since there's just four of us and being out here, where there's no cover but this reed grass. We've got no backups, no artillery or air patrols. Who knows what we'd be walking into? According to the Apache pilot, there's an entire battalion of surface-to-air missiles hiding in the village. Do I believe that? Not at all. But I'm not willing to bet on the lives of my men. Not going to risk it. Too dangerous right now."

"Okay, boss, but you realize if we jump in the HUMVEE and go tooling off across the grass, we're going to give whoever is waiting in the village an awfully long time to know that we're coming. If they haven't seen us already—and they might have, it's amazing how good these natives' night vision can be—they'll hear us at least five or seven minutes out. That's an awful long time to announce we're coming if there are hostiles hiding there. Lots of time to hide or plan an ambush. Lots of time to lock us in their sights."

"Yeah," Bono muttered. "And you know what really ticks me off. There's no one hiding in the village. I'm sure there's nothing there. I mean, look at it. If you were an Iraqi soldier and wanted to pop off a couple missiles at passing U.S. aircraft, can you think of a *worse* place to do it! No cover. No escape routes. No place to hide. You telling me those starving fishermen are going to offer you any help? What have they got to offer! A couple dry fish? I don't know what our Apache driver saw, but if it was a missile it *didn't* come from this place."

Sam nodded. He agreed. "But you know what will happen if we don't check it out," he said.

"Yeah, I've been around long enough that I figure I do. If we don't check out the village, if we don't turn every stone and look behind every door, those aviation grunts will never relax. Every time they fly over this area, they'll be on edge. They'll zoom down and fly low, harassing these poor guys every chance that they get. One of their fly boys *saw* a missile and it *was* launched from here, so the first time they see smoke from the village fire or a flash of reflected light in the sun, bang! they'll come in, their guns blazing to take care of this place."

Sam nodded sadly. It was true. As a grunt he had learned the value of a pause, the value of evaluating a situation completely before he lifted his gun. But the aviation guys weren't so careful. They just didn't have the time. And because of that, they were much more likely to pull their triggers on their missiles and guns. More, they were so much more vulnerable, sitting like metal ducks in the air. And they never saw the results of their bullets. Sam suspected it was impossible to fully appreciate the ugliness of death when one imposed it from the air.

He stared at the village in the distance as he thought. "What do you propose?" he finally asked.

Bono started unstrapping his web belt. He laid it on the bumper of the HUMVEE, then stripped down to his fatigue pants and boots. "I'm going to float down the river," he explained as he walked to the rear of the HUMVEE where the tool kit was stowed. Pulling out a black garbage sack, he wrapped his BAR-15 assault rifle, then secured it with tape. "If I can get into the current, it will carry me across the channel and down to the village . . . "

"Unless you miss it, and then some oil tanker will find you somewhere off the coast of Kuwait," Sam replied. He knew the river was fast and deep in the middle.

"Yeah. Unless that happens. But assuming it doesn't, then this is my plan. Give me ten minutes in the water, then fire up Bertha and head out across the road. Make lots of noise, gun the engine, whatever it takes to let them know you're here. I'll set myself up on the northwest shore, opposite of your approach. I don't know for certain what kind of cover I'll have, but I'm assuming there will be marsh and weeds, about like what we have here. I'll keep in the cover, but get as close to the village as I can. You guys come screaming in. If any bad guys are there, I can cover you from their rear. If they try to retreat, we'll have them surrounded . . . "

"Surrounded! With four men! And from only two positions?"

"Whatever."

Sam looked at Bono, his dark face camouflaged to match the night. "You should take someone with you," he said.

"No. I won't need it. I'm only acting as a safety value, you know, just in case it turns out I'm wrong. But I'm sure there's no hostiles in this village. This will be nothing but a cakewalk, a chance for a nice moonlight swim."

Sam nodded slowly. "You know, sir, treading water for fifteen minutes in a snake-infested lagoon while holding a rifle and radio above the waterline to keep them from getting wet is hardly my idea of a good time. But hey, that's just me. If this is the way you want to do it, then I'm with you, man."

Bono was slipping toward the water. "It's cold," he said.

"Do you want me to—" Sam started to question, but it was already too late. The lieutenant had slipped through the marshes and already disappeared.

Sam glanced at his watch. He fingered his radio nervously, then paced back and forth. He waited eight minutes before climbing into the HUMVEE. "Let's go," he said.

"The boss said to give him ten minutes," the other NCO answered.

"Yeah, yeah," Sam shrugged. He hated the lieutenant being out there alone. He hated waiting. He hated being so far away from the boss. He counted to sixty. "Let's go," he said.

They fired up the HUMVEE and headed out across the deeply rutted road. One man rode shotgun, standing at the open hatch at the roof. All of the men were wearing night vision goggles, and they kept their headlights off as they drove. No sense illuminating themselves like a target in case there *were* bad guys in the village. "Ranger One, what you got?" Sam questioned over his radio, but Bono didn't answer, and Sam's chest tightened up. It took longer than they had hoped to forge their way across the swampland, pushing dead tree trunks and palm leaves like a dozer before them, but they finally pulled into the village, their engine racing like a drag machine.

They found the lieutenant waiting, sitting on a log next to the fire. The village leader was next to him, and the two men were talking like they were old friends. Bono motioned to his comrades as they came racing in. He pointed to the fire, where some fishes were frying on sticks that had been laid across the fire.

The other Deltas got out and walked toward him.

"So . . . I'm assuming there aren't any bad guys?" Sam started to question.

"Not so much as a pea shooter," Bono answered him. "And *Sayid* ell-Marhsif here has assured me that he loves the Americans and would never aid the terrorists. He had four sons; they are all gone, taken by Saddam's army. He has nothing but his fishing now. No grandchildren. No wife."

Sam bowed to the old man, who grinned toothlessly back at him.

"And ell-Marhsif has been kind enough to offer us dinner," Bono said.

Sam looked down at the fish. "They look like carp."

"Yeah, but if you cook them long enough, they taste like chicken," Bono said.

* * *

Standing in the Operations Center, Sam smiled as he remembered that first night on patrol. Yes, Bono had proven thorough, ingenious, and ready to think outside the box. He would do anything to get the job done. Put him in a firefight and he wouldn't hesitate. But he cared about the Iraqi people almost as much as he cared about his own, and he had the reasoning ability to think about the larger picture at hand. If there was one thing Sam had learned, it was to respect and appreciate the opportunity to work with men such as that.

Sam took a deep breath, then walked toward his friend. "What's up?" he asked as he sat on a metal chair next to him.

The lieutenant looked up. "Three hundred and eleven," he replied.

Sam stared straight ahead. "Fifty-four days to go."

"Unless I get extended."

Sam took out a handful of bubble gum, offered one to the lieutenant, then shoved a couple of pieces in his mouth. Double Bubble. Delicious. He'd been an avid chewer since his days in Little League. "Not going to happen," he answered after softening the gum in his mouth. "You're on your way home, my friend. They're not extending soldiers any longer. They won't keep you here more than your year."

The Mule smiled. "Boy, I hope so. Not that I don't love you, you know that . . . " he reached over and slapped a desert cockroach off his knee, "but baby, unless you're willing to dye your hair blonde and start wearing a dress, then I'm outta here."

Sam chewed, blew a little bubble, and nodded his head.

The two men were quiet a minute, both of them lost in thought. Talk of home had a way of doing that.

"Three hundred and eleven," the lieutenant repeated after a while.

"Fifty-four and counting," Sam answered again.

The unit radio crackled with static behind them and Bono looked at it, expecting something, but no voices came through.

"You've got TOC duty all day?" Sam asked him.

"Until noon, is all."

Sam motioned toward the nearly empty Operations Center. Two young specialists were working at computers, and there were some voices from behind the commander's closed door, but other than that, they were the only ones there. "Not a bad day to have desk duty," he offered. "You're not missing any action. Nice and quiet. If you've got to sit at a desk, you got a pretty good day."

Bono nodded slowly.

Sam looked down in the lieutenant's lap and saw the tiny set of scriptures there—the serviceman's edition of the New Testament and Book of Mormon. Bono was one of a dozen LDS soldiers at Camp Freedom, along with a couple of other officers and enlisted men. There were a few women, some with children, but most were young, single men. "What you got planned for our services this morning, Brother Bono?" he asked.

Bono shook his head. "Some fascinating stuff," he said.

"Hey, maybe I'll come, then, depending on what you're serving after the service for treats."

The lieutenant laughed, but didn't push it. The truth was, he'd seen Sam slip into the back of the tent that served as a chapel the last three weeks or so. He had seen him hide in the back (as if he could hide in a group of fifteen men), then slip out before anyone could talk to him. Sam always took the sacrament, and always bowed his head to pray, but seemed unwilling to socialize with the others. The lieutenant knew it wasn't because he was embarrassed to be associated with the LDS group. Quite the opposite, it seemed Sam made a point of telling anyone who asked that he was a Mormon. And if anyone dared to speak impolitely of the Church, he let them know immediately they'd have to deal with him.

So the Mule couldn't help but wonder what was going on in his head. Sam was clearly uncomfortable around them, as if he were embarrassed for himself. And though he didn't hide the fact that he was LDS, he clearly didn't feel part of their group.

The tactical radios crackled again as one of the teams called in their position report. The lieutenant keyed the microphone and acknowledged with a sharp "roger," then noted the time on his log.

"Who's out there?" Sam wondered, hunching his shoulders toward the radio.

"That was the Snowmen. They and the Tiger team are on security patrol around Al-Attina and Tirkish. We heard last night that—"

The radio crackled again. "Breadman, Tiger Two . . ." a soldier cut in.

Bono picked up the small FM microphone and answered, "Go, Tiger."

"Breadman, we've got something here." There was an unmistakable hesitation in the radio operator's voice. "We've got a small car," he went on, "license plate reads Juliet, Romeo, niner, niner, four, Romeo. Take a look at it, will you? Something's not right."

The lieutenant sat up instantly. If there was one thing the U.S. soldiers had learned, it was that danger could be found anywhere. He motioned to one of the young specialists sitting at the computer four empty seats away. She had already copied the license plate information and was entering the query into the INMEDS computer, the multi-unit, multi-service database of automobiles, names, addresses, phone numbers, locations, aliases, Iraqi driver's license numbers, anything that could be used to track an individual or group of people in Iraq.

While the specialist tapped at her computer, the lieutenant spoke again into his microphone. "What's the situation there, Tiger Two?" he asked. "Do you need some support?"

There was a moment of silence until the soldier came back.

"Negative, Breadman. It's probably nothing. We've got a small sedan parked in a private driveway on the south end of the block . . . " While he spoke, Sam reached over and pulled out a large urban map showing the narrow alleys and crooked roads that made up the small town of Al-Attina, an old industrial town seven kilometers south of the international airport. He slid the map across the desk to the lieutenant, who turned it 180 degrees so it faced him, then tapped his pencil on a narrow alley off one of the main thoroughfares.

"Tiger," he interrupted, "confirm your location is Twenty-one and Lashihhia?"

"Roger," the soldier came back. "And, like I was saying, we've got an abandoned vehicle on the street. It's got a small child locked inside. Looks like he's no more than two, maybe two and a half years old. The windows are rolled up, and he's dying in there. We've tried to open the doors, but they're locked. I've got some of my guys going house to house along the street here, but so far either no one is home or they claim they don't know who he is . . . "

The lieutenant straightened up, his face turning tense. He looked at the specialists, who shot a quick look back at him. "Anything in the INMEDS?" he demanded.

"Nothing so far, sir. The license plate isn't in the database. The vehicle, or at least that license plate number, isn't associated with any terrorists or insurgents that we know."

Bono dropped his head as he thought.

Sam moved toward him, glancing down at the map.

"Breadman," the radio crackled again. "You know, we've got to do something. This kid's dying in there. It's over ninety on the street. It must be more than one-twenty inside the vehicle. He's lethargic and sweating. Now he's just lying on the seat. He's flushed and dehydrated. We've got to get him out of there."

The lieutenant didn't hesitate. "NO!" he replied. "DO NOT TOUCH THE CHILD! This is a family issue. You've got to find his parents. They have to be in one of the houses somewhere."

The soldier hesitated, then called back again. "Breadman, we've been up and down this block twice already. There's almost no one home, but you know how it is, most of these guys are too scared of us. They won't answer their doors, and we don't want to bust them down. And yeah, I know we don't want to get involved in some lousy child-abuse thing, but I'm telling you, this is a cute little boy and we've got to get him out of this car. Sergeant Brunner is standing here beside me. He's going to bust the front window, then we'll unlock the door. We'll be careful not to hurt him, but we've got to get him out of there . . ."

"NO!" the Mule screamed.

But it was already too late.

Sam and Bono heard an incredible explosion before the radio went dead.

* * *

The car bomb had been planted inside the passenger's side of the door. The terrorist had rigged the device to explode when the window was broken or the car door unlocked. Based on the power of the detonation, the explosives forensic specialist estimated that the bomb was between ten and twelve pounds of dynamite, enough to kill everyone within twenty meters of the car.

Four U.S. troops, all members of Sergeant Brighton's unit, had been killed trying to rescue the little boy from the car. Another seven were wounded, almost the entire Tiger team, some of them critically burned and scarred. The entire afternoon was spent evacuating them, with Dustoff medivac choppers deployed from as far away as Kirkuk. While the wounded were cared for and evacuated, two more Delta teams, Sam's included, were deployed to the area, where they searched house to house, questioning everyone they could find within four blocks of the explosion. They learned the automobile had been parked and deserted late in the afternoon of the day before. Apparently, the little boy had spent part of a day, a night, and the morning alone in the abandoned car packed with dynamite, and all for the opportunity to blow a couple of U.S. soldiers to bits.

The terrorists knew the soldiers would help the little boy when they found him. No way they would leave him to die in the car.

Though Sam and his team interrogated everyone in the neighborhood, they learned little else and took no one into custody. This was a battle-worn area, with an explosive mix of Sunnis and Shiites, and the locals had learned it was far better, and much safer, not to say anything.

The most of the little boy they ever found was one of his shoes, which had been blown across the street and through a small apartment window, where it landed on the floor.

* * *

Late that night, Sam lay awake on his cot. His gut burned inside him, and his fists were clenched at his side.

He pictured the scene again and again. His dead comrades blown to pieces. The shoe of the little boy. The fire and the smell.

He cursed in frustration, a rage that boiled over inside. He cursed the whole war. It was pointless and worthless, a complete waste of time. What were they doing, losing good men like this, all in a fruitless attempt to save the population of this stinking country from themselves.

These people simply weren't worth it.

They should pack up and leave them to rot in their hell, leave them to canker in this cancer they loved so well. They were cowards, afraid to fight for themselves. Leave them. Not look back. Write them off, every one.

* * *

As Sam cursed bitterly, the black angel hunched beside him, kneeling, his arms at his side, his mouth pulled into a tight and hideous frown. His teeth flashed, the only white on his face, for his eyes were as dark and lifeless as the black hole in his soul.

"You hate them," Balaam whispered in the soldier's ear. *"These people are all idiots. Savages. Animals. They aren't capable of freedom. They're too stupid, too weak. They aren't like you, so clever, so capable, so strong. You are so much better than they are, so much smarter and good. Look at them all. Take a look at this place! Is there anything worth fighting for here? Is there any good in this land?"*

Balaam took a deep breath, thinking as he glanced at the other American soldiers that were sleeping around them. How he hated them all. How he hated what they stood for and the things they had done. How he hated their kindness and the reasons they fought.

* * *

Sam wrestled on his cot, stretching his legs uncomfortably. He felt so agitated and angry. Hatred was building inside. He sat up on his cot and rubbed his hands through his hair, his bare chest glistening in the dim, moonlit night. His dog tags hung from his neck, and the chain swayed against his chest as he rubbed his eyes.

* * *

"You hate them!" Balaam continued to hiss in his ear. *"They smell. They are dirty. These people are not like you. They are not as good as you are, nor as strong. They are lazy. They are stupid and evil and stubborn and weak. They aren't really God's children, they are . . . you don't know . . . something else . . . something less . . . something unworthy of democracy and the things you fight for."*

* * *

Sam shook his head and frowned, forcing the thoughts from his mind. He knew they weren't true, and he was ashamed for even thinking them.

But the little boy. The youngest martyr. How could he reconcile that!

He struggled again, trying to force the depressing thoughts from his mind. And though Balaam kept hissing at him, he wasn't listening anymore.

Yes, there were times when he wondered . . . times when he had his doubts.

But he knew that it was not the Iraqi people's fault. For almost three thousand years, these descendents of ancient Babylon had lived through a nearly endless cycle of subjection and strife. The idea of democracy was completely foreign to them.

But they wanted it. At least most of them did. It was just that there were enough of the others to make it *so* difficult.

Sam shook his head in frustration, thinking of the dead little boy. That was the real tragedy. All the children. They were innocent. And far too often now, they took the brunt of the war. Not from the U.S. soldiers, that was never true; the U.S. military took exceptional pains to protect civilians and innocents. But these insurgents, these evil men who claimed to be fighting for the people but were clearly fighting for the power they craved, they were all too willing to fight their battles between the arms of another man's children, using them as shields or as bait, as diversions or screens, taking any advantage the children might give them to spring a surprise.

Maybe because he had suffered as a little boy, Sam had an exceptional soft spot, an almost deadly weakness, for the children he saw. He wondered again, and not for the first time, if there wasn't something he could do for these innocents. He had seen far too many suffer—the little boy in the car, the young girl in Iran, so many others through the last year. If he could just think of something, anything, that might make a difference in even one of their lives.

He paused suddenly.

He had an idea.

He stood up instantly. He was going to need some help.

* * *

Four tents down from Sam, the lieutenant also lay awake on his cot. He thought of the little boy, then turned painfully to his side.

He thought of his daughter, and felt a cold quiver inside.

Then he heard a knock on the post outside his tent door. "Lieutenant! You awake?" It was Sergeant Brighton's voice.

"What's up?" he answered quickly, and Sam slipped through the tent door.

"Lieutenant, I really need a favor," Sam said in a hushed voice.

chapter ten

CAMP FREEDOM
IRAQ

A blazing sandstorm had wrapped Camp Freedom in a miserable blanket of suffocating brown dirt and sand as fine as talcum powder. It turned the afternoon a dismal brown while coating everything in fine grit, bringing security operations to a slow and gloomy crawl.

Sam stood alone in his tent. He tied a brown handkerchief over his mouth and nose, pulled his combat goggles down over his eyes, fastened the Velcro collar on his combat jacket, and headed out the tent door. As soon as he stepped into the wind, he felt the sand blowing down his collar, up his sleeves, around his fastened pant legs, and into his ears. He lifted a hand to block the wind as he made his way to the Operations Center. Before stepping inside, he shook off his clothes as best as he could, then dropped the handkerchief from his face and squeezed through the door, sliding in quickly to keep the sand at bay. A temporary shield had been put up between the door and the interior of the tent, and he brushed himself off from his boots to his hair, then pushed the heavy cloth back and stepped into the room.

The Ops C. was crowded and noisy. The sandstorm had

significantly complicated combat operations, and the officers and senior enlisted men were busy working their contingency plans. Sam saw Bono sitting at a makeshift plywood table in a quiet corner at the back of the center. Spread out on the desk in front of him were half a dozen satellite photographs, his next patrol order, a communications plan, and several other items.

The patrol order included the detailed Rules of Engagement (ROE) for the mission: a three- or four-page analysis of the anticipated enemy action, the purpose of the mission, the position of friendly forces, including the location and availability of air force fighters for ground support, ingress and emergency egress routes, communications plans, radio frequencies, code words and the meanings of various smoke and illumination signals, and a list of the teams that were assigned for backup and support. Written in large block letters across the cover page of the patrol order were the words *Prepare Now or Die,* a fairly effective means of reminding the squad leaders of the importance of preparing for their patrol. And though reviewing the patrol orders was one of the least liked tasks for most officers, Bono took the responsibility very seriously.

As Sam walked toward him, Bono kept his head in his work. Watching him, Sam thought he seemed to be nervous. Sam knew that the previous squad leader had been reassigned to logistics or chow hall or some other non-combat duty, and that Bono was determined not to make a miserable mistake, though it wasn't his career he was worried about nearly so much as his men.

Bono was writing notes in the margin of his tactical map; Sam watched over his shoulder as he worked. In the corner of the desk, Bono had placed a picture of his wife and daughter. Most soldiers had some kind of charm or pre-mission routine that was supposed to bring them good luck: Some wore the same color underwear each time, some spit in the wind, some chewed the same gum, kissed a cross, wrote a letter, or listened to the same song. Bono's ritual was to tape a picture of his family on the wall next to the table while he prepared for patrol. Sam didn't know why, but, of course, he never asked. It was considered extremely bad form to question another's pre-combat routine.

Staring at the picture of the beautiful little family, Sam felt a tiny sinking in his gut. He moved toward the picture, looking closely while Bono kept his head down.

Will I ever have this? he wondered. He could only hope that he would.

Family was something Sam rarely talked about. His biological father, the old drunk who occasionally made a little money as a charter fisherman on the southern Virginia coast, and his mother, who had deserted him to the old man when he was only eight, had never been anything but a stress in his life. Yeah, they were back together now, and it seemed they were getting along, but after years of abuse, it was impossible for him to think of them as his mom and dad. If it hadn't been for the Brightons . . . Sam hated to even think. They had literally saved him. They were his family now.

But still he felt, deep inside, that he wasn't really one of them. The Brightons seemed to have something that he would never have, some innate goodness, some moral bearing that he just didn't possess. They were as straight down the line as anyone Sam had ever known, and he wasn't quite like that, though he had really tried. Sometimes he thought there was something inside them, something that literally ran through their veins, that made them different from him, even better somehow. He had tried. He had tried really hard. He was still trying. But he fell short so often, it seemed it just didn't work.

Sam's thoughts were interrupted by Bono's finally looking up. "Still blowing out?" he asked wearily.

"Yeah," Sam nodded. "No choppers will be flying tonight."

Bono looked down at his map and mumbled. That meant no air support. He shook his head.

Bono's desert fatigue shirt was open, showing the dog tags that dangled from the chain on his neck. Hanging next to the dog tags was a small silver shield. Lots of soldiers wore them. They called the little charm the Shield of Strength. *Joshua 1:9* was etched on the back—not the entire scripture, just the reference. Sam, who also wore a Shield, had the scripture memorized:

"Have not I commanded thee? Be strong and of a good courage; be not afraid, neither be thou dismayed: for the Lord thy God is with thee whithersoever thou goest."

Subconsciously, he reached under his fatigues and felt for the Shield there. Squeezing it, he asked Bono, "You thirsty?"

"Feels like I've got half the desert stuck in my throat."

Sam cocked his head toward the rear door of the Operations Center. Bono nodded, stood up, and followed him through a wooden door that opened up to a wide canvas hallway, then to another tent, which was set up as a lounge for the unit's soldiers. Once inside the second tent, they made their way to the refrigerator and grabbed some sodas, then dropped onto a couple of cheap, folding chairs. It was quiet here, and the two men relaxed for a while. Bono finished his soda in three long gulps, then took the picture of his family, which he had been holding in his hand, and tucked it inside the chest pocket on his shirt.

Sam watched him. "Do you always think of them?" he wondered.

"You know, it's funny," Bono replied. "When I'm out

there in the fight, I don't think about my family. I don't think about my wife, my kid, nothing like that. I don't think about going home, the reason I'm fighting, the idea of freedom or America or any of that. All I think about is the guys in the team. Protecting each other. Keeping each other safe."

Sam didn't answer. He felt the same way.

"We are the only men in the world who know what that means, to fight and die with your brothers. It's a huge privilege, man."

Sam held his cold soda bottle to his cheek, feeling the condensation cooling his skin. The lounge wasn't air-conditioned; despite the strong wind, it was hot inside.

"You know what I've been thinking?" Bono asked, staring blankly ahead.

"What's that?" Sam replied.

Bono crushed his plastic bottle, walked to the fridge, pulled out another soda, then came back and sat down. "People say American soldiers fight to protect their freedoms," he started. "Some people write us letters and thank us for keeping them safe. The politicians back home always thank us. Some are even sincere in their thanks. They say we are fighting for their freedoms. But I don't think that's true."

Sam laughed. "You going Jane Fonda on me, baby?"

"No, really," Bono answered. "Think about it, man. When was the last time Americans were actually fighting for *their* freedom? You might have to go back to the Revolutionary War. That might have been the last time."

"I don't know, Bono. How about the Civil War, boss?"

"I understand the North was fighting to protect the Union, but I think most of those men were fighting for something else. The freedom of others. I just don't believe, I can't believe in my gut, that men were laying it on the line there, laying it down like they did, just to protect the Union. I think there was more to it than that. They were freeing the slaves. Fighting to free other men."

Sam remained skeptical. "What about the first and second World Wars?" he asked.

"World War One was plain and simple a fight to save Europe. We had no national interest, nothing really at stake. World War Two? The Japanese were our enemy, the ones who attacked. We could have confined our war to the Pacific and won easily. We could have let Stalin and Hitler divide Europe, knowing they would eventually turn on each other and devour themselves. But we put our own interest aside and saved Europe first. Again, another fight to save other men.

"I know a lot of people like to talk about the Vietnam War, but can anyone make a serious argument that we were fighting for imperial power? I mean, come on, man, what did the Vietnamese have to offer if we *had* conquered them? Nothing. Nada. Not so much as a bowl of white rice. So why were we there, if not to save the South Vietnamese? And if you want to know what happens when we fail, you should look no further than Indochina. How many million Vietnamese and Cambodians were slaughtered because we failed in that war! The Killing Fields should haunt us for the next hundred years."

Sam didn't answer, he just listened, content to sip his soda for now.

"Kuwait?" Bono continued, his voice rising now. "Afghanistan and Iraq? Yeah, we needed stability in the region, but if all we were interested in was the oil, we could have been like the Germans and French who propped up Saddam to keep the oil rolling in. Heaven knows he would have sold us all that we needed. That isn't the reason we came here. There was more to it than that. Yeah, I think we needed to double-tap the Taliban and take out the madman, Hussein, and yes, in that sense, you might argue that we went into those countries to protect the freedoms we had. But though that might have been why we *came* in, it is not why we *stayed*. We could have eliminated the threat, then skipped out of town. But that's not how we work. We stay to protect the freedoms of those left behind. We stay to help them build a government that will keep them *free*.

"Now think about that, Sergeant Brighton. I believe it is true. We don't fight for *our* freedoms. We fight for much more than that. We fight for the freedom of *others*. We fight to free other men."

Sam shifted on his chair, adjusting the sidearm in the leather holster that was strapped to his side. "I guess that makes us the good guys," he said.

"Which is what makes it so hard."

Sam looked confused. "I don't get it," he said.

Bono looked away, then rolled his neck to crunch out the kinks. "Going home," he answered. "I mean, I want to see my family in the very worst way. I want to hold my daughter. I know that she needs me, and I want to be there for her. But I can't reconcile the way I feel at home with the way I feel about being here too. This mission. My comrades. The thrill of the fight." Bono leaned forward awkwardly and looked into Sam's eyes. Sam could see that this was his confession, he was getting it out, and Sam let him talk. "I would give anything in the world to be home *right now*. But when I get there, I know I'm going to miss being here. I'm going to miss the battles. I'm going to miss the thrill. But mostly, I'm going to miss the feeling of doing something right, something that helps another. I'm rock-solid on that, Sam. I know what we're doing here is part of God's work. And I'm going to miss it. Now tell me, is that wrong?"

Sam thought a moment, then raised his head. "I don't

know, Lieutenant. I think maybe you're asking the wrong guy."

Bono sat back and waited, and so Sam went on. "Is it wrong to be a warrior? Maybe it is. We are so steeped in violence, it can be offensive sometimes. Americans like their heroes soft now, you know, soft and cute. I don't know, but it seems there's almost a victim mentality in our heroes today: A POW who was taken captive and suffered, a soldier who died for his friends—these are the heroes Americans are most comfortable with. They don't like their warriors too battle hardened. That scares them now. But that's you and me. That's what you and I are. We find and kill the enemy. That is a day's work to us. Is that evil? It can't be. Not when it's for the right cause. Was Captain Moroni a hero? Darn straight he was. So you want to go home, but you want to stay in the fight. You feel the claws of this calling because they have latched into you.

"I don't know, Bono, but this much I believe. There aren't many people in the world who get to do something like this. Most will miss it. Most are never given the chance. But you and I and a few others, we've been given this opportunity to do something for others that they can't do for themselves. Are you wrong to appreciate that? I don't think you are. Sometime you'll go home to your family and hold each of them close. And you'll know you did your duty. How many people can say that?"

The two men fell into silence, listening to the wind blow. "You know what I look forward to more than anything else?" Bono said after they had sat for a while.

"What's that?"

"There are a thousand things I miss: my wife, my own bed, watching the Yankees on TV, getting up in the morning without having sand fleas in my hair. But there's nothing I miss more than holding my little girl. More than anything else,

I miss picking her up and holding her in my arms. She lays her head on your shoulder. She clings to your arms. She has a way of molding to my body, like she was meant to be there. That's what I look forward to more than anything else, when I step off that airplane and she runs to my arms. When that happens, I will feel like the luckiest man in the world."

Sam took a drink of his soda, which had grown warm and a little flat. "You *are* lucky," he answered.

Bono nodded and smiled.

"Fifty-two days," Sam muttered.

"And counting," Bono said.

The men stared at the floor. A convoy was just loading up, engines rumbling outside, and the wind howled like a monster trying to rip through the tent.

Sam thought awhile, then said, "You know, Lieutenant, the other night I came to your tent and told you what I was planning to do."

"Yeah," Bono answered.

"Are you going to help me?"

"Of course. Was there any doubt in your mind?"

"Not really. But it's good to know you're on board."

"So when we doing it?" Bono asked.

"It's got to be soon. We may not have enough time as it is."

"So, you're thinking . . . ?"

"Neither of our squads are scheduled for patrols this weekend," Sam said.

The lieutenant smiled wryly. "Cool," he replied.

chapter eleven

One measure of any tyrannical government's willingness to control its people is the completeness with which it suppresses the rights of its most vulnerable citizens. Throughout the entire Persian Gulf, the ruling mullahs, presidents, and kings have enforced humiliating and sadistic rules on women and girls, enslaving them in a system that, at best, demands segregation and second-class status and, at worst, treats the daughters of Heaven no better than beasts in the field. In far too many locations, women cannot be educated, work, or drive. In many places it is illegal and immoral for a woman to be examined by a male doctor, but since there are no opportunities for education, few women doctors can be found. And there are many places where lashing and stoning are appointed for the most minor infraction of law.

It would be easy to presume that a thriving sex trade inside a theocracy would be an unsustainable contradiction. Most would think that a country founded and ruled by Islamic fundamentalists would decry such a practice. But a substantive look under the surface reveals why just the opposite is true. Exploitation is not only possible, it is almost inevitable in a culture that tolerates repression, a lesson that has been demonstrated again and again.

Although it is impossible to determine the number of victims, U.N. officials who have worked inside Iran say there has been a nearly 500% increase in the number of teenage girls in prostitution since the revolution. In Tehran alone, there are nearly 100,000 women and girls in prostitution. Most of them live on the streets. The lucky ones live in brothels. Many Iranian girls, some as young as age ten, have been sold into slavery in various nations around the world. The Interpol bureau in Tehran reports that the trade in young women and girls is one of the most profitable business activities in Iran. Many of the young women who find themselves caught in this evil web are girls from the countryside, where poverty and ignorance abound. Worse, slave traders seem willing to take advantage of any tragedy in order to fulfill the demand. Following the tragic earthquake in Bam, a disaster that claimed some 50,000 lives, orphaned girls were swept up and transported to slave markets in Tehran.

And Persian women aren't the only victims of this flourishing trade. Young women from the ghettos of Gaza, the remote villages of Egypt, and crowded Kuwaiti city streets have been taken from their families, some even sold by their parents, and forced into prostitution in other areas of the world. Victims have been found in Qatar, Kuwait, and the United Arab Emirates. In the northeastern Iranian province of Khorasan, local police report that girls are being sold to Pakistani men. In the southeastern border province of Sistan Baluchestan, thousands of Iranian girls reportedly have been sold to Afghanis. Perhaps the most creative justification of prostitution takes place inside Tehran, where, in order to control the spread of HIV, officials of the Iranian Social Department of the Interior Ministry have proposed setting up "morality houses." There, using the traditional religious customs, a couple may be married for as little as one hour.

And the West is not free of this sin. Police in Tehran have uncovered prostitution and slavery rings with ties to France and Germany, England, and Spain. Turkey is a hotbed of trade heading to the United States, with underground auctions not unlike those that operated in northern Africa some three hundred years ago. And the prices are astounding. A young girl may be bought for as little as a few thousand dollars. But, as with everything else, beauty commands a much higher price. Someone with just the right look might fetch ten or fifteen thousand dollars, maybe more.

GHESHA GHETTO
EAST OF KIRKUK, IRAQ

The store was a dilapidated slab of concrete floor and plywood and cement walls situated in the southeastern ghettos of Kirkuk. It was a dark place, a mean place, a place where the light didn't shine and the darkness of evil settled on even the brightest day.

The Ghesha ghetto was a small, isolated triangle created by a fork in a slow, nasty river and some low hills to the north. There were only two roads leading to the ghetto, and a wall of rundown buildings and old warehouses formed a broken barrier that concealed most of the occupants within. The ghetto was off-limits to the U.S. military—the area was considered too dangerous and without any tactical interest—and even the local police rarely strayed between the banks of the river. Occasionally, when the sniping or pirating became entirely untenable, the regional Iraqi leaders would send in a heavily armored patrol, but they never stayed more than a few days before fleeing again, leaving the ghetto to feed on itself. Like a starving rat snake that was slowly swallowing down its own tail, the ghetto consumed all its young in turf battles and hate until there was very little left that was worth fighting for.

There was no law or authority in the ghetto, and the insurgents and foreign mercenaries took advantage of that, creating a world of darkness and pain for all of the residents. The business deals that were done here were nearly unspeakable. Everything was for sale in the ghetto: weapons, drugs, old women slaves, little girls, stolen pieces of art, counterfeits . . . other things. And the prices were cheap.

The store owner sat near the back wall of his shop, alone, smoking a hand-rolled cigarette. The shelves were mostly empty though there were a few things to buy: cigarettes from Europe and Turkey, a few canned goods and household supplies. Outside, the streets were cluttered and noisy with the sound of belching autos, tiny motorcycles, and many people, their shoes thumping along on the ancient brick streets. Children could be heard laughing and calling to each other from where they played down the narrow street, and the store owner couldn't help but scowl at the sound.

The owner's face was rough and pockmarked and sunken under his eyes. His lips were fat and dry, with tiny specks of dry spit at the corners of his mouth. He glanced at his watch, then turned his eyes on the door. Five minutes later, exactly on schedule, the two men walked in, one American, the other . . . he didn't know, maybe Middle Eastern, probably Afghani, judging by the way he was dressed, with his silk trousers, black vest, and thin canvas boots. The American was young and thick. He could be strong, or he could be overweight, it was hard to tell, for he hid his body under a loose-fitting jacket and oversized shirt. His long hair was bleached and tangled, as if he spent a lot of time in the sun. A beach kid. Venice Beach. The Arab had heard about them. Spoiled, rotten children with too much money and too much time, corrupted and carnal, thinking they could buy whatever they fancied in the world.

Yes, he knew about them. And yes, they were right. If they had enough money, they could buy anything.

The old man stared but didn't say anything as he continued to smoke. The dark-skinned man, the Afghani, pretended to shop, picking up a rusted can of potatoes (one of the many supplies stolen from a U.N. relief convoy), but the other one nodded to the shop owner, then moved to the back of the store.

"You Kiraddak?" the Caucasian asked quickly. Being the customer, the one with the money, the foreigner was in the superior position and he wasted no time with small talk or friendly conversation.

The other man, the dark one, watched anxiously from behind a low shelf, his dark eyes always darting as if he expected disaster to strike. He was there to cover his master's back, and he kept his head moving, searching for the ambush.

The shop owner didn't answer but stared arrogantly. Yes, they were the buyers, and there were many other places these men could go (too many men now sold the same thing as he), but he also knew that they were desperate and hungry and anxious to close the deal. His contact had warned him. "These men are amateurs," he'd been told. So though they held the money, the Iraqi knew he was in a position to take advantage of them.

He stared at the Caucasian. "Who sent you?" he asked.

The foreigner reached into his pocket and pulled out his own cigarettes. The Iraqi recognized the red and white packaging of the American smokes, the best cigarettes in the world, and stared as the American flipped the pack with his wrist. A single cigarette protruded from the half-opened top, and he extracted it with his lips, then took the cigarette in his fingers and offered it up. The Iraqi reached up with brown fingers and took the smoke, tucking it in his shirt pocket, saving it for a later time when he could enjoy the rich flavor by himself.

The American slipped the cigarettes back in his pocket. "You Kiraddak?" he asked again, this time more tersely.

The old man patiently placed his hands on his knees. "Who sent you?" he repeated as he leaned back against the cold wall.

The American fidgeted again, then answered. "Al Mohammad. From Istanbul. He said you would be waiting for us."

The old man smiled slightly and nodded. "Okay," he said.

The American moved toward the Iraqi. "We want to see the product," he said.

The old man scowled and answered, "I promise, you will be satisfied."

"No. We want to see some pictures before we close the deal."

The Iraqi grunted and pushed himself up. Moving to the front counter, he lifted a key from a pewter key chain hanging around his neck and unlocked the bottom drawer. Sorting through a thick stack of pictures, he extracted a few and threw them on the counter. The two men moved forward. They were far too anxious, though they tried to hide their emotions behind their cold stares.

"These are from the territory we asked for?" the American asked.

The Iraqi grunted. "That's what I've been told. They were emailed to me a couple days ago."

The American leafed through the pictures quickly and tossed them aside. "No," he said angrily, "none of these will do."

The Iraqi grunted. Really, he thought, was it that big a

deal? The shelf life of his product was just a few years anyway. Did it make that much difference? He grunted again. "What?" he asked with sarcasm. "Too young or too old?"

The American looked away, a flash of anger in his eyes.

The Iraqi shook his head. Turning back to the pile, he sorted again, then threw a couple more photos on the counter. The American looked at them quickly, then pushed them aside too.

"Help me," the old man scolded. "What are you looking for?"

The American told him, and the Iraqi snorted, then thumbed through the photos again. "This is your last choice," he huffed as he tossed a handful of black-and-whites on the counter.

The American froze as he stared at the pictures, his hands shaking heavily. He nodded, his eyes burning bright. His buddy gritted, his jaw closing in a smile.

This man was so anxious.

So close to a deal.

"How much?" the American demanded.

The Iraqi stared at the anxious eyes and doubled the price quickly in his head. "Twenty thousand," he answered. "U.S. dollars. Nothing else. And we want half up front."

The American scowled. "That's not what we agreed!" he protested.

The old man nodded to the pictures. "But that was before you saw those," he replied. He continued to study the American, who continued to stare.

The Iraqi knew that he had them; there was no doubt in his mind. Ignorant American, he laughed to himself as he watched the Yankee stare at the floor. He could have had the same thing for four or five thousand if he had just played it cool. But no, he was stupid. And the old man would make a huge profit, which would make his masters proud.

"Twenty thousand," the Iraqi repeated firmly. "Half now and half later and not one penny less. Cash. All American. And you must decide now."

The two men glanced at each other, and the American swore bitterly. "When will you be ready?" he demanded.

"The pipeline is in place. It will take only a few days. I only wish it was as simple to smuggle whiskey or cigarettes."

The foreigners glanced again at each other.

"Okay," the American finally said. "Twenty thousand. But I want delivery this week."

The old man grunted. "It will take another ten days."

"Ten days!" complained the American. "I thought you said it was easy . . . "

"It is easy, friend," the Iraqi replied. "But this is a special order, and custom orders take time. So stay, enjoy our hospitality. Sightsee for a while. Come back in ten days with the rest of the money and you will get what you want."

The American picked up the photographs, his hands shaking again.

Though they had been taken from a long way away, the photographs had been cropped to show Azadeh's face very clearly. She looked very scared in the first photograph, her lips drawn and tight as she gazed past the camera at something unseen in the distance. The second photo showed her checking through the in-processing desk at Khorramshahr, her dark eyes shining intently, a white scarf covering her hair. The last one showed her walking through the muddy camp, a burlap sack under her arm.

She looked vulnerable and lonely, yet there was a light in her eyes.

How long would that light shine? Not very long, the

American was sure. Khorramshahr was a hard place, he knew very well.

The American's voice took on a deadly edge. "Don't disappoint me," he threatened the Iraqi as he leaned toward him. "I want the girl in ten days, or you and I will have issues, my friend."

chapter twelve

The Orchid Flower Presidential Palace
Riyadh, Saudi Arabia

The royal Saudi family had been on a nonstop program of palace building since 1990. The king and his sons had been spending billions of dollars on their homes, including man-made lakes, gold trim, diamond-studded fixtures, marble floors, and other luxuries that beautified their palaces and those of their supporters as well. The security features, extensive, in some cases even formidable, were designed to protect the royal family from their own people as much as from their enemies around the world. Incredible gardens surrounded each of the dozens of palaces, gardens that required large amounts of water, often in drought-stricken areas. Beyond that, there were sophisticated waterfalls, interconnected swimming pools, aquariums, and deer farms, all of which required enormous quantities of water, all dredged up by the powerful pumps that had been dropped into the underground aquifer.

The Orchid Flower Presidential Palace had always been one of the king's favorite retreats. Built over 4.2 square kilometers and completed in 1998, the palace compound contained a fabulous central home, with five smaller palaces for various wives and family members, a presidential compound and VIP residences for visiting dignitaries, all surrounded by three lakes, five man-made waterfalls, and two fishing holes.

But though the palace had been a favorite of the king, he was dead now, and the new king, Abdullah Al-Rahman, didn't care for it much. It certainly wasn't what he would have built, but it would have to do for now.

King Abdullah Al-Rahman sat in his enormous leather chair, smoking a thick brown cigar and sipping the illegal Jack Daniels whiskey his brother had brought back from his recent trip to New York. As he looked at the huge office around him, the Saudi king couldn't help but smile.

If this was what it felt like to be king, he was going to like it. He was going to like it a lot.

Sitting there with his smoke and his whiskey, knowing the throne was now his, was the happiest moment in his life—a life that had, so far, been altogether too dull.

Prince Abdullah Al-Rahman was the second son born to King Fahd bin Saud Aziz, monarch of the House of Saud, grandson of King Saud Aziz, the first king of modern-day Saudi Arabia. From a young age, it had been clear that Prince Abdullah Al Qaeda-Rahman was not the preferred son. Highly intelligent and strikingly handsome but with an infrequent smile, the young prince had always fallen in the shadow of his older brother, Prince Saud bin Faysal. From the time they were old enough to compete in soccer or wrestle together on the tile floors, the younger son had been overshadowed again and again, always beaten by his older brother no matter what they did. And Prince Abdullah knew from a very young age who would be the next king: the first son. The loved son. The preferred son of the king.

The first son owned the birthright.

The second son did not.

The first son owned the kingdom.

The second son didn't own a thing.

But all that had changed. Death had changed everything.

King Abdullah thought, How many years, how many lives, how much pleasure and pain had gone into this moment? How much effort and planning had brought him to this point, when he could sit on the throne and go where he pleased, when he could hold the reins of power without constant fear—fear of his brothers, his father, fear of their kin, fear of the secret Palace Guards or one of the other half-dozen security organizations his father had created to maintain his great power.

The young king considered his brother, whom he had recently killed along with his brother's family, his wives and their children, even most of his friends (better to make a clean sweep than to have to spend his nights wondering if he had missed anyone). Yet, here he was now. The first step complete.

Was he satisfied with his work? Almost perfectly so.

Was he anxious for the next action? He could hardly wait.

Smoking, the new king thought of his dead older brother and shivered with pride. Swiveling his office chair, he turned east. From where he sat, the Persian Gulf was a little more than two hundred miles away, but he had walked the gray sands that lined the Saudi beaches at least a thousand times, and he could picture the scene perfectly in his mind, the blue-green water, the pebbled beaches, the burning sun in the sky. The waters were infested with sea snakes and eels, and he knew that, even now, some unseen sea scavenger was nibbling on his brother's corpse.

I waited. I was patient, he told himself. *I paid the price, I bore the burden, and I deserve what I have.*

The new king of Saudi Arabia took another quiet drag on his *Cabana,* sipped at the alcohol, and leaned back in his chair.

The truth was, Prince Abdullah had first thought of killing his brother at a very young age. Indeed, one of his earliest memories was of sitting on the edge of his bed, looking down at an open cut on his knee. He and his brother had been wrestling on the hard, wooden floor, and, being older and larger (his brother had always been more physically powerful), Prince Saud had flipped him over his shoulder and Abdullah had landed on the knee, splitting it open nearly down to the bone. He had grabbed his leg and caught his breath, clenching his teeth, the blood oozing through his fingers as his eyes grew wide in pain. But he hadn't cried. Not a tear. Not a whimper. He would have died before he would have let his brother see him cry.

Ten minutes later, sitting on the edge of his bed, he had applied a thick bandage, wrapping the white cotton tightly around his bloody leg. As he doctored his wound, the thoughts had first come into his head.

"He is stronger than you are," the voice seemed to say.

The young prince was crying angry tears now that he was secluded in his room.

"He is stronger than you are," the thought came again. *"He will always be stronger. You must not fight him anymore. Every time you fight by his rules, you end up on the floor."*

The prince shook his head and wiped a quick hand across his eyes.

"He is the oldest, born of the first wife, in every way preferred. Have you seen how your father looks at him! Have you seen the look in your father's eye?"

Abdullah hung his head, taking in a deep sob.

"You might as well get used to it. This is the way it is and the way it will always be. This anger you are feeling, it will never go away. He is the oldest. He is chosen. He will get everything!"

The young prince finished wrapping the bandage and tightened the knot with a quick, angry pull.

The thoughts continued in a low voice, a cold buzz in his head. As he listened, Abdullah felt a sudden surge of emotion in his chest, a hard, growing knot that seemed to pump up his heart. It was cold and unpleasant, but . . . tempting, somehow. Like a moth drawn to fire, he knew it could hurt him, but he wasn't afraid.

He could have shaken it off. He could have stood up and walked away. He could have fallen to his knees and prayed for the voice to depart. But he didn't. He wanted it. And he listened carefully.

"He will be the next king . . . " the voice was hissing now. *"He will be the next king. Unless . . . unless . . . There might be a way. . . . If you are strong enough. If you are brave enough. If you do what I say . . . "*

And that was how it had started, such a long time ago. He had been just a child, but he was old enough and smart enough to know. These thoughts didn't come from Allah. They came from somewhere else.

As the years went by the thoughts came more frequently and with even more force. And the thoughts—no, they weren't just thoughts now, it was a voice, full and clear—seemed to know how he felt. The voice seemed to understand him, his doubts and his fears. It seemed to understand his frustration far better than anyone else.

The day before Abdullah's sixteenth birthday, the day he was to become a man, the voice came again. *"I too was a second son,"* it spoke in a dry hiss. *"Like you, I wasn't chosen. I was rejected by my father just as you have been rejected by the king. I was rejected by a father who also had wild plans, just as you have been rejected by the king. I know what it is like to live under a father who is bent on destroying everything. A fool of a father who was blind to the price we would pay, blind to the pain he would cause us—blind or too cruel to care.*

"So, yes, I understand you. I too have been pushed away, forced in the shadows at the back of the room, forced to listen while others proclaimed their great love for Him. I too have been forced to watch as the oldest son absorbed all the attention and power, as if it were his right just because of when he was born. I too have been forced to watch in silence, forced to be still, as the chosen Son grew in power and majesty and might. I know the pain of being rejected, of not being the Chosen One."

The young Abdullah sat on the top of a fortified wall that surrounded his father's mountain palace, looking down on the dry and barren desert below. The sand stretched for miles, and the sun was unbearable. A hot breeze blew up from the desert, and the mountain smelled of dry pine. Abdullah stared. His dark skin was dry and he was used to the heat, but he had to squint at the hot sun, and he frowned as he thought.

"He will be the next king." The voice always came back to this point. *"He will leave you with nothing. You will never be anything."*

Though he was smarter than his brother, more capable, and far more willing to work, more willing to do what it took to protect the kingdom from its enemies, both at home and abroad, none of that mattered, for he would never be king. That thought was the most vicious cut, the deepest wound he could feel. *"You will not be king,"* the voice hissed again. *"Unless . . . unless . . . there still might be a way. . . . If you are strong enough. If you are brave enough. If you do what I say . . . "*

Thirty years in the making.

And the voice owned him now.

But none of that mattered, for now he was the king.

* * *

King Abdullah al-Rahman sucked the last puff of smoke from the tight, brown cigar, glanced at his watch, and smashed the glowing orange ash on his desk. The executive committee would be gathered. It was time to get back to work.

He walked down three flights of stairs, deep into the underground bowels of the palace, to the secure briefing room. There his three younger brothers were waiting, along with four of their closest advisors: the commanding general of their military forces, the communications czar, the foreign minister, and, most important of all, the head of State Security and Palace Police.

The underground command center had cinderblock walls and a bare cement floor. It was crowded with banks of phones and computers along three sides and a series of large maps along the back wall. Several command consoles sat in the middle of the room, each with a square metal desk and a row of three or four phones. A ten-foot plasma screen illuminated the front of the room. But the screen was a deep blue; all it showed was the time, the seconds and minutes ticking by on a digital clock in the center. There were no windows in the command center and only one exit, a heavy steel door along the east wall. Though the room had been designed to accommodate the king's entire security staff, there was no one in it now besides the king's three brothers and his top advisors, all of them waiting around a dark conference table. They stood when the king entered and remained standing until he had walked to the head of the table and sat down. His three younger brothers sat at the far end of the table. The advisors sat on each side. To the king's immediate right was General Abaza, head of the State Security and Palace Police.

Out of all the men in the room, General Abaza was the king's most trusted counselor, the only man he could truly depend on, the only man whom he didn't suspect he might find standing at the foot of his bed one night, a grim look on his face, a long knife in his hand.

Abaza was a large man, brawny if not particularly bright, and with the instincts of a badger huddled in the back of its cave. Leave him alone, and he was okay. Crowd him, and he would fight to the death. General Abaza and Abdullah had known each other since they had been in primary school and by the time they had reached adolescence they were best friends. The general had proven extremely loyal over the years. Of course, he owed everything he was or ever would be to Prince Abdullah, but both men understood that, so the relationship worked.

King Abdullah al-Rahman smiled as he thought of how he had recently tested the general. It was simple, yet brilliant, and he was proud of the plan that had been carried out just three nights before.

A group of hooded men broke into General Abaza's home. Brandishing rifles and swords, they rounded up the general, his wife, and his four children and herded them into the basement, all the time screaming obscenities and flashing their guns. The children howled in terror. His wife nearly fainted in fear. After gathering the family in a back room, the men pulled back their hoods to reveal painted faces in black and red camouflage. They looked like raging devils, their eyes circled in dark rings, drops of blood dripping from their painted lips. The men stood over the terrified family, all the time screaming and shoving, giving Abaza no time to think, no time to analyze, no time to wonder who they were or what was going on.

The leader moved forward and grabbed the youngest child. Looking into the general's eyes, he lifted his sword. "Prince Abdullah al-Rahman has killed our king!" he screamed. "He poisoned him. We know that. And he killed the crown prince as well. Now we are going to kill him. And we are going to move tonight. Are you with us, or against us? You've got five seconds to decide!"

Abaza stared, his eyes wide in terror, his mouth dry as sand.

"Who will you die for!" the terrorist screamed. "Are you loyal to Abdullah, or are you on our side? Pledge you will help us kill Abdullah, or you and your family are dead!"

Abaza stared, his Adam's apple bobbing like a bubble in a sea. Then he bowed his head, took two steps forward, and dropped to his knees. "I cannot betray Abdullah," he muttered. "If you are going to kill my family, I only ask that you kill me first."

The leader raised his sword over the general's head. Abaza's wife screamed. The children cowered in the corner and covered their heads. But the swordsman only grunted, then laughed and fell to his knees. He moved to the general and took him in his arms. The general looked up, staring into the man's eyes.

The man rubbed his face, removing part of the paint, and threw back a tight wig. It was Abdullah, the new king. His eyes danced with delight.

"So you are with me, General Abaza?" he laughed to his friend.

The general stared in disbelief while nodding his head.

"Good. That is good. You have won my respect, General Abaza. You have won my trust, too. I will never forget you and what you have shown me tonight."

And King Abdullah al-Rahman had meant what he said. Abaza was now his most trusted advisor, the only man in the room he knew he could trust with his life.

He glanced at the general, giving him a knowing look,

then turned back to the others. Standing, he lifted a finger and held it menacingly in the air. "Brothers," he said, "my father has passed. The kingdom is secured. We have saved our people, our family, and most importantly the Holy Cities of God from an unspeakable catastrophe, a disaster that would have set us back four hundred years."

The king's men grunted in false agreement. It was a cynical rationalization, and each of them knew it. They weren't in this for religion, their nation, or their god. They were in it for the power—the power and the money. It was as simple as that. They wanted to control their people. They wanted to control the hundred trillion dollars' worth of oil that sat under their sand. They wanted to control the significant events in the world. They craved to have other nations adore them, or, if they didn't adore them, then to fear them, it mattered not which.

Power was their opium. And they were as addicted as any group of men in the world.

So though they grunted in agreement, their eyes remained dull and dim. The king could lie to them if he wanted, but it didn't change anything. They knew what they had done, and they knew why they had done it.

Abdullah stared at his conspirators, then jabbed his finger at the air. "There is a tide, a stinking tide, that rises in our world. We have seen it in Iraq. We've seen it in Egypt and Lebanon. It's starting to belch up in Libya, Pakistan, and Iran. And we've got to staunch it before it goes any further."

"Yes," the youngest prince answered. "We must stop it now."

The other men remained quiet, though they nodded their heads.

"The stink of democracies seems to lift everywhere. It is evil. It is vile. *And it is not God's will.* It is not the will of Allah for these people to govern themselves. That is why he provided royal families. That is why he provided Holy Law. That is why he provided religious leaders and gave them power. We are the protectors of Mecca, guardians of the most sacred Shrine. It is our responsibility, it is our duty, it is *our right and our power* to stop the flow of democracies in this part of the world. *That* is the will of Allah. And we will see his will done!"

The men fell silent. None of them dared to speak. The youngest prince stared at his brother, then lifted his chin. "Our father . . . " he started saying.

It was a deadly mistake. The king exploded, leaning across the table, his eyes growing pale, almost yellow with hate. "My father," he screamed, "was an evil, foolish man! He was going to decapitate our kingdom. He was going to give it to them!" Abdullah stabbed his finger once more, motioning to some unseen beings. "He was going to take my birthright and give it away. But Allah will curse him. I have seen a vision of his special hell. He is there. He is burning. And you will not speak his name. You will not mention our father. I will not hear his name again!"

The young prince fell back, pressing against the back of his chair. The king's eyes burned through him, practically searing him with their heat. Abdullah's hatred was almost a buzz, a deadly sense of blackness that seemed to suspend in the air. He glanced at his brother, then dropped his eyes to the floor.

Abdullah remained suspended, leaning on the table, his knuckles clenched and white from the weight of his hands. He stared at his brother, then slowly stepped back to his chair. He moved his eyes around the table, taking in each of the men. "My father was a traitor. My older brother was too. They were traitors and fools. And we will never speak of them again!"

The room remained silent until General Abaza answered

simply. "Yes, my *Sayid,*" he spoke for the men. All of them nodded. It was a fine plan to them.

Abdullah was silent a long moment. He stood at the table, leaning toward his men. "The battle against democracies has grown bitter, my friends. Bitter as acid. And we are losing, you must know.

"And yes, I know, we were going to move against Israel. That has been our hope all along. But this thing . . . this idea . . . this cancer of freedom they call democracy is a looming crisis that we cannot ignore. And if we don't strike at the root, then we are only fooling ourselves. We can run around chasing sprouts of democracies until we die of old age, dashing from one nation to another, trying to kill each new bud. We can run around, fighting battles in half a dozen nations throughout the Middle East, from Jakarta to the West Bank and everything in between. But while we run around on the surface, the problem is taking root under our feet. After watching the problem, I am sure of one thing: We can't kill all the sprouts until we kill the mother tree. And we have to kill the mother before she sprouts any more."

The room fell into silence until the youngest prince spoke again. "But, my Blessed Brother, if we are able to cut off their oil . . ."

The king raised his hand, suddenly distracted. *Blessed Brother.* Where had that come from? He'd never been called that before. It was a new name. A good name. He liked that a lot.

The younger prince paused, then dared to go on. "My brother . . . if we cut off all oil shipments through the Persian Gulf, we would hit the Americans where it would hurt them the most. As you have said, our oil is the fuel that drives their economic machine. Without it, they are helpless. They would be brought to their knees. They would crumble like a tower built out of sticks on wet mud. We are sitting on the fuel the entire world needs to survive. If we cut off that power, we can show them where the *real* power lies."

Abdullah nodded, but his eyes remained firm. "There is no time, brother. Things are changing too fast. The race is on, and we are losing, so we have to be quick. We have to be more bold, more ambitious, more willing to take dangerous risks.

"So yes, we could cut off their oil, and we will do that, no doubt. But there is another way, another plan, that is even more beautiful. So listen to me, brothers, come and listen to my plan."

The seven men all leaned forward. They were listening, yes.

King Abdullah turned toward his foreign minister. "What do you want more than anything in the world?" he asked. "More than life itself, what is the one thing that you want in this world?"

The minister didn't hesitate. They had discussed this before. "I wish to see the world cleansed of the pig-Jewish state," he replied.

"Yes. That is right. That is our mission from Allah. And there is only one way to do that. Can you tell me what it is?"

Again, the answer came quickly. The minister knew the king's thinking, and he regurgitated it nearly word for word. "We must destroy her evil mother, the betrayer of Muslim nations, the mother of all whores, our greatest enemy, the U.S."

King Abdullah nodded. Though his lips turned into a tight smile, his eyes remained dull and black. "Yes. And I hope you can see that, brothers, for it is *so* clear to me. We can never eradicate Israel as long as the U.S. exists. The Americans will stand by the pig-dogs, even at the sacrifice of their lives. Evil binds together, and they are bound with strong cords. And worse, we cannot eliminate the rotting stench of democracies until we eliminate the U.S. Can you see it? Can you? Do you believe it is true?"

A heavy silence fell over the room. The youngest prince moved nervously in his seat and diverted his eyes. The general cleared his throat, keeping his eyes on his friend. He didn't doubt for one moment that what the king said was true, he just didn't understand what they could possibly do.

"But how, my dear brother?" the young prince finally said. "You are talking about the most powerful nation in the world! The most powerful nation that has ever existed since the first man walked this earth. And you think we can destroy them. It is not possible!"

"Yes, it is, brothers. And not only is it possible, it is possible *now*."

"But my brother, I don't—"

The king raised his hand, indicating for the other man to be still. He raised his other hand beside him and extended his palms. "Yes, yes, I know what you are going to say. But what if . . . what if there was a way, a final way to destroy the U.S.! What if there was a way we could get the entire world to hate them as much as we do? What if we could get the world to hate Israel *and* the U.S.! What if we could unite every people against the most powerful nation on earth! And what if we could even get their own people to hate and resent their government!

"Can you imagine such a war? The entire world united against the great whore and her little sister, the Israel pigs. Imagine it, brothers! Then, if you can truly imagine it, if your minds are strong enough to contemplate that it can be done, then consider what I have told you and stand up and follow me!"

The king turned suddenly and walked out of the room.

The underlings watched in silence a long moment, then stood and followed the king.

WASHINGTON, D.C.

It was Sunday afternoon. Ammon was waiting in the hallway of the church, just outside the bishop's office. Dressed in a dark suit and white shirt, he was feeling pretty good. Though not the first suit he had owned, it was the first one he had ever paid for himself, and it suddenly hit him: He was getting old. In three months he would turn nineteen; shortly after that, he'd be gone. Not just gone away for the weekend or the summer, he would be gone for good. His mission would mark the true beginning of his own life.

He couldn't have been more excited.

Then he glanced at the empty chair next to his.

The door opened, and the bishop stepped into the hall. "Hey, Ammon, thanks for coming," the white-haired gentleman said.

"Thanks for inviting me, Bishop Sanders."

"This is very exciting, you know. We're going to start on your mission paperwork. This is it! The real show!"

"I'm excited. I can't wait. I am ready to go!"

The bishop shook his hand and smiled, then looked up and down the hall. "Where's your brother?" he asked.

Ammon shook his head, embarrassed. "He isn't here," he said.

"Did you remind him about the appointment?"

"Yes, Bishop, I did. But my brother's been kind of a conehead the past couple weeks. Sometimes he doesn't think. He's got this girl, and she's got him whupped. It's a bad case. Worst I've seen. He forgets a lot of things lately."

The bishop smiled, but a look of concern passed over his

eyes. "Well, then, I'm just going to have to do a better job of reminding him," he said solemnly. Then, switching gears, he clasped Ammon by the hand and pulled him along, saying, "Come on in!" They walked through his office door.

chapter thirteen

AL HUFUF MILITARY WEAPONS STORAGE COMPLEX
EASTERN SAUDI ARABIA

One of the king's private helicopters was waiting on the asphalt at the end of the circular drive on the east side of the presidential palace. It was a monstrous machine, American made, with deeply tinted windows and black paint with gold trim around the cockpit and along the smooth tail. Two powerful engines sat just behind the midsection, their chrome exhaust ports glinting in the afternoon sun. A set of small steps had been extended from the aft cabin door, and a line of military guards stood at attention on both sides of a narrow stretch of deep blue carpet that extended from the steps. Two military pilots were waiting, one of them watching the palace anxiously. As the king emerged, he nodded. The other pilot hit the start button, and the twin turbine engines started to turn. The pilot moved the throttles to idle, and the engine caught, emitting a sudden roar from the jet engine exhausts. As the engines rolled up, the rotors started to turn. By the time the king was climbing into the cabin, the helicopter was ready to go.

The king's men followed quickly, half a dozen steps behind. They hurried into the cabin and sat down on the reclining leather seats situated throughout the interior of the helicopter. A steward lifted the collapsible steps and quickly disappeared behind the forward bulkhead. The massive chopper lifted into the air before the men even had a chance to buckle themselves in. It turned immediately east, flying over the palace grounds, kicking up biting pieces of dirt and sand in a swirl of hot air.

Overhead, a flight of two Royal Saudi Air Force F-15s circled at fifteen thousand feet. The lead pilot, one of the king's four dozen cousins, kept a close eye on his radar while his wingman, half a mile behind and to his right, watched the low-flying chopper make its way east.

Turning to his window, the king glanced up at the sky, thinking of his brother lying at the bottom of the sea. In his death, his brother had taught him one final lesson. Never again would he fly in a helicopter without fighter escorts. A helicopter was completely defenseless when attacked from a jet. So the king searched the sky carefully, anxious to know that his escorts were there. But he couldn't see the fighters. They were too high and too small.

Fifty minutes later, the chopper set down on an unmarked landing pad in the middle of the Al Hufuf weapons storage facility. It was a peculiar complex—high cement and concertina-topped walls, layers of security with wire, and guard towers every fifty feet or so. And there were dozens of military police, some in the open, some hidden behind protective walls. Inside the triple fences, there was not much to see: a few low brick buildings, open sand lots, roads large enough to support heavy convoys, two rows of cement bunkers half buried in gravel and sand, a small supply building, and not a whole lot more. But most of the facilities had been built underground; the complex was much larger (and far more important) than it looked from above.

A small military escort was waiting, five military HUMVEES surrounding two black Mercedes SUVs. The king rode alone in the first vehicle. The other men crammed into the second SUV. The convoy rode through the military compound to the headquarters building, a long, single-story brick building. The men got out, entered the building, and took the elevator to the tenth floor below ground.

* * *

King Abdullah stood before the group in a small conference room. Behind him, a 28-inch television emitted a pale, gray light. Reaching under the table, the king tapped a button that activated the video equipment, and the television screen came to life, showing a live video feed from one of the nearby underground bunkers. The bunker was a large room and brightly lit. Cement floor. Cement walls. No visible entry. No guards. It appeared spotless, almost sterile, with not a smudge on the floor or speck of dust in the air. Sitting in the middle of the room were five lead-plated crates. The king's men stared at the screen. They did not understand.

The king broke into a sinful smile as he looked at the TV. "Our deliverance," he muttered lustily. "Our great gift to our people. Our great gift to the world."

The men only stared, their eyes wide. Though they didn't understand yet, every one of them sensed an overwhelming power in the air.

The very world that they lived on was shifting right under their feet. They could smell the revolution in the air.

The king moved forward until he was standing next to the screen, his face eerily illuminated by the subtle light. "The objects you are looking at," he explained in a low, even tone, "are five nuclear warheads. Fifty-seven kilotons. One-hundred fourteen *million* pounds of explosives each. There are five. You stare at those weapons and do the math in your head, and then tell me, my brothers, that we can't bring our enemies to their knees. Look at those weapons and tell me we can't do what we want."

The men fell into a stupor. It was not what they had thought. Things were moving too fast. "Where did you get them . . . " the foreign minister muttered. The king waved him off. No time to go through that. It didn't matter anyway.

The minister leaned against the back wall, his face turning dark gray. His mind raced, trying to absorb everything. The king. The crown prince. Both of them killed. A new king among them. A new direction. A new track. And yes, King Abdullah al-Rahman was a strong man, but he was also as driven and ambitious as any man in the world. And now this, now these weapons . . . it was a terrifying prospect. He sucked a deep breath, giving his mind time to think.

The room was deadly quiet. The men only stared. It was all they could do. After a full thirty seconds of silence, the oldest prince breathed. "When?" he asked dryly.

Abdullah hesitated. He didn't know. "Soon," he finally answered. "A few months. Maybe more. I haven't decided, and the timing is critical."

The younger prince shook his head. "No, King Abdullah!" he muttered in terror. "It would be suicide. You will destroy the kingdom. You will destroy Medina and Mecca! I don't know what you're thinking, but it is suicide."

Abdullah moved toward him, his lips pulled back in a sneer, his hands clenching, his breathing labored and fast. "Haven't you heard anything I've been telling you?" he demanded. "Haven't you understood anything?"

"But brother, if you attack the U.S., their position is clear. They will retaliate. They will kill us. They will destroy the entire Middle East. They will not absorb a nuclear detonation on their country and not retaliate."

King Abdullah looked at him, his eyes burning bright. "Oh, my brother, my dear brother, if you only understood. If you only knew what I know now, if you could only see what I see. It has all been so long in the making. And we are not alone. We have so many allies; so many men are on our side, men you don't know about, unseen advocates and sponsors. There are many who will be working to ensure we succeed."

The younger brother shook his head. He was growing more scared, even angry. He trusted his brother, but he was not an incompetent fool. And he resented being dragged here, to this underground hole, to be shown a row of weapons that, if used, would only guarantee they were destroyed.

His heart skipped, the spit in his mouth turning suddenly sour. "Brother, you know I love you," he started to say. "But if you do this thing, if you attack the U.S., then we all are dead men. You must certainly know that. This *isn't* good news. These weapons are not our salvation, they are our destruction, I'm sure."

The king stared at him a moment, angry thoughts rolling around in his head. The young prince looked away cautiously, seeing the emotion in his brother's eyes. "King Abdullah," he mumbled, forcing himself to look at the king once again. "I trust you. You know that. I would do anything for this cause. I would die for you, brother, you know that I would. Give me a knife, say the word, and I would thrust it deep in my heart. I would cut out my own intestines if you commanded me to. But I have to tell you, dear brother, I simply do not understand. I do not understand what you're thinking, I do not know your plan, but I am certain of this—if you choose to use these weapons, if you detonate an atomic warhead anywhere in the U.S., they will find out who did it, and we will all be destroyed."

Abdullah shook his head, showing a smile. "Yes," he answered tartly, "without the right preparations, then we would be destroyed. If it was us against them, then I would be a fool.

"But you see, Prince Mohammad, there is something more we can do. Preparations. Arrangements. And before we use these weapons—*and we will use them, my friend*—we are going to change the world in a magnificent way. We are going to realign every thinking, realign every ally, every enemy and friend. We are going to change the geopolitical world in a fundamental way.

"Then, when we have completed our work, it won't be us against them. It will be the U.S. against the world, it will be the U.S. against the Middle East, the Arab nations, every Muslim on earth. It will be the U.S. against most of Europe and Asia as well. It will be the U.S. against China and South America too. It will be the Americans and their lapdog Israelis against the rest of mankind. And *they* will be the criminals. *They* will be the ones who are feared. It will be the Americans and the Jews who will be hated and despised.

"When we are finished, the world will not only support us, they will see justice in our cause. Then they will not only allow it, they will help us see our enemies destroyed."

Camp Freedom
Central Iraq

Sam sat with Bono at the end of the dining hall table. It was early morning, and the two had just come back from patrol. Though they were not on the same team (Sam's immediate commander was the captain who lived in constant fear of taking his father any unhappy news), they had been on the same mission, patrolling on the western edge of Baghdad, where there had been reports of insurgents recruiting from among the poorest neighborhoods. Both men were exhausted, their faces blacked with camouflage and dirt. The patrol had been fruitless, and all they had found were two dead Chechen soldiers (easily identified by their Russian boots) who had been bound, their faces covered, and then shot in the head. They were finding more and more of this kind of thing now, and it gave them a little hope. If the terrorists were killing each other, that clearly made their job easier; more, though, it indicated the growing divisions between the various terrorist groups. Though bound by their common hatred for the U.S., they also hated each other, and it wasn't unusual to find the results of their fratricide.

Sam rested his arms on the table, sipping a 20-ounce bottle of imported water from some unpronounceable desalinization plant on the eastern shore of Qatar. It tasted like saline solution, but Sam had grown used to it. It was cold and wet, and that was all he required anymore.

The chow tent was a little cool—it had been a cold night—but it was growing warmer as it became more crowded during the change of patrols, some on their way in, some getting ready to go. Bono was hacking into a huge pile of scrambled eggs and dry toast. He kept his fork moving while Sam sipped at his drink. They didn't talk much until Bono was nearly through.

"You hear about the Lizards?" Bono asked, referring to one of their battalion's other combat teams.

"What's that?" Sam looked up.

Bono laughed as he leaned across the table. "A couple of their guys were working one of the checkpoints leading into the airport. Some fool comes speeding toward them, doesn't even slow down. They fire the warning shots, take out his tires, you know that routine. At the last second, the guy steers the car toward them, opens the door, and bails out. They drop behind their cement bunkers, expecting a huge explosion; I guess little ol' Lieutenant Ramirez nearly jumped out of his boots. The car screams toward them, hits the cement barricade, and . . . that's it. No car bomb. No big explosion. Nothing. The guys come out from behind the barricade, wondering why they aren't dead. They see the Iraqi running away, but he's gotten too far for them to shoot. Then they see the money scattered all around."

"Money?" Sam wondered.

"Yeah. A couple hundred thousand. Cash. U.S. bills."

"What? Why!"

Bono shook his head. "No one knows."

Sam thought a minute. "So some crazy guy goes careening toward the checkpoint, refuses to stop, gets his tires shot out, steers toward the barricade, jumps out, and runs away, leaving behind a couple hundred thousand dollars in cash to spill on the ground?"

Bono nodded and smiled. "Yeah. That's what I was told."

"They don't know what—"

"They don't know squat, my good friend. Just another day in this paradise that we all call home."

Sam shook his head in disbelief as a stranger approached them and sat down at Bono's side. Though there was plenty of room at the table, he sat close to them. Bono looked up and nodded, then turned back to his eggs.

The man was dressed in dark jeans, heavy boots, and a tan jungle shirt. He looked to be in his mid-forties, with short black hair and overly dark skin from too many days in the sun. The stranger caught Sam's eye, dipped his head in greeting, and turned back to his coffee, blowing over the hot brew. Sam studied him while he sipped. Who was he? Definitely not one of the civilian contractors from the States. Too lean. Too relaxed. Those guys all drove around with a target on their foreheads, and every one of them was as skittish as a chicken in a yard full of wolves. Support staff from the Civilian Affairs office in Baghdad? Maybe. But if he was, he was new to the country. It would take him a couple weeks to get that scared look in his eye, the darting pupils, the constant swivel, the unremitting suspicion that most of them couldn't hide. *Got to be CIA,* Sam thought. *Plenty of them around.*

The man looked up and caught his eye again, then leaned toward him. "Sergeant Brighton?" he said, keeping his voice friendly but low. "I've come a long way to see you. Could we get away and have a quick talk somewhere?"

Sam hesitated. "And you are . . . ?" he asked.

Bono stopped eating and looked over. The stranger turned and nodded to him. "And you too, Lieutenant. I'd like to talk to you both."

"What about?" Bono demanded.

The man extended his hand. "Colonel Gass," he answered with a crushing grip. "Come on, men," he said, pushing away from the table. "Like they say in the movies, I'm going to make you an offer that you can't refuse."

WASHINGTON, D.C.

It was a little after nine in the evening, and General Brighton was just getting ready to leave his office when his computer chimed, telling him he had another batch of email. He had already turned his monitor off, and he hesitated to turn it back on. He was supposed to meet Sara at a dinner party for the new Chairman of the Joint Chiefs of Staff, way out in Chevy Chase, and he was already more than an hour late. But he couldn't resist.

Fourteen new email messages had been loaded into his

inbox, but there was nothing so urgent it couldn't wait until morning. Then he saw the last message, this one from Sam. It was short and ambiguous:

Dad,

Things are going well here. Nothing earth-shattering to report (or dangerous, Mom will be happy to hear).

Thought you might want to know that I had a very interesting conversation yesterday morning. Met a guy who made me a very tempting offer. It looks like all those days of playing cowboys and Indians when I was a kid will come in handy, if you know what I mean.

I'm very excited. I think this is my calling in this world. And if I can help in this battle between good and evil, then that is a good thing and I will feel proud.

Just thought I'd let you know.

Tell the family hi for me.

Tell Mom I'm happy and doing well and that I think of her every day.

Sammy

Brighton read the message quickly, then typed a short reply:

Very good. I am proud of you. It is an incredible honor, but one you have earned.

I pray for your safety every morning and night. And if God could save his Stripling Warriors, I pray he will do the same thing for you.

Be safe. Be good.

Come home when you can.

Dad

chapter fourteen

Azadeh walked toward the bright sun, which was just cresting the top of the great Zagros Mountains. The craggy peaks, topped in dark granite, had sloughed off ten million years' worth of broken rock, and a huge boulder field spread across the foothills on the west side of the range. Above the Zagros, the sky was clear and open, a deep blue that had not yet taken on the lighter hue of mid-morning. Azadeh breathed the air, smelling hints of salt water and rotting seaweed mixed with the deep musk of junipers and pines from the dry forest on the mountain ridges to her right. The morning was crisp and clean, and though it was still chilly she felt the soft rays of the sun beginning to warm the skin on her face and the backs of her hands.

This would be a good day. She felt it inside.

Earlier in the week, she had talked to one of the U.N. headmasters, a stern Muslim woman from some unknown village along the Pakistan border, about being allowed to attend classes at the improvised school. High school classes were held in the cafeteria tent between meals, but so far only the young men had been allowed to attend. There was talk now of letting the young women attend the classes as well, and Azadeh had been the first to sign up when the list of those who might be interested had been passed around. Today she would get her answer, and she was full of hope.

Standing outside her tent, a small, aluminum, semipermanent structure mounted on a plywood platform and covered with a wide sheet of canvas to keep the rain off, Azadeh sniffed the spring air, then glanced around, realizing she was going to be late for breakfast if she didn't hurry along.

She was just turning toward the chow line when something seemed to stop her. She paused, thinking a long moment. Then words she had spoken in her morning prayer repeated themselves in her mind:

Show me someone I can help, for I would like to do something for You today.

She hesitated, wondering why the words would come back to her now.

Show me someone I can help.

She looked quickly around.

There was no one there. No one who needed her.

No. There is someone. The thought was clear in her mind.

Turning left and right, she confirmed once again that she was alone; the row of small tents under the canvas sheet appeared empty, and the dirt path that ran between the rows of tents was deserted as well. She could hear the low sound of the gathering crowd in the distance, up near the top of a small hill where the refugees were forming up in the chow line, but no one was around her, and she didn't understand.

But she couldn't shake the feeling.

No. There is someone near.

She shook her head, thinking, then put the feeling aside. Turning, she started walking to the cafeteria hall. She was already late, and those last in line got very little to eat.

somewhere else, and the thought of leaving Khorramshahr was almost distressing to her now. Knowing she would never leave, she had accepted this place and sought to make it her home.

Pari's assigned quarters was a small plywood and tin-roofed hut with prefabricated pieces of foam insulation tacked to the ceiling and walls. Most of the 600 refugees in Camp Khorramshahr lived in these permanent structures—the newest refugees stayed in tents only until a plywood hut came open—and Pari had decorated her small home to an almost ridiculous degree. A single, small window and door took up most of the front wall, but she had taken colored chalks and paste and painted fantastic murals on the other walls, the only paintable surface available to her in Khorramshahr. The colors were bright, with oranges, pinks, and soft hues depicting a sunrise over the mountains, spring flowers, and the black sand and deep green water of the Persian Gulf. The paintings were awkward (whatever talents Pari had, painting was clearly not one of them) but they were certainly more pleasant to look at than the bare, foam-insulation walls. Under the murals she had placed tin cans filled with wild chrysanthemums and croton plants she had gathered along the fence, back where a small stream kept the ground wet and agreeable. In one corner of the hut she had set up her small, foot-operated sewing machine (the only object from Iran she had brought with her to Khorramshahr), and through the years she had taken odd scraps of cloth and crafted dresses for the younger girls in the camp as well as colorful quilts, one of which was on top of her cot. Her clothes were neatly folded and arranged on top of a small bureau, and the only pair of shoes she owned was placed neatly at the foot of her cot. The floor was covered with a threadbare Persian rug, a gift to her from one of the U.N. volunteers who had worked in the camp some eight or nine years before. On the bureau was a black-and-white photograph of a young man, handsome, light-haired, with blue eyes and a thin nose, clearly not Persian. A silver cross, highly polished, hung over the head of her cot.

It was a home of poverty by any measure, humble but clean, warm enough but never quite comfortable, adequate, but without even the simplest luxury. But it was a home filled with as much love and beauty as she was able to create from the barren environment around her. Despite its lack of elegance, Pari was satisfied.

These walls are large enough for someone such as I. It is but one room, and not grand, but I have felt Christ's spirit here.

And unlike many of the huts in Khorramshahr, this one had an air of permanence, as if Pari had accepted that this was the place she would die.

Through the years, Pari al- Faruqi had seen many come and go from Khorramshahr—a thousand children, a hundred families, far too many to remember. She had known orphans, single mothers, tiny babies, and old men who had lost everything. Few of them spent more than two or three years in the camp before they were assigned a patron outside Iran or Iraq, someone who was willing to sponsor them in their country, provide them with a job, a little money, and someplace to live until they could get on their feet. But Pari hadn't been so lucky and she never would be. She would die in Camp Khorramshahr, of that she was sure, for there was something inside her, something deep in her chest, that guaranteed she would live out her days here.

Though she was only sixty-six, she looked older, with frail shoulders, thinning gray hair, and so many lines on her face that the creases seemed to fall into each other. But her neck was long and slender, her fingers thin and elegant, and she carried herself with such confidence that it was clear to anyone who studied her for more than a moment that one day, long before, Pari had been very beautiful. And though she was now an old woman, her eyes were bright and alive, and they danced as if she knew a special secret that she would never tell.

Resting on her cot, Pari coughed deeply again. She had been coughing all night and she held a small cloth sprayed with blood in the palm of her hand. She lay there and wondered if she should get out of bed. Maybe not. Not this morning. Not until the sun had warmed things a bit.

Pushing herself against her pillow, she looked around the room and shivered. The inside of her hut was cast in a pleasant light from the sun filtering through the thin fabric over the window, but she still felt so cold. Turning, she saw that the flame on the small propane heater in the far corner had gone out again.

Wincing at the cold, she hacked through a coughing fit, then lay back again.

* * *

Azadeh followed the sound of the coughing.

Behind her tent was a double row of huts, all of them identical, with rain-stained plywood walls, tin roofs that were now rusting, and small prefabricated doors. She had never spent any time in this part of the camp, and she made her way carefully, not knowing if she would be welcome.

She listened, hearing the sound again, then stopped in front of the unpainted door. Knocking gently, she squared her shoulders and waited.

A long moment passed, but no one opened the door. She knocked again, the sound echoing off the wood walls. Then she heard a small voice answer, and she pushed back the door.

Azadeh poked her head tentatively into the room and saw the old woman waiting on the side of her bed.

"Hello, hello," Pari said in a bright voice. She motioned

with her hand, beckoning Azadeh to come in. "Well, well, what is this? Who is this beautiful girl?"

Azadeh smiled shyly. "I heard . . ." she hesitated. "I heard you coughing and I wondered if you were all right?" She glanced around quickly, taking in the murals and flowers.

Pari adjusted herself on the side of her bed, then looked up, her dark eyes flickering in the morning light. She was wearing a deep blue cotton robe, and she pulled it tightly around her waist. Azadeh watched her, standing shyly at the door. "I'm sorry," she tried to explain. "I was just wondering if . . . you know . . . if there was anything I could do?"

"Oh, how wonderful," the old woman exclaimed. "I've been hoping to meet you. Your name is Azadeh, am I right?"

Azadeh nodded in surprise. "Yes, my lady, but how did you know?"

The old woman smiled. "I know most of the people in this camp. And someone as beautiful as you, well, it would have been hard for me not to take note."

Azadeh lowered her eyes. She was not used to being complimented so easily and she did not know how to respond. "*Bânu* . . . madam," she started, but Pari broke in.

"Your last name is Pahlavi?"

Azadeh looked up in surprise, instantly on guard.

Pari read the worried look on her face. "Come in, will you, please," she said, gesturing toward the younger woman. There was a single chair in the corner, near the portable loom, but Pari patted the cot beside her. "Come, Azadeh, please sit down."

Azadeh entered the hut carefully, leaving her shoes near the door, and stood in the center of the room.

"I knew several Pahlavis," Pari began gently, as if she knew she was on tender ground. "It was many years ago. And a long way from here. I used to live in Tehran. When I was a little girl . . . " she studied Azadeh's face as she spoke.

Azadeh kept her eyes on the floor. "My father . . . ," she started to say.

" . . . was a grandson of the Shah?" Pari finished the sentence. Though the inflection in her voice indicated it was a question, it seemed she already knew.

Word spread easily through the camp; among people with little to do, there was plenty of talk. *Badguyi*. Gossip. Everyone knew everything. Azadeh had heard some of it already, the quiet whispers, the sideway looks. But she lifted her head defiantly. She would not apologize, nor would she try to hide who she was. She nodded, her lips pressed firmly, her chin held high.

"They were good men." Pari offered in a soft voice. "A good family." She paused and stared at Azadeh, choosing her words carefully. "I knew some of your family, Miss Azadeh, a very long time ago. My husband was a very . . . " She stopped, thinking, then continued slowly. "Your grandfathers were treated poorly, very poorly, I'm afraid. I think they had the best intentions for our country, but most of them are . . . gone now."

Azadeh nodded but didn't say anything.

Pari patted the cot again, motioning once more for Azadeh to sit down. "Okay, Miss Azadeh Pahlavi, that is all we will say of that for now. We will talk of it later, if you want to, but come and sit down."

Azadeh motioned to the door, still uncomfortable. "*Bânu*, I was just . . . I heard your coughing and I thought I might be of some help."

Pari smiled. "Yes, well, that is a coincidence. You see," she pointed to the propane heater in the corner and coughed. "I'm afraid I've taken a chill. It feels so cold in here. Yet I can't seem to get the flame on my heater to be anything more than a flicker."

Azadeh moved toward the propane heater and knelt down. It was very similar to the heater her father had kept in his bedroom, and she saw instantly what she had to do. Reaching around to the back of the unit, she turned off the gas. "Have you got a file? A toothpick, perhaps?" she asked. Then she saw a broom in the corner and she quickly stood up, removed a single straw, and went back to the heater. "Your outlet is clogged," she explained as she worked. "We had a heater like this at my home. You have to clean the gas outlet every once in a while." She ran the strand of straw carefully through the propane outlet, rubbing it against the sides of the valve, then broke it in two and ran both straws through the narrow hole. After several moments of this, she reached behind the heater and turned the propane on again. Pushing the igniter, she heard a sudden *snap* as the igniter clicked and the pilot light fluttered, a light blue flame at the base of the porcelain retainer. She turned up the valve and the flame kicked on, spreading bright and yellow across the base of the unit. She felt the heat instantly and stepped back and smiled.

Pari clapped her thin hands in delight. "Do you know how long, my dear Azadeh, I have been trying to get that heater to work? Too many nights I have shivered under the blankets in the cold."

Azadeh smiled. "It was easy, *Bânu*."

"Thank you, thank you. You have really brightened my day."

Azadeh moved away from the heater. "You know, *Bânu* . . . " she paused, not knowing her new friend's name.

"I am Pari al- Faruqi."

Azadeh bowed politely while bending her knees and holding her hands across her chest. "*Bânu* al- Faruqi."

"You don't have to call me madam. Miss Pari will be fine. We are all equals here, Miss Azadeh. There is no rank in Khorramshahr; we all tread the same ground."

Azadeh smiled, beginning to feel comfortable. "Miss Pari, were you intending to eat breakfast this morning?"

The older woman's shoulders slumped. "I was feeling a little tired. And cold, as you know. I was thinking I might skip breakfast today."

Azadeh looked at her new friend. She was so tiny and frail. The last thing she needed was to skip another meal. "I was just going up," Azadeh offered. "I would be happy to bring you something."

Pari smiled instantly. The warmth from the heater was beginning to spread through the small room, and she already felt better knowing she could get warm if she wanted without having to crawl under the quilts on her bed. She turned to Azadeh. "Perhaps it would be nice to eat. If you will bring me something, I would be very grateful. And we could eat here together. Would that be okay with you?"

Azadeh smiled. "What would you like?" she asked.

"Do I have a choice this morning?"

"Probably not," Azadeh said. The breakfast menu was very basic.

"Then I'll have a wheat roll and spice jelly, if you really don't mind."

chapter fifteen

Azadeh set a small plastic plate and two cups of steaming coffee on the bureau. While she had gone for their breakfast, Pari had put on a white dress with overly extravagant blue trim and white lace. She sat by the heater now, her feet near the flame, a thick, woven sweater covering her lap. Her hair was combed back and tied with a blue ribbon, and she looked a bit more alive than she had just twenty minutes before.

"You look lovely," Azadeh said as she stirred the hot coffee. "Blue is a good color for you, Miss Pari."

Pari looked proud as she pressed the long trim. "You think so?" she asked, moving her hand to the ribbon in her gray hair.

"Oh, yes," Azadeh smiled, then bit her lower lip. The ribbon and lace looked oddly out of place in the bare hut, but then so did the flowers and the colorful quilt. She handed her new friend a coffee, noticing as she bent toward her that Pari had patted some foundation to cover the crow's-feet at her eyes. Azadeh tried not to stare as she set the tray down. Makeup was forbidden, didn't Pari know?

"It's been so long since I've had a visitor," the older

woman said excitedly as Azadeh placed a warm cup in her hand. "I'm getting too old now. It's harder and harder to get out anymore."

Azadeh almost laughed. As if there were someplace to go!

Pari took a careful sip of the coffee. "This is so nice of you," she said.

Azadeh nodded, then sat down on the corner of the bed. The hut was so small that she could reach across the room and touch Pari's knees.

Pari took the tray and a plastic knife and began slicing the bread. The Iranian bread, or *nân,* was round as a pancake but thicker and brown and made of hard wheat, well cooked, without yeast. It had a brittle crust that crumbled in her hand, leaving a soft, spongy middle, which she then broke in two. The brown spread was half butter, half jelly, and heavy with spice. Azadeh smelled the jelly and her belly grumbled. Pari took a piece of the bread and smothered it in spice jelly, then handed it to her.

Azadeh waited until the older woman had prepared her own piece before lifting the bread to her mouth.

"Could we offer grace?" Pari interrupted before Azadeh could take a bite.

Azadeh hesitated, not understanding.

"Thanksgiving," Pari explained.

Azadeh nodded, and Pari bowed her head. Azadeh kept her eyes open, but she bowed her head too. "Father, I thank you for this meal," Pari said. "I am grateful that I don't have to be hungry today. And I thank you for sending me a new friend. Bless her for her kindness. In your Son's name, amen."

Azadeh hesitated as Pari lifted the bread and took a small bite, then followed her lead and began eating. The crust was hard, almost bitter, but the inner portion was soft, the jelly sweet, and she savored each bit. The coffee was black and heavy with sugar, and she held her plastic cup tightly, letting it warm her hands.

Looking around the small room, she noticed the young man's picture on the bureau. "One of your sons?" she asked politely.

Pari laughed. "Oh no, Miss Azadeh, that picture is much older than that. That is my husband, Yitzhak Nakash. Both of us were much younger when that picture was taken, as I'm sure you can see."

Azadeh leaned toward the picture, which showed a tall man standing between two marble pillars. A crystal-clear pool shimmered in the background, and exquisite granite tile was under his feet. She studied the man in his white suit and white hat. "He is very handsome," she said.

"Yes, dear, he was. And smart. Oh, so smart! He read everything. He had more books, oh, you should have seen them, his library reached up to the ceiling. I used to tease him that he loved them more than me. He assured me he didn't. And I usually believed him; he could be *so* convincing, you know." Pari stopped and smiled shyly, and Azadeh noticed her dancing eyes—those eyes with their secrets that Pari would never tell.

"Yitzhak was such a beautiful talker," Pari went on wistfully. "He was so smooth and sweet. He used to tell me—" she stopped suddenly, then took a slow bite of her *nân*. "It was a long time ago," she concluded with a firm shake of her head.

Azadeh hesitated. "He is not with you?" she wondered.

"No, Azadeh. He died years ago."

Azadeh nibbled politely. "I'm sorry, *madam* Pari."

"No, no, it's all right. In my prayers sometimes I ask God to scold him for leaving me alone for so long. It hardly seems fair, him leaving so soon and the way that he did. When I see him again, believe me, I'm going to let him know. But I'll reprimand him only for a moment, and then I will rejoice."

Azadeh was silent a moment, then motioned to the silver cross over Pari's bed. "You are a Christian?" she asked carefully, not knowing if it might be an inappropriate question.

The old woman hesitated and Azadeh sensed her tightening up. Her shoulders had been slumping, but now she sat square and placed her arms on her lap. "Yes. I am a Persian Christian. There are a few of us left."

Azadeh took a bite of her bread and chewed slowly, still fearful of saying the wrong thing. But it was so . . . fascinating. She felt drawn to the cross, and she stood up and moved closer, leaning over the head of the bed. She touched it with both hands, running her fingers down both sides. It felt so solid, so heavy, as if it was ten pounds of pure silver. "This represents the suffering of the Great Prophet Jesus?" she asked.

"Yes, child, it does."

"He was killed on the cross? Crucified?"

Pari nodded in answer.

"You celebrate the death of your God? I do not understand."

Pari thought a long moment. "We do not celebrate his death, but we remember it, yes. His death was important because he died for me."

"He died for you?"

"He died for all of us, Miss Azadeh."

Azadeh shook her head. It seemed horribly cruel. What kind of religion believed that men would crucify their own god? What kind of religion would worship such a powerless being, a god who could not even defend himself against his own creations? And what kind of religion would worship a god who was dead? She didn't understand it, but she didn't question it now. Odd as it seemed, she didn't see any particular evil in this belief; it seemed foolish, perhaps, but not wicked. And Pari certainly didn't seem like a devil, though Azadeh knew that was what most of their people would have considered her.

"There were no Christians in my village," Azadeh continued after some thought. "But I went to private school outside of my village, and I had a friend who was a Christian. We called him Oman, but his mother called him David. He was a good friend. Bright but quiet. I thought he was honorable."

"So you can be honorable and still be a Christian?" Pari asked with a laugh in her voice.

"My father said you could," Azadeh quickly replied, anxious not to offend.

A warm wisp of steam lifted from Pari's cup, and she smelled it deeply before taking a sip. "There have been Christians inside Persia for more than 800 years," she said. "We have been part of the government, business leaders, traders, craftsmen . . . most anything. We have flourished and we have famished, depending on who is in power. But since the rise of the ayatollahs, we have been nearly destroyed."

Pari glanced at her surroundings and concluded, "You realize that is why I am here."

Azadeh nodded. She had suspected that.

"Our countrymen will no longer tolerate us," Pari said. "We have been forced to leave our homes, cast out from our people. It has always been dangerous to be a Christian in Persia, but it is most deadly now. There is much to fear if you believe as I do."

Azadeh nodded sadly, thinking of her own village and her status of an outcast. She remembered her father and his whispered conversations with Omar in the night. Both of them feared. Everyone feared in Persia. It was the way that they lived. "Tolerance is anathema to their teachings," she said, not needing to specify who she meant by *they*. "They believe there is a battle between Allah's teachings and the influences of the world. There are true believers and heathens, and you must choose which side you are on. You are either with them or against them, but there is no middle ground."

Pari pressed her lips. "I guess that is a fairly accurate description," she said. "But I had some neighbors, good friends, and they were not always so intolerant. A few of them were not good people, yes, but most were simply afraid. So they did what they had to. But there were some good people too."

Azadeh shook her head, thinking of her own people in Agha Jari Deh. "Not enough of them," she replied bitterly, her voice hard and low. "They will betray you. They will hate you. They will take everything."

Pari watched her a moment, noting the look in her eye. There was a bitterness, a hard squint, that had not been there before. "Who are you talking about, Azadeh?" she asked quietly.

Azadeh moved angrily to the edge of the bed. "I'm talking about everyone!" she said in a bitter voice. "Maybe there are some good people out there, but they are few and far between. And what chance do they have? They are *always* destroyed. The bad ones are stronger! They will always win. It is better to be quiet. It is better to hide. It is better to quietly do what it takes to get by and live."

Pari took another slow bite of bread and studied her younger friend. "You know, little Azadeh, you are going to have to decide."

Azadeh moved her head to the side. "Decide what?" she asked.

"Will your heart be softened, or will you let it become hard, like a wet stone in your chest, like an ice chip that is too cold to hold? Will you turn bitter—or will you remain happy despite the things you have had to endure?"

Azadeh didn't answer, though her eyes remained narrow. She shifted her weight on the side of the bed. "Sometimes I wonder," she admitted. "Does God really love me? And if he does, then why this? My father was a good man. He didn't deserve to die. And did I really deserve this . . . " Her voice trailed off.

Pari watched her, then leaned forward on her chair and rested her rough hands on Azadeh's knee. "I know you've been wronged, Azadeh," the older woman said. "That is clear in your face. I've seen that look many times before. You are alone here, deserted. There is a long story inside you that perhaps one day you will tell. But regardless of your story, Azadeh, this much I know. You have to decide how you are going to respond. Will you let your heart grow hard and bitter or will you look to the future and remain able to love?"

Azadeh looked away. "Sometimes I feel angry. I know that God has always helped me, but sometimes . . . I don't know . . ." She looked away sadly. "Sometimes I don't understand."

"I can't answer that, Azadeh. Many things I don't know. Why we hurt. Why we suffer. I know that life isn't fair. But I've also learned that there is more equity in our struggles than we may believe; there are hidden hurts in those around us that we may never see. Everyone has to suffer—that is part of the plan. But it *isn't* the outcome and it *isn't* why we are here. So remember that, Azadeh. There are better days ahead. Don't give up. Don't grow hard. That is not God's will."

chapter sixteen

Azadeh got out of bed long before the sun came up and dressed quickly, then slipped out of her tent and moved up the hill. Keeping to the shadows, she waited outside for the U.N. contract workers to show up at the cafeteria. The head cook, a thin woman from Algiers, nodded to Azadeh as she plodded up the trail in the darkness, then held back the tent flap and let her slip inside.

Putting on a stained apron, Azadeh went to work. She cleaned the grease drains and ovens, brought in and stacked thirty-pound sacks of flour and ten-pound sacks of sugar and salt, then prepared and kneaded huge blobs of dough. The ovens were warm by the time she finished the first batch, and she pulled off and shaped the *nân* into flat cakes, then set them inside. Two hours later, just as the sun was rising and the refugees were lining up for breakfast, Azadeh cleaned her hands, wiped the flour off her cheek, and turned to the head cook, who reluctantly paid her the agreed-upon wage.

Azadeh stared at the commodities, then took the dripping pork sausage, scrambled eggs, and white cheese and arranged them carefully on a paper plate. She placed the food in a small box, covered it with a clean cloth, and slipped out of the tent.

Walking quickly, she made her way past the line of hungry refugees, nervous in the knowledge that she was hiding a treasure. She hoped the smell of the sausage wouldn't penetrate the box or she would be mobbed. Pushing through the crowd at the end of the line, she walked past the administration building, off the low hill, and toward the long row of plywood huts. It had rained the night before, a cold and misty drizzle, and a low fog hung over the hills on the east side of the camp. The ground was almost slimy from the powder-fine mud, and she walked carefully, occasionally slipping as if she were walking on ice.

Down to the second row of huts she walked, then turned left past the latrine and showers, over the small bridge that protected the exposed water pipes and gas line, and east to the fifteenth hut on the right. She stopped in front of the shelter and noted the heavy moisture on the inside of the window. The propane heater created its own condensation, and it appeared that Pari had the heat turned up full blast again.

Which meant Azadeh wasn't the only one who had woken up covered in sweat in the night.

As she pushed the door open, Azadeh was met by a warm wave of moist air. The older woman was still sleeping. The hut was built on a platform elevated six inches off the ground, and Azadeh stopped on the threshold to take off her muddy shoes, which she left outside the door. Stocking-footed, she stepped quietly into the hut and pushed the door closed.

Pari rolled over to face her as Azadeh walked into the room, then struggled to push herself up on the side of the bed. Azadeh walked to the small bureau and placed the box down. "Good heavens, darling Azadeh, what are you doing here so early?" Pari said.

"I brought you breakfast," Azadeh smiled as she helped the older woman sit up. Putting her arms under Pari's shoulders, she looked quickly around, searching for the handkerchief Pari always tried to keep hidden from her, seeing the tip of the red-tinted white cloth sticking out of her clutched hand. As she lifted her weight, Azadeh felt the dampness of the smaller woman's night clothes. Pari's gray hair was matted to her neck, and Azadeh reached for the small wash basin on the bureau. The water was cool, and she dipped a gray washcloth inside. "You didn't sleep, *Bânu?*" she asked as she washed Pari's face and neck.

"I slept very well, Miss Azadeh," Pari answered in a weak voice.

Azadeh shook her head. "No, *Bânu,* I can see that you didn't."

The older woman didn't argue but sat, her shoulders slumping, while Azadeh washed her face and combed her hair. "That feels so nice," she said simply.

"I'm glad," Azadeh answered.

The two were quiet a moment until Azadeh said, "I brought you a surprise for breakfast."

Pari's eyes brightened up. "What? Extra jelly?"

"Even better," Azadeh said. "And you'd better eat it now before it gets cold." She washed her own hands in the clay bowl, then picked up the box and removed the cloth covering, exposing the sausage, eggs, and melted white cheese that had been hidden inside. The aroma immediately filled the room, and Pari leaned forward, a sudden smile on her lips. "My goodness, Miss Azadeh, how *did* you arrange that?"

"I guess even we homeless refugees deserve more than bread and jelly once in a while," she said.

The older woman stared at her. "They are serving this for breakfast?" she asked in a disbelieving tone.

"They are this morning," Azadeh replied.

Though she had gotten up at 3:00 A.M. and worked in the kitchen for two weeks for this single meal, she didn't tell Pari. The woman would not have enjoyed it, would perhaps even have refused to eat it, if she had known.

Pari stared at the scrambled eggs and sausage, then up at Azadeh, her eyes wide with excitement. "I haven't had eggs for . . . I don't know . . . years and years. And sausage. I can smell it. It makes my mouth water. How could we be so lucky!"

Azadeh spread a paper napkin on Pari's lap, then settled the single plate in front of her and sat on the bed.

"Oh, no," Pari said as she saw the plate, "you have to eat too!"

Azadeh looked at the scrambled eggs and the finger-thin rolls of pork sausage. "I ate at the chow tent," she said.

Pari shook her head, then took a clean fork and divided the eggs in two, moving one of the sausages toward the second pile. "Then you will eat again. You must eat with me, Azadeh, or I won't feel comfortable."

Azadeh glanced at the eggs and anxiously nodded yes. The two said grace, then ate slowly, savoring each bite of the special meal. "Delicious!" Pari murmured as she tasted the egg.

"So good!" Azadeh agreed as she took a bite of sausage.

They ate in silence. It took only a few minutes before all the food was gone.

While Azadeh cleaned up, Pari got dressed (same old dress with blue trim), and then they sat together, Pari on her chair, Azadeh on the corner of the bed.

"*Bânu* Pari," Azadeh said, looking her square in the eye. "I want to ask you something, and I need you to be perfectly honest with me."

The older woman smiled. "Now, Miss Azadeh," she

teased, "you know a lady of proper upbringing and stature can never be *perfectly* honest. There are always a few secrets one must keep to herself."

Azadeh smiled, but only barely. "Don't worry, *Bânu* Pari, I'm not going to ask your age."

"As well you shouldn't, my dear friend, or I would have to ask you to leave."

Azadeh looked stern. "*Bânu,* I need to be serious for a moment."

Miss Pari sat back "All right, Miss Azadeh, what can I do for you?"

Azadeh nodded toward the red-tinted handkerchief Pari still hid in her hand. "You are sick. You try to hide it. But in the little time I have known you, I have watched you grow frail. I touch you, you have a fever. And the cough. That horrible cough. Now I want you to tell me what is wrong."

Pari leaned forward. "Don't worry for me, Miss Azadeh. I'm not contagious, I promise, or I would never have let you come into my home. Yes, I am sick, but there's nothing you can do. So let's not worry about my health, dear. There are other things we can talk about, other things to plan: getting you back in school, getting you out of Khorramshahr, what you will do with your life. So many good things to talk about, so many interesting things. Things of promise and optimism. There are many things we can discuss, but my health is not one of them. We must speak of something else."

"No," Azadeh said firmly. "We will talk of this. I want to know what is ailing you. I want to know why you have come to accept that you will never leave this camp."

"Miss Azadeh, why waste our time—"

"*Bânu,* you must tell me. And I want to know now!" Azadeh's eyes grew fierce with a hard light from the fire within. She sat on the edge of the bed, determined, her lips pressed and tight. She had learned—she knew now—that sometimes she had to fight, and she wasn't going to sit passively and let this thing pass. "You are my friend, *Bânu* Pari. I trust you. I hope you trust me. But if you feel any affection for me, if you have any feeling for me at all, then I deserve to know."

The older woman sat still a long moment, though she seemed to deflate. "I really wish we didn't have to," she said in a quiet voice.

"I have many wishes, *Bânu.* Sometimes our wishes don't come true."

Pari hesitated. "That is something I could have said to you, dear."

"Then we understand each other, *Bânu.*"

The old woman was still.

"Now please," Azadeh begged now, her voice soft and low. "As your friend, as my friend, I have a right to know."

Pari swallowed awkwardly from the tightness of her throat. "All right then, Miss Azadeh, if you really must know. I have tuberculosis. And there is nothing they can do."

Azadeh hesitated, then asked, her voice sad, "You are going to die, *Bânu?*"

Pari laughed quietly. "We're all going to die sometime, Miss Azadeh."

"No, I mean . . . you know, are you going to die now?"

"No, I don't think so. If you had asked me five years ago, I would have said I'd be gone by now. But it seems this old body just keeps slogging along. Another month. Another year. Another five years. I don't know."

"Tuberculosis . . . ?" Azadeh wondered, an uncertain look on her face.

"Tuberculosis is a bacterial disease that usually affects the lungs," Pari explained, "though it can affect other parts of the body as well—the lymph nodes, kidneys, or bones."

"And this tuberculosis is the reason why you have never left Khorramshahr?"

"Well, yes and no. Having TB is what keeps me here now, but it isn't that simple. The reason I've never been able to leave Khorramshahr goes back even further than that.

"Being a Christian means it has always been much harder for me to find a sponsor so I could leave the camp. But for me it was even worse. I had other issues as well. You see, Azadeh, my husband . . . he was a very good man, but good men have enemies. A list of enemies is but a list of the battles one has fought. If a man has no enemies, then he was a coward, I think.

"And my husband fought many battles. He was a very . . . controversial man. Very wealthy, very strong, a man of great means. He was courageous and ambitious. And, well . . ." her voice trailed off. "Let's just say it is a very long story that I may tell you someday."

"*Bânu,*" Azadeh said softly, "I don't understand."

Pari took a pained breath. "You asked if my tuberculosis is the reason I have never left Khorramshahr, and the answer is no, at least it wasn't at first. My husband had many enemies in the government who had great interest in keeping me here. If I were to leave, I could hurt them. They owe me many things.

"But some of that eventually passed, and after many years I was told that I could apply for release. I started making arrangements. A few more years passed while I searched for a sponsor. Again, I am a Persian Christian. It was difficult. Then I was diagnosed with tuberculosis, which was the final delay. A refugee cannot immigrate with an infectious disease. And untreated TB is infectious—"

"Untreated," Azadeh interrupted. "So there must be a treatment. There is a way you can be cured!"

"Yes, Azadeh, there is. People with TB can be treated effectively. Treatment usually includes taking a combination of anti-tuberculosis medications for six months or so. It takes time. It takes money. And the exact treatment plan must be determined by a highly qualified physician."

"Then we will do that!" Azadeh shouted, standing up from the bed. "We will arrange a treatment plan. I don't care what it takes. I am smart. I can do it! We will figure a way."

Pari smiled and pulled her back, setting her on the edge of the bed. "Yes, Miss Azadeh, you are smart, maybe even brilliant. But more, you are determined and willing to work." She nodded quickly to the greasy paper plates. "How long did you have to work to get that simple meal?" she asked. "I've been here long enough to know it was a long time. Which only proves what you said. You are very capable.

"But this is different, Azadeh, different. And much more difficult."

"But why? I don't see! There must be something I could do."

"But you see, there is a thing now, a complication," Pari tried to explain. "After years of waiting and begging and standing in line for the U.N. doctors who visit Khorramshahr every six months or so, I finally began to receive treatment for my disease. But it turned out . . . poorly, I guess. The doctors gave me inferior quality drugs, drugs that were old and half strength. I should have taken the anti-tuberculosis medications for several months, but I only had enough medicine for two or three weeks. So the virus in my body wasn't eliminated. Instead it grew strong. Six months later, the doctors came back again. Same weak medicines. Once again, not enough. And the virus grew stronger and even more powerful. They call it

MDR-TB: multiple drug-resistant tuberculosis. It is nearly impossible to treat."

Azadeh looked confused. "Then what does it mean? Isn't there something they can do!"

Pari shook her head slowly, coughing into her handkerchief. "From what I can learn, patients with a drug-resistant disease can sometimes be treated with drugs to which their organisms are still susceptible. But it is difficult. Very rare. And very expensive. I need an expert who has experience in treating drug-resistant TB, and not many of those can be found around Khorramshahr, my dear. And even if they were somehow to provide me access to such a specialist, the effectiveness of treatment for MDR-TB is very uncertain. It might work, it might not. Knowing that, do you think they are going to spend the money to treat an old woman such as me?"

Azadeh was silent as she stared at her hands. "There is nothing they can do, then?"

"No, dear, there's not."

Azadeh hesitated. Then, lifting her eyes, she asked, "Might I be in danger?" Before Pari could answer, Azadeh cut in again. "It doesn't matter to me, *Bânu*. I will not leave you either way. But if there is something I could do to lessen the risk of infection . . ."

Pari shook her head. "I cannot spread the disease anymore," she said. "The TB has done its damage inside me, but I have no germs in my sputum anymore and I cannot spread the disease."

"Then why won't they let you leave Khorramshahr!" Azadeh exclaimed.

"Once you are on the list of the contagious, it is very difficult to be removed. I've been fighting them for years, I have notes and reports from a U.N. doctor, but the paperwork is suffocating, and I just can't fight anymore. I'm tired, Azadeh, worn down, and it is hard for me to care anymore."

"No," Azadeh mumbled. "Pari, you can't give up like that."

"Azadeh, I won't be the first one to get lost and die in a refugee camp." Pari nodded to the west. "There is a camp cemetery out there, and I won't be its first occupant."

"No, Pari, no. If you are no longer contagious, you can get your name on the release list. But you've got to keep trying. You cannot give up. And you *cannot* die here. "

Pari took a deep breath and closed her eyes. She sat unmoving, then slowly said, "Listen to me, child, and let me try to explain." She opened her eyes and stood up, took two small steps, and bent down to look into Azadeh's eyes. "It's all right. I'm not unhappy. In fact, I think I might be better off in this place than anywhere else I could be. What else would I do? Where would I go? I am too old to start over. I have no children left alive now. No family. I have nowhere to live. No friends to take me in. No matter where they sent me, I would be a stranger in a lone and strange land. Where would I stay? How would I eat? I must be realistic and consider these things. And there are worse places than Khorramshahr, believe me, I know. It isn't much, but over the years I have come to think of this as my home.

"And I don't have much more time left, Miss Azadeh. I know you are young and that makes it very difficult for you to understand, but I have accepted my fate here and I am satisfied."

Azadeh shook her head. "It is not fair," she whispered, speaking more to herself. Feeling a bitter swell of emotion, she wiped at her eyes.

Pari pressed forward and kissed Azadeh's cheek. When she pulled back, her face was peaceful and she smiled, her eyes calm and bright. She reached for Azadeh's hands and wrapped her fingers in hers. "You know, Azadeh, you and I are so much alike. I keep smiling. You keep smiling. We both see the good in this life. And we have so much in common, I mean right here and now. Your entire life lies before you, bright, perhaps uncertain, but still beautiful. We have both seen our share of shadows, but there are such bright days ahead. You have so much to look forward to. I know that you do.

"But listen to me, Azadeh, for you have to know this is true. You have so much to look forward to. But so do I, dear. You have this life. I have another. You have this world. I have the next. There are bright days ahead, bright days for you, but bright days for me as well."

Azadeh nodded slowly, her eyes rimmed in red.

Pari pressed her fingers, then kissed her cheek again. "Now, listen to me, Azadeh, for I *know* this is true. You have a special mission, a special work in this life. I can see it in your manner; I can see it in your eyes. And God will direct you, I know that he will. Perhaps you have felt his presence, maybe even seen the angels he has sent to your side. And though I haven't seen them, Azadeh, I know they are there, for I can feel them. They are near.

"I can see from your eyes that you do not understand. But you will. I promise one day you will know what I mean."

Listening to Pari, Azadeh felt scared and confused. The words made no sense, and it frightened her to hear Pari talk this way.

But then Azadeh felt it—a warm burn in her chest, a pleasant and comforting feeling that she couldn't explain. Like a glowing ember that had been gently blown over until it burst into flame, an inexplicable warmth blossomed inside her.

She never forgot the feeling.

And she would recognize it instantly when she felt it again.

* * *

The stranger stood on the low hill outside the fence, looking over the camp. The sycamore branches hung low, and he kept in the shadows. He was an Arab, poorly dressed, but the gear in his pockets was worth a great deal.

His master wanted a final confirmation that the target was still in Khorramshahr. So he waited and he watched, ever patient.

A little more than an hour after entering Pari's cabin, she appeared at the door once again. She paused on the threshold to pull on her shoes, then shut the door behind her and made her way down the path. Even from the distance, he recognized her. She was too beautiful.

He quickly pulled out the camera with the powerful telephoto lens and snapped a single picture.

Yes. It was her. There was no doubt in his mind.

Twenty thousand dollars was a very fine sum. But she was worth it, he could see that. She was worth that, and more.

chapter seventeen

For several days after learning of Pari's disease, Azadeh worried and stewed, the frustration simmering until she could no longer sleep. After three days, she walked up the hill to the camp administration building and talked to a burly man standing guard, who told her she would have to wait.

Hours later, she was admitted through the front door and escorted to a small office near the back of the building, where a worn and tired man was waiting behind a worn and cluttered desk. His nameplate read:

MR. SEBASTIAN RAULE
Special Assistant to the Administrator

The assistant studied her carefully. This one, he remembered from when she had first come to Khorramshahr. He smiled at her, a wry and pleasureless turn of his lips. "How may I help you?" he asked as he sat forward in his chair.

Azadeh spent the next twenty minutes explaining the situation with Pari. Raule appeared only to half listen while he doodled on a yellow pad.

"There was political influence that tried to keep her here,"

Azadeh concluded in a determined voice. "Then she was diagnosed with TB, and improperly treated, as you surely must know. But she is no longer contagious. There is no reason to make her stay here anymore."

The thin man checked his watch and impatiently bounced his pen.

"Can you help her?" Azadeh begged him. "There must be something you can do!"

Without answering, Raule swung around in his chair and pulled a small, leather binder from the cheap credenza at his right. He flipped through the pages until he came to Pari's name, reviewing the administrative notes, though he pretty much knew what they said.

"Her case has been sent to the review panel in Kuwait," he explained. "From there it was passed on to the Red Cross office in either Belgium or Washington, D.C. Once the paperwork leaves the camp, there's not a thing I can do."

"You could call. Write a letter. The poor woman has been waiting for years!"

The assistant shook his head and forced a look of sadness onto his face. "I'm sorry. There is nothing. Now if you have anything else . . . "

"NO!" Azadeh shouted, leaning toward the old desk. "You can't dismiss her with a simple wave of your hand! You can't dismiss Pari al- Faruqi as if she were some nameless thing!"

Mr. Raule shook his head. "I'm sorry, but she's a problem. We do the best that we can."

"She isn't a problem, she's a woman! A human being, you fool!"

Raule sat speechless for a moment, then lifted up in his chair. "Let me remind you . . . " he started, his voice low with rage.

Azadeh's face had already turned gray. She huddled in the chair, her eyes wide in horror. "I'm so sorry," she muttered, almost falling to her knees. "It was wrong . . . I was wrong to say what I did. I'm sorry, my *Sayid*." She kept her head bowed as if expecting a blow, not daring to look. "It is not like me to say such a thing, Master Raule. It is not how I have been taught. You are no fool. I was wrong. I'm very sorry, *Sayid*."

The thin man sat back, glaring at the young girl. He let the moment linger, the silence hanging painfully in the air. Azadeh waited before carefully lifting her eyes. The man had returned to his seat. She wondered if she dared go on. "Master Raule, please," she finally whispered, "couldn't you try to find some way to let her go home?"

"She has no home now, Miss Pahlavi."

Azadeh started to speak, then fell silent again.

"She has no home," Raule repeated. "She has nowhere to go." Azadeh looked up, her dark eyes growing wet. Raule shifted his weight as he pulled uncomfortably on his pen. There was something about Azadeh that he couldn't resist and he finally leaned toward her, placing his arms on his desk. "She is better off here," he said, his voice soft now. "I'm not just saying that, Miss Pahlavi, I believe it is true. She has nowhere else to go."

He stopped and watched her. "But even if what I just said wasn't true, I am but one tiny cog in a world of grinding, meshing gears. There is very little I can influence. Very little I can do.

"Now, if you will let me be honest, I will tell you the truth. It is extremely unlikely that your friend will be granted a release from Khorramshahr. She is old. Perhaps contagious. She has little to offer, and no family or friends to take her in. Even if she were to leave Khorramshahr, she would only end up in some other camp, a different name, but another place just like this. I'm sorry, Miss Pahlavi, but I have seen this before. It would be best to accept it. I know Mrs. al- Faruqi has."

"But she has only accepted it because she knows nothing else. You have beaten her down, robbed her of any hope. If you were to give her the option, if you found her a home, I believe she would leave here. Look around! Wouldn't you? Please, isn't there something, isn't there *anything* you could do!"

The assistant stared a long moment, then slowly shook his head. "I am powerless," he answered. And it was the truth. The U.N. bureaucracy was the largest and most vicious in the world. He knew the old woman would die here; she wouldn't be the first.

He stared blankly at Azadeh.

The young girl closed her eyes and cursed.

chapter eighteen

Were some people born with a predisposition to do evil? Did some men's decisions in the premortal world make it practically inevitable that they would come into conflict with God once they arrived here on earth?

Did some leave their best friends on the other side of the veil, friends who had followed after Satan and fought against Christ? Did they miss those wicked ones? Was that where their hearts actually lay? Did they yearn for the pleasures those old friendships could bring?

Did some skirt the boundary even in the premortal world, always looking back, hoping to catch a glimpse of how the other side lived, yearning for the enticements only the Great Liar could give? Did some watch their best friends, those whom they truly loved, choose to worship Satan and understand why? Were some of these people disappointed when their friends were punished by God? Did some come to earth confused, even bitter, over the battles that had taken place in the premortal world?

If the veil were to be lifted, would some of these men run

with open arms to join their premortal friends, their seduction coming easy, almost laughably so, because they recognized the hissing voices of those who had known them so well?

Was that why some human beings were so evil they would do *anything*?

GHESHA GHETTO
EAST OF KIRKUK, IRAQ

The two Iraqis stood facing each other in the back of the store, the sounds of the overcrowded slum penetrating the thin windows and cracks around the poorly fitted door that faced out on the alley. The faint smell of sewage and stewed cabbage drifted through the shutters of the darkened window, and the room was still chilly from the cold cement walls.

The men wore dark, unsmiling faces.

Former lower-ranking members of Saddam's ruling Baathist party, for years these men had ruled through intimidation and fear, assisting in the rape of their country and her daughters as they sought to satisfy their slightest desire. Now they were left with nothing but bitterness and hate. Having been drugged on power, they were going through the equivalent of heroin withdrawal, and it was clear from their actions they valued nothing now—not their families, not their country, barely even their lives.

The leader was a short man with a thin neck whose head strained awkwardly when he looked up to talk. Though he had a dark beard, his dome was bald and shiny and it reflected the light of the single bulb overhead.

"Why is he willing to pay so much for this girl?" the short leader demanded, his voice thick with *sha,* the opiate tea he drank every day.

The store owner frowned. "I don't know," he replied defensively, many years of resentment boiling in his thick voice.

A former army officer, he was not used to being questioned, and his eyes flashed with anger, his brow furrowing into a deep scowl.

The leader gritted his teeth. "I don't like it," he sneered. "You can buy a girl, any girl, I don't care how young or beautiful, for ten thousand American dollars. He is paying two times the market. Something is going on." The leader stared at the shop owner, who hunched his shoulders and scowled. "Who is he? Where did he come from? Why does he want her so much?"

The shop owner stood square, staring into the young leader's face. "I'll tell you why he wants her! Because she is young and beautiful, and he is American. They think they can buy anything! Twenty thousand dollars! That may be little more than a month's wage to him! I don't know. I don't care!" He swore bitterly. "Who are you to question when I make a good deal? If I had sold her for ten thousand, you would be angry too. I bring you a deal with enormous profits, and you are worried because I don't know *who* the buyer is! Do we know any of our buyers? No. Not a one. Now, are you going to get the girl, or should I go somewhere else!"

The smaller man stared defiantly, glaring into his subordinate's eyes. There were issues here, he could see that, issues he could not ignore, but he would deal with them later. There was always time to make adjustments in the attitudes of his men. Working in Saddam's political chambers had taught him many things.

He took two deep breaths, then frowned and nodded toward the wooden door that led into the shop. "The whitey is out there?" he asked.

The other man nodded yes.

"I will talk to him," he said, walking toward the door.

* * *

The American was waiting beside the counter near the front of the nearly empty store. Emerging from the back door, the Iraqi leader walked toward him; the American turned and waited until the two men stood face-to-face. This was the Iraqi's land, his neighborhood, and he stood with confidence, not intimidated by the American's money or wealth. Whitey was the stranger in this part of the world, and the Iraqi stood too close, knowing it would make him uncomfortable. He studied the stranger, making a swift appraisal of him. Soft hands were a sign that a man could not take care of himself, and he glanced down. This man's hands were dark and hard. Many days in the sun. A long way from soft, and certainly not manicured. The Iraqi grunted, a little surprised; most of the whities he had dealt with were soft-padded poodles from the city who couldn't change a flat tire or load a weapon if their lives depended on the result. He moved his eyes up to the man's shoulders, which were broad and strong. Many Americans strengthened themselves—part of how they worshipped their bodies—and there was nothing unusual about the strength of his arms. But there was something lean in the muscles. They were taut and quick. These were the muscles of a fighter, not a fool who spent his time mindlessly lifting weights.

The Iraqi felt the first stab of fear.

Then he studied the face, the shaggy hair and hard eyes.

There was something about this American, something familiar. He had not seen this face, but he'd seen *that look* before.

The Iraqi bit his lip, even more uncomfortable. "You came to discuss the girl?" he snorted in barely understandable English.

The American nodded toward the shop owner, who was

standing near the back of the store. "He said he could get what I wanted, but it would take ten days. Things have changed. I want her now."

The Iraqi was suspicious. "What's your hurry, good master?" he asked.

The American glared. "Does it matter?"

"No, my *Sayid,*" the Iraqi answered sarcastically as he bowed. "But these things can be difficult . . . "

"Can you do it? Yes or no?"

"Yes, yes, of course. It's just that . . . "

"I'm leaving the country in three days. Can you get her by then?"

"Oh, no, my *Sayid*. It will take longer than that."

"How long?"

"At least a week. She is inside Khorramshahr, which you must know is a U.N. refugee camp. If she were in Iran or a village under Iraqi control, I could have her tonight. It would be easy, my friend. But the refugee camps are much more difficult—you must know that is true. Perhaps I could interest you in another one of our . . . "

"No," the American snapped. "I only want her."

The Iraqi stepped back and forced a smile. "You must be buying for a very, ah . . . how do you say in your language? . . . a very particular buyer."

"Who I buy for doesn't matter. All I want to know is, can you get her by Saturday? It's a simple question, Mr. Zubaida."

The Iraqi scowled with anger. How did this man know his name?

He shook his head. "Very difficult. Maybe, if we were to pay the right people, pull a few strings here and there—but it will be much more expensive. Our cost would go very high. I will say we can do it, but it might cost another five or six thousand dollars."

The American leaned toward the Iraqi, his eyes bright and intense. "Then you will take it out of your profits, which were already *very generous,* my friend. I will come back in three days, and I want *that* girl. Have her here, we are all happy. Disappoint me, and I shut you down."

"Shut me down!" the Iraqi scoffed as he turned away. "Don't make me angry, you American fool! You cannot touch me, not here. If we were in Baghdad, in the American sector, then maybe, but this is not your world, my friend." He snorted again. "Shut me down! What an idiot! What are you going to do!"

The American took a step forward. "I did not mean shut down your business, *my friend.*"

The Iraqi took another step back, glancing anxiously toward his partner, who was standing quietly near the back door. Who *was* this American? His gut tightened up.

The American moved his hand, flipping aside the open flap on his jacket. The Iraqi saw the weapon and glared angrily.

"There are things I could do," the American said through clenched teeth. "Things you are familiar with. Things you have done too." His eyes glinted in the dim light, and the Iraqi saw that look once again, that look he had seen too often before.

"You and I are the same," the American hissed. "We understand each other. You know that we do. Now, I'm coming back on Saturday, and I want that girl."

The Iraqi pressed his lips together and nodded.

The American turned and walked out the front door.

The Iraqi cursed at him, keeping his head down until he heard the door close.

Oh, how he hated the Americans. How he hated them all!

KHORRAMSHAHR REFUGEE CAMP
IRAQ/IRAN BORDER

Twenty hours later, the former Baathist party leader was escorted through the front gates at Khorramshahr. The camp looked like any other he had been to, and he kicked his feet through the dirt and dead grass, not noticing the few trees and wildflowers along the fence on the east.

The man wore dark pants, white shirt, and black turban. He didn't remove his dark glasses, which he wore to hide his red eyes. He waited impatiently on the wood porch of the administration building, listening carefully to the sounds of the camp. It was afternoon, and the sun was hidden behind a thin haze, enough to soften his shadow and reduce the afternoon heat but not enough to keep him from sweating profusely, a steady stream of perspiration beading on his heavy brow.

The administration building was built on a small hill overlooking Khorramshahr. A ten-foot barbed-wire fence surrounded the camp, but it was in disrepair and generally unnecessary, as none of the camp's occupants had anywhere to go. To the north were the cafeteria and improvised school. Rows of identical plywood huts had been built on the flats to the west, and south of them were rows of multicolored tents, which housed the newest refugees. The stranger stared at the tents, hoping to get a glimpse of the girl. Behind him, up near the trees, some refugees were burning the contents of the latrines, an inky black smoke drifting from the fifty-gallon drums.

A little after 3:00, Mr. Raule, special assistant to the camp administrator, came out on the porch where the Iraqi was waiting. "The administrator will see you now," he said. The Iraqi followed the pasty-looking French officer into the building.

The admin building was simply laid out, with small

cubicles lining both sides of the tile-covered room. Little furniture, no decorations, a small clock on the wall. Four larger offices took up the space at the back of the building, and Mr. Raule led the Iraqi to the largest of them.

The camp administrator was a French career civil servant, a man who had spent his entire professional life working through the monstrous bureaucracy that was the U.N. He had finally, and proudly, reached a place where he owned his own kingdom, and he exuded an air of smugness that was almost tangible. He was an overly neat man, small, with a tightly trimmed white mustache and a hairline that had receded past the midpoint of his head. His office was sparse, clean, and all business: metal desk, metal cabinets, metal wastebasket, metal chairs. A single window looked out on the camp, but the blinds had been closed. As the Iraqi was escorted into the room, the U.N. administrator stood and moved quickly from behind his desk, every motion efficient. He had little time.

The men shook hands, but the French administrator did not invite the Arab to sit down. "What can I do for you?" he wondered, getting right to the point.

"I'm looking for someone. A young girl, about fifteen, maybe a year or two older. Pretty. Long hair. She came here from the western mountains of Iran."

The Frenchman studied the Arab, noting the sunken cheeks and rough skin, the dark and lifeless eyes. He wanted to step back from him. "We have many young people here," the administrator replied, offering little help.

"She is my master's niece. She was recently orphaned, and my master has reason to believe she might have come here. He has sent me to find her and bring her back to her family in Pakistan."

"What is her name?" the administrator asked.

"Azadeh Pahlavi."

"Have you checked with the front desk?"

"No, my *Sayid.*"

The camp administrator turned to the door and called. Raule appeared almost instantly. "Azadeh Pahlavi. Young girl. See if she is here."

Raule didn't move. "She's here," he said.

"You are certain, Mr. Raule?"

"Yes, sir, I am. She in-processed no more than a few weeks ago."

"Really?" the administrator said. "Just curious, Mr. Raule, but how can you be so sure?"

Raule blushed and dropped his eyes. "I helped her with some of the paperwork when she in-processed. She's . . . I don't know. I remember her. I've talked with her a time or two since then."

The administrator stared, a curious look on his face. "Very well then, Mr. Raule." He nodded to his Iraqi guest. "This gentleman, Mr. Ishameil, has come for Miss Pahlavi. He works for her uncle. He brings good news for her. He wants to take her with him."

Raule shook his head and answered, "Sir, that can't be."

"And why not?" the administrator questioned. The Iraqi frowned.

"The young woman that I'm talking about had no next of kin. Her father had been recently killed. Her mother died in childbirth. She said she had no family. No brothers. No sisters. No one, she said."

The camp administrator cocked his head to the Iraqi and raised a curious eyebrow. "Perhaps we are talking about two different people," he offered.

The Arab shook his head and pulled out a picture, dropping it on the desk. The Frenchman picked it up, then handed it to his assistant, who looked at it carefully as he nodded his head. "Yes, that is her. I remember her very well."

The administrator extended his hand, asking for the picture again. It showed a close-up of Azadeh's face but no background or other identifiable feature that would give context to where the picture had been taken or how long ago. "This is a recent photograph?" he wondered.

The Arab shook his head. "Perhaps a few months old. Her father sent it to my master sometime last winter, I believe."

The administrator turned to his assistant. "Mr. Raule, are you certain she said that she had no kin?"

Raule answered quickly, "Oh, yes, quite certain, sir."

He lifted the picture and shook it. "And you are certain this is her?"

"Very certain, sir." Raule shot a glaring look at the stranger.

The administrator leaned against his desk, took out a cigarette, and placed it between his lips. But he didn't light up, sucking on the filter instead. "It seems, Mr. Ishameil, that we have a discrepancy here. Either your master is a liar, or this girl has an uncle that she is not willing to claim."

The Arab's shoulders slumped. So insulting. So demeaning. His eyelids drooped with hurt.

His act wasn't particularly convincing, and the U.N. officer pressed his lips together.

"*Sayid,*" the Arab pleaded, "my master is an honorable man. He has sent me at great expense, and he is not a wealthy man, my *Sayid.* He sent me to find this girl. He only wants to help her. He has her interest at heart. And it may not be surprising the girl wouldn't mention her uncle, for my master has lived in Pakistan his entire adult life. It has been many years and, though I can't say for certain, it seems possible Miss Pahlavi and my master may never have met."

The administrator finally lit the cigarette and pulled in a long drag of smoke. He had heard so many stories, most of them filled with grief, that it was difficult to tell him something that he wouldn't believe. This was certainly possible, yet it just didn't ring true. In his gut, he knew the Arab was lying. But he didn't how he could prove it. And he didn't much care.

"Do you have papers proving relationship?" he asked quickly, ready to move on to his next task.

"Of course, *Sayid.*" The Arab pulled out three stapled forms and handed them to the administrator, who immediately passed them to his aide, Mr. Raule.

"Now, my *Sayids,*" the Arab went on as Raule scanned the documents. "I would love to spend the afternoon discussing my master's family tree, but I know you are busy, and frankly, I am as well. If you would sign the papers and release forms, I will take custody of the girl. And of course, I also have a copy of a signed U.N. form 12–22." He reached into his pocket and pulled out another neatly folded form. "I believe that is all you will need," he concluded confidently.

The administrator eyed the forms as he smoked. "It seems, Mr. Ishameil, that you might have done this before?" His voice carried just enough sarcasm to show his disdain.

"Oh, no, my *Sayid,*" the Arab shot back. "But as I said, my master is very anxious. The news of his brother's death has been very hard on him. They were . . . not friendly. Estranged. There was a bitter divide in their family, and my master is hopeful that his brother's death, in Allah's mercy, may have the power to bridge the divide. My master believes that caring for this young girl is part of his penance, and he means to make good. So he has taken great care to find out what has to be done. Thus, I have my instructions: find his orphaned niece and bring her back to him."

The administrator pulled another drag, then turned

toward Raule, who lifted his eyes. He had studied the documents. They were in order. He reluctantly nodded his head.

The administrator knew then that, despite his suspicions, he could not stop the stranger from taking the girl. The camp directives were clear: U.N. officials were to make every effort to repatriate underage refugees to their families. No exceptions to the rule. Families had precedence. And no agreement was required from the underage refugee to go. Even if minors didn't want to go back to their families—and the administrator knew there were many good reasons some of them did not want to return—they had no choice. If a family member appeared with proof of relationship, the camp directors had to release the minor to that person's care.

The Frenchman knew that some of the young women he released from Khorramshahr ended up in very bad circumstances: prostitutes in Iran; sex slaves in India, Pakistan, and Thailand; suicide bombers in Gaza; prisoners in forced labor camps. The list of places they could be sent was as long as the list of sins. But worrying about the children who left Khorramshahr was not what the U.N. paid him to do. Such concerns fell under the Office of Children's Advocate on the twenty-first floor of the U.N. building, which was eight thousand miles to the west.

Eight thousand miles from Khorramshahr. A very long way, indeed.

He glanced at the photograph of Azadeh. She was beautiful and smiling. Beauty was a dangerous thing, he knew. He turned to the Arab. Did this man really represent Azadeh's uncle? He had serious doubts. Would she end up in a brothel in Karachi? It was certainly possible.

Would he spend even five minutes worrying about her once she had been taken from Khorramshahr? Not a chance in this world.

He had other worries than one more lost girl.

He walked back behind his desk, sat down, and began to sign the release forms. The Arab smiled as he watched the administrator work through the papers.

Without looking up, the administrator asked Raule, "Do you know which living quarters Miss Pahlavi has been assigned?"

Raule hesitated, shooting a look at the stranger, who was watching him now. The two men locked onto each other with unblinking eyes. The hostile moment lingered.

"Mr. Raule . . . ?" the administrator prodded, still looking down.

The assistant's jaw tightened up, and the Arab scowled as he leaned his weight toward the smaller man and pressed his lips in a frown.

Raule cleared his throat, his mind racing ahead. "Miss Pahlavi is still in the temporary quarters," he finally said.

The French administrator signed the last document, then looked up and said, "Then will you go fetch Miss Pahlavi. And tell her to pack all her things."

chapter nineteen

KHORRAMSHAHR REFUGEE CAMP
IRAN/IRAQ BORDER

Raule walked through the neat rows of plywood and tin shacks, making his way down to the tent-city where the newest refugees were housed. Approaching the tents, he slowed his pace, then glanced down at the note he had written on a small piece of paper. *Row B, tent 12. Azadeh Ishbel Pahlavi.*

He stopped outside one of the tents. It was set back six feet from the main road, and a narrow, rock-lined path curved toward the half-open flap. The rocks that lined the small trail, none of them bigger than his fist, had been painted green and blue by some previous occupant, and a ten-inch plywood sign had been posted in the dirt at the head of the path. *Tent 12* was painted on the worn plywood, though the dark letters were so faded they were barely readable. Underneath the tent number was a long line that was blank. Years before, the tent occupant's name would have been written in grease pencil in the now-empty space, a small gesture of welcome and ownership, but the habit had long since been abandoned, overcome by events. Raule stood outside the tent and called Azadeh's name. He listened. It was quiet. He called her name again, then moved toward the tent, careful not to disturb the painted rocks on the narrow path. He pushed the tent flap aside and looked through the netting. The tent was empty inside.

Raule felt a sudden surge of relief. She wasn't here. He couldn't find her. The stranger in the admin building would have to come back another time.

A horrible image flashed like a dark movie in his mind. He knew the truth. Like his boss, the camp administrator, he knew that the burly Arab was not who he said he was. A lost uncle. A paid servant sent to find an orphaned child. The lie was so thin, it was like peering through a torn veil. Yes, the Arab's paperwork was flawless, but that didn't mean anything. In his heart, Raule knew they were about to send Azadeh into a dark and terrible world, a world where she would spend the next ten years working for her masters, then be tossed on the street if she had not died already of disease.

He stared at the empty tent and smiled. The Arab would have to come back another day.

He would go back and lie. He would tell the stranger waiting in his office that she had left the camp. He could say that she might have been gone for days; some refugees came and went, it wasn't as if there was any kind of roll call. He could pretend to mount a search, buy a little time. His boss would know what he was doing, but he might play along. He had many more things to worry about than his assistant's efforts to save a young girl.

Raule's hands started to tremble as he worked out the plan. He would delay a few minutes, then go back to the admin building and report that Azadeh was gone. Feigning surprise and distress, he would tell the Arab to leave while they searched, to come back the next day. He didn't need much time to get her out of the camp. When night fell, he would take her away. After that . . .

He heard voices behind him and quickly turned around. Azadeh was walking toward him, her hair covered with a white scarf. Raule glanced down the trail toward the admin building, then around at the crowded pathways and dirt roads that wound through the camp.

"Master Raule," Azadeh said brightly as she walked toward him. Then she saw the look on his face and came to a stop. "Is there something I can help you with?" she asked in a worried tone.

"Miss Pahlavi," Raule started, then halted for a moment. Did he really have the nerve? He quickly stepped toward her. "Miss Pahlavi, come quickly. We need to talk." He pushed her toward her tent, but she resisted his hand.

"*Sayid*, what is it?" she asked him. Raule looked around nervously again.

"You have an uncle?" he asked her.

She shook her head. "I told you, Master Raule, I have no one."

"No, Miss Pahlavi. Think. You came from a large family. You have many uncles and cousins. They scattered to the wind. When your grandfather left Persia, all of them followed him. Now think, did your father have a brother who went to Pakistan?"

Azadeh didn't hesitate. "No, my *Sayid*. My father had no brother."

Raule nodded firmly. It was as he had thought. "Listen to me, Azadeh," he started to say, his hand squeezing her elbow in a firm grip. "There is someone here for you . . . " Then he looked back.

The Arab was standing twenty feet away, at the head of the dirt path. The camp administrator stood beside him, an irritated look on his face. The Arab scowled, then moved quickly, making his way down the trail. "Miss Azadeh!" he shouted, extending his arms to the girl. "Thank Allah, I have found you! Grace and peace be to Our God. Allah has protected you. And I have found you safe."

Azadeh stared at him, a puzzled look on her face. "Do I know you?" she asked as the stranger swept her up in a powerful embrace.

"No, Miss Azadeh, you do not," he whispered quietly in her ear. "But my master is waiting. You will come with me, my dear."

Azadeh pushed herself back. "Who are you?" she asked anxiously.

The Arab didn't answer as he turned to Raule. "Thank you," he said, victory flashing in his eyes.

Raule looked away, conceding defeat. The Arab had known his intent, or at least he had suspected. There was nothing to do now. He glanced at his boss, who nodded to his watch and spun his fingers in a circle, indicating, "Let's go." Time was wasting. He was pressured. There were important papers to sign, important decisions to make, and his office hours ended at four.

Raule glanced at Azadeh, his shoulders slumping in defeat. "Miss Pahlavi," he told her, "this man represents your uncle who lives in Pakistan. He has come to retrieve you and take you to his home."

Azadeh's face was a blank. "I have no uncle," she said.

"Yes, Azadeh, you do. We have the paperwork. It is in order—"

"I have no uncle!" she cried. She turned to the stranger and shivered, looking into his dark eyes. "I do not know who this man is, but I will not go with him."

"But he carries proof. We have checked it."

"Come!" the administrator called from the path. "Pack

your things. We are waiting. You're going to your new home, child."

Azadeh's face grew taut, her eyes glaring and bright. "I will not go!" she answered, backing up to her tent.

And that was all that the stranger would have. "In *my* master's house, a young woman is taught to do as she is told," he said icily. "She does not challenge her master. She may do it once, but only once; she'll never do it again. The rules of *Sharia* hold true in our home. It is not your place, as a woman, to tell me what you will or won't do. You will do as we tell you. And you will remember what your place is in this life."

The Arab seemed to swell as he stood over her. She shrank, pulling back, conditioned to retreat. Raule stepped between them and looked Azadeh in the eyes. "I'm sorry," he whispered, "but it's true. You must go."

Azadeh shook her head, not in defiance but in disbelief. "I cannot. I cannot. Look at him," she whispered, leaning into Raule. "You know what he is. You know it, I can see. Please, Master Raule, please."

"Come!" the camp administrator shouted, growing angry now. "Tell her to gather her things and let's go!"

Raule nodded sadly. "I'm so sorry," he said.

The Arab stepped between them, pushing Raule to the side. "You should be grateful," he sneered as Azadeh stepped away. "My master sent me here to save you. I've traveled many days. We have both sacrificed, and this is the thanks that we get. Now get your things, Azadeh, and come gratefully."

Azadeh shot a pleading look toward Raule, the only man who could help, but he did not look at her now. He had done all he could. He had done more than he should have. He glanced back at his boss, who was walking toward them, an angry glare on his face.

The Arab opened the tent flap and moved inside. It took him less than two minutes to throw her things into a rough burlap sack and reappear, ready to leave.

"Miss Pari," Azadeh gasped, thinking of her only friend. "I need to tell her good-bye."

"Who? What?"

"There is an older woman. My friend. Please, you must let me tell her good-bye."

The Arab looked around, then huffed impatiently. "What time is it?" he asked. Arab people rarely wore watches; time seldom mattered to them.

"Four-twenty," Raule answered.

The Arab shook his head. "No time," he said impatiently as he moved down the trail. "The train heading north from Khorramshahr leaves in less than an hour. We will have to hurry to catch it even now. And I will not spend another night in this land."

"But *Sayid*, please, I have a friend. She lives not more than a five-minute walk from here. Please, if I could just go and tell her—"

Her new master shook his head again. "Come now!" he said, as if speaking to a disobedient dog. "And remember, Miss Pahlavi, what I said about *Sharia* and accepting your place in this world. We can do this easily, or with difficulty. It is up to you."

GHESHA GHETTO
EAST OF KIRKUK, IRAQ

The meeting had been arranged for 9:40 P.M., enough after sunset to be dark but still early enough to allow the parties to get off the streets before the 10 P.M. curfew. Not being a fool, the American had refused to enter the ghetto—not while carrying $10,000 cash, not with the enemies that he had already made there. And the Iraqi had been reluctant to allow the transfer without his supports around. After bitter negotiations, they had decided to meet on the ghetto side of the bridge that joined Ghesha Ghetto to the main highway on the other side of the river. There was a turnoff there, a dirt road that led down to the river and was out of sight of the main road.

At 9:40, the American was standing in the middle of the dirt road. Behind him, forty meters in the distance and hidden behind a stand of stunted trees, his friend was waiting, his automatic weapon trained on the road. The moon was still low, and the dirty air stole most of the starlight, leaving the night dark and still. The American glanced at his watch as he waited, then turned his eyes back to the road. At 9:43, a dusty Mercedes moved slowly toward the bridge and turned off onto the dirt turnaround. The American didn't move from the center of the road, and the driver of the Mercedes kept his lights on bright as he approached. The American turned away and closed his eyes, anxious to retain his night vision.

The Mercedes rolled to a stop not more than two feet from him. The driver cut the engine and then finally the lights. The American turned back to the automobile. His face was dark and hard and he watched silently as the back door opened and his contact got out. The American peered past him through the deeply tinted glass. Another man was sitting in the front seat, but he was barely a shadow behind the dark glass. There was movement from the backseat, but he couldn't see who it was.

The Iraqi slave trader approached the American and stood near the front of the car. They summed up each other with menacing glares.

"Where is she?" the American asked, a hard edge on his breath.

The Iraqi didn't answer. "You got a cigarette?" he asked.

The American shook his head. Not tonight. No time to be nice.

The Iraqi nodded to the low trees. "How many men do you have back there?" he asked.

The American bent down, pulled a blade of dry grass from between the ruts in the road, and stuck it between his teeth. "Where is she?" he countered, ignoring the question altogether.

"Where's my money?" the Iraqi asked.

"Who's in the car?"

"Where's your other man?"

The two men stared at each other, neither of them wanting to give. The American finally tightened his jaw and said, "I've got one friend with me. You met him before. He's back there in the trees. Other than that, we're alone."

The other man nodded. He believed it was true. They had been watching the riverbank for the past two hours or so. They had seen the American, but not his buddy hiding down in the trees, although it didn't take a genius to figure that was where he would be.

The Iraqi studied the American and smiled. There was something about him that he simply didn't like, that made his skin crawl. He had no right to be here. Ghesha ghetto was for Iraqis, not Americans. So he would rob him, then kill him, along with his friend in the trees.

The Iraqi looked around, searching for their car. "And how are you proposing to get out of here?" he asked.

The American nodded to the river. Up against the bank, mostly covered over with cattails and brush, a low boat had been hidden, small but speedy and perfectly adequate.

Glancing at the boat, the Iraqi sensed for a fleeting moment that something was wrong. If the American was a stranger to Iraq, where did he get the boat? And why was he always with his buddy? The Iraqi's military background suggested the pattern of working in teams this way, but he didn't dwell on the thought. His mind was too full with the prospect of a pile of thousand-dollar bills. "Where's the money?" he demanded again, shrugging off the boat.

The American reached under his jacket and pulled out a thick wad of cash.

The Iraqi stared and then turned, slapping the hood of the car. The back door swung open and a huge man emerged. Azadeh followed, a dark coat over her shoulders, a burlap bag in her hand. She looked up in fear.

And the American smiled.

Forty meters upriver, the man hiding among the trees adjusted his weight on the ground. He was lying on his stomach, his elbows at his side to support the weight of the automatic rifle with its night-vision scope. Watching through the scope, he saw the scene as clearly as if it were day. From his angle, he had a clear view of the American's back and sometimes the side of his head. He also had a clear view of the Iraqi and the front of the car.

He saw his target slap the hood of the Mercedes, then another man crawl out, followed by the young girl.

The woman beside him rested her hand on his arm. "Is that her?" she whispered directly into his ear.

The shooter nodded slowly.

The woman breathed a sigh of relief. "Please, will you put the gun down now?" she asked.

The man only grunted. No way he would leave Sam exposed.

"Please," the woman begged him. "We're here to save someone, not get anyone hurt."

"No one's going to get hurt. Now, will you be quiet, *please.*"

She recognized the command, knowing it was not a request, and lowered her head to the grass, peering all the time through the trees.

Sam Brighton looked at Azadeh, and for some reason he winked. She stared at him, bewildered. Where had she seen him before! Then she faltered as the memory came flooding back. The soldiers. Her father. The helicopter. His smile.

"I know you," he had told her.

It couldn't be true!

Not him. He was a good man. She felt her heart break.

The Iraqi watched her carefully, noting the recognition on her face. "You know this man?" he asked her in surprise.

Azadeh dropped her eyes, but the man could see that she did.

The Iraqi was confused. Then his heart slammed in his chest, his instinct for survival finally slipping into gear, forty years of training standing the hairs on his neck on end. The smugness about him melted into a feeling of fear.

All the questions washed over him, the things he should have thought of before. The boat. The American. Far too fearless. Too confident. Willing to pay too much money. In a hurry. Insisting on *this* girl.

Now it was clear that she knew him.

A chill ran down his spine.

He reached for the handgun that was strapped to his chest. But the American had already pulled a pistol from some unseen holster under his jacket. A 9-mm Beretta, U.S. Government issue. A Special Forces handgun.

The Iraqi feinted for his weapon, but Samuel Brighton moved forward with amazing speed, grabbing his hand in a crushing grip. The Iraqi felt a jab of cutting pain as the

American put pressure on the joint of the thumb and his wrist. He tried pulling back. The grip tightened. "I wouldn't," Sam said calmly. "Not if you want to live."

The huge man next to Azadeh reached out and grabbed her by the throat, his fat fingers crushing into the soft skin. He jerked a small pistol from his sleeve and jammed it to the side of her head.

Sam stared at him coolly, his eyes narrow, his face firm and blank. He showed no emotion, no anxiety, not a worry in the world. The Iraqi watched him, noting the look in his eye.

That look! How he hated it. So smug and so cool. They all walked with the same swagger and carried the same arrogant glare.

Looking into the American's face, he finally understood. This wasn't some rich boy from the city looking for a sick thrill. This wasn't some Yankee thug looking to make a quick buck on a deal.

This was an American soldier.

His world came crashing down.

He felt the American's grip on his wrist, firm as cold steel. He saw the handgun, U.S. issue, and the confident smile.

And he panicked, his mind clouding, his thoughts irrational, paranoid. Who were they! What did they want?

Why was the American armed? Was he going to kill him? Who was his friend in the trees?

Were they going to steal his girl? After all the work he had done! No. They couldn't have her.

Not if she was dead.

And he would certainly kill her before he would give her away.

"Let's keep this simple," Sam said in a calm voice. "No one needs to get hurt here. All I want is the girl."

The Iraqi hesitated, years of hatred and resentment

bursting inside. "You're a U.S. soldier," he stammered in fury, staring into Brighton's eyes.

"I just want the girl . . . "

"You're going to steal her, *my friend!*"

"Of course not, you fool . . . "

The irrational panic welled up in the Iraqi's mind. He didn't have that much to live for anyway. He could die now, he could die later, he didn't care that much anymore.

The hateful pride inside him took complete control. "Kill her!" he screamed over his shoulder to his friend. "Kill her! They will take her. Kill her before they do!"

The man holding Azadeh tightened his grip on her throat. It was clear from the rage in his eyes that he was going to shoot her. He jammed the blunt end of the pistol into her temple, moved his finger for the trigger, and pushed her head down by his hip, not wanting to get splattered when he blew out her brains.

Sam heard the electric whiz of a bullet speeding by not more than a few inches from his ear, and the huge man suddenly slumped, a red dot on his head. The sound of the gunshot crashed from the trees half a second behind the sound of the shell. Sam instantly twisted the Iraqi's wrist, hearing the bone snap in the night, and the Iraqi dropped his weapon and cried out in pain. Continuing the movement, Sam lifted his pistol and fired through the side window of the car, aiming at the shadow in the backseat. Another shot echoed from the trees behind him and the front window shattered, two bullet holes pocking the passenger side.

The Iraqi screamed, his face pulling in pain and fear. He knew he was dead. He bent down for his weapon, but Sam had already kicked it away.

Sam leaned toward him, twisted his broken wrist, and grimaced, unable to hold in his disgust. "You sell little girls!" he screamed, slapping the man on the head, his anger and resentment snarling his breath. "Little girls! Little children! What kind of sick man are you!"

The Arab fell over, holding the top of his head. He whimpered like a puppy that had been beaten with a stick.

Sam reached down and grabbed the Iraqi's chin, jerking his head around until he was staring at his dead friend. "You couldn't fight *me*. No! You couldn't fight like a man! You had to go for the girl, and now look what you did!" Your friends are dead. You are alone here. So now, tell me, big man, what are you going to do!"

The Iraqi whimpered, begging, "My *Sayid*, my *Sayid* . . . "

"Shut up!" Sam cried, releasing the grip on his face.

The Iraqi fell to the ground and lay on his stomach with his arms spread wide, a familiar position he had forced many others to endure.

Azadeh didn't move. She was quiet. And a long way from tears.

She moved toward Sam, saying something in Persian that he did not understand.

He was five inches taller than she was and he looked down, holding her shoulders in his hands.

"You . . . " Azadeh started, her face crunching as she struggled to find the right words in English. "You . . . remembered me," she finally managed.

"Yes. I came for you," Sam answered in joy.

"I," she pointed to her chest. "I did what . . . you tell me."

Sam broke into a wide smile. "You did good, my girl. You got to Khorramshahr. And now you are safe."

chapter twenty

The woman rushed to Azadeh, sweeping her up in her arms while turning her head away from the dead man who lay crumpled on the dirt. Bono followed her quickly, his M-16A in one hand, the barrel pointing upward, his other hand on the holster that was strapped to his chest. Sam stood over the last Iraqi, who lay very still.

Bono moved to Sam's side, breathing heavily. He studied the dead man, then turned away. "I'm sorry," he mumbled. "I know you didn't want this to happen. But he was going to kill her. I saw it all through my scope. Trust me, Sammy, it was him or her. I made the right call."

Sam nodded grimly. "Yeah," was all he replied. He looked down at the dead man, then placed a hand on his friend's shoulder.

Sam glanced at the car and the shattered windshield. The side window was so heavily tinted it was impossible to see through; the bullet had entered it cleanly, leaving a single, tiny hole. Sam had a good idea what was in there, and he didn't want to look. He nodded toward the front seat. Bono shook his head. "He had a gun on you the entire time," he said.

"They were going to kill you, get the money and, as a bonus, keep the girl. They set us up. You know it. You could smell it. We've been here before."

Sam didn't argue. He knew it was true.

He turned to Azadeh, who was standing a few feet from him now. The woman still held her, her arms wrapped high around her shoulders, her hands covering her eyes. It was as if she wanted not only to protect her but to blind her as well, as if it would all go away if Azadeh didn't see it.

But Sam could see that the woman was far more shaken than Azadeh. *She's new to this,* he thought. *Azadeh's seen this, and worse. She's been around now.*

He walked slowly toward her, holding his hands out at his side. The woman kept her arms around her shoulders, but Azadeh had turned her head. She watched Sam carefully. He stopped three feet away. She pushed away from the woman, turning to face him again.

"Do you speak English?" he asked her.

She shook her head. "Tiny. Tiny."

He turned to the woman. She was thick and husky and wore a heavy jacket with a hood on her head. She had dark hair with light streaks of gray, dark eyes and dark skin. She too was an Arab. "Tell her," Sam said. "Tell her who I am."

The woman looked surprised. "Tell her? How much? What do you want me to say?"

"Tell her I remembered her from the village in Iran."

Azadeh was listening intently, and she started nodding before the woman could speak. "American . . . soldier," she said, pointing at Sam.

"Yes," Sam nodded. "American soldier."

Azadeh nodded again.

"Ask her if she is alone now," he told the woman.

The older woman spoke in Persian. Azadeh answered in a low voice.

The woman looked at Sam. "She said these men took her from Khorramshahr. And yes, she is alone."

"Tell her who you are," Sam instructed.

The woman spoke quickly. Sam listened, catching as much of the conversation as he could. "My name is Amina," the older woman began.

"Miss Azadeh Pahlavi," Azadeh introduced herself.

"Yes, of course, I already know that," Amina replied. She forced a tight smile, though it was clear she was still close to tears.

"I'm with an organization called *No More,*" Amina went on. "Have you ever heard of that, Azadeh?" Azadeh shook her head. "We are a private group based in London," the older woman continued. "We work throughout the Middle East, some in Pakistan, some in India and Malaysia. We work to free children, both boys and girls, who are being bought and sold as slaves. We intercept them; we buy them and set them free. The slave trade is a nasty, nasty business." Amina paused. "Do you understand what I mean?"

Azadeh pressed her lips and nodded, her eyes growing narrow, her forehead creasing tight.

"Do you realize, Azadeh, that's what these men were going to do? They brought you here to sell you. To sell you as a . . . slave."

Azadeh nodded grimly. "I know that," she answered. "But I would have died before I would have let them do that to me."

Amina was silent a moment. "Azadeh, I don't think you really realize what they could have done."

Azadeh shook her head. "No, Miss Amina, I do understand. I knew what would happen the first time I saw that man." She nudged her shoulder toward the Iraqi who lay on the ground. He kept his head down and his eyes closed, though it was clear he was listening carefully. "He claimed he worked for my uncle." She spit the words in his direction. "What a filthy, simple lie. I have no uncle, no family, no one who knows or cares. I knew what he had in mind. But I determined when I met him that he would not succeed."

Amina held her tight once again. "You are brave," she said simply.

"No. I am not brave. I am not strong. But if that was what was in store for me, then I didn't want to live."

Sam looked away. He had caught enough of the conversation to understand. He passed a hand in front of his face, rubbing his eyes.

Bono stood behind him, clearing his throat. Sam looked quickly over his shoulder. The lieutenant was standing guard over the Iraqi, a small pistol comfortably in his hand. He nodded anxiously, indicating that he wanted to go. Sam motioned to him, a barely noticeable move of his head, then turned back to Amina. "Tell her my name," he said.

"No, you should not do that," Amina said emphatically. "There is no good that can come if she knows. You endanger her. You endanger yourself. Some things are better left unsaid."

Sam shook his head. "Tell her," he repeated.

Amina hesitated, then put her hands on Azadeh's shoulders. "This is Sergeant Brighton." She nodded to the man who stood at Sam's back. "That man is an American soldier too. They are friends. Close comrades. Do you understand?"

Azadeh nodded as she stared at Sam.

"Now you need to understand something," Amina continued in Persian. "What he did here tonight, he did on his own. The U.S. government had nothing to do with any of this.

Nothing at all. In fact, Sergeant Brighton would be in very big trouble if they ever found out. It isn't his purpose, it isn't his mission, to try to save the local citizens from the effects of this land. But he came to me, Azadeh, a few weeks ago. He asked me to help him. I told him if he could get you out of Khorramshahr, I could take you from here. I helped him when I could, but it is mostly him you should thank." Amina paused, then asked, "Do you understand, Azadeh?"

Azadeh nodded, lowering her eyes as if she didn't dare look at him.

"Now listen, Azadeh," Amina went on. "I'm going to take you from here. You are safe now. *No More* has the funds and organization. You are going to leave Iraq. We are going to send you to the United States."

"The U.S.," Azadeh repeated. She couldn't believe it was true.

Sam watched her and bent down, reading the look on her face. "It's true, Azadeh," he said. "They're going to send you to the U.S. There are people there who are willing to take you into their homes . . . " Amina translated in a low voice, interpreting as quickly as she could. "You will be safe," Sam continued. "You will have a new life there, a new start."

Azadeh thought a long moment. Behind him, Sam heard the lieutenant stomp his feet on the ground. He quickly glanced at his watch. "Sammy," Bono said, "we've got to be going. We've got to get back to camp."

Sam lifted his hand, gesturing for his friend a minute or two.

Azadeh stared at him, her eyes wide. "Will you come with me?" she asked.

Sam shook his head and laughed. "I wish I could," he said. "Believe me, Azadeh, there are plenty of days when I want nothing more than to get out of here. But I have other obligations. Remember, Azadeh, I am not here on my own. I am a soldier. I have a duty. This is where I belong."

She nodded. "Who will go with me, then?" she asked.

"Amina has arranged it. She will go with you, introduce you to your new home, help you get situated inside the U.S."

Amina touched Azadeh's hand, and the girl shot a quick look at her, but then turned back to Sam. "But who will I stay with?" she wondered. "What will I do?" She did not look happy. She looked terrified.

Amina translated. Sam shook his head, pushing his dirty hands through his long hair. "I don't have all the answers, Azadeh, but this much I know. You will happy. And free. You will be warm and fed. You will be placed in a home with someone who loves you and wants you to be there."

"No," Azadeh said. "They will not love me. I am not their child. I'm not one of their people. I do not come from their tribe. They might show sympathy, even kindness, but they will not love me, I'm sure."

Sam listened to Amina translate, then took a step forward and knelt down in front of Azadeh. He stared up into her dark eyes and saw the loneliness, the sadness of being on her own. She was a young woman, but in that moment she looked like nothing more than a child. Lost. Alone. Full of deep fear. He wanted to hold her, to pull her to him. He wanted to help her.

That was why he was here.

"Azadeh," he started. "I know this has been hard—"

Azadeh shook her head abruptly. "No, no. I am grateful," she said.

"I know you are, Azadeh. But you still need to know. Your difficult path is over. You have walked through the dark. There are others now who will help you. You will not be alone."

Azadeh kept her eyes down, staring at the black dirt under her sandals, not daring to look into his eyes. The night was quiet and, up the river, a loon cried, a long, mournful sound. She lifted her head and looked at the low moon, a dull yellow sliver against the Iraqi sky, then turned to Sam, her eyes crunching now. "But I will . . . I will leave my people. I will leave my home. If I go to your country, will I ever come back again?"

Sam hunched his shoulders and thought a long moment, wanting to say the right thing. He pictured himself in her circumstance, barely escaping with her life, losing everything along the way, her family, her possessions. Everything she owned had been stuffed in the burlap bag she was clutching under her arm. And now she was losing her country, her people, everything she'd ever known. He imagined himself in her situation at such a young age.

But maybe we are not so different, he then thought. He considered his own father and mother, who had beaten and deserted him by the time he was ten. By age thirteen, he had fully expected to live his entire life all alone, with maybe short visits from his addicted mother or occasional brawls with his old man.

His mind flashed back to the evening when he had been taken to the Brightons' house, the next stop on a long list of temporary homes. He fully expected this visit to last not more than a few days—maybe a week, if things went unusually well. And even now, he remembered what it felt like to be a terrified little boy, standing in the hallway of a stranger's home, looking around him, a young animal in a new cage, always expecting to take another blow, another heartbreak, another push back down the road. Yes, he remembered the feeling. He wouldn't allow himself to forget.

Looking at Azadeh, he saw himself in her eyes. He remembered. And it hurt him, feeling the loneliness again.

But somehow, in ways that even now he didn't understand,

God had led him to the family that had been waiting for him. Once he understood that, it had changed everything.

Could Azadeh be so lucky? He really didn't know. Most weren't. He knew that he was one of the lucky few.

But he couldn't help but think of how he had felt the first time he had seen her. He could picture it so clearly, Azadeh hiding in the brush and dirt, the smell of death and the smoke of destruction all around. He had known her. No . . . he *knew* her. This was his sister, he was sure.

He didn't believe that their meeting had been left up to chance. He didn't believe that, out of all of the places he could have been sent in the world, he had been sent to her tiny village in the mountains of Iran out of pure happenstance. And he didn't believe, he *couldn't* believe, that he'd be able to save her only to send her off on her own and never see her again.

A long moment passed. Azadeh watched him all the time. Then he finally looked up. "Azadeh," he started. Amina translated quickly, whispering in Azadeh's ear. "Sometime you will understand. Until then, you're going to have to believe me when I say that I know what you are going through. I have been where you are. And I know, I understand, I remember how hard it is. But you live. You always live. And as long as you live, then you fight. You live and you fight, and it gets better. I can promise you that."

Azadeh nodded slowly as Amina translated the words.

"You live and you fight," she answered. "That's something I can understand. And I will believe you. I will trust you. I will do what you say."

Sam smiled and pulled her close. "Go with Amina," he whispered into her ear. "She will help you. She is your friend. Trust her. Keep your faith and it will turn out okay."

Sam felt her head move as she nodded. Although he had spoken in English, it seemed she had understood.

Pulling back, she touched his shoulders. "Will I ever see my home again?"

Sam shook his head. "I don't know, Azadeh. Maybe . . . but probably not. The world is changing quickly. The days are growing shorter, and there is evil all around. Events have been put in motion that will never come to a rest. Where it leads, we don't know; sometimes all we can do is hang on. But this much I can tell you: It is not in our hands. So have faith, and be hopeful, and maybe you will come back here again."

Sam stood up and nodded to Amina. It was past time to go.

Bono walked to him. "What do we do with him?" he asked, pointing to the Iraqi on the ground

Sam thought, then moved forward and nudged the man with his boot. "Stand!" he commanded in Arabic. The Iraqi pushed himself to his feet.

Sam glared in his face. "You were going to kill me here tonight, weren't you, my friend?"

The Iraqi returned his cold stare, a deadly rage in his eyes. "I would kill you even now if I were given the chance." He spoke in a guttural, almost animal sound. "Give me the chance, you ***harâmzâde*** Yankee, and I would reach down your throat and crush your heart in my fist."

Sam stood back and smiled. "Yes, I suppose that you would. And maybe one day, if you're lucky, you just might get the chance. But until then, let me give you some advice. I have friends. We have ears. We have eyes. We have feet. We get around. We listen and we watch. And I will be listening and watching for you. And know this, my merchant friend, if I ever hear your name, if I ever hear even a whiff of a rumor that you are back in business, I will send you to your master who is waiting for you in hell. I will hunt you and kill you. I promise I will.

"So remember me, *harâmzâde,* because I will remember you. Your first day in business will be your last day on this earth. I will hunt you like the sewer rat that you are. I know you believe me; I can see it in your eyes. You know I'm not afraid of the sewer. It doesn't matter where you hide, I will come after you."

The Iraqi glared at Sam, then slowly nodded his head.

"Go!" Sam commanded.

The Iraqi turned and ran.

Sam took a breath and turned to Azadeh again. "You be careful, Miss Azadeh. But be happy, too. You are off on another adventure, but this is a good one, I swear. Now go with Amina. She's your friend.

"I'll remember you, Azadeh, and one day I'll check up on you. And when I do, I want a good report. I want to hear you speak in English. I want to hear that you're doing well in school. I want to hear about your new friends and your family. But mostly I want to hear that you're happy. That's all I ask."

Azadeh smiled and nodded, wiping a tear from her eye.

Sam stood and nodded to Bono, then turned for the riverbank. He climbed into the small boat, and his friend pushed it back. Reaching into his vest pocket, Sam pulled out a small pen flare, held it away from his body, and turned his head. Pulling and releasing the firing pin, he sent the flare into the dark sky, where it exploded with a burst of red light.

"Wait here," he commanded as his boat drifted away. "A friend will come to get you in a blue Nissan pickup. You can trust him. You go with him. He will take you back to Baghdad and deliver you safe."

Azadeh started to run toward him, but it was already too late. The dark hull drifted into the current, then disappeared silently, slipping into the dark.

chapter twenty-one

The new king of the House of Saud sat alone in a small office in the presidential penthouse atop the Royal Saudi Oil company headquarters building in Riyadh. He slouched at his desk, his head low, his eyes tired. A small reading lamp was the only light that illuminated the dim office, and there were deep shadows in the corners and across the wood furniture. The king preferred the semi-dark. He didn't know why—it was just more comfortable to him now. He liked how the dim light softened all the features, making everything a little less harsh, a little less intrusive. The darkness invited open conversation. People were less aware of themselves, more willing to say things. The king had learned a lot of secrets from conversations in the dark, and he had grown comfortable with the night.

King Abdullah al-Rahman was holding a highly classified document in his slender fingers. The report had been brought to him by General Abaza, and though he had read it already, he read it again, this time more slowly, considering carefully.

It was a handwritten report by General Sattam bin Mamdayh, head of the ultra-secret Iranian Interior Police. As director of the highly classified security force, the Iranian general was in a very powerful position, able to operate almost entirely on his own. But he was also three or four layers down in the food chain and, like everyone, he had many superiors whom he had to please. And though his commanders were all powerful men, they had one thing in common: fear of the Saudi king.

King Abdullah al-Rahman was not Persian, but he controlled many things. Many people. Many organizations. His reach extended much further than the borders of his land, and there was much he could influence beyond his own shores.

Reading, the king had to squint, for the general's handwriting was thin and imprecise, the Arabic adequate but barely readable. It told of the general's attack at Agha Jari Deh: the destruction of the village, the burning of the man, the search for the young one. It told of their frustration, briefly describing the failure of his men.

Though they had done everything possible, they had not succeeded in finding the child. Then the American soldiers had appeared, forcing his men to flee.

American soldiers! Abdullah thought, his mouth growing dry. U.S. soldiers had dared to move openly inside of Iran! There had been rumors, even sightings of Special Forces units working inside the borders of Persia, searching for hints of their nuclear program, listening, watching, looking for things, but this had been different—these were combat troops. And they had shown up at the village at the very worst time.

The king swore angrily, his gut burning inside.

The Americans were watching. No, they were doing more than that; they were actively working against him, all of it under the table, all of it in the dark. And they had stopped the Iranian general before his work was complete.

The king finished the report, stared a moment into the

darkness, and then glanced at his watch. At a predetermined time, the general was going to make contact, and the king was going to wait up for him.

At ten past one in the morning, the secure telephone rang. Abdullah let it ring five times, then picked up the receiver.

"Yes," he said simply.

The Iranian General Sattam bin Mamdayh's voice filled his ear. It was a deep voice, powerful and demanding. "This is General Sattam . . . " he began.

"I know who you are," Abdullah cut him off in a sarcastic tone. After reading the general's report, he was not in a good mood. "I've been waiting for your phone call. Now, what's going on? It's been almost three weeks; I want to hear some good news."

The general cleared his throat. "My men have been through the village again. They have searched all the mountains . . . "

"Save me the details. I'm a very busy man. It's late. I've been waiting. Did you find him or not!"

The general paused another moment. And with the silence, the king knew.

"You have failed me," Abdullah said before the Iranian general could respond.

"I have not failed, my *Sayid*, but it is proving difficult. Much more difficult than we expected, more complicated, I'm afraid."

"We're talking about a *child!*" Abdullah sneered in disgust. "A little four-year-old boy. I didn't ask you to take over the Persian army. I didn't ask you to conquer some foreign land. I asked you to do one little favor, to take care of one simple thing. I told you where to find him. I told you how I wanted it done. I did everything but pick up the gun and pull the trigger for you. And you're telling me this is difficult. You're telling me the child still lives!" The king cursed again bitterly, his voice hard and dry.

"But," the general defended, "the Americans came with their—"

"You can't be serious, Sattam. Please, tell me you are not that incompetent."

"The child was taken to the mountains. A local man was helping them. He warned the family we were coming, then helped the boy and his mother escape. They are up there somewhere, hiding in the mountains. It has been a difficult task. And then . . ."

"And then what, General Mamdayh! What terrible thing happened then? Your gun jammed? You broke a nail? Got some dirt or blood on your hands! *Xodâvând,* General Mamdayh, this was such a *simple task!*"

"He had friends. They were helping him. I know the Americans are watching, which means my superiors will be watching. I have to be careful now."

The Saudi king shook his head. He had heard more than he could take. If the handwritten report from the general weren't discouraging enough, listening to his whining explanations was simply more than he could stand.

The phone was silent a moment as both men fell into thought: the general on how he might save his neck, the king on how he would kill the Persian general when he was given the chance.

The soft hum continued until the king finally said, "General Mamdayh, you understand, of course, that I can do good things for you?"

"Yes," the general answered. "You can help me, I know."

"You know I have friends at the Iranian Ministry. The mullahs. Friends at the Iranian palaces as well. There is no place in all of Persia that my hand can't reach. And money, General

Mamdayh, I have plenty of that. And I am willing to help you. I am a man of my word. I can reward you generously. I can do many things. Do you understand that, General? Do you know what I'm saying is true?"

The general hesitated. He saw what was coming next, and he didn't want to respond.

"Answer me, Mamdayh. Do you know what I can do for you!"

"Yes," the general answered, his voice low and cool.

"Then you also understand, General Mamdayh, there are two sides to my sword. I can help you if you help me, but I can hurt you as well. One word, and you would simply disappear. One phone call to my friends in Tehran, and you would never be heard from again. And not only could I have you killed, General Mamdayh, I could determine how. Fast or slow, I could tell them. If I wanted, I could have them cut off one of your fingers every day for ten days and have them deliver it to me. Then your toes. Then your elbows. Then your knees and your arms. I could have you taken apart, General Mamdayh, piece by piece, bit by bit, and have you delivered to my palace in an overnight pouch. And then I could turn to your family and do the same thing to them. I could do all this and more. So I want you to listen to me, General, and consider what I have to say."

Abdullah heard the general swallow painfully on the other end of the phone.

"You made a pact," the king sneered harshly. "Now, do you understand what I want?"

"Yes, *Sayid*, I understand."

"And do you remember what I told you?"

"You said you wanted him dead."

"Yes! That is right. He is the last of his offspring, the last of his seed. He will remember, he will grow, and he then will come after me. So I asked a simple favor, and now I'm going to ask you again: Can you find this young child? Can you find him and kill him? It is a simple thing, General Mamdayh. And it's all that I ask."

The general didn't hesitate. "Yes, King al-Rahman, I can do this for you."

Abdullah nodded slowly. "That is good, General Mamdayh. Now, go back! Search every mountain. Search every rock, if need be. You have taken too long already! I want to see results now. I want to see some bodies. I'll give you three days, General Mamdayh, that is all you will have. Find this young boy and his mother and see them destroyed."

The general was silent.

It would take months to search the mountain.

He knew it was not enough time.

* * *

The Iranian general slumped in terror as he hung up the phone. His eyes watered with fear, red-rimmed and dreary, while his hands shook uncontrollably on the top of his desk.

He should have known better than to enter an alliance with someone like Abdullah al-Rahman. He should have known it was dangerous to jump into such a slimy swamp. He had heard things; he had been told things. He should have known better than this.

He had tried to kiss the snake, but now he had been bitten.

A helpless, hopeless feeling sank into his dark heart. The truth was, he and his men had already done everything they could do. They had searched every corner, every canyon, every inch of that mountain. They had torn apart the village, interrogated everyone.

There was nothing more he could do.

He thought of Abdullah al-Rahman's words, a cold sweep of terror running down his spine: *"I can help you if you help me, but I can hurt you as well. . . . One word, and you would simply disappear. . . . I could have you taken apart, General Mamdayh, piece by piece, bit by bit."*

It was true. The general acknowledged the king as a man of his word.

Which left him no choice. Not if he wanted to avoid a most excruciating death. Not if he wanted to protect his family and himself from such pain.

He could not choose if he died; that decision had been made for him now. But he could choose the timing and the method, which was a worthy thing to do. And in a society that didn't place that much value on life, the decision was not especially difficult.

* * *

General Mamdayh's body was found early the next morning by one of his maids. He had slumped at his desk as if he had simply fallen asleep at his work, his hands resting peacefully on his lap. The empty bottles of Valium and OxyContin were found on the floor. And though he died with his eyes open, his lips were pulled back in almost a smile of relief, as if the life he expected could not be worse than the one he had left.

chapter twenty-two

He knew it was coming. The forecast had warned them: *Di kulâk* on its way. Devil's Storm. The Sudden Darkness. It would be here within the hour.

It happened two, maybe three times every year. The great sandstorms rolled in from the desert to fall on the city like a wave.

Something about the *Di kulâk* excited the king to the bone. In the old days, his ancestors had lived in terror of the storms. But Abdullah loved them. They connected him with his land, making him feel as if he were a part of the desert that he cherished so much.

So he stood at the window, waiting for the great sandstorm to appear. He knew it would come from the east, across the great plain, and he stood watching, surrounded by luxury while waiting for the huge wall of sand.

King Abdullah al-Rahman thought as he waited. There was much on his mind.

He was standing at a window in the presidential penthouse in Riyadh. Surrounded by gold and teak and every fine thing in the world, the king was alone in his private lounge. To his left, a twenty-foot, custom-made plasma screen—one of the largest privately owned plasma screens in the world—showed a satellite feed from Al Jezzera TV. Under his feet, fifteen other television screens had been inlaid in the marble floor and covered with glass. Each television was tuned to a different satellite feed from the West, and the flashing images on the screens added an unnatural texture to the light in the dimly lit room, creating shifting shadows and flashing contrasts everywhere. The muted televisions inlaid in the floor were obviously not designed to be watched, but they did make a statement as to how the king felt about the western culture that flashed on the screens. To his right was an exquisite bar stocked with the finest liquors of the world. The liquor was only for his foreign guests, of course, alcohol being prohibited in the kingdom, but if the king were to indulge from time to time, who would dare question that?

Did it bother King Abdullah that his kingdom developed, funded, taught, spread, and advocated Wahabbi fundamentalism, the strictest and most repressive interpretation of Islam anywhere on earth, while the king exempted himself from almost all of its teachings—the use of alcohol, for example, or, say, murder for another? The answer was clearly no. The king was not bothered at all. Abdullah did what he did for the good of the kingdom, and he had long ago gotten past the irony of his hypocrisy. To those around him, his closest advisors, his brothers, his few friends, the king made his personal feelings very clear: Allah had given his fathers religion as a means of controlling their people. That was its only purpose. It meant nothing more. The only thing their god truly cared about was keeping the kingdom pure to sustain the royal family, his chosen vessels on earth.

Wahabbi Islam, with all its teachings and prohibitions, was a tool given to them. And it was a good tool. Important. But it was not the only tool they had. God had provided other means to keep his children safe from the great influences of the world.

And King Abdullah would use them. He would use every one.

The new king stood at a tall window, twenty feet from ceiling to floor, and looked out on the city he loved. He could see it coming in the distance now, the great, rising storm. Thick sand was moving slowly toward them like a huge wall of brown water, boiling and mean. It stretched from north to south as far as the king could see and rose upward to four or five hundred feet. It rolled and raged as it moved across the land, swallowing everything in its path, a terrifying brown wave of sand. It was small now, still in the distance, but it was coming fast. The king's heart skipped a beat. It was a terrifying sight, like something out of a nightmare, except this was real and moving toward him. The king stood and watched.

Above the wall of sand, the sun was rising over the desert and the buildings of Riyadh were splashed in bright colors of the early morning light, the predominant browns of the Arabic arches and porticos mixing easily with the pastels, desert pinks, and light blues. Some of the main buildings in the city were fascinating works of architecture, almost playful pieces of art, but even the tallest buildings seemed to shrink from the coming wall of sand, the billowing wall looming over the tallest building in Riyadh.

The buildings on the outskirts of the city were swallowed as the storm moved toward him.

He heard his office door open behind him. He turned his head just a bit, lowering his chin to the side, but he did not turn around, and he could not see who it was. Then he heard the shuffle of soft feet, and his heart jumped in his chest. He heard the deep breathing, the rattle in the chest, and his lips turned up in a smile. Then he smelled him. The stale clothes.

The smell of medicine and disinfectants. The smell of sour breath.

He turned around slowly.

The old man was standing there.

The king bowed at his waist. He didn't think, he just did it; it was an instinctive reaction, one he could not have explained. Yes, he was king, but this was Master, the only man on the earth that Abdullah feared. He bowed his head, then rushed forward and took the old man by the arm. He felt the thin flesh, the tender skin and weak muscle hanging like limp cloth on the bone, as he guided the old man toward the nearest chair.

"Old friend!" he cried. "I did not expect to see you here!"

The old man smiled sarcastically. "What you really mean, *King Abdullah*," he accentuated the title with obvious satisfaction, "was that you did not expect to see me *at all*. Here. Somewhere else. You thought I was too close to death to be seen anywhere."

Abdullah didn't deny it. He knew he couldn't lie to this man. "I did think, my good friend, that you were too weak to travel. So, yes, I'm surprised to see you anywhere."

The old man looked up and grinned, his teeth brown from a lifetime's worth of drinking dark tea. "Have you got any whiskey?" he asked impatiently.

Abdullah nodded and fixed the old man a glass. He sipped, then leaned back his head. "Your little episode with the Iranian general was a disappointment, my friend."

Abdullah hesitated.

It had been twenty-four hours since the Iranian general had chosen to kill himself. What a coward! What a woman! The king cursed to himself.

The old man watched him carefully, studying the look on his face.

Abdullah shrugged in frustration. "He failed me," he said.

"He did more than that. He failed us all."

"He said he would find him."

"Yet the young one still lives."

Abdullah stared in silence. Was there anything the old man didn't know? No. There really wasn't. He had learned that before. "It is a disappointment," he answered slowly. "I needed him. He deserted me. There is nothing I can do about that now."

The old man nodded slowly. He didn't accept it so simply—that was clear from the look in his eyes.

Abdullah looked at the old man, though he tried not to stare. There was something about him, something strange and powerful. He still looked old, that was true, but he looked more healthy somehow. Last time they had met, he wouldn't have given the old man a full week to live. Yet here he was once again, sitting with him in this room. And not only was he here, he looked better. Not younger, but . . . *recycled.* Freshened and new, as if, through some miracle, he had been granted more time.

It was unnatural. Abnormal.

And Abdullah wanted to know how it was done.

But there was a lot about the old man that the king wanted to know.

Once, years before, after too many questions, the old man had taken his hand and squeezed it so hard that it hurt, all the time looking him straight in the eye. "It is better if you don't know too much," he had said. "It is better for you and it is better for me. Let's just do our business. That is all that you need."

Through the years, Abdullah had accepted that he would never know about his friend. But looking at him now, with his renewed energy, he was certainly curious as to where he had been.

The old man looked at him, then took his hand. "You have been a good student," he said in a raspy voice. "From the first time we met, that wonderful day on the beach, I knew you would be one of our stars. From that first night outside the embassy building, when you told me to kill your countrymen, I knew you would be someone our team could count on. I would lay my life on the table for you, Abdullah, and I know you would do the same thing for me."

"Yes," Abdullah answered. "I would lie down for you."

The old man stared at him, his dark, sullen eyes boring into the king's soul. Abdullah held his gaze the best that he could, but he finally looked away, unable to match the older man's stare.

"You are frightened," the old man mumbled. "I can see it in your eyes."

"No," Abdullah answered. "I am careful, that's all."

The old man shook his head. "You are hesitating. Always thinking. Waiting for the exact time to move. You can't do that, Abdullah—you have to move now. We've been waiting for this moment for way too long. There will be no sign from heaven. Nothing will fall from the sky. You have to take a breath, be committed, and stay with the plan. And you must do it now. It is time that you move."

"But I was thinking—"

"No more thinking, Abdullah, it is time to act!"

"But if we wait until . . . "

"You have only a few days," the old man almost sneered. "The U.S. is suspicious and they are watching you now. Your older brother had a friend. He works for the American president. He knows about you, and he is watching. Every day that you hesitate gives him more time to think. Far too many people around you have died suddenly. Too many bodies can be found in your wake: the Pakistani general who provided the warheads, the Iranian general who killed himself recently, your brother, your father, all of their kin. You are surrounded by death, and they will want to know why. And though the U.S. intelligence apparatus isn't perfect, they are not nearly so stupid as their critics think. They will figure it out if you give them too much time. So you've got to move quickly for this thing to work. You've got to strike the U.S. and strike them where it counts. If you take out D.C., you can take out their entire government. Then you can turn your eye on Israel. She will be waiting for you.

"But you can't wait a few months. You don't even have days. If you haven't moved within 72 hours, it may be too late."

"All right," Abdullah answered. "I can see that is true."

"Three days. Maybe four. You must move by then."

Abdullah only nodded.

"You are ready, then?"

"I am."

"I hope that you are."

The king turned and looked out the window again. The sandstorm was almost upon them. It moved across the city like a great tidal wave, swallowing everything that fell in its path. It was a block away, then half a block, a hundred feet. It was here. The sandstorm washed over the building. The light turned orange, then deep brown, then as dark as the night.

The old man moved forward, standing beside the new king. They watched the storm together without saying anything. The sand beat against the windows like a billion pellet shots, and the wind howled across the roof, causing the building to sway.

The two men stood in silence until the old man turned

around. "There are still some things I must teach you," he said in a solemn tone. "They will strengthen you in your weakness, provide you comfort and strength. They will give you support when you need it to see this thing through."

Abdullah nodded, waiting. "Then teach me, my friend."

"There are secrets we should talk about. Secrets that go back many years. They are sacred and chosen, and they will change your life. Once you have learned them, you will be bound to your oaths. You can never deny them. They will bind you, my friend, like the web of a spider wrapped around her sleeping prey. They will bind you forever. But you are ready, I am sure. You have been ready for a long time. And now I'm ready too."

Abdullah waited, submissive, and the old man stared at him.

"You do not believe in a god," the old man went on, 'but I'm here to tell you that is a terrible mistake. There are two gods in the universe. They are eternally locked in battle and they are both powerful. One god is the spirit of freedom that has threatened your land. He is your enemy, your destroyer—he seeks to bring you down. He brings the idea of democracy and freedom, which will destroy the kingdom you've built. If he wins, he will leave you homeless and destitute. He will destroy your family and everything that your fathers have built.

"Some people will claim that freedom belongs to all mankind. That is a lie. Don't believe it. From the beginning of time that lie has been deceiving the world.

"Some will say that all people have been given the power to choose. Another lie. Don't believe it. Life is *not* a matter of choice. It is a matter of *strength*. It is *not* a matter of freedom. It is a matter of *power*. That's the only thing that matters: who is strong, who is weak, who can convince enough of the others to follow. That is all that matters in this miserable world.

"If you could remember, you would know that. I remember! You were there. You heard the counsel. You've heard the arguments. And now it is your turn to take up your arms.

"And know this, young king, for there may be times when you will doubt. It is no sin, my brother, to defend what you have: your kingdom, your family, this place in this world, the riches and privileges that your forefathers built. It is no sin to protect them, and protect them you will.

"Now, listen to me, Abdullah. There are things you must learn. Certain oaths and combinations that will unlock special doors."

Abdullah moved toward him. "I am ready," he said.

chapter twenty-three

THE WHITE HOUSE
WASHINGTON, D.C.

Major General Neil Brighton stood anxiously in the narrow pantry outside the Oval Office. He glanced at his watch: 10:16. He had only twenty minutes with the president, beginning at 10:20, and as always he found himself standing outside the office early to make sure he was ready to go. It was a courtesy he felt the president deserved, and an easy one to offer, since he worked just down the hall. More, he didn't want to waste a minute of his allotted time. Twenty precious minutes. He needed them all.

Leaning away from the wall, he glanced down the hall toward his own office. The West Wing was quiet; it was a Saturday afternoon, and most of the staff wasn't in. He studied the hallway, with its heavy blue-and-white window coverings and imposing paintings—former presidents, western landscapes, the D.C. landscape in 1822—all of them set in large, gold-gilded frames and spaced evenly between the high windows.

Halfway down the narrow hallway was a display of military photographs. But there were none of the typical pictures of speeding fighters, powerful ships, or deadly battle tanks.

Instead, the photographs showed soldiers—mostly young men, a few women—all of them battle weary, with dust and sweat and dirt on their faces. The pictures were tender: a young rifleman, his heavy M-16 under his arm, bending down to pet a small kitten with his fingers while anxiously surveying the battle damage around him; a multi-ethnic group of soldiers standing in a circle, their heads bowed in prayer; a young soldier sitting cross-legged in the dirt dressed in full battle gear—flak vest, helmet, protective goggles, and gloves—while holding a tiny baby in his arms. Smoke was wafting in a stiff breeze behind him and debris had been scattered everywhere, but the soldier looked almost peaceful, as if he were holding his own child. There were pictures of soldiers handing out candy, giving a young boy a high-five, kissing a letter from a loved one, helping an old woman across a battle-scarred street. There was a picture of a young medic wrapping the broken leg of a small dog, a little boy standing nervously at the side, one hand on his puppy, another on the medic's arm. In the middle of the pictures was a handwritten note:

This is why we do it.
And let us never forget.

It had been General Brighton's idea to put up the display. Most of the national security staff had been against it. Too political. Too sentimental. Too emotional, the National Security Advisor had said. But Brighton had insisted, even going to the president when the others told him no. Upon seeing the photographs, the president had immediately agreed.

The general considered the display one of the better things he had done. Members of the press, congressional delegations, cabinet secretaries, White House staff, all of them passed the display every day. Most of them stopped. The pictures were simply too compelling to pass by casually without a look. And some of those who stopped to look at the pictures studied them for a long time. The images caused them to think. Brighton was happy about that.

Looking farther down the hall, Brighton could see the open door to his office, a tiny cubbyhole at the far end of the West Wing. It was hardly more than a closet, with old wood floors, a single narrow window (sealed shut and covered with shatterproof Mylar coating), and a small wooden desk dating back to the Civil War. It would have been an embarrassingly tiny office had it been in any other government or business building in D.C. But it wasn't. It was in the White House—which made his 80 square feet of space more valuable than any piece of real estate in the world. Many people would have happily paid a million dollars, ten million dollars, even more, in order to work this close to the president.

General Brighton considered that fact as he stared down the hall. It was fifty-three steps from his office to the Oval Office door. He knew that. Fifty-three steps. He had counted them many times.

Fifty-three steps away from the president, the most powerful man in the world. Fifty-three steps away from some of the most pivotal moments and decisions of the last two hundred years.

Most people had no idea how big the White House really was. Hidden behind carefully planted landscaping, and with much of it built underground, the 55,000 square feet of office space and living quarters were spread across six stories and 134 rooms, with eight staircases, three elevators, and 35 bathrooms. Out of all of this space, Brighton had but one tiny office.

Fifty-three steps from the president.

Sometimes it felt like a mile.

He glanced again at his watch. 10:18 now. He fidgeted, moving from one foot to the other. He wasn't nervous, but he was restless; that was just the way it was. One didn't enter the Oval office without feeling a little on edge.

Four minutes later, the heavy door to the Oval Office swung open and the president's chief of staff let him into the room. Behind the chief of staff, next to a white Elizabethan couch, the president was standing, his back to his desk. He wore a dark suit with a striped shirt and red tie, and he was bending over while an assistant held a document for him to sign. Behind him, the National Security Advisor, Johnny "Bo" Grison, Brighton's co-worker on the national security team, was leaning against the gently curved wall, his right arm tucked across his chest, his left elbow resting in his right hand, his fingers touching his lips. The NSA was staring at the floor, deep in thought, and he paid no attention as Brighton walked into the room.

The NSA and General Brighton had a mutual respect for each other, but they were not close friends. They were on the same side of the battle, yes, but they tended to see things from very different points of view. Although the NSA was the man who had recommended to the president that he bring Brighton on as his personal security advisor (he had argued for a long time that the president needed an informal and less structured link between his intelligence and military chains of command), Brighton knew that sometimes the NSA now regretted the move. Grison thought Brighton was a pessimist: too skittish, too fast to react, too willing to see ghosts when there was nothing there. Brighton, on the other hand, thought the NSA was too slow, too methodical, always waiting for more information and never willing to act.

"Bo!" he once exploded in exasperation. "You can't wait for perfect intelligence. It doesn't exist. We get what we can, but you will never know everything. If you demand perfect information, then you are demanding the impossible.

Sometimes, Bo, you've got to go with your gut. Sometimes you have to close your eyes and jump off the cliff. If we always have to wait until you are perfectly comfortable, we'll never move. Things are changing too quickly. Our enemies are quick and cunning. We have to be quick and cunning too. We've got to stay up with them, Bo, or this whole thing falls down."

"You're talking like a fighter pilot, ready to blast into the air," the NSA had shot back. "This is different, Neil. We've got to be careful. If we don't get it right . . . if we make a mistake, then we all pay the price."

Brighton had stared, his face tense with frustration. "Our enemies aren't afraid of making mistakes," was the only thing he had said.

So the two men served in nearly constant conflict, and the president knew it. But he didn't mind. In fact, that was precisely what he was hoping to get. It gave him the conflicting voices, the different points of view, the balance he needed to make the best decisions he could. And the president was a strong man. He was capable of listening and thinking, then making a decision for himself.

After signing the last document, the president tucked his pen inside his breast pocket, and the aide disappeared through a narrow hallway door, leaving the four men alone. Brighton glanced at the president as he sat down. Not tall, but with the square shoulders of a boxer, the president was, for the first time in his life, starting to show his age. His eyes were accented by crow's-feet, which a few years ago hadn't been there, and his temples were turning white now.

The men sat in their customary chairs: the NSA and General Brighton on the white couch, the president and his chief of staff facing them on two padded armchairs. The president was holding an iced tea with lemon. A Diet Coke was waiting for the general. The NSA sipped his water. The chief of staff chewed his gum.

"How's Sara?" the president asked as the general sat down.

"She's fine, Mr. President. Thank you for asking, sir." Brighton shifted in his seat, then added, "She sends her warmest regards."

The president watched Brighton squirm, and he smiled.

Brighton's wife, the lovely Sara, had met the president on many occasions, and she always seemed willing to give him advice, something that made Brighton cringe but that the president loved. She was engaging and pleasant, and the president had a warm spot in his heart for her.

"She still not reading any newspapers?" the president asked.

Brighton smiled. "Still too many, I'm afraid. I can tell as soon as I get home if she's been reading the *Post.*"

The other men looked at each other questioningly, and the president leaned over to his chief of staff and explained. "Sara is, and I'm not just saying this—" the president eyed Brighton under a creased brow—"one of the most politically perceptive people I know. She seems to have a sixth sense, a real feel for the country out there. But, as I understand it, she recently swore off reading the papers or watching the news. Said she couldn't take it any longer. Too frustrating. Too maddening. It was driving her nuts. But I knew she wouldn't make it. She's a news junkie."

The other men smiled. They could relate. The president turned more serious, looking at the general again. "Did she . . . ah, did she see the photograph of your son?"

"Not yet, sir."

The president leaned forward. "Yeah, well, you tell her, if someone ever shows her, it's so much garbage, nothing more. It's nothing. It means nothing. It's all garbage press."

Brighton thought of the newspaper image of his soldier son that had appeared on the front page of the *Post,* the carnage and death of the village around him. Were most of his fellow Americans willing to believe that their soldiers would assault and kill dozens of villagers in Iran? Apparently not. Though the cynic inside him was a little surprised, Brighton was extremely relieved that the story hadn't grabbed any traction inside the U.S.

The truth was, General Brighton didn't much like the press. Left or right, it didn't matter, he had little respect for any of them; he had seen how they worked, he knew the agendas they had. But as he looked at the president, his face remained neutral and calm. His was a nonpolitical position, and he took great pains to be careful of everything he said.

The president watched him carefully. "Is your family okay then, Neil?" he asked in a caring tone.

"Yes, sir, they are."

"You've been working long hours."

"We all have, sir."

"You've been working longer hours than most."

"I'm not sure that's true."

"I'm sure. And I appreciate it."

"Thank you, Mr. President, but really, I'm just doing my job. Like everyone else, we're just trying to make this whole thing work."

The president pressed his lips together. "Your other boys, they're going to be leaving on those church-service things . . . ah, what do you call them . . . ?"

"Missions, sir."

"Yes. You were telling me a few months back that they would be leaving this winter."

"Luke and Ammon will be leaving right after Christmas, sir."

"Now, how does that work? How much do they pay them? Will they earn some money for college?"

"Actually, sir, it is volunteer service. They don't get paid anything."

"Really!" The president whistled. "Not even expenses?"

"They pay their own way, sir."

"I didn't know that." The president glanced at his chief of staff, who had been raised in the West. "Did you know that, Charlie? Pretty impressive, huh? I wish we could get more kids to take on such a challenge. Think of what kind of leaders they could be!"

The chief of staff nodded but didn't say anything. He fidgeted anxiously, ready to get to the point of the meeting. As the unofficial timekeeper, he took his responsibilities seriously.

But the president wasn't ready. "Can your sons choose where they go?" he continued. "Do they want to go somewhere in Europe? I'll bet Florida's a pretty good place to serve. Anything I could do? I'd be happy to put in a call to headquarters out there in Salt Lake. You know, I know a few people, I could pull a few strings."

Brighton had to smile. In fact, he almost laughed out loud. It was just an absurd proposition: the president of the United States making a call to Church headquarters in Salt Lake in order to pull a few strings on where his sons would be called to serve. He shook his head and waved off the offer with his hands. "Thank you, Mr. President. You are very generous. This doesn't really work like that, sir, but thank you again."

The president cocked his head to the side. "All right," he said. "But if you change your mind . . ."

"Yes, sir, I'll remember your offer."

The men were silent a moment, then the chief of staff said abruptly, "Mr. President, we only have a few minutes."

"Yes, yes, of course," the president answered. "A few

minutes, a few minutes, never more than a few minutes. It's the way we all live." He turned to General Brighton, then glanced at his National Security Advisor, a middle-aged man with slender shoulders and thin hair. "You got something for me, Bo?" he asked.

The NSA straightened himself. "Yes. A couple of things."

The president nodded. "Go," he said.

"First, we wanted to update you on the situation in Saudi Arabia. As you know, sir, Crown Prince Saud and his entire family seem to have entirely disappeared. Now, we know the crown prince's helicopter went down a little more than a fortnight ago, but we haven't been able to confirm his status. As to his family, it's very likely most of them are simply laying low. In fact, the entire royal family has dropped out of sight. There is upheaval in the kingdom, no doubt about that, but the workings inside Arabia are nearly impossible to track, and we haven't been able to find out anything more."

The president frowned. He had been a huge fan of the Saudi king, but he disliked his sons. "What about that little jerk, Abdullah?" he asked. "What's going on with him?"

"Sir, we're hearing a few rumors—Jordan's King Mohammad has been very helpful and a few others as well—but that's all we have right now, rumors and whispers. Still, it appears that Prince Abdullah al-Rahman has ascended or soon will ascend to the throne. But again, that's only rumor; we really don't know. The House of Saud is a tight little family. They hate each other, yes, but they never talk, and it was easier for us to crack the atom than to crack the secrecy around the royal family. There could have been a nuclear explosion in the kingdom, they all might have been killed by falling meteorites, and we wouldn't know it. Until we hear something definitive, all we can do is guess. So while we are attempting to make contact with Abdullah or his subordinates, right now we have to sit tight."

"I've never liked Abdullah," the president said. "He's a spoiled little brat. He's got a few guns, he feels invincible, but he's nothing without his posse and some cash in the bank."

"If he's the next king, we have problems," the NSA replied.

"Oh, don't you worry about Abdullah. I can take care of him," the president said.

Brighton sat forward in his chair. He knew the royal family perhaps better than anyone, and the president's estimation of Abdullah was clean off the mark. "Mr. President," he said, "I must respectfully disagree. Abdullah is a dangerous man. We'll have to approach him carefully."

"He's nothing!" the president shot back. "He's a spoiled kid, oversexed and over-moneyed. No brains. No ambition. No direction. No core. If he's the next king, that's fine. I know how to deal with him. I've dealt with worse men before."

Brighton shook his head slowly. "No sir, that's simply not true. You don't know Abdullah. None of us do. It would be foolish, even stupid, to underestimate this man."

The room fell suddenly silent, the general's words hanging like a chill in the air. The NSA scrunched, counting the offensive words in his head: *No sir . . . you don't know . . . foolish . . . stupid to underestimate this man.* No one talked to the president of the United States that way. It was . . . undiplomatic, unacceptable, at least to most of these men.

The president stared at Brighton, then smiled. The general returned his gaze, never blinking an eye. "Sir," he continued, "forgive me for speaking so bluntly. I certainly don't mean to offend. But the truth is, Mr. President, something is going on here. We've got high leaders throughout the Muslim world dropping like flies in a bucket of swill. The Saudi king. The crown prince. Now it has spread beyond Saudi shores. General Sattam bin Mamdayh, head of the ultra-secret Iranian Interior Police. Abu Nidal Atta, deputy director of Pakistan's Special Weapons Section. Both of them dead. Their governments deny it, but we know it is true. And the one thing all of these men held in common was their association with Prince Abdullah al-Rahman."

The general sat back, feeling a tiny trickle of sweat move down the side of his ribs. He thought of the dream, the grass and explosions, and his mouth went dry.

It was nothing, he repeated again in his mind. *The dream means nothing. It means nothing.*

But that wasn't what he really believed. In his heart, he knew he was being warned.

How to convey that to the president, though? *"Mr. President, I had a really scary dream . . ."*

The men he worked with were analysts and politicians, some of the smartest men in the world. They were professionals, the highest ranking officers his government had. They were ambitious and powerful men, men who did not bet their future on *dreams.*

It was impossible to tell them. The president needed facts, hard intelligence, analysis that was sharp as a knife. He needed solid counsel from his advisors and all the information 80 billion dollars could buy. He needed details.

He didn't need someone's dreams.

But that was what the general had to give him. He lowered his eyes, trying to think.

The president placed his fingertips together and lifted his hands to his face, covering his mouth and resting his chin on his thumbs. Muted voices could be heard in the hallway, and a security chopper flew overhead, vibrating the windows gently against their old wooden frames.

Brighton lifted his eyes and leaned forward in his seat. "I'm just saying, Mr. President, and you'll forgive me for being so frank, but I've got a bad feeling. I think we need to presume the worst case."

"You always do, General Brighton."

"That's why you pay me, sir. That's the only reason I'm here."

The NSA stared at Brighton, then cut in anxiously. "There's another little thing, Mr. President, that we need to talk about. It may be nothing, it may be something, and we hate to bring this to you when it is so preliminary, but some of my staff . . . " the NSA glanced at General Brighton again . . . "particularly General Brighton feels this is something worth bringing to you."

The president waited, sipping his southern tea.

"You remember our Jackson Teams?" the NSA said.

The president frowned. "They are what, some guys up in New York? They monitor the SEC or something, right?"

"Sort of, Mr. President. The team consists of Homeland Security agents, SEC investigators, some guys from Justice as well. But the team leaders are all FBI agents, and the team is under FBI control. The Jackson Team is tasked with monitoring suspicious trends in trading, securities, currency markets, that sort of thing."

The president sipped again at his tea, studying his security advisors over the rim of the glass. "Sounds like law enforcement," he said. "Why are you guys involved?"

Brighton sat back in his chair as he explained, "Sir, the Jackson Team was put together with the 9/11 commission's recommendation. It is based on the theory that, before we would see another major attack, there would be some indicators on Wall Street."

The president scowled. Out of the hundreds of issues he

discussed every day, national security was by far his highest priority. But there were ten thousand security programs and procedures that had been put in place, or were being put in place, or were being considered, or were being funded, or studied, or talked about by his staff, and there was simply no way he could remember them all. So while this whole Jackson thing was faintly familiar, it was still full of holes. "I don't see how Wall Street can give us warning?" he queried suspiciously.

Brighton continued. "Sir, the Jackson Team operates on the premise that before a terrorist organization or hostile government were to launch a major attack against the U.S., they would provide some kind of warning to their financiers. You have to consider, Mr. President, every terrorist organization, whether al Qaeda or a hostile government, gets its funding from *somewhere.* We know that a lot of that money comes from wealthy individuals throughout the Middle East. And we hope that, before we would see a major attack on our soil, we would see some movement in the market as these individuals begin to liquidate their U.S. assets . . ."

"Their terrorist comrades would warn them before they attacked?"

"We think that they might."

"So they could cash in their assets? Jump like a rat from a ship?"

"A ship that was sinking very fast, sir."

The president shook his head. It seemed unlikely to him, that was clear from the look on his face.

"You have to remember, Mr. President," General Brighton went on, "the financial cost of the 9/11 attacks to our nation was more than ten *trillion* dollars. The market tanked. The dollar fell. The recession lasted almost three years. Then, after 9/11, when we were going back through our records, we discovered a very interesting thing. Several extremely wealthy

Saudi princes started diversifying their U.S. assets just a few weeks before the attacks."

The president sipped quietly. "So they made money predicting how our markets would fall!"

"Not really, sir. It appears they weren't so much interested in *making* money from the market's collapse; they were interested in not *losing* everything they had invested over here."

"Okay," the president answered. He glanced at his watch, then turned back to his NSA. "So, where are you going with this, Bo? What do I need to know?"

The NSA folded his hands on his lap. "Mr. President, our Jackson Team has seen indications that have caused us concern. Significant Saudi holdings have been moved from U.S. markets to various holdings overseas. Almost ten billion dollars have left our country in just a few weeks."

"Are you telling me the Saudis are dumping their U.S. assets before another terrorist attack!"

"We don't know, Mr. President. But we think it is worth looking at."

The president caught his breath. "It might be a purely financial decision," he countered. "I mean, you have the Saudis, the Europeans, the Chinese and Japanese, half the world moves in and out of our markets every day. We live in a global economy; trillions of dollars cross our borders in any twenty-four-hour period. Our unemployment rate ticked up last month. Gas prices keep climbing through the roof. Don't you think it might be nothing more than a reaction to the current market?"

The general moved his head slightly but didn't say anything. This wasn't a reaction to high oil prices—he was certain of that.

"A purely financial adjustment?" the president prodded again.

"We can never be certain," the NSA replied. "But it is a significant adjustment, if that's all it is."

General Brighton leaned forward again, but the NSA's eyes warned him off. He had been cautioned before the meeting not to say too much, and he had spoken too much already. But General Brighton knew there was something else—something the president really needed to know.

The royal families of the House of Saud weren't the only ones dumping U.S. stocks and securities. A firm up in New York City was dumping as well—dumping so much and so fast, it would have been impossible not to take note. Jackson Team or no, it was obvious.

Which meant one of two things: They were either stupid or scared. And these men weren't stupid.

So the general swallowed hard.

chapter twenty-four

KHORRAMSHAHR REFUGEE CAMP
IRAN/IRAQ BORDER

Mr. Sebastian Raule, special assistant to the camp administrator at Khorramshahr, stared at the paper that he held in shaking hands. His mouth went dry as he stared. His heart beat like a butterfly wing in his chest.

He didn't believe it! It was not possible! He read the dispatch again and again, then held it up to the light to study the signature.

It appeared to be real.

What was he going to do?

He put the paper down and turned to his phone. The yellow light in the corner of the black receiver was blinking weakly; there was only one line into Khorramshahr and it was already in use. He was almost relieved. He didn't know what he would say when he made the call anyway. He turned back to the dispatch and read it for the fifth time, then turned again to the phone. The light was out. He picked up the receiver and dialed with a shaking hand, his pointer finger jammed into the round slot on the rotary dial.

His knees bounced anxiously as he waited for the phone call to go through. The phone clicked and hummed through forty-year-old communications switching machines, then fell silent. He was just thinking he might have been cut off when he heard a man's voice: "U.N. Baghdad mission headquarters."

"Yes, this is Sebastian Raule calling from Khorramshahr. I need to speak with Mr. Conner. Is he available?"

"Mr. Conner. Let me see. May I ask again who is calling?"

"Sebastian Raule. I'm the assistant—"

"Yes, Mr. Raule, I know who you are. Let me see if Mr. Conner is in."

The phone hummed again as he was placed on hold, then he heard the American pick up the phone. The director of the U.N. mission in Baghdad answered in a hurried tone. "Conner," he said.

Raule swallowed tensely.

The director of the U.N. mission in Baghdad was the big dog at the top of the pile. The Americans were calling all the shots in Iraq—a fact that drove the other U.N. representatives crazy, especially those from the E.U.—and Conner was the point man for all the U.N. officers working in-country.

"Yes, Mr. Conner," Raule began, his voice diminutive and polite. "My name is Sebastian Raule. I'm calling from the Khorramshahr refugee camp . . . "

"Yes, yes, Sebastian." The American chuckled. "I know who you are. And I think I know why you're calling." He laughed again.

Raule couldn't help feeling that the American was laughing at him. He hesitated, then asked, "Well yes, sir, I don't suppose you are surprised I might call. I have the message from your office, and I must say I find it remarkable. It raises so many questions. Honestly, I'm not sure how to proceed. But before I did anything, I wanted to confirm that this was legitimate?"

"Oh, yes, Mr. Raule. It is perfectly legitimate, I assure you."

"And you think I should . . ."

"What I think, Mr. Raule, doesn't matter a lot. She is your responsibility. But I have every confidence you will handle the situation with appropriate courtesy and dispatch."

Raule was silent a moment, then said, "Sir, there is the issue of repatriation."

"Yes, I'm aware."

"Then, sir, you might also be aware there is the possibility she may not be amenable to an offer."

Conner wasn't surprised. He had been briefed by his staff, and they had indicated that might be the case. Her family, all killed. Nowhere really to go. Miserable as it was, after half a lifetime of waiting, Khorramshahr had become her home. "After almost twenty years, I can see why she might have lost some interest," Conner said. It wasn't a personal dig at Raule, just a dig at the system that could fail so miserably.

Raule exhaled, embarrassed. "Yes, Mr. Conner, it's been a long time."

"Too long," Conner answered, a bit more acidly. "The U.N., I'm afraid, is not very good at these things."

"Yes, yes," Raule answered, then let his voice trail off. "But sir, that could create some . . . ah, interesting issues if she does not want to go."

"Yes it would, yes it would. With that consideration in mind, maybe you ought to head down and have a long talk with Mrs. Pari al- Faruqi."

Raule was silent again. "It is an awful lot of money," he then added, almost speaking to himself.

"Yeah, you could say that. And I understand she isn't well?"

"No, sir, not well. Not well at all."

"Then I wouldn't hesitate, Mr. Raule. I would talk to her today."

The French assistant to the administrator was silent. That was one of the problems with the Americans. They were so sentimental. They all loved a good story, an underdog, come-from-behind, happy ending. But this might not end so happily. He thought of Pari and how poorly she had looked the last time he had seen her. Since Azadeh had been taken, her health had fallen dramatically. And now this. It complicated things. It complicated things a lot.

"Mr. Conner," Raule questioned, "if I could, sir, just one more thing before I let you go. Can you tell me why the sudden change of mind? I mean, not only about the money, but also clearing her husband's name. After all these years, can you tell me what changed?"

Conner hesitated. "The administration is exerting enormous pressure on the regime," he finally said. "The E.U. is also pushing. The president of the E.U. had a meeting with the Iranians last week. Apparently one of the messages he gave them was to clean up the camps. 'Take care of them or the U.S. will take care of them for us,' he said. It would be much worse for the mullahs if that happened, much worse for everyone. So the Europeans, your countrymen, are running interference for the Iranians. God bless their wicked little hearts, the last thing they want now is for the U.S. to get involved. So the Iranians have decided to clean up the camps, and they know they can't leave her out there. Her old man knew too many people, and they're not going to forget. Better to free it up and get it behind them, then move on to the next phase."

Raule listened, shaking his head. He knew there was something more to the story, something much deeper—not obvious, but something he didn't know. Did Conner know the story? Maybe. Maybe not. But this much was clear to anyone who could think: The mullahs had not made their decision because they were afraid of the U.N. Nor had they agreed because they suffered from a streak of sudden generosity.

The U.S. had something on them. He was certain of that.

There was an untold story unfolding somewhere under the dirt. But it really didn't matter. It was what it was, and now it was in his lap.

The silence grew long as Raule considered.

"Anything else, Mr. Raule?" Conner asked, ready to end the call.

"No, sir," Raule answered.

"Call if I can be of any help."

"I will, sir, I will."

"You know, Mr. Raule, I wouldn't delay meeting with Mrs. Pari al- Faruqi. Maybe I'm going out on a limb on this," here Conner stopped to laugh, "but I suspect she might be one of the wealthiest women in your camp." Conner laughed again. So delicious. A happy irony. "She's not an everyday refugee," he continued. "Never was. Never will be. Maybe it's time some of your folks down there realized that was true."

"I suppose so," Raule answered dryly. "Good day to you, sir."

He hung up the phone. Staring at the receiver, he took a deep breath. And, as he thought, he couldn't help it. His lips slowly turned into a smile.

Justice, she was a fickle lady, moody and unpredictable. Sometimes she was gracious, but far more often she was vague and ambivalent, even apathetic, always ready to turn a blind eye. Raule had seen it, grown used to it, and accepted it; he had seen too much injustice not to have grown cynical. After forty-five years, he knew that justice was not the norm, although he conceded that God still might wield it in the next world.

But the stars had aligned before his very eyes, and, for whatever reason, justice was going to be served. Yes, it was late, but it was justice, and he couldn't help but smile.

* * *

Later that day, Mr. Sebastian Raule made his way down the hill to the long row of huts below the administration building. Picking out Mrs. Pari al- Faruqi's quarters, he knocked, waited, then pushed the door back and found Pari lying in her bed in deep sleep, her chest moving the thin blanket as she labored to breathe. Raule entered the small hut and woke her gently, then pulled the small chair over to the side of her bed.

"Miss Pari," he started, "I have something to tell you." She tried to sit up, then lay back again.

"Miss Pari, there's been a significant change with the government of Iran's disposition toward your late husband's standing and estate . . . "

Pari lifted her hand, pushing herself up on the bed.

The old woman and Raule talked through the late afternoon. The sun eventually set. Raule turned on the small lamp, the only light in the room, and they talked an hour longer. Then Pari fell asleep, exhausted, Raule at her side.

He stared at her, his face tight, fantasies of sudden and unexpected wealth dancing around in his mind.

He watched her sleep for a few minutes, then pulled the blanket up, tucking it under her chin. Standing, he checked the heater to make certain it was on, cracked the window half an inch to let in just a breath of fresh air, and moved back to the chair by the side of the bed.

Listening to her labored breathing, he was suddenly terrified.

She couldn't die. Not tonight. Not for at least a few days.

It would take that long to put everything in order. She *had* to live until then.

He stood guard a few minutes, then leaned down and planted a dry kiss on her bony cheek.

Walking out the door, he had no doubt that Mrs. Pari al-Faruqi had just become the most important person in his life. More important than his children. More important than his wife. Far more important than his boss. More important than anyone.

She was his best friend, his salvation, his ticket out of this hole. She was the unexpected rainbow in a dark world of storms.

So she'd better not die now—at least, not for a few days.

chapter twenty-five

KHORRAMSHAHR REFUGEE CAMP
IRAN/IRAQ BORDER

It was late at night and the camp was very quiet. A warm wind moved gently up from the sea, moaning sadly as it moved through the cracks in the poorly sealed windows of the camp administration building. There was a smell of fresh rain in the air, and Sebastian Raule couldn't help but stop and take a deep breath. He glanced at his watch. Almost 4:00 in the morning. He had napped quickly between 1:00 and 3:00, but the fire inside him kept him going now—that and a constant supply of harsh coffee, black, with huge spoonfuls of sugar, thick bread, and even an occasional cup of cheap wine from his secret stash in the bottom drawer of the file cabinet.

Raule sat back and rubbed his eyes, then glanced at his desk. The papers were piled high: thick government folders, excerpts from history books, newspaper clippings, files he had printed from the net (Khorramshahr had a single computer connected to the internet, and the time on it was rationed and strictly enforced), transcripts of conversations with government representatives in Tehran, Belgium, Baghdad, and France, and notes from bankers in Europe, Persia, and the U.S. The paperwork spilled off his desk and onto the floor, arranged in a semicircle around and behind his chair. At first glance it appeared that Raule was surrounded by an indecipherable mess, but each pile had been neatly organized, alphabetized, and listed in priority order. Atop every pile were pages of his personal notes, each written in his careful script, a synopsis of the information that little stack of papers contained.

Raule listened intently to the sound of the wind. He sniffed again, taking in the smell of the coming rain. In one sense, he hated the rain—it turned the camp into such a muddy and miserable mess. But he did love the smell of the coming storm, which reminded him of his home and his growing-up years on the small farm, the rolling hills around him, gray in the late winter but green as a postcard from early spring until fall.

He pushed his weight back and pictured his own fantasy farmhouse in his mind: small barns in the back, ducks in the yard, two sheepdogs resting on the front porch. As he thought, he imagined, almost slipping into a dream. There was light smoke from the chimney. A warm fire inside. Stacks of neatly cut wood near the front door. A small fishpond in back. A few cows, a few goats, a horse, maybe a sheep or two.

It was not enough land or animals to live off, but that was not the point. It was an ideal situation for a gentleman farmer, a man of means who needed nothing, not money, not attention, not interaction with the world.

He shook his head again, bringing himself back to Khorramshahr.

His fantasy was reachable, if he could just make this work. He looked down at the papers and grunted again.

The death of Master al- Faruqi many years before had left an incredible mess. The years had tainted too many memories, and the paper trail had grown cold, but he thought that he had it. Most of it was here. Now he needed lawyers and bankers to take the next step. He was close; he had the basis. They could take it from here.

He squeezed his lips with his fingers as he thought. It was an incredible story. At one time, Pari's husband, the late Master al- Faruqi, had been one of the most wealthy and ambitious men in all of Persia. Special assistant to the Shah, responsible for developing the Parsi oil fields, some of the largest oil fields in all of Iran, he was rich and connected, which had been his downfall. Being too closely tied to the Shah was a dangerous thing in 1978, and when the Shah had fled Iran, his friends had been left out to dry. Stripped of his power, wealth, position, and prestige, his in-country financial assets stolen by those men who had ousted the Shah, his out-of-country assets frozen by every foreign bank, Master al- Faruqi had been left with nothing. He died soon thereafter, leaving his widow, Pari, utterly destitute.

Now many of his enemies had also passed away, and, thanks to pressure from the U.S. and U.N., what remained of his foreign assets, any money that had not been looted before, was being released. Released to his widow, the longest tenured resident of Khorramshahr.

Raule considered the story while he studied the papers around him, then went back to work. He wasn't focused any longer on locating the money left behind by Master al-Faruqi—that task was complete. He had accomplished all he could there.

He had a more unpleasant work now: verifying his mistake. Bending over his desk, he started reading again.

At 7:00 in the morning, he sat back in his chair and stretched, lifting his hands high above him, then took a deep breath. He stared at his papers, realizing there was nothing more he could do. It was what it was. His actions might kill the deal, but he couldn't change that now.

He took a quick sip of coffee, then headed down to Pari's hut.

* * *

"You don't know where she is?" Pari demanded, an unbelieving tone in her voice. She was growing weaker, Raule could tell, but she was animated now, her eyes burning, her face agitated, her hands constantly moving in frustration and anger.

Raule hesitated, then answered, "No, Miss Pari, we do not know where she is."

"But you said she had been released to her uncle!"

"Yes, well, that was what we had been led to believe." Raule's voice had turned suddenly quiet, and he paused now too long. Pari stared at him, the heavy silence a great weight in the air. She had been in the camp long enough, had seen enough young girls come and go, that she immediately understood. Her face became more tense, her jaw set tight as she struggled against the emotions that were building inside.

"You knew, didn't you, Sebastian." She wasn't accusing. She just wanted to know.

"No, Miss Pari, that simply isn't true. Did I suspect? Yes, perhaps, but even if I did, there wasn't a thing I could do. Our rules are straightforward and my superior is very demanding. I could not ignore our protocols. I had no choice. The man had documents proving the family relationship. He had the release forms; everything was in place. There was an uncle in Pakistan. We had to follow procedures . . . "

"Then what is the problem!"

Raule looked away. "He does not exist," he explained. "Miss Azadeh Pahlavi has no uncle in Pakistan. We know that now."

Pari shook her head and coughed weakly, keeping her eyes on the floor. She had to bite her tongue or she would regret what she might say. Money or no, she had a place in the world. She took a couple of deep breaths, pushing her anger down.

Raule watched her carefully, knowing he had to get everything out. This was his chance at redemption, and he wanted to make a clean start. He had one chance to convince Miss Pari al- Faruqi that he was on her side. But to do that, he had to come clean and tell her everything.

He stared at the close walls, the murals and flowers, then turned back to Pari. "The documents he provided were forged," he said. "We know that. He is gone; he took the girl. He didn't go to Pakistan. He went to northern Iraq."

Another long silence filled the air. Pari struggled to breathe, then fell into a violent coughing fit. Raule looked away as she hacked, each lunge of her chest a little weaker than the one before. When her fit had passed, he stood, moved to her bed, and knelt on the floor. He handed her a handkerchief and wiped the cold sweat from her brow with another cloth.

She looked at him desperately, her anger gone now. They sat silently for a while, staring into each other's eyes.

"I'm sorry," Raule said in a soft voice. "I mean that, Miss Pari. It tears at my heart. Yes, I suspected. I thought that something wasn't right, but please, you must believe me. I tried to help her. I did all I could. Was it enough? Clearly not. But I ask you to forgive me and let me help, if you will."

Pari stared at him, then took his hand in hers. She held it a moment, measuring the feeling in his soul. Looking into his eyes, she saw the pain and anguish there. Was his disappointment for real? Was he a good man? Was he loyal? Was he a man she could trust?

She looked at him a long moment, then concluded that he was.

chapter twenty-six

Khorramshahr Refugee Camp
Iran/Iraq Border

It took several more days for Sebastian Raule to gather the lawyers, bankers, and government representatives and have them draw up the documents. It was very complicated, more so than he ever could have predicted, and the more he got into it, the more complicated it became. Yet he worked frantically, sometimes twenty hours a day, all the while watching Pari anxiously as she was slipping away. He tried convincing her to move to his private quarters where it was warmer (but not cleaner) and much more comfortable. But she would have none of it. Her hut had been her home for more than twenty years, and if it was good enough for her last week, as a penniless pauper, then it was good enough for her now, as a multimillionaire.

So Raule worked while Pari died. It was a race against time.

As he worked with her, Raule came to realize that if it hadn't been for the young Azadeh Pahlavi, Pari would already have given up, letting herself slip away. "I'm tired of watching those I love come and go," she explained. "I don't want to be left alone here anymore. I want to go home to my husband. I hear him calling my name."

Raule understood. But still, he watched Pari linger, fighting for a few more days. She wanted to live until she could sign the paper. It was as important to her now as it was to Raule.

So he prayed and he worked like a man on a ship that was taking on water at a terrifying pace. He made literally hundreds of phone calls, drove more than a thousand miles, and scheduled dozens of meetings each day. He worked and he dug, trying to uncover half a generation of old records and bank receipts.

Yes, the government of Iran had agreed to release Mrs. Pari al- Faruqi's family assets. Yes, they had agreed upon the amount—12,456,987 U.S. dollars. But the fact that they had agreed did not make them amiable to the idea. Everyone Raule talked to wanted a piece of the pie. Some wanted a large slice, some a sliver, some just a cherry, but he didn't talk to anyone who didn't want a cut. So he promised and pleaded, he threatened and cursed, he signed secret contracts and illegal documents and did some things even worse.

But in the end, eight days after the first message from the U.N. headquarters in Baghdad, he had a draft agreement and the appropriate players in place.

The five men were met by a driver at the front gate of Khorramshahr. They were directed to park their Mercedes and immediately driven in a large van to the headquarters building, where they were met by Sebastian Raule and his boss, who was bitter now and angry that he had not gotten in on the deal. The camp administrator waded through the introductions, then turned the time over to the lead attorney who had drawn all the contracts together.

The men reviewed the paperwork for the last time. "Do we agree everything is in order?" the lead attorney asked when they had finished. He was a British officer, round-shouldered but aggressive as a hungry pit bull, who had volunteered to work in Iran right out of law school and ended up staying for nearly ten years. He was a young man, with a soft face and eyes that were as clear and cool as his work.

The other men nodded, some reluctantly, some ambivalently, some anxious to proceed.

"Then let's do it," the attorney concluded. "It's time that justice was served."

Raule, who had been fidgeting nervously on the edge of his chair, smiled now as the attorney stood. He loved this man. He really loved him. And if this worked out, he planned on sending him birthday gifts for the next fifty years.

The government agent nodded to Raule. "Bring her in," he said.

Raule stood and moved quickly to a side door. He pushed it back and disappeared, and the men could hear the sound of soft voices from the next room. Then Raule returned, pushing a weak Mrs. Pari al- Faruqi in a new wheelchair. The men stood and waited as Raule positioned her at the head of the group.

"Mrs. al- Faruqi," the young attorney said as he moved toward his client, "you are looking a little stronger today."

Pari smiled and held her hand out toward him. This was their fifth or sixth meeting, and she had come to like him a lot.

The attorney moved to stand beside her and got right to the point. "Pari," he said, kneeling in front of her chair. "We have completed all the documents. I want to review them for you."

Pari raised her hand to stop him. "You still represent me, right?"

"Of course, Pari. I am your representative here."

"And you have carried out my wishes?"

"As best as I could."

"Then we don't need to review them. I am ready to sign."

The attorney nodded, pulled a chair over, and sat by her side. "Pari, it's going to take a while, maybe a few weeks, maybe longer, before the Iranian government actually releases your funds."

"But they will."

"We believe so. Everything indicates that they will comply."

"You know you can't trust them."

"Yes, ma'am, I know. But we have made progress, and we believe that they will act in good faith this time. We have the initial agreements in place, signed and on file. And they remain under a lot of pressure from the E.U."

Pari smiled wearily. "Are they going to pay me interest?" she asked.

The government agent shifted his weight in his seat. The lawyer shook his head. "No, Pari, you know they will not. Now, we could try to seek interest and damages, but I strongly recommend against it. Trying to get additional monies will certainly poison the deal."

"They're crooks and cheats—and they're cheap ones at that."

"Yes, ma'am, I will not dispute that. But I believe we are better to just let it go."

"Twelve million. Ten percent. I would have tripled my money. Better than that. I was a good investor, you know."

"I suspect that you would have, Pari."

She stared at him. He finally grinned, recognizing that she was only teasing.

"Okay, let's do it," she said. "I could die any time. Heaven knows we all want to do this before it's too late."

The men laughed uncomfortably. Pari looked at them and smiled.

The lawyer pulled out the first document. "This authorizes me to act as your agent in disposing your assets."

Pari didn't read the document but turned to the last page and signed. Though she was weak, her signature was smooth and flowing, filling the line.

The lawyer took the document and placed it inside his briefcase. He pulled out a stack of other documents and placed them in his lap. "A final review, then, Miss Pari, of your intentions. Upon your passing, you are leaving all of your assets, less the cost of disposal, which I will administer, to Miss Azadeh Pahlavi. Does that remain your desire?"

"Yes," Pari answered. "I want it all to go to her."

"You realize, of course, that we have no way of knowing where Miss Pahlavi is?"

"Yes, I know that is true."

"And you are commissioning Mr. Sebastian Raule, who is sitting in the chair opposite me," the attorney nodded toward Sebastian, "to locate Miss Azadeh Pahlavi, wherever she may be."

Pari hesitated. "He is the only one I have," she said.

The attorney remained quiet. Pari looked over at Raule. He shifted anxiously in his seat.

The attorney started again. "Does it remain your intention, Mrs. al- Faruqi, to commission Mr. Sebastian Raule with the responsibility of locating Miss Azadeh Pahlavi—for which, if and *only* if he is successful in locating Miss Pahlavi, he will become eligible to collect a finding fee?"

Both Pari and her attorney smiled at the phrase. "Well, I guess that is a more literal application of the phrase than you might normally use," Pari weakly laughed.

"Yes," the lawyer smiled. "As to the question, Mrs. al-Faruqi?"

Pari paused and then answered. "Upon hearing the news of my late husband's assets being released, I did agree with Mr. Raule that I would pay him one million dollars if he could locate Miss Azadeh. I intend to honor that agreement. He is to find her and direct her to you. Once you have verified her identity and transferred the funds to Miss Azadeh, then Mr. Raule is to be compensated one million U.S. dollars."

The attorney nodded. "Anything else, Pari?"

She shook her head. "No. I'm getting tired. Too tired to think."

The attorney placed his hand on her shoulder. "Then we are ready to sign." He thumbed through the stack of documents on his lap, organized them, and handed the first one to his client. It took a few minutes for her to sign every one. The documents were then passed on to the other men. Two of them acted as the witnesses: one a Turkish lawyer who represented the Iranian government, the other a lawyer from the E.U. The final signature was from the representative of the consortium of European banks where the money was currently held.

Fifteen minutes later, the paperwork was done. The attorney knelt again at Pari's side. "Mrs. al- Faruqi," he whispered. "Please, will you consider coming with me. I could get you to London. I could get you to the United States."

"So they want me now. Ironic. They didn't want me before."

"It's not only that, Mrs. al- Faruqi. There is more to it, as you know."

"I understand. I understand. And I'm grateful for your concern. But I made my decision a fairly long time ago. I'm okay here. I am comfortable. There are worse places to die. I do not mind spending my last days here; it won't be very long anyway. So please, let's let it go. I don't want to speak of it again."

The attorney squeezed her hand, then nodded and stood up again.

Twenty minutes later, Sebastian watched the men drive away in their Mercedes Benz. Watching them go, he felt his heart skip a beat, and he looked down at the contract he held in his hand.

One million U.S. dollars. He would be a rich man. He would retire. He would fish. He would read all day long. He would listen to his operas. He would smoke fine cigars.

Now all he had to do was find her.

How difficult could that be?

He would start in Baghdad. Then Karachi. She had to be here, somewhere in the Middle East. He would track down her uncle and her family.

And he would make them both rich.

chapter twenty-seven

Azadeh Pahlavi sat next to the window of the 767–300 wide-body aircraft, her eyes shining and wide in anticipation, her hands fidgeting nervously. She stared out the window, then glanced over to Amina, who was watching her intently, evidently taking great pleasure in the look on her face.

The two women had the seats next to the left window. To Amina's right was an aisle, then four seats, another aisle, and two more seats on the far right. The cabin was crowded, and more than half a dozen languages could be heard as the business travelers and tourists talked among themselves. The 767 was high, still above 30,000 feet, but it had begun its descent into JFK, and the air grew more turbulent as the plane passed through a thin layer of frozen cirrus clouds. Multiple rows of small television screens suspended from the ceiling of the cabin showed the aircraft's flight progress, direction, and altitude. Thirty-one thousand feet. Heading west by southwest. One hundred thirty miles from the U.S. border.

One hundred thirty miles from freedom. One hundred thirty miles from her new home.

Eight thousand miles from her people. Eight thousand miles from everything she had ever known.

Azadeh turned and smiled nervously. Amina leaned toward her, bending over her seat to peer out the window. All she could see were white clouds and dark water a long way below. No land was in sight—no dark ribbon of coastline, no sand-bars, no white tops, nothing. But, looking west, she could see the water turn a slightly different shade, the tint changing from almost black to deep blue. Sitting back, she smiled at Azadeh. "It won't be long now," she said.

Azadeh nodded anxiously, twisting her fingers together.

"Pretty exciting, isn't it."

Azadeh nodded again in awe but didn't reply. She had grown progressively more quiet since the flight had taken off some seven hours before, lifting off from London's Heathrow airport in the dark of the night. Now she was almost silent, trying to take it all in. Amina studied her young friend. She recognized the racing emotions from the look on the girl's face. Azadeh was nearly sick with equal amounts of excitement and dread.

The young Persian smiled weakly and the older woman took her hand. "I'm so excited for you," she laughed.

"Thank you, Amina. Thank you for everything."

Amina nodded.

Azadeh thought quickly of Sam. "One day I want to thank the soldier too," she said.

Amina didn't answer. She knew that was impossible. Azadeh picked up the small cup of lemonade on her fold-down tray and sipped, puckered her lips, and sipped again. "It's so sweet," she said, placing the cup back on the tray. Amina watched her intently, not wanting to miss a single expression on her face.

Watching Azadeh, she remembered why she had dedicated

her life to saving lost children. This was why she did it, the reason she worked as hard as she did: the excitement, the new pleasures, the feeling of awe. And it all started when she watched their looks of excitement as they approached the U.S.

So, though she tried not to stare, it was hard to take her eyes off of Azadeh. She wanted to see it, the smile of anticipation and excitement that even the fear couldn't hide.

The moments passed. The aircraft descended, breaking below the clouds. Azadeh continued to stare out the window. Suddenly she reached over and grabbed Amina's arm. "I can see it!" she whispered. "I can see the U.S.!"

Amina gripped Azadeh's fingers tightly as she leaned across the seat. There, far in the distance, a thin ribbon of dark blue land and white surf was barely coming in view.

Ten minutes passed. Azadeh kept her head glued to the window, though she squeezed tighter now. "Oh, my . . . " she gasped as the city passed by.

The aircraft turned, a few thousand feet above the ground. Azadeh stared until the outline of the city filled the entire oval window. It was an incredible sight: deep canyons of buildings so thick and tall, it looked like a dream.

She fidgeted anxiously as the beautiful buildings passed by, just a few miles off the left wing. It seemed as if the tops of the buildings reached almost up to the aircraft. The Brooklyn and Williamsburg bridges, black steel structures that spanned the East River, were crowded with multicolored vehicles, large buses, and trucks. The river shimmered, catching the slants of the sun that slipped through the partly cloudy skies. Central Park slipped under the wing, a huge rectangle of green among the enormous buildings, a contrast of nature among the workings of man. Half a dozen of the tallest skyscrapers had their tips shrouded in a low bank of clouds, a transparent layer of silver that was illuminated from the top by the sun.

Azadeh stared down silently, then turned back to Amina. "It looks perfect," she said.

Amina shook her head. "No, Azadeh, it isn't perfect. There are problems, you will see that, but I believe it is good."

* * *

The two women moved through customs without incident. Azadeh noted the cautious stares, but she didn't mind them; Amina had warned her to be ready for intense examination. The security situation in the U.S. had changed things for many immigrants, especially those from Arab-speaking or Muslim countries. It was the reality. They would deal with it. Still, the scrutiny was a fraction of what Azadeh had come to expect. Inside her own mind, she had prepared herself to be questioned, taken into a small room and threatened, forced to sit under a bright light, perhaps even beaten if she did not answer correctly. When nothing like that happened, and they had passed through the last control booth and into the airport concourse, Azadeh looked around anxiously.

"That's it," Amina told her.

Azadeh shook her head. "Nothing more?" she asked in disbelief.

"Nothing more. You are here. You are a free woman, Miss Pahlavi."

Azadeh shook her head again. No interrogation. No religious police. No threats or violent hazing. No comments on the inadequacy of her white scarf or the immodesty of her knee-length black dress. No questions of her father or the whereabouts of her man. No questions of her intentions, her religion, where her allegiance lay. She glanced down at her thin sandals, then placed her hand to her breast. "I can't believe it's over. My heart is beating like a hammer," she laughed to her friend.

"Come on, Miss Pahlavi. Let's get something to eat."

"No, please not now. Can we do the other first?"

Amina hesitated, then glanced up and down the concourse. Crowds of people jammed the corridor, most of them dragging small, wheeled suitcases behind. The crowd brushed by them, pushing the two women toward the wall. Eighty feet to their right, the concourse opened into a huge open area with bars, restaurants, fast-food spots, luggage shops, newspaper stands, bookstores, expensive clothiers, even a small sporting goods store. Amina took two steps forward and craned her neck, looking for an exit sign.

Azadeh touched her shoulder and nodded. "Exit and baggage claim," she read.

Amina turned toward her. "You can read that?" she asked in surprise.

Azadeh nodded.

Amina cocked her head. "That's pretty good, Azadeh. You're going to pick it up very fast."

"My father tried to teach me. I remember some of what he said."

Amina glanced at her watch. Four hours until their connecting flight to Chicago. She nodded to the end of the concourse. "Come on," she said.

Azadeh led the way, almost running, and Amina had to rush to keep up. The two women left the concourse and walked out of the main airport building to where dozens of yellow taxis were waiting in line, trapped against the curb by the flow of heavy traffic. Amina was directed to the first cab in line, and she and Azadeh climbed in.

The driver was Pakistani, and when he saw Azadeh's scarf, he looked back with a friendly grin. *"Salâm,"* he said happily, showing a brown, tea-stained smile. Azadeh nodded shyly, and Amina answered in Arabic. The two talked a moment as the driver pulled away from the curb, but Azadeh didn't pay any attention, her eyes wide in wonder as she looked around.

"Where to?" the cabbie asked them.

"Battery Park," Amina said.

The driver glanced back, smiling widely again. "Oh, a new one, have you?"

"Yes," Amina answered.

The driver nodded eagerly as he accelerated through traffic. "Good, good. This is good. A very good day," he said.

* * *

The taxi drove through the mass of traffic moving in and out of JFK, hit the Long Island Expressway heading north toward Queens, and followed the freeway as it turned west and then south through the very heart of Brooklyn. Azadeh stared out the window, watching the buildings roll by. The taxi followed the Expressway south along the East River. Azadeh caught a glimpse of the enormous docks along the western shore of the river and she couldn't help but think of the docks at Bandar-e Bushehr. She remembered the many times she and her father had taken the bus down to the port city, and for a moment she was transported back in time. She remembered walking along the ancient docks, feeling the salt air, smelling the brine and rotten seaweed. She felt a sudden surge of homesickness and took a deep breath.

The taxi turned west, heading toward lower Manhattan across the Brooklyn Bridge. The bridge's enormous, double-arched towers and thick steel cables passed high overhead as the skyline of Manhattan came into view. Azadeh sat forward, watching in awe. The buildings looked even more incredible from the ground, their reflected images shining on the dark water where the East River and Hudson River met.

At the apex of the bridge, when lower Manhattan was

most clearly in view, Amina nudged Azadeh and pointed to a sudden break in the skyline. "Do you see that?" she asked.

Azadeh brought her hands to her face. The taxi's wheels hummed across the steel plates on the bridge. "I've seen . . . pictures. Many stories. But seeing it in person . . . it looks different somehow."

Amina sat forward in the seat, straining to keep the break in the skyline in view. The reconstruction was nearing completion, but the new buildings were smaller—more beautiful, but somehow less grand.

The two fell into silence as the new buildings passed, neither of them willing to speak as the taxi crossed over the riverbank and turned south on FDR Drive.

Ten minutes later, the taxi stopped in front of Battery Park.

Amina bought them tickets for the ferry and they stood in line for forty minutes. When the triple-decked ferry arrived, they hurried to the top deck and moved to the front of the boat.

The great lady loomed before them, growing grand and tall as they sped toward her through the water. She stood majestic and valiant, her patina complexion a resonating green against the blue and white sky. Her pedestal was tall and imposing, almost taller than she, the rock stacked underneath her in a fitting platform. Solid. Firm. A beautifully carved pedestal.

As the ferry moved toward the island, Azadeh kept her eyes on the Statue of Liberty, the one symbol of America that was known throughout the world, the one symbol of liberty and justice that could not be clouded in lies. She shivered as the statue grew, looming over her head. The lady held her arm high; she was not merely confident, she was defiant and proud. She held the book close to her body, protecting it in her other arm. Her crown was beautiful and yet dangerous, the spikes reaching out from her brow. At her feet, the broken shackles lay, the metal rings torn in two.

Azadeh stared at the lady, repeating the words her father had secretly taught her so many years before:

"Keep, ancient lands, your storied pomp," cries she . . .
"Give me your tired, your poor,
Your huddled masses yearning to breathe free,
The wretched refuse of your teeming shore,
Send these, the homeless, tempest-tost to me,
I lift my lamp beside the golden door!"

Azadeh felt as if the Great Statue were speaking to her now. *"Keep, ancient lands, your storied pomp . . . "*

Keep your mullahs, your landowners, your shahs and religious police. Keep your grand officers of society, your rich and powerful. Give us your human trash, those whom you hate, and we will take those wretched souls and create the greatest nation on earth. We will take your destitute and homeless and build the most free nation in the history of man.

Azadeh was one of the masses, homeless and tired. She was poor and, like the others, she had yearned to be free.

She was part of that wretched refuse: she had been left to die.

Yes, she was *outcast.*

But now she had a home.

She started to weep.

Her father would have been so proud.

Al Kuwayt International Airport
Kuwait City, Kuwait

Sebastian Raule stood at the ticket counter, shifting his weight anxiously from one foot to the other. He smoked, keeping an unending chain of French cigarettes in his mouth. It would be a long flight, non-smoking, and he had to stoke up before he got on the plane. While he waited for the ticket agent, he pulled another smoke from the black-and-white carton and stuck the brown filter in his mouth.

It irritated him that he'd had to come down to Kuwait to get on a flight to Kirkuk, but it was far easier to make the two-hour drive to Kuwait City and then fly to northern Iraq than to chance the four-day, life-and-death adventure of trying to make his way north in a car.

It had been a long time since the liberation of Iraq from the madman Hussein, but the country was still a far cry from safe. Since the U.S. had pulled out most of their troops, things had only gotten worse. It was clear now that it would be many years before the nation's infrastructure was put fully back in place, if indeed that could ever happen. There were too many gunmen, too many bombs, too much confusion as to who was in charge—the government or the insurgents who fought against their fellowman.

The Kuwaiti ticket agent typed a moment, then looked up to Raule with a disinterested stare. "Sir, it appears that all of the flights into Kirkuk are completely booked for the next week or so. I apologize, but you are traveling without any notice, and the flights in and out of Iraq are always very full."

Raule knew he would have to pay the *bâj;* the only question was how much it would be. He decided to start out low. Who knew how many flights he would be on for the next couple of weeks? He nodded to the ticket agent, then slipped a ten-Euro bill across the white counter. The attendant slipped the bill in his palm, then turned back to his screen and hit a few keys.

"Mr. Raule," he continued after tucking the Euro into his vest pocket, "it looks like we might have something . . . maybe tomorrow afternoon." He didn't look up, but continued to stare at his screen.

Raule slipped another twenty Euros across the top of the counter and the attendant typed again, hardly missing a key as he reached up and pulled the money down to his side. "Good news, Mr. Raule, it looks like something just opened up on the 12:15 flight. It is in coach, however. Is that acceptable to you?"

The attendant looked up and waited, measuring the French U.N. officer. If he demanded first class, then he would bump him again. No way he'd let this guy into first class for a mere 30 Euros.

But the foreigner didn't hesitate. "Coach is fine," he said in remarkably good Arabic.

"Fine, sir, fine." The ticket agent continued typing, holding Raule's U.N. passport in his left hand, then looked up and said, "Mr. Raule, I see you have requested follow-on travel to Baghdad and Pakistan. You realize, of course, that it will be very difficult to book these flights. Travel is fairly restricted in and out of Pakistan, and I'm not sure even your U.N. papers are going to be enough to get you there."

Yes, Raule realized that, and he smiled sarcastically. He had been working on the travel arrangements for more than a week. The greedy ticket agent hadn't told him anything he didn't already know. "Can you do it?" he demanded.

The agent shook his head. "I'd suggest putting your travel itinerary on request when you get to Kirkuk."

Raule shook his head, then huffed as he placed his suit bag next to the counter. The agent started tagging his bag. Raule thought as he watched.

Yes, he was aware how difficult the travel arrangements would be, but the truth was, that was the very least of his concerns. Trying to find Azadeh would be far more difficult than arranging a flight to Pakistan.

And he had a lot of work to do before he even knew where he would be flying to next. He knew that the man who had taken Azadeh had bought his forged documents from a black market printer in southern Kirkuk. (It hadn't been difficult to determine the origination point of the documents; the U.N. had seen enough of the forgeries to trace them fairly easily now.) And though he suspected the printer wouldn't help him, he felt like he had to try. So he would climb on a flight to Kirkuk, track the printer down, ask a few questions, be rejected, then go on his way, knowing nothing more after the trip than he knew right now.

Where would he go after that? He really didn't know. The stranger who had taken Azadeh had mentioned a small town in western Pakistan. He figured he would likely start there, not because he was overly optimistic but because he lacked a better plan.

The truth was, he knew Azadeh could be literally anywhere. Once she had been taken from Khorramshahr, she could have been smuggled to a dozen locations in the world: Asia, the Middle East, Europe, even the U.S.

He smiled at the irony.

Who did he think that he was! Some kind of special super agent? An undercover spy? This wasn't the movies, this was real. He was no hero, and certainly no superman.

He stared at his worn-out, brown suit and rubbed his thin knee. He was none of those things. He was a mouse of a man who had spent his entire life pushing papers from one steel desk to the next. From one U.N. assignment to another, it had been the same thing. He had never shot a gun, never interrogated anyone, never investigated so much as a misplaced marking pen. Yet here he was, seeking to locate one single girl, a girl who had been taken from his refugee camp and now could be anywhere.

He shook his head in frustration. What were the chances of success? Maybe one in a thousand. Maybe much more remote.

chapter twenty-eight

Hyif El-Irbid Military Complex
Amman, Jordan

It was the last time these nine men expected to see each other on this side of the veil. It was the last time they would meet, for their association would be shattered once the final war had begun. Some would be dead. Others would be in hiding. And it would be far too dangerous for them to ever meet again.

But it no longer mattered. Their preparations were complete; there was nothing more to discuss. All they needed now was the king's final word.

The meeting took place under the most secret conditions that could be possibly arranged. The various leaders, some of the most powerful and power-hungry men in the world, traveled alone, without their normal entourage of aides, assistants, secretaries, butlers, advisors, protectors, consultants, gunners, communications specialists, snipers, drivers, and security forces. Each man came to the meeting completely unescorted, except for the king, who even himself brought only one man. And they traveled in secret, disguising their faces underneath various hoods, veils, dark glasses, and long, flowing robes. They came in small vehicles, rusted taxis, and worn-out desert Jeeps. The commander of the Popular Front for the Liberation of Palestine (PFLP) actually traveled as a woman, covered from the crown of his head to his toes in a flowing black *burka*. He took on the disguise easily, walking with small steps and deferring to any male who approached him while keeping his rough hands, clearly manly, hidden under his long, full sleeves. And though he was one of the most cruel and bloodthirsty men in the world, the leader of the PFLP wasn't the most notorious terrorist in the group. The disgraced imam Ali Omar al-Harazi, leader of al-Fatah, sat near the front. The presidents of Palestine Liberation Front (PLF) and Force 17 were in attendance as well, as was the leader of al Qaeda, the most wanted man in the world. Second only to the leader of al Qaeda on the most-wanted list, the leader of the counterinsurgency in Iraq sat quietly in a corner, his head low, his dark lips parted, his thin arms folded impatiently on his chest.

The blood of a hundred thousand innocents had washed over these hands: Americans, Europeans, Arabs, and Persians; Christians, Jews, and Muslims. It didn't matter to them who they killed, their brothers, their kin. It wasn't a matter of religion. It was a simple matter of power.

Taken together, the nine men were some of the most dedicated and evil men in the world. And they all sat around the king of the House of Saud, waiting for his final command.

The room, with only a few candles on the table to provide any light, was a small cement edifice with thick steel doors and a single metal shutter over a small, broken window. It was cool and drafty and the candles flickered and swooned, sometimes bending left, sometimes dancing in the swirling air. The half-buried munitions bunker, a cement structure that was used to store contraband weapons and ammunition bound for the terrorist organizations inside Gaza and along the West Bank, was indistinguishable from the three dozen other bunkers in the compound. Located near the center of a tightly knit web of underground tunnels, semi-buried bunkers, raised wooden warehouses, and squat administration buildings, surrounded by barbed wire and guard towers, the Hyif El-Irbid Complex served as the conduit between the innumerable terrorist organizations that operated inside the Middle East and their suppliers in various locations throughout the world. During any given week, a hundred thousand dollars' worth of military equipment might pass through Hyif El-Irbid, and on any given day, perhaps a million dollars in cash, all U.S. dollars, could be found in various hiding locations through the complex.

The meeting began a little after one in the morning, allowing time for all the participants to travel under the cloak of darkness while also allowing enough time for them to conduct their business and disperse before the sun would lighten the desert sky.

The king stood before his men, who sat on the floor on small wicker mats. As they assembled around him, he eyed them carefully. The old man had warned him to look for any sign of squeamishness, any hint of weakness or hesitation, which could be so deadly now. And he had also prepared him. If he needed to make a statement of conviction, even among these most trusted men, then he was perfectly ready and capable of doing so. He would kill every one of them, right here and right now, if they so much as hesitated when discussing the plan.

But though he was cautious, he was not overly concerned. He knew in his heart that these men would follow him. Driven by the same lust, they were in one accord, and the king didn't expect to lose any of them.

As the men gathered, they mumbled in excitement, though none of them knew exactly why. The king was the only man in the room who knew the entire plan, the only one who understood completely what the process would be. Each of them held a tiny piece of the puzzle, each had been assigned a critical task to perform, but none of them understood entirely what the king was planning to do. All they knew was the outcome, which was enough for them now.

Standing at the front of the barren bunker, the king looked out of place in his elegant clothes. He was dressed in an Arab *Dishdashah,* a beautiful robe with a silver sash that was tied at the side of his waist. His *Gutrah,* a scarf-like head cover, was held in place by a diamond-studded *Ogal,* a narrow leather band surrounding the top of his head. He had grown a goatee, and it was perfectly trimmed. His teeth were white and perfect, his jaw broad and strong. He wore diamond rings on the middle fingers of both hands, and his dark eyes reflected the flickering light in the room. He looked absolutely magnificent. The king of his world.

The other men bowed as he stood, a sign of subjection and respect.

Abdullah glanced at his closest advisor, General Abaza, who nodded almost imperceptibly at him from the back of the room. The king knew that underneath his garment, and against every arrangement, General Abaza was armed with a 9mm Glock, one of the most reliable and accurate handguns in the world. He didn't expect they would use it, but he wanted to be prepared.

Abaza stared at the king steadily and with just a hint of concern. The general didn't like open meetings, not when he wasn't able to confront or search all the participants or secure the surroundings with a team of his men. Abdullah read the look in his eye and felt an almost tender moment of affection. Abaza had proven so trustworthy, so reliable, the king felt almost a kinship for him. More than any of his younger brothers, more than any of his wives or his children, he cared for this man. He knew he could trust him, and if there was any man in this world for whom he felt grateful, Abaza was that man.

The king cleared his throat and started speaking in a low, even tone. "Brothers, we are ready. The time has finally come."

The room took a sudden chill, and the men stared up at him.

The king nodded to the leader of the PFLP. "Your team in Jerusalem is ready?" he asked.

The PFLP commander nodded.

The king turned to another who was sitting directly at his feet. The commander of al Qaeda rested his hands on his crossed knees. Everyone in the room knew the al Qaeda leader hated the king. He hated all the Saudis, for they had betrayed him many times. More, he considered their stewardship over the holy relics a dismal failure of oversight. But as much as he hated the Arabs, he hated his other enemies more, and he was so weak now, he could no longer effectively fight them on his own. So he sat in subjection, still proud, a holy warrior in the holiest war.

"You have made arrangements with our yellow-skinned brothers to the east?" the king demanded in an impatient tone.

The al Qaeda leader nodded. His beard was dark, but thin, with patches of gray beginning to show at the chin, and it brushed against his chest as he moved his head. "I will have the face-to-face meeting with them in the morning," he said. "I remain optimistic they will do as we ask."

The king leaned toward him. "It is important, my brother, that you close the deal. The shipments have to go east through China! It is the only option we have!"

The al Qaeda leader nodded. "I swear to you, my brother,

I will see to this task. But to seal the deal with the general, you might have to meet with him yourself."

Abdullah nodded. "I will do it. Make the arrangements. I want it done by tomorrow."

"I will see to it, I swear."

The king's dark eyes lingered a moment, then he turned to another man sitting at his right side. "The first of the warheads has been hidden?"

"It is in place, my *Sayid.*"

"They do not know?"

The man didn't hesitate. "They do not, my Good King."

The king nodded, a feigned look of sorrow beginning to furrow his brow. Though his heart remained cold and unfeeling as a glacier, his face appeared to soften by the thought of the approaching death of his brothers. "There are many valiant men among them," he said, referring to those who would die. "They will be granted mercy in the heavens. A just title will be written and a generous home given them."

The mullah nodded in agreement, though he kept his eyes low.

As the king studied the head of the mullah, he couldn't help but think. Yes, many of their best men would die. Tens upon thousands. Maybe many more. The price of their brothers' blood was substantial, but it was a good price to pay, for what blood was too precious to see their mission complete?

In a week, maybe less, they would see the destruction of their enemies throughout the Middle East. They would see the Great Satan literally brought to his knees. They would see the destruction of his offspring, the goatish daughter herself. She would be pushed into the deep sea, forever destroyed.

Yes, they would pay a price. Many of their men would die. And their wives. And their families. But what choice did they have? The final battle was upon them. The time of the goat's blood was here.

* * *

Lucifer watched his earthly angels, proud of their determination and pleased with their work. They were so open to his whispers, so swallowed up in their pride, that they were as malleable to him as wet clay in his hands.

He smiled as he watched, feeling their dark power. Through the centuries, he had deceived many men; many foul and evil souls had scrapped their way to his hell, but there weren't very many he was more proud of than these. Who else had been so willing to cause the death of so many souls: their own people, their loved ones, even their own families?

A cold shiver ran through him.

How he loved this dark war!

As the Master gloated, Balaam stood behind him, listening to Abdullah give his final instructions to his men. Standing between Balaam and his Master was a crowd of dark souls, Satan's most trusted advisors from the previous world. Balaam stared at their backs, feeling small and alone. It made him so angry not to be part of his Master's inner circle. How many centuries had he tried now! How many things had he done! He'd given up everything to be one of his Master's trusted ones. But still the Master ignored him, always pushing him away, and Balaam finally realized that it would never be. The Master would never reward him for the sacrifices he had made. Lucifer had deceived him. It was that simple.

A feeling of deep sadness seeped into his lost soul. He often felt alone now. He knew that all of them did. But under the depression was the constant, burning rage: rage at his Master for excluding him, rage at being robbed of all hope.

As Balaam glared at the angels that stood at Lucifer's side, one of the favored spirits turned around and looked back at him. Her arms were so thin that he could see every bone, and a mat of long hair fell in a rat's nest at her back. Her yellow eyes were wild and burning, her crooked smile fanged with rotting teeth. She stared, then smiled smugly, as if she had read his mind. "Get used to it, my friend," she seemed to say with her smile. Balaam nodded at her and turned away.

Why they all had turned so loathsome, he didn't understand. But they had and they knew it; they were ugly, raging souls. Without the light, they were nothing but dreadful, deadly cores.

Balaam considered the angel, staring at her mat of hair. She had once been a striking woman with blue eyes and dark hair and a face so fine and beautiful she could get anything she wanted with just a wink and a smile (which had been one of her problems, Balaam thought with a smirk). But now she was nothing but a loathsome, lying mess. She had no beauty. She was not happy. There was no light in her eyes. The only thing that she wanted was to make others share her pain, to cast her darkness on them, making them as unhappy and miserable as they could possibly be.

As Balaam's mind raced, his lips cracked into a thin smile. He didn't have a sense of humor—that had been lost years ago—but he had a bitter sense of irony that was sharp as a pin. And the irony was so obvious it simply could not be ignored. "We rebelled against the Father," he cried in desolation to himself. "We fought against the Father! We fought against his Christ! We did everything in our power to take the kingdom from them. *And they would have given it to us anyway! They were willing to share!*"

Everything the Father had, every kingdom and power, every pleasure and joy, every good thing in life had been offered to them. Everything they had fought for, the Father had offered anyway. He would have given them *everything*. But that wasn't enough.

The Great Master and his angels wanted it all for themselves. Greedy, selfish spirits, they wanted to take it from him and give nothing back.

Balaam shook his head and shivered at the ironic truth.

Then the mortals in the bunker began to stand and shake hands. The meeting was drawing to a close; the men were getting ready to go.

As the men gathered in a circle to say their final good-byes, Balaam heard a low chuckle, an evil, empty sneer. "Go, my sweet angels!" the Dark Master laughed. "Go! I command you! Follow your hate and your wrath!"

The words cut inside Balaam like a knife to his soul. "*Vessels of wrath*, the Father called us," he cried to himself. He shuddered, almost reeling, weeping in despair. "I am a vessel of wrath. That is all I am now. If the mortals really knew how I felt, if they could feel what I feel and see the darkness inside my chest, they would run and hide in terror from the pain in my soul. They would never listen to me. They would run from my lies."

But the mortals didn't understand that. They couldn't see into his soul. So they still listened to him, always believing his lies. They would never understand him—until they had joined him in hell.

chapter twenty-nine

WASHINGTON, D.C.

Ammon Brighton walked out onto the porch and saw his twin brother sitting on the front steps in the dark. Ammon stood there a few seconds. Luke looked up and grunted wearily but didn't say anything. He had turned off the porch lights, and the lights of the city hung over them like a soft, fuzzy bowl. There were rain clouds in the air, flat layers of low clouds that reflected the bright city lights, causing a hazy, white glow. Their old Victorian house was built at the end of a narrow brick street lined with huge oak and sycamore trees growing in old cement planters, and the soft wind blew now through the enormous branches. Some creaked as they moved, and their leaves fluttered lightly, creating a soft, rustling sound.

Ammon stared at the clouds. "Think it will rain?" he asked.

"Supposed to," Luke answered as he lifted his eyes to the wet sky.

"Going to be cool tomorrow."

"Yeah." Luke spit. "You know what the temperature was in Baghdad today?"

Ammon shook his head. "No. But it should be cooling down by now."

"Hundred and seven. Will drop to forty-nine in the desert tonight."

"SWA's a lousy place to be, ain't it, bro." SWA, pronounced "swah," short for southwest Asia, was only one of the dozens of military acronyms the brothers had picked up from their father. It was the military designation, and a more accurate geographical description for what most people called the Middle East.

"Got a short email from Sam," Luke continued as he stared into the dark. "He said he's done some very cool missions the past couple weeks. Said he met a girl. Said it broke his heart, she was so beautiful, seeing how she lives and all."

"Hmm," Ammon hummed. "That's kind of funny. Doesn't sound like him. Think he's falling in love?"

"Who knows. It's a strange world. Maybe he'll come home with a wife."

The brothers stared at each other and started to laugh. *Yeah, right!* they were both thinking.

After a minute they settled down and were quiet. "You couldn't sleep?" Ammon finally asked.

"I woke up a little after two. I've been kind of . . . you know, waiting for Dad."

Ammon glanced at the driveway. His dad's car was there, but that didn't tell him anything since he was always chauffeured. "You check his bedroom?" he asked.

"Yeah. Mom's in bed alone."

Ammon nodded. He went into the house, walked to the fridge for a couple of sodas, over to the pantry for a bag of chips and some salsa, then back outside to the porch. Sitting down, he heard three soft chimes and glanced through the glass and oak door to the old grandfather's clock that sat on the marble floor. Three o'clock in the morning. A pretty good time to eat.

He pushed one of the sodas toward his brother. Luke nodded thanks, popped it open, and grabbed a handful of chips. Dipping into the salsa, he grunted and stood, disappeared into the house, and returned with a miniature bottle of Tijuana Fire Sauce. The bottle was lime green, with a Spanish label featuring warning signs with a skull and crossbones. He took the bowl of salsa and, like a chemist mixing a dangerous mixture, let the drops fall slowly. "How many?" he asked, counting each drop by the light of the street lamp.

Ammon felt his stomach. "It's pretty late. I would like to sleep at least a couple hours. Better keep it to five."

Luke huffed. "O ye of little gastrointestinal capability. I scoff at your five." He counted ten drops, added one more for good measure, then began to stir the Tijuana Fire Sauce into the salsa with his finger.

"Nice," Ammon said, nodding at Luke's index finger that was dipped in his sauce.

Luke hunched his shoulders, pulled out his finger, and stuck it in his mouth. "Don't worry, brother, this stuff is more powerful than alcohol. They used to use it to clean the open wounds of rebel soldiers during the Civil War. There isn't a germ alive that can survive contact with this Tijuana Green."

Ammon scooted over, took a chip, dipped it, and shoved it in his mouth. "Not bad," he mumbled through his mouthful of food.

"Want another couple drops?" Luke asked.

The delayed reaction of the peppers, or the dynamite, or whatever was in the sauce, began to kick in. Ammon started sweating, his mouth on fire, and he grabbed a mouthful of chips, knowing he had to suffocate the flames with something dry; the soda would only wash the burn down his throat.

Luke, having destroyed most of his taste buds already, watched him and laughed, then dipped another chip.

"Good," Ammon said after his mouth had cooled down.

Luke laughed. "You can't fake it with me, bro."

"No, really. I would have stopped at eight drops, but this is okay. Just kind of caught me off guard is all."

Luke laughed again.

Looking at the two brothers, one wouldn't have known they were twins. Ammon, blond and tall, cut his hair short and combed it back in short tassels. Luke was shorter but thicker, his arms dark and tan. Luke acted fast. Ammon acted slow. Luke was always looking for something exciting. And he loved having friends around. In fact, it almost seemed he hated being alone. Ammon, on the other hand, sometimes had to lock his bedroom door and just sit by himself. He just had to get away, even if only for a few minutes.

Luke stared at the driveway, then leaned forward and looked down the empty street.

Ammon watched him, reading his mind. "You know, buddy, Dad must not be coming home tonight. Mom didn't even wait up for him, so you know what that means. I'm sure he called and said he got stuck at some meeting or ended up having to fly off somewhere."

Luke nodded as he sipped on his soda.

Ammon thought of his father. He used to think it was so cool, the fact that his father worked for the president. The first time the White House sent a military helicopter to land in the intersection at the end of their street to pick up his dad for some emergency meeting, it had nearly blown his mind. He remembered watching from the corner, the police escorts stopping traffic to let the chopper land, his dad ducking under the blades and then turning around to wave good-bye. He had nearly dropped dead with pride. How could anyone compete with that!

But the glamour of his father working for the White House had worn off a long time ago. His dad was gone so much now. He worked all the time. And even when he was home, he was still far away. How many times had Ammon been talking to him, only to see that far-off look in his eye?

His dad tried to compensate—he really tried. But he was crushed with responsibility and it was very hard.

Ammon stared up. It was just starting to rain, more a mist than anything serious, and he watched the sidewalk grow wet. "Dad's got it tough right now," he said.

"Yeah," Luke answered. There wasn't much more to say.

"It's hard on Mom too. She wants to help him, but she can't. And it's hard on her, being alone all the time . . ."

Ammon stared at his brother in the darkness, knowing it was hard on him too. Luke needed their father more than Ammon did. It had always been that way, even when they were young.

When they were little boys, Luke would wake up in the night and want to sleep with his mom and dad. They let him for a night or two, but soon had quite enough of that. "You've got to stay in your own bed," his mother had explained. "No more sleeping with Mommy and Daddy. You're a big boy now, Luke. You need to sleep in your own bed."

Next night, Luke had tried slipping into bed with them again. No good. They brought him back. He claimed to have had a nightmare. His mom had handed him his favorite stuffed toy, turned on the night-light, and told him to stay in his bed. Ten nights in a row he had tried to slip in bed with his mom and dad. Ammon had watched, enjoying the marathon contest of wills, though he never said anything. After it became obvious they were not going to give in, Luke had taken to slipping into the hall in the middle of the night, curling up by their door with his blanket, and sleeping there. That went on for a long time.

Ammon didn't think his parents ever knew.

The older twin smiled at the memory, but it made him kind of sad. Sitting there on the front porch in the middle of the night, he realized that some things hadn't changed. The front porch, the hall near their bedroom door, it was pretty much the same: Luke was missing his dad.

Luke took a final drink of his soda. "I read something today. Really ticked me off," he said.

"What's that?" Ammon asked.

The clouds broke, a thin line of clear sky showing above the streetlight before falling behind the low clouds again. Luke kicked his legs out, extending them to the bottom stair. "Okay, there's this agency in Pakistan," he began. "They work with refugees, orphans, that sort of thing. They're trying to get food to this refugee camp. Have to haul it out there in these old, beat-up trucks, the only vehicles the Pakistani government will let them use. Yesterday, after a couple aid workers had taken a load of food to the camp, the bread and water ran out before everyone had a chance to get some. I guess a riot broke out. Here you have all these starving, dying people. No food. No water. So what do they do? They riot. Attack the relief trucks. Both of the aid workers were killed. One of them was trampled, the other one was dragged from under the truck and beaten to death.

"Now, I don't know, Ammon, call me stupid, but I just don't get it. Those aid workers were there to help them. It wasn't their fault that they ran out of food. Yet the refugees went so crazy, they trampled and beat them to death . . . "

Ammon stared at his empty soda can. "I guess people have to be pretty desperate for them to act that way," he said.

"Desperate or crazy."

"I don't think you can say they were crazy. Have you ever been really hungry, Luke? I mean really, seriously hungry? The most we do is miss a couple meals on fast Sunday, and even then we cheat, but you'd think we hadn't eaten in weeks. We skip two meals and think we're dying, while lots of people in the world, maybe most of the people in the world, skip one or two meals *every* day."

"Yeah, well, I still wonder what those people are thinking sometimes."

"Have you ever been so thirsty that you thought you might die? Have you ever been so dehydrated that you couldn't even sweat or spit or swallow because your tongue was so thick? Have you ever slept out in the desert with only the clothes on your back? Have you ever looked at a tiny cloth sack and knew it contained everything that you owned? Absolutely everything! You had nothing else! Have you ever been so scared for your family's safety that you would have done *anything*?

"Think about this, Luke. I'll paint a picture for you. You're a young father. You used to live in a small village that was taken over by the resurgent Taliban and now you've been chased from your home in Afghanistan because of another war. The same thing happened to your father. Same thing happened to your grandfather before. Your wife was killed by Taliban rebels because she dared to appear in public showing part of her hair. You flee with nothing but a bundle and your little girl. You sleep in the desert for three days until you get to the refugee camp. When you get there, there's no food and no water. Your little girl is going to die unless you get some for her. She's crying. She's begging. Then she doesn't cry anymore. She just kind of lies there. Sometimes she'll reach for your hand. She squeezes your fingers, but she doesn't focus her eyes on you anymore. She's dying and she knows it. She needs water now! The trucks show up, but there's not enough, and neither of you get anything. You're wild-eyed crazy with hunger. And you *love* your little girl. You would die to protect her. That's not an American thing, a white thing, a Christian thing, or anything else—that's a human thing. A father thing. You would die to protect her. But they have run out of food. She's dying. She needs water, or she won't live through the night.

"Think about that, dude, and maybe it will make it a little easier to understand what happened over there."

Luke scrunched his face. "That's a pretty horrible picture."

"It takes place every day."

"I know. And it helps to remember the whole story. But it doesn't explain everything."

Silence returned for a moment. "I guess there are some things we may never understand," Ammon said.

Luke crossed his feet. "There's a lot I don't understand."

"Me too," Ammon said. "But let me tell you something important, Luke. I've been watching over your shoulder, and I know more about you than you may think. I mean, come on, dude, why am I out here with you tonight? You can't sleep, and I feel that. You get a cold, I do too. I know your moods. I know what you're thinking. I sometimes think I know you even better than you know yourself.

"And I want to tell you something I've been meaning to tell you for the past couple days. You have a great destiny, Luke, a great mission, a reason you're here. Think about it, bro—do you think it was the outcome of mischievous luck or blind fate that brought you to this time, to this world, to this place! It couldn't be! There had to be a reason. I think we used to understand it, but we've forgotten what it was.

"But why do you think you were born here, to this time

and place? Why did Mom and Dad join the Church? To bring us to this place. You have a destiny and a mission, a reason you were saved for these days. And you can control it. You have the power to decide your fate.

"But just as you can seek out and complete your mission, you can screw it up, too.

"That cute little girl who likes to hang on your arm? She isn't right for you, brother, and you know it. Play with fire, and it burns you; any fool knows that's true. And the first step in falling is choosing the wrong friends. I don't care how cute or good-looking or rich or cool they might seem, this young thing and her buddies, they are poison for you.

"I know that. You know that. Now stand up! Be a man!"

Ammon stopped and glanced at his brother, but Luke didn't say anything. Ammon turned and stared forward, looking into the dark night. "Don't you dare screw this up, Luke," he threatened, "or I'll kill you, my friend."

* * *

For the next couple of days, Luke spent a lot of time in his bedroom and driving around in his car. He was sullen and moody, and he seemed to glare a lot. But more than once, Ammon caught him on his knees by his bed in the middle of the night.

On the third day, he woke up in a very good mood. He came downstairs, kissed his mother, and made breakfast for them all.

Later that night he called her. "Alicia, I *really* like you," he said in a determined voice. "I've been happier since I met you than I have ever been. You've been good to me. You've been good *for* me in a lot of important ways. I would do almost anything to keep seeing you, but I can't. It's not right. I've got something I've got to do now, something very important that you can't understand. I'm sorry, babe, I really am, but we've got to back off."

She cried. She protested. She called him names and said he'd lied. She begged more than once, then started crying again. She said she loved him, but it seemed that he loved his church more than her.

He said she was right.

They talked on the phone until almost one in the morning. Luke held firm, though he was in tears by then. When they finally hung up, he was frazzled and frustrated. But he was not confused.

He had done the right thing—not the easy thing, but the right thing—and inside he was calm.

It would be a very long time before he would see her again. The world would be different. So would Luke. So would Alicia. Everything would have changed.

chapter thirty

The timing of the attacks had to be precisely coordinated and extremely compressed. Like an enormous tsunami that would crash over the land, the attacks had to be unexpected and devastating, with no chance of turning them back. The destruction had to be wide and deep, completely demoralizing and debilitating in every way. And they had to create a sense of passing, as if the old world was gone, leaving normal life shattered like broken glass on the floor.

They had to leave the world utterly breathless, with no chance to respond, no chance to think or debate or wonder or prod. This wasn't a military battle, King Abdullah knew that, it was a battle of wills, a test of resolve. So there was no desire on his part for measured escalation, no strategy of attacking, then sitting back and weighing the response, attacking and negotiating, trying to score a political point. Indeed, just the opposite. The entire purpose of the plan was to create a sense of complete vertigo, overwhelming devastation, as if things had immediately and irreparably spun out of control. At the end of the day (and a day was all it would take) his plan had to shatter the old preconditions, leaving no sense of proportion at all.

It had to be quick: *BANG! BANG! BANG!* and then it was through.

Then would come the opportunity to rewrite the rules.

Then would come the opportunity to reorder the world.

* * *

The first attack would never have been successful but for the fact that the enemies of Israel knew a secret that no one else knew.

And though the terrorists had long been aware of the quirk in the aircraft hangar construction, they had waited, ever patient, for the right time to hit. With such an ace up their sleeves, they had been willing to delay, willing to stay at the table and keep their hand in the game until the stakes were the highest and they could win the whole thing.

So the attacks had been in the planning for just over nine years. Logistics, munitions, communications, materials, recruitment, decoys, reconnaissance, explosives, and hardware—the list of technical specialists involved in the planning was very long indeed. And though almost a hundred men had been involved in the preparations at one time or another, only a handful ever knew all the details.

Unlike the Israeli military, that had to rely on its superior technology and advanced weapons to protect its lands, the Islamists kept it simple and did it the old-fashioned way. Nothing new. Nothing fancy. A simple and straightforward plan.

All they needed was a man who was willing to die (there were many) and a single opportunity to fire. Then great patience. And a rifle. And just a tiny bit of luck.

BEN GURION INTERNATIONAL AIRPORT
TEL AVIV, ISRAEL

The Israeli prime minister's aircraft touched down at nineteen minutes past four on a hot afternoon. The aircraft, one of five different, unmarked airplanes the prime minister used for his out-of-country travels, was a small corporate twin-engine jet with civilian markings and an untraceable tail number. It touched down on the thousand-foot marking on runway 08, the sun at its back, decelerated slowly on the twelve-thousand foot runway, then took the high speed taxiway to the right, which led toward a large steel hangar on the west side of the airport. As always, the perimeter around the government hangar had been secured with uniformed soldiers, though there were plainclothes security officers also on patrol. Three black sedans waited in a line in front of the hangar, where the enormous metal doors had been rolled almost shut, leaving room for the automobiles to squeeze through but not so much as to reveal the outlines of the other four Israeli aircraft that were hidden inside: a white G-4, a highly modified Boeing RC-135 provided by the United States government, and two blue and red C-21s with "Mediterranean Airways" painted on their tails. As Talon One, the call sign for the prime minister's aircraft this day, taxied toward the hangar, the three black vehicles waited until the enormous doors began to roll back, allowing enough space for the aircraft to taxi inside. Following the taxi lines, which changed from yellow to red once inside the threshold of the hangar, the pilot taxied quickly, then cut his engines and switched to auxiliary power, allowing the waiting vehicles to follow the aircraft without fear of having their windows blown out or being rolled over by the jet engine blast. Inside the hangar, the vehicles swung around to the right side of the aircraft, and the hangar doors were rolled shut again to avoid exposing the prime minister to any view from outside the hangar.

Thirty seconds after the aircraft had come to a stop, the cabin door opened and the small, chrome steps extended automatically from the aircraft's floor. Two security men stepped from the aircraft and moved quickly down the stairs, but the prime minister and his wife did not emerge.

Outside the hangar, the uniformed servicemen moved on patrol. Three sniper teams had been positioned on the roofs of nearby hangars, and a single military helicopter flew slowly overhead. A thousand feet farther out, another security perimeter had been established with motion sensors, infrared detectors, and ultra-sensitive listening devices. Behind an enormous civilian airline hangar on the south end of the runway and hidden behind a row of trees, two Apache attack helicopters were waiting, their rotors spinning, ready to escort the PM's convoy to Tel Aviv. Each of their munitions winglets was crowded with air-to-ground rockets, and their nose-mounted Gatling guns swung quickly, following the movements of the gunner's eyes. The single airport road that led to the hangar had been secured. Beyond that, the main airport road was crowded with cars, taxis and buses. Half a dozen unmarked police cars moved through the traffic. Inside each vehicle, police officers watched the other cars carefully through their deeply tinted windows.

The security measures around the prime minister of Israel were extraordinary even during the most peaceful times—and things were not peaceful now. The Israeli security operations were operating in DEFPOS (Defensive Posture) Two, the second highest state of alert. The security apparatus protecting the state of Israel had heard enough rumors and seen enough message traffic to have their ears to the wall. Over the past week it had only gotten worse. They had seen too many suspicious travelers moving in and out of Gaza and picked up enough troubling information from Iran and Saudi Arabia not to be on an increased state of alert.

Although they had their suspicions, they didn't know exactly what the threat might be. But they had learned from experience it was best to be prepared. So the chief of security had ordered additional precautions, demanding extra layers of security to be added to an already impenetrable security machine.

* * *

Because the aircraft hangar had originally been designed and built for civilian purposes and only later converted for use as the prime minister's official hangar, it had not been constructed with security as the primary concern. And though the hangar had been modified and upgraded by the Israeli Secret Police (the agency responsible for protecting the PM and other government leaders), there remained tiny gaps in the security wall.

One of those gaps was up high in the structural beams of the hangar, the huge steel girders that provided the skeleton structure the sheet-metal coverings were fastened to. Deep behind the girders above the hangar's rolling doors, four of the crossbeams joined together and formed a tiny crawl space: fourteen inches wide, six feet long, and twelve inches high.

This was the little secret that the terrorists knew.

Though the entire building was always searched multiple times before the PM ever arrived in the hangar, none of these patrols climbed up to the rafters to check the girders above. And because these security patrols were always initiated five days before the PM was scheduled to use the hangar, any other time the hangar was more or less accessible to the airport at large. So if a man were to arrive before the regular security patrols had begun, and if he were extraordinarily patient, he could conceal himself in the dead space of these girders, making it impossible for him to be seen from the ground. Then, once the security patrols had begun, if he remained in a prone position, the thick steel beams would protect him from both the infrared scanners and the motion detectors that were used to sweep through the hangar every two hours or so. If he were very quiet, he might even avoid the sensitive listening devices that were planted throughout the hangar but only turned on once the PM was inbound.

* * *

The assassin had been waiting in the rafters of the hangar for almost eight days, hidden above the section of crossbeams almost directly above the hangar doors. He had not eaten in two days now, and his water was gone. The batteries on his radio had grown so weak as to make it completely unreadable, so he had taken out his tiny earpiece and let it fall to the metal beside his shoulder. It didn't really matter. There was no one left to talk to anymore. He had received the final instructions, and his commander had long ago slipped away.

Eight days before, under cover of night, the assassin had infiltrated the prime minister's hangar. Because the Israeli leader hadn't been expected for more than a week, the security forces were on their lowest state of alert. Once inside the hangar, he'd used a small crossbow to shoot a thin rappeling rope over the crossbeams above the hangar floor, pulled himself up, secured the rope, then hidden in the tiny crawl space directly above the rolling doors. There he had waited. He had enough water for a week, enough food for five days, a radio so he would know when the prime minister was expected to arrive, and a high-powered rifle to kill him when he did.

Now, after all of that time lying on the hard metal, his

muscles were cramping miserably, leaving his body to hurt all the way to his bones. He was exhausted and weary in his body and soul. The yellow pills he took to keep him constipated had tied his stomach in knots, and the little plastic bags he had filled with his urine were beginning to leak.

Worse, though, was the problem of having far too much time to think. Too much time to lie there and consider his standing in the next world. Too much time to stare up at the girders and wonder what he'd been taught.

It was difficult to consider murder-suicide for eight days without slipping into a funk. And the pain of lying on the steel girders, wallowing in his own sweat and urine, only added to the blackness and the ache in his bones.

But the painkillers helped, and the Valium seemed to mellow the fear in his head.

And now it was almost over.

He lay there and listened to the aircraft's jet engines spool down and the hangar doors begin to roll closed. His heart skipped a beat when he heard the voices below.

His muscles were so cramped from lying on the metal that he didn't know if he could stand or even push himself to his knees. But that didn't matter. He didn't need to. From where he lay, he had a perfect angle on the prime minister's jet. All he had to do was lift his head half an inch above the girders.

Despite the pain and depression, the assassin was ready to complete the mission he'd spent years training for. He was in extraordinary physical shape, knew how to operate and repair his own radio, could take apart and reassemble his collapsible rifle in less than fifty seconds (fifty-two seconds in the dark), and could pull himself up a sixty-foot rope with just his hands and his feet. Most important, he was an expert marksman who could shoot a bullet through the face on a twenty-dollar bill at three hundred feet.

Now, after years of training, his mission was here.

The PM would be emerging from the aircraft any moment now.

The Palestinian adjusted his weight to his side, his muscles and joints screaming with every move. He was so hot and dehydrated that his vision was blurred. But he saw well enough. And the target was so close.

Peering over the metal crossbeam, he had a clear view of the door to the prime minister's jet. It was forty feet below him and thirty feet to his right. It would be like shooting a pig with a shotgun from three feet away. He wouldn't miss. He couldn't miss. Not from this range.

When the two security men emerged from the aircraft, the shooter had already positioned his weapon over the edge of the beam. He steadied the barrel on the metal rafter, then placed his finger on the trigger, feeling the pressure of the metal against his skin.

Four days before the Israeli prime minister had been scheduled to return from his two-week trip overseas, the aircraft hangar had been swarmed with regular security patrols. Two days before his arrival, security agents had taken control of the hangar from the officers and mechanics whose job it was to maintain the prime minister's jets. Beginning twelve hours before the prime minister had been scheduled to arrive, the hangar was swept with regular security patrols using IR detectors and explosive sniffing dogs.

This was the easy part for the security team. Out of all the possible locations the PM could be hit, inside his own hangar seemed the least likely of all. So the Secret Service men relaxed just a little as the aircraft taxied in.

The Israeli prime minister stepped to the open aircraft door. He was old now, and not as agile as he used to be, so he held the handrail carefully as he descended the narrow stairs.

His wife was walking behind him, her hand on his shoulders to help steady him. Four feet below him, two dark-suited men waited. They faced away from the steps, their backs to him. A half-dozen other agents formed a circle around the jet. The rear door swung open in the third black sedan, and one of the agents at the bottom of the stairs turned around. The prime minister reached the cement floor and started walking, his wife at his side. It was only twenty feet to the waiting vehicle. The security forces closed in around him as he walked to the jet.

After more than two weeks touring through Europe, the prime minister was exceptionally happy to be back in his country again. He always felt safe here. And this was his home. He took a deep breath, smelling the tang of salt in the air, then glanced at his wife and smiled happily.

The prime minister of Israel received death threats almost every day. He'd been living under the constant threat of assassination for almost five years. Before that, as an army and intelligence officer, he'd lived through combat and covert missions, including the bloody 1967 Six-Day War. Through it all, it had never occurred to him even once that he would not die from old age.

But the Palestinian watching from above him knew he had just drawn his last breath.

Union Station
Washington, D.C.

Union Station was always crowded with travelers and tourists as well as locals who worked in the District, mostly on Capitol Hill. The station was a large and beautiful building, built on three levels, with a classical stone and pillar entrance, dozens of restaurants, a movie theater, and a shopping center as well. The Amtrak station fed the busy eastern corridor between Boston, New York, and D.C., and the Metro provided easy access for those who commuted to work.

And though Union Station was a standard tourist location, it was popular with the locals as well. A couple of the restaurants were very good, and it was close enough to the Capitol and the congressional office buildings that it was an easy walk for lunch.

Neil Brighton and his guest sat at a small table in the third level of the Americana restaurant. Their table, very private, was positioned in a small alcove looking over the main floor, surrounded by potted flowers and plants. Brighton was wearing a blue Air Force shirt, with his pilot's wings on his chest and two stars on his shoulders, but not his formal blue overcoat. Sara was wearing a blue dress with white pearls. She looked younger than he did, he knew that, but he had grown used to the fact. "Is this your wife or your daughter?" How many times had he heard that line before? But he didn't mind—in fact, it only made him more proud of his wife. He had wondered all his life why she had agreed to marry him, and the marvel of her enduring beauty only made him love her more.

So he gazed at his wife, her blonde hair and white smile, and wished once again that he could go home with her. They could sit in the backyard by the pool and absorb the afternoon sun. She could talk. He would listen. That was all he wanted to do. He didn't want to think, solve any problems, or make any decisions right now. What would he give to go home, throw on some shorts and sandals, squeeze some lemonade, and just sit and not have to think? What would he give to lie in the sun, close his eyes, and just listen to her voice? What would he give to spend an afternoon just watching the sun in her hair?

How much had he given up already? How much had his family sacrificed?

Sara stared at him and he forced a smile. But she didn't

buy it. She knew that he was concerned. She picked at her salad, piercing a marble-size tomato and placing it in her mouth. "You look tired," she said.

He nodded. He knew that. And he felt worse than he looked.

"I got an email from Sam this morning," he said, not wanting to talk about himself.

"Good. How is he? Anything new?"

Brighton thought of the Cherokees, knowing he couldn't say anything. "He's fine," he answered simply. "He didn't say much. You know, he's a man of few words."

Sara didn't say anything, but her face lighted up. Any mention of her three sons always made her smile.

She picked another tomato, then said, "I was talking with Ammon this morning. Did you know Luke is planning on going to Europe after Christmas? He wants to go see some of his old friends from Germany during the break."

Brighton's forehead scrunched. "Is Ammon going with him?" he asked.

Sara shook her head. "He doesn't think that he can afford it—"

"But Luke thinks that he can!"

"Neil, you know how he is."

"He's supposed to be saving his money for his mission."

"He says he's got it figured out. He can use some of our frequent flyer miles and stay with his friends. He told me it wouldn't cost him more than a couple days skiing, which is what Ammon plans to do."

"Hmmm," Brighton said as he stared at his plate. He looked up at Sara. "How do you feel about Luke? Do you think he is ready? Is he on the right path?"

Sara hesitated, then answered, "He reminds me of you."

"Me!" Brighton cried.

"Come on, baby, it hasn't been that long. Try to remember. He is you through and through. You were a rancher from Texas, determined to see the world, determined to knock off the cotton balls that were stuck to your boots. If there was anyone less focused than you were at that age, I don't know who that would be. I mean, look at our romance. I was ready to get married, but it took you three years—"

"I would have married you after the first date, except I had to finish college . . ."

"Yeah, that's a responsible line. You're responsible now, Neil, but it's not the way you were then. You were terrified of getting married. It makes me laugh sometimes to think of how you used to act. Here you are now, a big-shot general in the White House, a fighter pilot who has flown as many combat sorties as maybe anyone in the world. And you were afraid of getting *married*. You were *afraid* of me."

Neil took her hand. "You still scare me," he said.

"Only when you really make me angry," she laughed. "But you know, Neil, you are so determined now, so focused and single-minded, you probably don't remember you weren't always like that. How many summers did you spend backpacking through Europe, going *anywhere* but home? You stayed away from west Texas like everyone there had the plague. You wanted to see everything that was out there, to experience the world. That's how Luke is, babe, but it's not a bad way to be. Even after we were married, we were pretty free spirits, you know. What did we do for our honeymoon . . . ?"

Brighton smiled as he thought. "Wasn't that great!" he said.

"Yes, it was the most . . . ah, how would you say . . . *entertaining* two weeks that we've ever had. And now Luke wants to go roam through the Alps for a while. I say that we let him. Besides, we couldn't stop him. He will do what he wants."

Brighton nodded while he thought, picking at the lemon in his water and sucking it between his teeth. "I just hope . . ." he said softly.

Sara waited. "You hope what?" she asked.

"I just hope he's getting ready."

"Luke will be okay. He has a strong testimony and a compassionate heart. He cares more about other people than anyone I know. He isn't focused right now, but he still has a few months. This thing with Alicia has really strung him out. I say let's let him stretch his wings for a few weeks. Then he'll come home, finish his mission papers, and everything will fall into place."

Brighton nodded and relaxed. He trusted her intuition more than he trusted anything; she was so keyed to the Spirit it was almost scary sometimes. "All right, then," he told her. "I guess it would be okay."

Sara squeezed his fingers lightly, then pulled back her hand. "I'm really, really glad that we could get away for lunch," she said. "I appreciate you getting away from the White House. I know how difficult it is."

"Sara," he answered, "I would rather be here with you than anywhere in the world. I am busy right now, but someday things will be better, I promise. One day soon I'll retire and then we'll have lots of time to spend together. After a while, you'll be so sick of having me around that you'll beg me to leave."

"I think not," Sara answered, "but it will be fun to see."

The two were silent for a moment. Brighton took a huge bite of his sandwich while Sara poked at her fish.

"Babe, I've got to ask you a question," she said.

Brighton stopped chewing. There was something serious in her voice.

"Were you ever going to tell me about Sam's picture in the papers? Or were you going to always try to hide it from me?"

Brighton swallowed hard, his throat suddenly tight.

Sara watched him struggle, then continued. "I know you were only trying to protect me, but it really doesn't help. I mean, if one of the largest papers in the country has a story about my son, claiming the possibility that he and some other U.S. soldiers were involved in some atrocities, don't you think that I'd like to know that? And I'd like to hear it from you, not my neighbor, and certainly not from the peace activist, military-hater, goober of a Greenpeace feminist who lives down the road."

Brighton swallowed again. He didn't know what to say. "The story wasn't true," he mumbled feebly.

"Of course. I know that. Everyone knew."

"I thought . . . I was worried . . . I just wanted to . . . "

"Protect me. That's very sweet, dear, but I'm a big girl now. I can take it. I take things like that better than you do. So don't ever do it again."

She smiled at him sweetly, but then cocked her head to the side. That was his signal to say "I'm sorry," and he quickly fell into line. She was right. He was wrong. It had been a dumb thing to do. It belittled her strength and courage, and though his heart was in the right place, it had been a mistake. "I'm sorry," he told her humbly. And he meant every word.

"That's okay, babe," she said. She smiled at him brightly. "This is very good," she said as she took a bite of her fish.

BEN GURION INTERNATIONAL AIRPORT
TEL AVIV, ISRAEL

It was a single shot to the head. The sound of the bullet hit like a *puff* and the prime minister's brains exploded out the back of his skull. The prime minister hit the floor in a heap, his knees buckling midstep.

His wife screamed in terror as she fell to his side. And though his arms twitched and jerked, she knew he was dead.

The young Palestinian followed his instructions perfectly. "Do not get caught!" they had told him. "Do not be taken alive. Do you understand us, Imir, you are not coming home! No man can resist them; they will force you to talk. So *do not* let them take you! You must follow the plan!"

Reaching to his side, the young Palestinian felt the beveled grip of the small handgun stuffed in the holster at his hip. He pulled it out, shoved it to his temple, and pulled his trigger finger again.

But before he pressed the trigger, a final thought rolled through his head: "If I cannot go home, I go to my god instead."

The two shots, less than three seconds apart, reverberated through the enormous hangar like rolling claps of thunder through the air. The echoes bounced off the metal walls, making it impossible to detect from which direction the shots had emanated. As the prime minister fell to the floor, the security men sprang into gear. Weapons extended from their bodies and steadied in their hands, they contracted the circle, closing in on their charge. Machine guns appeared out of nowhere. Shouts and screams filled the air. The security men moved constantly, their eyes searching, ready to shoot instantly. As the dead man slumped to the floor, his terrified wife fell at his side, her voice choking on a scream. Two of the bodyguards fell on top of her, driving her to the floor, the guards placing their bodies between the woman and the shots. Another guard fell on the prime minister to protect him as well, but he quickly saw the mess and knew he was lying on a dead man.

Another body fell from the rafters with a sickening thud.

Sirens wailed from outside the hangar, and the doors rolled open again. Security men began to swarm through the hangar, seeming to emerge from everywhere. There were machine guns and rocket launchers, grenades, shotguns, and radios.

Less than fifty seconds after the first shot had been fired, an ambulance screeched through the half-closed hangar doors, retrieved the body, then screeched out again. Another ambulance followed, but this one was a decoy that would take another road. Both of the ambulances were escorted by dozens of wailing sirens and police, some on motorcycles, some in cars. The prime minister's wife was shoved into one of the waiting sedans, which made its way to the hospital by yet a third route.

Twelve minutes after being shot, the prime minister of Israel's body arrived at Tel Aviv's closest hospital.

UNION STATION
WASHINGTON, D.C.

General Brighton's cell phone went off, then his emergency beeper as well. Sara hesitated, mid-bite, as he punched a small button to quiet his beeper and flipped open his cell. "Brighton," he answered in a no-nonsense voice.

He listened a moment, his face growing tight. "Are you certain?" he demanded, then listened again. "How long ago did it happen?" He looked at his watch. "Do they know who did it?" he asked. Then he gritted his teeth. "All right," he said grimly. "You know what to do. Tell the NSA I'll be there in five minutes. Keep the recall going. Get everyone in . . . no, no, no, don't send an escort, I'll catch a cab instead. Be there in five minutes. Keep this line open and call if you get any word."

The general flipped the phone shut, pushed back his chair, and stood. His face was ashen and he had that long-distance stare in his eyes; though he was looking right at her, Sara knew he didn't see her anymore. "What's going on?" she asked timidly. She recognized that look, and it scared her now.

"Let's go," Brighton answered.

"What is it?" she said.

Her husband dropped a couple of bills on the table, took her by the hand, and pulled. "You had Ammon drop you off, right?" he asked her.

She nodded as they ran.

"Okay. Take the Metro home. I'll have Sybil pick you up at the station. Go home and turn on the TV. It might be on by then."

"Neil, you're scaring me," she told him.

He pulled hard on her hand. "It's okay," he answered.

Then he thought of his dream. And he came to a sudden stop right there in his tracks.

He knew. Though it didn't make any sense, he knew that it had begun. He shivered and looked at his wife, staring into her eyes. "Go home," he said simply. "Don't worry. It's okay. Everything will turn out all right. If I come home, it will be late, but I'll call when I can."

They had stopped at the bottom of the winding marble stair that led down from the Americana restaurant. He had to go right to the street. She had to go left to the Metro station. He turned and started walking, then came back to her. He held her shoulders tightly, looking into her eyes. "I love you," he told her.

"I know, babe."

Brighton turned and ran through the enormous brass doors that led out to the street. A small taxi turnout had been built in front of the station and he ran immediately to the front of the line. Two older men, both of them foreigners, were climbing into the first cab, but Brighton held their door open and bent down to them. "Please," he begged desperately, "I must have this cab."

The two men scoffed at him. "Get lost," one of them said, his English halting but still self-assured.

"Please, I work for the White House. There is a problem. I really need this cab."

The foreigner took in Brighton's military uniform and scoffed again. "Are you military?" he asked.

Brighton nodded eagerly.

"Then forget you," the other sneered, and both of them laughed. One of the foreigners slapped the thin Plexiglas. "Let's go, cabbie!" he said.

The cabbie looked back and frowned. He was a huge black man with arms as thick as tree limbs and he didn't look happy now. He stared at Brighton's uniform and then scowled at the men. "Get out," he told them.

The two men glared back at him. They didn't move, but they cursed bitterly.

Brighton reached into the cab and grabbed one of the men by his shirt, pulling him out of the cab and onto the street. The other man cried out, then rolled out of the other side of the cab. Brighton fell in and pulled both doors closed, and the cabbie turned around again. "Stupid French guys," he muttered. "For one thing, they never tip. And their wives never shave."

Brighton almost laughed. "Get me to the White House," he said.

The cabbie looked surprised. "The White House. Okay. You look like you're in a hurry, mo'n."

"You've got no idea, friend."

"This some kind of national emergency?"

"You got it, mo'n."

"Cool," the cabbie smiled as he turned around and

dropped his foot on the gas. "No worries," he called back over his shoulder as he accelerated away. He started honking his horn to clear traffic before he even hit the main street. Brighton held on to the armrest as the cab sped along. The Jamaican screamed through the first red light, his horn blaring all the while. He bobbed and weaved and cut through traffic, driving like a madman.

Six minutes later they came to the White House. Brighton slapped him on the shoulder, threw some money in the front seat, then jumped out and ran.

TEL AVIV, ISRAEL

The surgeons, a couple of the best in the world, worked frantically to save what was left of the prime minister's brain. The surgery was chaotic and desperate, delicate and painstaking and frustratingly slow. But when it was over, they had failed. There was simply nothing else they could do.

The respirator breathed for him. The artificial heart pumped his blood through his veins. The sensors looked for brain activity, but there was nothing there.

The truth was, the prime minister had died the moment the bullet had passed through his skull. Now there was no heartbeat, no breath, no life left in him at all.

The spirit had departed his body, leaving lifeless flesh and still blood.

Both of the surgeons recognized it. They had grown sensitive to the subtle changes that take place in the body when there is no more life there. So, though they fought frantically, in the end they knew they would fail.

Two hours after his hurried arrival at the hospital, the president of Israel spoke with the surgeons. He asked a few questions, nodding while he listened to the answers, then placed his hand on one of their arms.

Walking to a chaotic reception area, he announced to the world that the prime minister was dead.

JERUSALEM, ISRAEL

The Israeli parliament, the *Knesset,* met in an emergency session before the sun had gone down. Outside the red limestone building in the center of the government complex at Gavet Ram, eighty thousand demonstrators had already gathered, a number that was growing by ten thousand every hour. Pockets of rioters had mixed with the crowd, and the National Guard had been called to help with crowd control. Though the city was technically in a lockdown, with curfew and travel restrictions imposed, it was impossible to know that from the size of the crowd. The mass was growing every minute in both numbers and rage, the Israeli people's emotions boiling like water over a white-hot fire.

Opposite the entrance to the *Knesset* building was an enormous menorah, symbol of the state of Israel. More than twelve feet wide and fifteen feet high, the sculptured menorah was carved with 29 scenes depicting significant events in Israel's history: the ancient prophets, the Ten Commandments, Ruth the Moabite, Spanish Jewry, the Warsaw Ghetto uprising, creation of the modern nation-state. As the mass of mourning and bitter people gathered around the large sculpture, they sensed they would soon add another monumental scene to the carvings on the Menorah's side. The history of their nation had been altered this day.

The crowd swarmed through the square, some chanting, some singing. A few prayed, but most cursed, pumping their fists in the air.

Not long after the sun went down, the meeting inside the *Knesset* was ready to begin. Only 93 of the 120 members were present, but it was a quorum, and the president stood at the podium and brought his gavel down. The dark wooden desks were positioned in a U-shape around him and the large chamber was noisy, the legislators talking and shouting and moving around. The president gavelled again, and the noise began to subside, though many still whispered in harsh, angry tones. The mood of the members matched perfectly the mood of the crowd on the street. Anger. Resentment. A demand to do something *now!*

At twenty past nine, the emergency session of the *Knesset* was finally brought to order.

At 9:38, a powerful explosion ripped through the room.

* * *

It had taken more than three years for the bombs to be slipped into place inside the *Knesset* building. Piece by piece, pound by pound, the powerful C-4 plastic explosive had been smuggled into the building by a single maintenance worker, an immigrant Russian Jew who valued the money more than his adopted home. In order to avoid detection, the explosives had been molded into various forms: plastic milk bottles, fake bananas, radios, cell phones, books, the heels on his shoes, combs, CD cases—dozens of deceptions were required to gather enough explosives to make the nineteen high-power bombs. Once inside the building, the former Russian munitions expert had hidden the powerful explosives inside small metal drums filled with mineral oil to avoid detection from bomb-sniffing dogs, then hidden the drums inside the ceiling air vents. The last thing he did before hiding the bombs was to attach the remote-controlled, long-life RD-182 detonators.

At 9:38, the detonation signal had been sent from a small transmitter outside the government square, bringing the ceiling on the *Knesset* building down.

Smoke, fire, dirt, and debris filled the night air. The

explosions were so powerful, and so brilliantly placed, that the entire roof collapsed, along with two outer walls. Nineteen powerful fireballs rose and merged together into one puffy, black ball, the outer edges illuminated by the heat of the core. The smoke rose, then drifted east, carried by the Mediterranean wind.

The explosions enveloped the crowd in a wave of smoke and heat. Those nearest the building were blown to the ground, pieces of broken tile and mortar piercing their skin and tearing at their clothes. Everyone felt the heat, but no one was burned, for the police had kept the angry crowd a safe distance away. The debris began to rain down on the people: chunks of sandstone and rebar, cement smeared in blood, pieces of human skin and hair. As the explosions rocked the air, eighty thousand people turned and stared together, watching the building come down.

The crowd stood in horror, their disbelief so complete that not one of them spoke. A silent hush fell upon them as the sounds of wailing sirens filled the air.

The crumbled building was on fire, the smoke black and thick. The crowd remained in a stupor of horror and awe. Then the moans could be heard from the wounded, their voices drifting through the flames to lift over the silent crowd.

chapter thirty-one

HEADQUARTERS, ISRAELI DEFENSE CENTER
12 KILOMETERS WEST OF JERUSALEM, ISRAEL

The senior Israeli military leadership had been evacuated to the underground bunker, a nuclear-hardened facility cut deep into the granite that had been exposed by ten thousand years of wind and rainwater washing toward the Soreq River.

The Israeli Central Command Center (CCC) seemed to cycle through moments of chaos and energy and uneasy silence. Three dozen officers manned their posts, taking in messages, coordinating rescue attempts, securing borders, and placing their military forces on alert. Outside the hidden facility, a dozen military helicopters circled in the air, ready for the orders to fly to Jerusalem and evacuate key members of the government to the underground capital.

Everyone knew things were different now. Israel wasn't just responding to another terrorist attack. They were going to war.

Inside the CCC, the commanding general watched the updates with a face of stone. He moved slowly and spoke in a calm voice, always in perfect control. While confusion and fear boiled around him, he was completely composed.

He knew what was coming. There was no doubt in his mind. He had prepared for this day for going on thirty years.

But still, in his gut, he quivered with fear. He had to move carefully. He had to be sure. So much depended on what he decided now.

His assistant moved toward him, an unlit cigarette in his mouth, his eyes burning with rage. He stood before the general. The two men stared at each other, but neither of them spoke. The colonel hunched his shoulders as if he expected something, but the general only watched him, giving nothing away. The colonel turned angrily, then walked behind his boss, pacing like a wild dog on a chain. He stopped suddenly, swept his eyes across the control center, and leaned toward the general's ear. "They're gone," he said simply, his voice grim with rage.

The general's face remained passive, almost unnaturally so, though he did move his head until he could see the younger man out of the corner of his eye.

"They're gone, Marshall, gone!" the colonel repeated. "The prime minister! The legislators! This isn't an act of terror. This is a savage act of war!"

The general turned away. "What's the final count at the *Knesset?*" he asked.

"Who cares!" his aide hissed. "If it turns out some survived—and I'm sure some of them will—none of that matters; our response *must* be the same. This isn't an original scenario, General Malka. We've thought this thing through. We've war-gamed this option for how many years? You know what to do now. What are you waiting for!"

"Have you talked with the Home Defense Network?" the general demanded.

The colonel hesitated, then nodded.

"What is the current tally?"

"They really don't know."

"What is their best estimate? I want to know!"

"Fifty, maybe sixty, dead. Another thirty wounded, most of them critically."

The general sat back and exhaled.

It would have taken a very powerful bomb blast to kill that many members of the *Knesset*. How did they do it? he wondered for the thousandth time. How . . . when had they been able to plant the bombs in the building? Security was so tight. The entire government complex secure! How had they done it!

Then his brain shifted gears.

He quit wondering how they'd done it and started wondering why.

His assistant moved around his chair, standing before him again, tiny beads of perspiration forming on the top of his bald head. He stared at the general, then lowered his voice. "You've got to Pinball this thing, General. You know that you do. You've got to Pinball this and you've got to do it now. They'll expect us to be paralyzed by indecision, unable to move. But you know what to do now. It's time to light the Pinball."

"We should wait to find out if the president survived before we—"

"No, General Malka," the colonel hissed impatiently. *"There's no one left to consult with. This is up to you!"*

The general stared ahead, then shook his head carefully. "I cannot act alone. And no one has confirmed that the president or the leadership of the *Knesset* are actually dead?"

The other man huffed, his rage burning through. "Are you *kidding!*" he stammered. "Do you think they would hesitate! You know what any of them would do! We have our instructions, General, and every minute you wait makes it that much more difficult. Every minute you hesitate makes it less likely that we are going to be able to finish this job."

The general thought for thirty seconds, then exhaled a long breath. "All right," he answered slowly. "It is time. Light the Pinball. You know what to do."

chapter thirty-two

Hatzerim Air Base

West of Beersheba, Southern Israel

Hatzerim has been the primary IDF/AF (Israel Defense Force/Air Force) air base since its construction in the late 1960s. Located in southern Israel, with the rocky Mount Dimona rising dimly in the east, it is a modern military installation with huge aircraft hangars, hidden bunkers, an enormous (and busy) aircraft parking tarmac, and dozens of administrative buildings running parallel to the main runway. On a normal day, the taxiways and parking areas would have been packed with dozens of fighter and attack aircraft. With thirteen flying squadrons, the sound of screaming jets and the smell of burning jet fuel constantly filled the air. But the stop-launch orders had been given when the prime minister had been killed. The military needed time to gen up combat sorties, time to get their pilots and their fighters ready to fight, so the parking ramp had fallen silent throughout the long afternoon.

As evening fell, the wind had picked up, blowing in from the Mediterranean Sea, kicking dust and humidity into the air. When the sun set, the western sky began to burn like a bloated fireball, the entire horizon turning an eerie purple and red. And then the wind quit, taking a breath before the storm.

A little after 10:00 P.M., the aircraft parking ramps became suddenly crowded again as dozens of crew chiefs began preparing their aircraft for the sorties ahead.

Twenty F-16 pilots were given the initial orders to attack. Their targets were an assortment of terrorist training camps, administrative buildings, homes, businesses, logistic centers, safe houses, and weapon storage facilities. From their girlfriends to their families, from their businesses to their cars, from their guesthouses and retreats to their military training camps—anything identified as being associated with any terrorist group—Israel was going after them all.

The list of terrorist organizations they could target was depressingly long: Hezbollah, Ansar al-Islam, al Qaeda, Qa'idat al-Jihad, the Islamic Army, World Islamic Front for Jihad Against Jews and Crusaders, the Islamic Salvation Foundation, the Usama bin Laden Network, 'Asbat al-Ansar, Hamas, Harakat al-Muqawama al-Islamiya, the Islamic Resistance Movement, the Organization of the Oppressed on Earth, the Revolutionary Justice Organization, Fatah Revolutionary Council, the Abu Nidal organization, Islamic Jihad, the Arab Revolutionary Council, the Arab Revolutionary Brigades, Black September, the Revolutionary Organization of Socialist Muslims. All of these organizations (and an unknown number of other unidentified terror groups) were pledged to the destruction of Israel, and any one of them could have masterminded the attacks against her government. Half had already claimed responsibility, anxious to get their names in the news.

As the Israeli pilots prepared for combat, none of them knew for certain who was responsible for the assassination of the prime minister or the brutal attack on the *Knesset*. But they didn't care any longer. All of these terror groups now were targets, and they were going after them all.

The Pinball had been fired. They were free to bounce around now, hitting wherever and whatever target they could find.

The first twenty F-16s had been divided into five flights of four. Some were tasked to fly north toward Damascus or Lebanon, while others were going east toward Amman. Two flights were heading south toward Egypt and the south Jordan border. And these would be only the first of many sorties. The bombing would continue for days.

* * *

Captain Aharon Elnecave felt a tightness in his gut as he walked to his jet. His flight suit was soaked, and he could feel tiny drops of perspiration running down the side of his ribs. It was almost full dark now, and cool, but he continued to sweat.

His F-16 was ready to go. He walked around the aircraft, lovingly touching the jet. The little fighter felt cool, the metal and composite materials smooth to his touch. He did a hurried pre-flight inspection, concentrating on the weapons tucked under the belly of the jet. Two enormous bombs—he stared at them, his throat tight and dry. Looking up, he nodded to the security man. The soldier watched him carefully, the overhead lights casting his eyes in dark shadows under the brim of his helmet. Aharon glanced left and right. Up and down the flight line, the security soldiers were everywhere, all of them dressed in full battle gear. He grunted a hurried greeting to the sergeant, then turned back to his jet.

Fourteen minutes after walking to his aircraft, the captain had completed the walk around and preflight inspections, strapped himself in, run up the engines, and completed all of his pre-takeoff checks.

He turned to his right, where his flight leader was sitting in another F-16. At 10:56, the leader nodded and released his brakes, and the jets started to move. Turning east on the taxiway, two other fighters fell in with the flight, taking up the #3 and #4 positions behind their leader and Aharon. After taxiing onto the hammerhead at the end of the runway, the flight leader stopped and the other jets pulled into position at his side. The munitions crews were ready, six guys in fluorescent yellow vests standing off the right side. The four pilots gave the "clear" signal by placing their hands on the cockpit, always keeping them in view. Confident the pilots couldn't hurt them by mistakenly moving the flight controls or inadvertently hitting the wrong switch, the munitions crews ran under the jets, where they pulled the arming pins from the weapons, then turned and ran back to the side. While they worked, Captain Elnecave glanced behind him and saw another group of fighter jets lining up behind him on the taxiway.

Once the munitions crews were clear, the flight leader signaled the other pilots and the four jets moved forward again. As the fighters accelerated down the runway, the pilots hit their afterburners, and a solid orange-and-yellow flame sprouted at the engines, then shot back fifteen feet. The calm night shattered as the sound echoed through the air, rolling over the airport like a long, thunderous roll.

The little fighters climbed to three hundred feet, then turned west, following in a half-mile trail.

It was a very short flight to their targets, and they had a lot to do. The pilots started their bombing checklist almost as soon as they were in the air.

White House Situation Room
Washington, D.C.

The Presidential Situation Room is a cramped series of offices built underneath the West Wing of the White House.

Unlike the Presidential Emergency Operations Center underneath the East Wing, which had been designed for use as a command and control center during a nuclear war, the Situation Room was fairly small. And all through the '80s and '90s, it had hardly been used. Now it seemed the president used it regularly.

There were half a dozen men and three women inside the main conference room. They sat around a large table that was cluttered with empty Coke cans, a coffeepot with plastic cups, scratch pads, and red-bound, top-secret security files. Three digital clocks on the wall showed the local times in D.C., Jerusalem, and Riyadh. Behind them, the faux wood panel walls hid various communications gear and television screens. A white curtain at the front of the room had been pulled back, exposing an enormous flat-screen monitor, which was presently showing a real-time relay from an American AWACS command and control aircraft orbiting sixty miles west off the coast of Israel, over the Mediterranean Sea.

Everyone watched the tactical screen as five blue triangles emerged from the Israeli air base at Hatzerim, each representing a flight of four fighters. The flights took off thirty seconds apart, then headed in different directions, flying north, east, and south.

A Marine four-star general, the Chairman of the Joint Chiefs of Staff, stood at the head of the table and to the right of the screen.

"What are they?" the president asked.

"F-16 fighters, sir. Block 60s. Air-to-ground role."

"So all of them are strikers?"

"Yes, sir, they are. We've been in constant contact with the Israeli commanders, and they have assured us that this first wave of attackers will be hitting well-established terrorist targets. After that, they will spread out, but we've got no problem with what they are going after right now."

The group watched in silence as the mass of blue triangles spread across Israel, seeming to saturate the skies. The country was so little, and the fighters moved so fast, it would take only seconds before they would be tossing their bombs.

The television monitor suddenly shifted, seeming to jump in its tracks, as the satellite feed from the AWACS burned through some electromagnetic static in space. The picture returned, a little more hazy and gray, but the president continued to stare at the screen. "Review the target list," he demanded for the second time.

The Marine general looked down at a sheet of paper and read the targets again. "The training camp at Rafah . . . General Karak's home in Khan . . . Hezbollah facilities along the Lebanon border . . . "

The list seemed to go on and on. Twenty aircraft. Forty bombs. Eleven separate targets in all.

The Chairman finished reading the list, then looked up at the president. "Sir, we have maintained regular communications with General Malka, acting director of the Israeli National Security Committee—"

The president lifted his hand impatiently. He wasn't interested in General Malka; he needed to talk to the civilian leadership, not a military man. He turned in his chair, brushing his hands across his face. "Still no word out of Jerusalem?" he asked his secretary of state.

The black-haired woman leaned forward. "I'm afraid nothing, sir."

"We don't know who is in charge there!"

"It seems that General Malka is, sir. At least for the moment, he appears to be in command."

The president hesitated as he considered the subtle meaning of her words. "In command." Yes, that was right. Civilians were "in charge." Military leaders were "in command," which was only one of the reasons he was nervous. His stomach fluttered again.

"What about Secretary Rabin?" the president questioned.

"No word from him, sir."

"The senior member of the Cabinet of Ministers . . . "

" . . . was presiding over the *Knesset,*" the SecState interrupted. "He hasn't been seen or heard from since the explosion. The Israeli press is reporting he is dead."

The president was desperately searching for someone inside the Israeli government that he could talk to. The last thing he wanted was for this thing to blow out of control. And who knew what the Israelis were planning to do!

"Defense Minister Fuad Ben-Eliezer?" he asked in desperation.

"We do have some information on him," the SecState replied. "Although he hasn't tried to contact us, we believe he is being evacuated to a secure command center west of Jerusalem. We've been told he's en route, but we don't know for sure."

The president fell silent, his shoulders slumping at the thought. He had a pencil in his hand and he rolled it absently, twirling it between his fingers, then letting it fall into his palm. "And you're certain," he demanded, "that you've tried every possible means of establishing communication with President Bier?"

"Yes, sir, we have. We have not a word of his status, which is clearly bad news. If he had survived the bombing of the *Knesset,* I think he would have emerged. We would have seen him, he would have made a statement, we would have heard something by now. The silence indicates—and this is just my opinion, sir—but I think we have to assume he is incapacitated if he survived the bombing at all."

The president moved his eyes around the table, inviting disagreement. No one said anything. It seemed they agreed.

"Then who's in charge over there!" he demanded in a gruff voice.

"No one knows, Mr. President. The Israeli people, the military, it seems that none of them know. Try to imagine, if you could, a parallel situation here in the U.S. Imagine, Mr. President, that one day you were assassinated, and the vice president as well. Then later that night, during an emergency session of Congress, an enormous bomb goes off, killing most—at least half—of the senators and congressmen inside. Our lines of succession would be in tatters. Who survived? Who was ranking? None of us could say. Yes, we have doomsday operations and contingency plans, but we have never envisioned our chain of command being severed two hundred leaders down the line. We would reach the end of the line of authority in very short order, sir.

"That is the situation Israel finds itself in right now. So it will take a little time for them to figure out who is really in charge."

The room fell into dreary silence, the air seeming suddenly stuffy and warm.

Brighton was sitting two chairs to the right of the president. So far he'd been silent, but as he watched his leader he noted the heavy droop of his shoulders. Sitting this close he could feel it, the nearly unbearable weight that crushed the president down. The president's light hair had turned grayer over the past couple of years, the lines on his face a little deeper, the flesh under his eyes less healthy and firm. Still, his eyes remained resolute, and his motions were quick and alive.

"A perfect strike," the president mumbled angrily to himself. "They have effectively taken down the entire government in less than a day."

No one said anything until the Chairmen of the Joint Chiefs announced, "The second group of fighters are launching."

The president turned back to the monitor to see another group of triangles lifting off from Hatzerim. "These are F-15E strike fighters," the general told him. "They are the second wave. There will be many more."

The Chairman held a laser pointer, which he flashed on the screen. "It looks like the first of the sorties are almost on target, sir." He moved the pointer in a circle over the first group of fighters, continuing, "This group is heading to the Gaza strip. They are eight or nine miles from their targets. That's just more than a minute, sir."

Brighton stood and started pacing as he watched the aircraft attack. The National Security Advisor moved toward him and stood at his side. But the two men didn't speak, keeping their eyes on the screen. Brighton coughed anxiously, then glanced as the NSA turned and motioned to him.

"This is it. They're going to do it," the NSA whispered in his ear. "The Israelis are going to finish this. They'll clean up in two weeks. Say good-bye to Hezbollah. They'll take care of this problem. You know they'll fight like madmen with their backs to the wall."

Brighton only nodded. He felt suddenly sick.

He moved toward the screen, then stood in silence. A deep, bitter darkness seemed to wash over him. His gut sank and his skin crawled up the back of his neck. He felt sick. He felt like crying. He felt like screaming in despair. He didn't know why—it was confusing, utterly out of character for him to feel this way, but he felt his knees would buckle, and he had to take a step back.

The blackness was so powerful it made it hard to breathe. It was as if the very jaws of hell were gaping open to him.

Then he felt the darkest evil enter into the room.

Perdition. Son of the Morning. The king of this world. He had come to watch his battle. He had come to claim victory.

Brighton felt him laughing, and he closed his eyes to pray.

chapter thirty-three

JERUSALEM, ISRAEL

The lone spirit looked over the edge of a deep glen on the downhill side of the old wall that had once completely surrounded the great city of Jerusalem. He sat at the top of a rocky lip that jutted over the dell, looking on the steep bank that fell below at his feet. The bottom of the dell was bowl-shaped, with jagged rocks jutting out from the parched, barren ground. Thorn bushes and needled grasses clung to the gravel on the opposite side. A large rock, three feet high, with a flat top and smooth corners, protruded from the center of the dell.

The spirit knew that the rock had been there for almost four thousand years. He knew that under the clinging grass growing up at its sides were the markings of ancient tools, as well as some faded names and symbols that were impossible to read, barely recognizable now as even being man-made. The rock also showed signs of ancient fires—its sides were blackened and the top smothered in soot that had been baked at such a temperature as to cook it into the stone.

Balaam stared at the stone, remembering, smiling as he thought.

His Master had enjoyed many playgrounds through all the dark years, but perhaps none was more special than this one.

The Greeks had called it Gehenna. The Jews had called it the valley of Hinnom. Lucifer had called it Eesh-al-Guturr. All of them meant more or less the same thing: the "valley of fire" or the "valley of death."

Balaam thought back on the things he had witnessed in this place, the blood, the crying, the shattered lives and broken hearts. This was the place where the idolatrous Jews had sacrificed their children to Moloch, one of the ten thousand imitation gods his master had created out of greed, lust, or fear. Sitting at the rim of the dell, Balaam relived a few of the happiest moments that he had witnessed here, letting the scenes play out in his mind: tiny babies, little children, dark-eyed boys, pretty girls. Why the ancient Jews had been so willing to offer their youngest and most beautiful to some powerless god had always escaped him, but the mystery had also added to the excitement of watching them die. He pictured the raised knives, the flowing blood, the songs and the smoke. He pictured the mothers as they watched their own children sacrificed, their eyes painless but opaque, as if they had already cast the very lives from their souls. He pictured the fathers who had participated, along with their priests, holding the arms of their children as the long knives came down.

He smiled again, a chill of happy memories slithering up his spine.

Years later, when the children of Israel had gone chasing after yet another false god, the valley of Gehenna had been abandoned, then avoided, then turned into a burning garbage pit. For hundreds of years, the citizens of Jerusalem had thrown in their trash, adding fuel to the fire that always smoldered in the dell, a stinking, smoky fire that burned their wet garbage and waste.

What a fitting monument. The city had sacrificed their children, spilling their blood on the ground, then covered their remains with garbage and set fire to the place.

Fire and smoke. Heartbreak and pain. This place was steeped in dark memories that could not be erased.

Balaam knew that both the ancient Christians and the Jews believed that hell was divided in two. The good went to paradise. The evil went to a place the Greeks called Gehenna, which was named after this dell.

Looking out on the little valley, he felt a swell in his chest. Would the good times come back? Almost certainly not. But the thing that was coming was even more grand—more compelling, more exciting, more intrusive and vast.

He raised his eyes to the great city and smiled once again.

The Arab fanatics who sought to destroy the Jews had a plan that would prove that Judaism was wrong. It was a simple plan, but brilliant, and, having contributed to its inception, Balaam couldn't help but feel proud.

For more than four thousand years the Jews had believed that their Savior would come to them in this great city. They had staked their future, their religion, on that desperate belief.

But Jehovah couldn't appear to his children in Jerusalem if Jerusalem didn't exist. If the city was destroyed, what would happen to their religion then? If the Islamists could destroy Jerusalem, that would prove their Jewish prophecy wrong, their core beliefs ridiculous, their faith utterly wasted on superstitions and lies. It would prove that Allah had prevailed and that their god had died.

Destroy their city, destroy their religion. It was as simple as that.

So Balaam looked out on the city in which he had spent so much time. He looked over the ancient buildings that he had watched the humans build. He looked over the temple and the mosques and the old city wall. He looked over it all, and then bid it good-bye.

Soon, the second sun would appear.

Weasel Four-One
Over the Gaza Strip

The Israeli pilot banked his aircraft to follow his lead. Their target was a group of four cement and brick buildings on the city square in Rafah, one of the depressing and squalid shanty towns that dotted most of the Gaza Strip. The buildings had been used for many years as a headquarters facility for Hezbollah, and since Hezbollah had been one of the first to claim responsibility for killing the Israeli prime minister, the Israelis were returning the favor by making their headquarters one of the first facilities to be attacked.

The pilot went through his pre-bomb checklist for the third time, then checked his targeting radar. The AN/AAQ-13 navigation pod combined a forward-looking infrared sensor with terrain-following radar to produce television images inside his cockpit, allowing him to fly at night as if it were day. The acquisition and targeting system maintained the white crosshairs on the southeast building, then automatically slew to the left, confirming the coordinates for the southwest building as well before using the information to program the flight paths of the bombs. Cycling one last time, the computer confirmed the location of the southern buildings in the compound. His flight leader would take out the two buildings on the north. These two buildings were his.

The pilot took a quick look to his right. Five seconds before, aircraft #3 and #4 of the formation had split off and were already out of sight, their aircrafts' deep gray skin melting into the darkness. They would hit their targets in the southern edge of Rafah; then the four aircraft would rejoin as a formation for the short flight back to base.

The pilot nudged his sidearm controller, a barely perceptible movement of his right hand, and the fighter's nose turned a little more than a single degree to the left.

He was alert, but not anxious, and certainly not scared. This mission was easy, and he felt in complete control. Flying above the Palestinians' anti-aircraft guns, and out of range of their feeble surface-to-air missiles, a bunch of old and poorly maintained Russian SA-2s and SA-3s that would have trouble targeting a 747 unless it was on fire, the pilot knew he was not in any real danger of being shot down. In addition, the target was easily identifiable—the computer would command the bomb run and automatically release the weapons at the exact dropping point. No, this mission wasn't particularly challenging, but still, he was glad to be in the air. The big party had started. *Let's do it!* he thought.

Two minutes from the bomb release point, the pilot quickly glanced over his shoulder, checking the air behind him, then turned forward again. He reached up and touched the instrument panel, gently stroking the jet. He loved the F-16 Fighting Falcon. It was a pure joy to fly. The bubble canopy gave him such an unobstructed view that it felt like he was riding on the tip of a spear. His seat reclined 30 degrees, and the fly-by-wire system provided the ability to exercise precise control of the aircraft during high G-force maneuvers. The warning system and countermeasure pods were exceptional at detecting and defeating airborne or surface electronic threats, and if everything else failed, the Fiber Optic Towed Decoy (FOTD) provided the aircraft with a final means of protection against modern radar-guided missiles.

But of course, he wouldn't see any of those buggers tonight.

Yes, an easy mission. Almost embarrassingly so.

"Weasel Two," the captain heard over his secure radio.

"Go," he shot back to his flight leader, speaking into the microphone in his oxygen mask.

"Confirm you got a good lock on buildings three and four."

"Roger. Two is ready."

"You see the vehicles outside building one?"

The pilot stared down at his air-to-ground mapping radar, which illuminated the target scene. He could see the headquarters complex, the vehicles, even the guards at the gate. His targeting crosshairs floated over building three. "Roger," he replied after taking in the scene.

The flight leader hesitated, then called back again. "Does that look like a school bus in the corner?" he asked.

The captain swallowed hard. He touched the pointer on his targeting radar, moving it fifty feet to the right. Then he saw it. A long vehicle. Could it really be a bus? He studied the image. It just wasn't clear enough to know for certain, but this much he knew: it would follow with the terrorists' rules of engagement to move a busload of children and park it at their headquarters in order to protect themselves. The captain swore in frustration, then tightened the shot on his radar, going to a .07 range. The picture came in tighter but more fuzzy and a little less clear. Then he saw the dual axles and a tractor on the back of the truck. He breathed a sigh of relief, pressing in his microphone switch. "Weasel, bogey looks to me to be a flatbed trailer. We're still good to go."

His flight leader hesitated, then came back again. "Roger that. I confirm. Fifty seconds to release."

"Two is ready."

"We are clear."

"Bombs in forty-five seconds now."

WASHINGTON, D.C.

General Brighton stared silently at the monitor on the wall, watching the Israeli pilots fly toward their targets. There were only seconds to release point, and he swallowed painfully against the knot in his throat. Taking a step forward, he muttered under his breath. "No. Call them back. It's not too late!" he said.

The National Security Advisor turned toward him. "What did you say?" he asked.

"Turn them back," the general repeated, a look of dread on his face.

"Turn who back? What are you talking about! What do you want us to do?"

"Tell the Israeli pilots to turn around. This will be our last chance!"

"Turn them back! Are you crazy! Why would we ever do that? Our last chance to do what! What are you talking about!"

But it was too late. And Brighton knew it.

He heard the guttered laughing again.

HEZBOLLAH AUXILIARY HEADQUARTERS BUILDING
GAZA STRIP

The man wasn't Palestinian, he was a Saudi; in fact, there were no Palestinians anywhere to be seen. The complex had already been abandoned, their leaders having warned them that the Israelis would attack. It hadn't taken a genius to know this headquarters building would certainly be one of the first casualties. So the complex was empty but for a few men standing guard outside the wall and on the narrow streets to the north.

The Saudi sat alone in the corner, waiting for his death,

which would come in an instant of fire and heat. He hunched in the corner, the electronic trigger sliding against his sweaty palm. He stared at the silver container that sat on a reinforced metal table in the middle of the room. He wanted to touch it, to feel it. He knew what was inside. He wanted to feel its heat, its power, its magnificent strength. The Destroying Angel. The Prophet's Horseman. The Tip of Allah's Sword. It was their Avenger, their angel who had been sent to them from God. He started inching toward it, reaching out with his hand, then stopped and pulled back, suddenly afraid. He stared at the container, changed his mind, and scurried back to the corner and waited for death.

While he waited, they started chanting, the hissing and bitter voices that seemed to fill every space in the room: *"Kill them! Kill them all! That is what you must do! You are good. You are righteous! This is the right thing to do!"*

He shook his head violently, then rubbed his hands at his eyes. But the voices wouldn't leave him. Indeed, they started screaming louder, their voices more hissing, their chants more intense.

Balaam stood with the others, forming a circle around the shivering man. They glared and pulled their teeth to each other as they concentrated their energy on him. What he was going to do was so evil, they could not give him time to think. So they kept up the constant noise and evil chants in his ears.

He was weak, they could see that, weak and vulnerable. Even now, he could still reason, he could think, and that scared them at the core. Though they could discern his thoughts only from the look on his face, they saw the hesitation and uncertainty, the concern for his brothers and the children he knew. They saw the soft light of goodness, and they worked in a panic to crush it out. It was critical now to keep their enemy and his bright soldiers at bay. He would certainly try to stop them, and they *could not* lose this man.

This was the moment they had been waiting for—for more than seven thousand years. This was the tipping point, the start of the Great War. So they had to keep this man panicked; they had to keep the hate and confusion in his head. They had to keep him from thinking of what he was about to do.

They hissed and they danced and they cried in the air. They swooped and leaned toward him, swearing and lying in his head.

"Do it! It is good!" they lied in his ear. *"It is the right! God will reward you! Now go! Go and kill!"*

Weasel Four-One

The Israeli pilot had his head down in the cockpit, watching his targeting screen. The time-to-go display counted down: fifteen seconds to go. The crosshairs lay exactly over the targets. Altitude, twenty-four thousand feet. Airspeed, four-eighty. On time. On target. The TTG now showed ten seconds to go.

He glanced up and checked his leader, who was half a mile ahead and twenty degrees to his right. He looked down and flipped the master arm switch, giving the final release command to his bombs. Then he felt a sudden snap as the pins fired and the two bombs dropped away. His aircraft bobbed up from the sudden reduction in weight, and he pushed the nose down. He banked the jet up and jammed the throttle up to military power, then watched over his shoulder, keeping the target in sight. He wanted to see the two explosions before he turned back to base.

The two bombs fell silently through the dark night. They separated gradually as they moved toward their targets, but always remained abeam each other as they slipped through the thin atmosphere. Two hundred feet after dropping from the undercarriage of the F-16, the bombs had reached terminal velocity. Their nosecones slowly dropped, the miniature steering fins at the back of the bombs guiding the weapons with adjustments that were too quick to see.

Fifteen thousand feet and falling. Twenty-one seconds to go.

The air turned from crisp and cold to warm and wet as they fell, the humidity and heat of the ocean warming the lower atmosphere. The bombs made no sound but a soft *whoosh,* like the wings of an angel that slipped through the dark night.

Eight thousand feet and falling.

Just more than ten seconds to go.

The Saudi's cell phone chimed, and he jumped. Startled, he stared at it, then shook his head.

So many voices. So much confusion. So many spinning thoughts in his head.

The phone continued ringing, its high-pitched tone seeming to pierce the dark night like the cry of a child from some tin-covered pit. Moving slowly, he flipped the phone open and placed it at the side of his head. "NOW!" he heard his master's voice scream in his ear.

The Saudi mumbled something, but he didn't do anything.

"NOW!" he heard his master scream once again. Though thirty miles away, his voice was as clear as if he were standing right next to him. "Now! Hit the trigger! You know what to do!"

The Saudi took a breath and looked down at the trigger in his palm. He closed his eyes and pressed the button. And that was all that he knew.

* * *

The nuclear flash illuminated the night, turning it into a brazen, white day. The light was unnaturally bright, like the surface of the sun, with tongues of white fire that flashed across the entire sky. Like a burst of stark lightning on the darkest night, the blazing strobe of nuclear power flashed, blinding and burning every eye that was unfortunate enough to see.

The Israeli pilot was turning over his shoulder as he banked his aircraft to the north, and though he didn't see the flash, he felt the piercing heat penetrating his eyes, as if a white-hot, burning needle had been jammed in his skull. Immediately blinded, he cried out in pain.

Confused, terrified, he rubbed at his eyes. He heard his formation leader begin to call him, his panicked voice crying over the radio. Then the heat blast fell upon him, tearing his little fighter apart.

The shock wave moved across the ground at the speed of sound, a wall of heat and energy that burned up or exploded everything in its path. Then the awesome wind followed, blowing out everything before it in a powerful explosion of superheated air that suddenly seemed to reverse itself and fall back to fill the vacuum that was left from the nuclear fireball.

Across the ghettos and slums and neighborhoods of Gaza, the nuclear explosion destroyed everything. There was fire and heat and nuclear radiation. There were crumbled buildings, burning rubble, and melted concrete and steel. Pain and death were everywhere.

From ground zero to four miles out from the core of the explosion, only a few were left alive. From four to seven miles out, most were burned or radiated beyond what they could survive. From eight miles out, the devastation was survivable, but 120,000 humans lay dead or dying inside the ring of fire.

The mushroom cloud rolled up into the night sky, an orange-and-red fireball that seemed to churn and boil and feed on itself, growing larger and more violent as it climbed into the upper atmosphere. The flash of white light and the burning fireball could be seen for hundreds of miles, each sign announcing the change of times to the world.

WHITE HOUSE SITUATION ROOM
WASHINGTON, D.C.

The radar picture from the American AWACS circling over the Mediterranean Sea suddenly collapsed on itself, seeming to suck into a small dot at the middle of the screen before it snapped and disappeared. The image was replaced by noisy static, and the members of the White House national security team seemed to pause and take a breath as one. A couple of them turned to each other and shrugged their shoulders. The watch supervisor sitting behind a glass-enclosed cubicle at the back of the room pressed a button under his desk, calling on the IT staff. The screen had blown a fuse, he figured, and he needed an immediate replacement.

General Brighton stood without moving, staring at the blank screen, a sinking feeling in his gut.

The president turned to the vice president. "What happened to our picture?" he asked.

The vice president looked concerned and confused, then reached for a button on the communications panel directly in front of him. But before he could do anything, the room was filled with a panicked voice that was filled with fear and cold dread. "Bull's-eye, this is Falcon," the pilot called before his voice was swallowed in static.

"Who the devil is Falcon?" the president demanded.

The vice president leaned toward him. "Falcon is the call

sign for the AWACS reconnaissance aircraft flying over the Mediterranean Sea."

"What does he—"

The president stopped talking when the AWACS pilot started broadcasting again. "Bull's-eye, this is Falcon. We've got . . . fire . . . into the sky!"

The president hesitated. What was he talking about? He jammed his finger against the broadcast button on the communications pod. "Falcon, what are you saying?" he demanded in a sharp voice.

"Bull's-eye. We've had . . . explosion over the Gaza Strip. Repeat, we've . . . nuclear fireball. It looks like . . . holy . . . " The pilot's voice trailed off, crackling with the static that was building from the electromagnetic disturbance in the upper atmosphere. "It looks like," his voice came back after a moment of white noise, "it looks like the Israelis have just nuked all of Gaza. And half of Egypt as well!"

chapter thirty-four

The world sat in stunned and breathless silence for almost a day. Shock. Trauma. Terror. The emotions boiled high. Like a man who'd been shot, the world seemed to look down in surprise, astonished to see the blood begin to seep from his chest. The pain would come, but it was slow, the shock keeping the anguish at bay.

Rescue operations were sluggish and cumbersome, for the area was so radiated that it was impossible to work. The dead remained in the streets and in the gutters. Without assistance, the sick and the injured started dying, and the stench of rot filled the air.

Devastation and destruction. More than 120,000 dead. Five thousand more had died in the first day alone.

Israel pleaded with the world, declaring her innocence. "We did not do it! We did not do it!" But no one believed her. The evidence was before them and it was crystal clear. Everyone had *seen* what had happened. It was too obvious to deny. The Jews had been desperate. They had acted. And now they had to pay the price. A hundred twenty thousand dead and dying Palestinians could simply not be denied.

The president of the United States made a quick statement, begging for a calm and measured response to the attack. "We don't really know what happened," he declared to the world. "We must be patient. We must be careful. We must not condemn until we know. And we will stand by our ally until we know who to blame. Israel is our closest friend and our most important ally in the region, and we will not desert them until we have proof they are responsible for the attack."

But everyone knew that was what the U.S. president would say, and no one was listening. They were through listening to him now.

The first world leader to speak after the U.S. president was the Secretary-General of the U.N. The lead diplomat stood before the General Assembly in an emergency meeting, his white hair shining brightly under the television lights. His voice rose and fell with emotion. He was on key, a perfect delivery, indignant and full of self-righteousness. "What we have just witnessed," the Secretary-General began, "is nothing but genocide. Ethnic cleansing and vile hatred of the very worst kind! Not since the last century has our planet, our home, been polluted by a nuclear device. Not since the closing days of World War II have so many innocent people died. How many guiltless Palestinian families were killed yesterday? How many more are dying even as I stand here? How many more will die before the death count is complete?

"We must identify and punish those Jewish leaders who have committed this crime. And we must ensure that the people who supported them will be held accountable as well.

"And then, my fellow leaders, we must consider the next step to take.

"For how many years now has the world been roiled in strife! Since the inception of the State of Israel, we've seen nothing but war. There is no peace, and there will be no peace, until we take the next step."

He left the next step undefined, but everyone knew what he meant.

"Do we need any more excuse," the Secretary-General completed, "or have you finally seen enough? Have we need of further evidence than what we were shown yesterday? I think not. I think not. You know what we have to do."

Within an hour of his speech, the European Union made a formal statement, condemning the state of Israel as well as any who had supported them in this most horrendous attack. Already, European Muslim immigrants, almost fifty million in all, were rioting in the streets, demanding justice, demanding punishment, demanding the destruction of Israel and the U.S. Watching their own streets erupt in Muslim fury, the European leaders cowered. They knew that the immigrants had been growing in numbers, but now there were so many, and they were so strong! So many Muslims. So much fury. What could they ever do! They could wield a furious power of destruction if the leaders didn't tread carefully.

On the evening of the second day, the United Nations Security Council met in an emergency session. It was almost midnight when the meeting got under way, and for the first time in the history of the U.N., the United States ambassador to the United Nations was not allowed to attend. A security delegation of the General Assembly stood at the doorway to keep him from entering the Security Council room.

The U.S. ambassador protested and argued, but it didn't change anything, and the meeting was called to order with him standing outside the closed door. For almost ten minutes he stood there, looking like a fool to the gloating press, then finally left in a rage, disappearing down the winding stairs.

The French ambassador called the meeting to order.

"Israel has created an enormous problem," he started. "One that will be extremely difficult to deal with, I'm sure you agree. And yes, it is true that Israel must be punished, and we, as a body, must soon turn our attention to that. What will happen to her, I don't know, I don't think anyone can predict. It will be dire. It will be unpleasant, but we have to remember this: The problem isn't only Israel. The much greater problem is the United States."

The German and Russian ambassadors all nodded, clapping their hands to agree. The Chinese delegate remained silent. This was all good to him. The English ambassador huffed for a moment, then remembered the twelve million Muslims who lived inside England now. He remembered the strident anti-American candidates who had gained so much power in the local elections. He considered the anti-Semites who had become brazen now, picking up power at almost every turn. He remembered the pictures he had seen of the nuclear explosion over Gaza, the charred and burning bodies, the dead children on the street. He remembered all this and more, and then sat quietly.

The German ambassador stood next to his European brother. Together, they proposed a joint resolution. The time had come for the world to move beyond the postwar perceptions and recognize things for what they were now. The United States, once a great and benevolent nation, was no longer a force for good. Instead, the Americans and their allies had become the greatest threat to peace in the world. Always arrogant and self-serving, they had grown far too powerful. And while their allies were few, they had grown evil as well, the puppet state of Israel having proved that beyond any doubt.

But if they could neuter the Americans, her allies would be neutered as well. Without the U.S., her puppets wouldn't have the power to wreak such havoc in the world.

Therefore, the two ambassadors proposed a drastic resolution.

Two hours later, after a nearly unanimous vote, the United States was kicked off the Security Council. It seemed the best way to indicate the world's disdain.

As the second most populous nation in the world, India would be given the old U.S. seat. And yes, the U.N. charter would have to be either amended or ignored to accommodate the resolution, but no one seemed particularly concerned with the governing rules right now.

The proposal was put before the General Council, where it passed overwhelmingly.

And while the U.S. protested angrily, the rest of the world seemed to cheer.

* * *

On the evening of the third day after the attack, King Abdullah al-Rahman of the House of Saud was given time to address the General Assembly. Before doing so, he informed the U.N. leadership that he had been asked to speak for the entire Muslim world and all Arab-speaking peoples. It would be his task, he told them, to provide their formal response to the nuclear attack.

The world breathlessly waited to hear what he would say.

The king stood at the enormous podium, looking down on the representatives from virtually every nation on earth. His comments were being broadcast throughout the entire world. Almost five billion people watched him as he stood tall and proud. He was a handsome man, well mannered. He even *looked* like a king! Strong. Compassionate and yet defiant. Confident and still kind.

"I stand here before you," the good king started to say,

"because I have been asked to speak for my people, to speak for my fallen kin.

"Now, I understand what you expect. You want me to stand and condemn the state of Israel. I should. And I will. But this is not where I want to begin. You see, we have been hacking at the leaves of this new evil for far too long now. We hack at the leaves, and they keep growing because we ignore the root.

"So I stand here, my brothers, my fellow human beings, to declare the need to let the leaves blow, for they will fall in the wind if we can destroy the root!"

A silence fell over the assembly. The cameras rolled. All sat grim-faced. A deadly hush filled the air.

"My oldest brother has been killed recently," the dark-haired king continued in a solemn tone. "My father killed as well. So I stand here as an Arab and a Muslim, one who has felt the harsh sting of death. I stand here as a brother to one hundred thousand Palestinians who have been mercilessly killed, as the son of a dead father and a dead brother, my prince. I stand here to cry out for justice and vengeance as well.

"We can talk all we want about Israel. We scream and condemn. We can point fingers and plan retaliations, we can pound our fists on our desks. We can do this and more, but we would be wasting our time. You see, my fellow world citizens, I know now, we all know, where the real problem lies."

The king paused and lifted a large photograph and held it for the cameras to see. "U.S. combat soldiers operating inside Iran," he explained. "A clear and warlike violation of this nation's borders and integrity. Now, how would the United States react were an Arab nation to secretly send its combat troops to operate within U.S. borders? You don't have to think very long. The answer is clear."

The king dropped the picture and lifted another. "Muslim men being tortured in a U.S. military prison," he explained. "This is only one of many U.S. gulags in the world; it just happens to be the most famous one: Guantanamo Bay in Cuba. But there are many more: Abu Ghraib in Iraq, Saud el-amin in Pakistan, and Bagram prison in Afghanistan, to name just a few. From one hemisphere to another, there are military prisons everywhere. Most are secret. None are open. The International Red Cross cannot get in. These torture chambers have become such a scourge, Hitler and Stalin would be proud. Tens of thousands of innocent victims sit and rot in these prisons where they are tortured, starved, and beaten every day. And why are they held? What crime have they done? Even according to many U.S. courts, they have committed no crime. Their only crime, their only sin, is that they are Muslim men. From this evidence, and more, it has become clear that the U.S. is waging a war against my religion and my people, against a culture and ethnicity that is different from theirs.

"Who will speak for these prisoners? *Who?* my people demand!

"That is why I stand here. I speak for them today!"

The king stopped and looked out on the delegates, their eyes all fixed on him. They all smelled the blood now, and they wanted to get in on the kill. The king's black-and-white headdress fell perfectly down his neck, and his dark eyes stared out as he brought his hand to his chin. "And now I must tell you, fellow delegates, that I have further bad news.

"I have been informed that we have evidence, even proof, that Israel coordinated its attack on Gaza with the U.S. president. In addition, the head of the International Atomic Energy Agency has informed me that the nuclear bomb that was dropped over Gaza was supplied by the U.S. Every nuclear detonation leaves a particular fingerprint, one that is traceable, and this warhead was almost certainly produced by the U.S. weapons facility in Tennessee. The head of the IAEA has assured me that they will know for certain very soon. But either way, the U.S. *must* have known what was coming. How could they not know! Israel would never have taken such a step without the express approval of her master. In fact, it is my opinion that the U.S. not only approved the attack on Gaza, they commanded it. Think about it, fellow delegates. Haven't we seen this before? Think of what the Americans consider an appropriate response: A few thousand Americans are killed in this city in an attack—an attack, I might add, that was roundly condemned by virtually every Arab state. Yet how does the U.S. respond? They invade an entire nation, causing an untold number of civilian deaths. They destroy an *entire* government. An *entire* nation is brought down.

"But does the U.S. stop there? No, they are merely getting started. We see Iraq was to follow. Who was to follow after that? Iran? North Korea? How do you know when they'll stop? Is this the American's idea of proportion? Is this the American's idea of a fair and appropriate response? Something nips at their heels and they crush their heads. 'Be our slaves, or we destroy you. Do our bidding or you die. You are either with us or against us.' How do you reason with that!

"But that, my fellow citizens, is the great lesson they have taught us today. That is the lesson of this new century.

"And now we have seen that Israel has learned the lesson from its master very well.

"But I reject it. I reject it! And we must stop them now.

"The blood of a hundred thousand Palestinians cries out from the ground. Ten thousand tortured Muslim prisoners cry for vengeance as well. Israel must be punished, and she will be. But so must her master, for the slave does not do but what the master bids it to.

chapter thirty-five

El Saud bin el-Aziz Auxiliary Air Base
Northern Saudi Arabia

The Chinese colonel was escorted across the dry airfield, a Saudi aide always holding an umbrella over his head, not so much to block the sun as to hide the rank on his shoulders from the American satellites that might be prying overhead. Yes, the Saudis thought they had a handle on most of the U.S. satellites, but they often varied their flyover schedule, and then there were always the high-flying drones.

As the Chinese general walked, he glanced around the remote airfield. A few trucks had been parked at the opposite end of the runway, and a couple of French Mirages and early version American F-16s sat on the far tarmac. A herd of white goats grazed in the center of the field, their shaggy coats attracting gnats and black flies. There were very few men around, and all were dressed in military attire. There were more guards than he could see, the general suspected, but if there were, they remained hidden from his view.

The general hacked and spit nervously. The king of Saudi Arabia had agreed to his demands for a personal meeting, which was very important in order for him to keep face. But with the kind of money they were talking about, he would have agreed either way.

The Chinese general was escorted down a long ramp that led under the desert sand, through a set of steel double doors, along a long hallway, down some winding stairs, and through some more steel doors. He ended up in a small conference room. No windows. One door. A single table. Nothing else.

The Saudi king was waiting. He stood when the general appeared.

The conversation was fairly short. It was a simple request.

"Do you understand what I am asking?" the king finally queried.

The general had a few questions. What was in the crate? Was it drugs? Heroin? Counterfeit American bills? Where was it going? What was the hurry? Why must it have an escort? All this, he needed to know.

The Arab king frowned as he raised his hand. "Too many questions," he answered bitterly. "Too many things, I cannot tell you right now. But what I ask is very simple. Only one crate. That is all. One crate to be shipped across your country, that is all I ask. If you can assure me of its safe arrival in Shanghai, then my people will take it from there."

The general smiled, mentally counting the money. Five million U.S. dollars. Twenty- and fifty-dollar bills. All for assuring safe passage of a single crate for the king. When he considered the money, his questions didn't seem so important somehow.

The two men talked a few minutes. Then the Chinese general agreed.

He would allow a single crate to transit his country. But only one. And only once. And, not knowing its contents, he insisted on measures that would guarantee deniability for both him as an individual and his government. No records would be kept anywhere along the way. A Chinese military transport would pick up the crate at a small airport on the border and carry it to Beijing. The transfer to the civilian freight carriers in the city had to be under the general's direct control. One of the Chinese intelligence organizations at the port facilities in Shanghai would see that the crate was cleared through customs without leaving a trail. Nothing would be documented or written down.

"And there will be no inspections," the king insisted again. "The crate will never be opened or inspected. You will see to this thing!"

The Chinese general nodded. For five million dollars he would.

"And you will get it across your country in twenty-four hours?"

The general bowed and nodded. He certainly would.

The Arab king smiled. Half the money would be presented up front, half when the crate was safe in Shanghai. The two men stood and shook hands, and the deal was done.

"Soon. Soon," the king emphasized as the general walked away.

The general left immediately to make the arrangements. Six hours later, he called the king with good news. He had taken care of everything and was ready to go.

That night, in the underground bunker beneath the expansive airfield, a Saudi technician went to work attaching the barometric trigger to the firing device. His work was monitored at all times by three mature and highly motivated Saudi military officers. The nuclear warhead was then carefully extracted from its box and put on a metal stand. A blanket of composite material, very difficult to get, impossible to buy, secretly built in a Malaysian factory outside of Kuala Lumpur, was wrapped around the warhead and heat-sealed with electric blowers. The composite material, a mixture of Mylar, Lenmex, and BHT, would absorb any leaking radiation from the warhead, making it impossible to detect for at least a few days.

The warhead was sealed, then carefully packed into a nondescript, reinforced wooden crate. Under cover of darkness, the crate was carefully put onto the back of a small military truck, carried across the airfield, and loaded on a Saudi military transport, which took off immediately.

Ten armed guards, all of them dressed in civilian attire, accompanied the crate, never letting it out of their sight. They were some of the great king's most trusted agents, but they worked under the clear threat of death.

The Saudi transport flew across all of southern Asia, eventually landing in a busy airport on China's western border

From there, the crate was loaded into a Chinese civilian transport, one of the undercover aircraft the general's organization used every day. The steel and aluminum aircraft took off a little after noon and made its way east toward the glimmering city on the coast. En route, the aircraft stopped to refuel and change crews. After it had taken off again, the original crew members were driven to a deserted spot on the airfield and shot.

Seven hours later, the aircraft touched down again. The new crew members were also silenced, and the crate was delivered to the general's men in Shanghai.

Shanghai International Airport
Shanghai, China

It took less than a day for the crate to clear customs at Shanghai, and that was a record, for normally it would have sat in a warehouse on the south end of the airport for a week or ten days before its paperwork would move to the top of the pile.

But a single call from a small brick and stucco office outside the fenced perimeter of the airport guaranteed that the crate would move through the international shipping terminal without delay.

Two hours after the phone call came through, the crate was inspected, approved, and stamped for shipment to Taiwan via PacEx Express, the largest commercial air transport that flew out of Shanghai. The freight manifest indicated that the contents of the crate were offshore oil drilling bits and platform braces from a manufacturer in central China. The inspectors at the customs facility were not surprised to see that there was in the system a computer-generated request for the parts from a Chinese-owned supplier in Canada as well as a receipt for the parts from the factory.

The crate was postmarked to Québec. Like most international package carriers, PacEx would make several stops along the way, including a stop in Taiwan, where the huge crate from China would be loaded onto another aircraft. That aircraft would in turn make stops in Honolulu, L.A., and Washington, D.C., before ending up in Québec.

* * *

The PacEx Express Airbus 300 lifted off the runway at Shanghai International Airport, its wheels dropping a few inches against their pistons as the aircraft elevated into the night air. The humid atmosphere, hot, wet, and steamy from the afternoon storms, created miniature vortices off the wingtips of the jet, misty horizontal tornadoes that funneled through the air and dipped toward the tarmac before fading away. The intricate maze of blue, green, and white airport lights receded as the Airbus climbed into the night. Onboard the aircraft were six crew members, four tons of mail, 12,700 small packages, each of them boxed in the bright green and yellow PacEx Express colors, and various larger boxes and industrial crates.

The crate from China was packed in the rear of the aircraft and strapped down carefully.

As the aircraft lifted into the air, the pilot, an English gentleman who had earned a whopping three hours of combat flying time during the first Gulf War, climbed to 500 feet, then pulled the nose skyward to an angle of ten degrees. With the leading edge slats at 60 percent and the engines at full power, the aircraft climbed quickly through 1000 feet while maintaining a perfect heading of 270 degrees.

"Departure, PacEx 687 is with you, passing through one-thousand for nine thousand feet," the pilot spoke into the tiny microphone attached to his headset. His accent was only one of many in the skies, for the Asian airways were filled with accents from all over the world, some barely understandable over the busy radios.

The departure radar controller answered immediately. "PacEx 687, direct to Ryukyu, climb to flight level one-two-zero. Switch over to my channel on one-two-four point six."

"Direct to Ryukyu, up to one-two-zero, switching to you on one-twenty-four point six." As he spoke, the pilot nudged the aircraft to the right, banking to 20 degrees. He was so smooth on the controls that the copilot didn't even notice the turn.

The copilot glanced at his instrument panel. The three lights depicting the main and nose landing gear turned momentarily red as the gear finally tucked into the belly of the jet. A solid *thunk* could be felt as the gear locked in place on their hydraulic arms. "Gear up," the copilot announced.

"Slats and flaps retracted," the pilot called back.

The sound of the rushing wind over the aircraft began to abate as the wings became a clean airfoil once again. The huge aircraft passed through a thin layer of smog and cloud around 1400 feet, creating another series of wingtip vortices. The pilot concentrated on flying the aircraft as he rolled out on heading.

* * *

Below, the East China Sea slipped into view, the moon illuminating the whitecaps against China's eastern shore. As the Airbus passed over the coast, the air became very clear, providing the cockpit crew members with an unlimited view. The lights along Shanghai's shoreline snaked both north and south, millions of flickering candles illuminating the night. As the aircraft turned, the towers of downtown Shanghai moved into view. The web of lights from the high-rise office buildings reached up for the aircraft, concrete barriers stretching into the sky. They looked dangerously close, as if they were scraping the jet's wings. It was a visual illusion that took the copilot's breath away. He reached absently up and touched his cockpit window, superimposing his hand over the outline of the buildings. Beneath the skyscrapers, the curving lines of the highways flowed continually with light. Shanghai never slept. It was the hub of so many international corporations, organizations doing business in virtually every corner of the earth, that there was not a time when business was not being done. There was no time to sleep when there was money to be made.

Continuing to climb, the Airbus turned on its heading. The lights along the Chinese shoreline faded in a thick bank of fog that had blown in from the sea. The pilot sat back, adjusting himself in the seat. The aircraft engines created a comforting and powerful drone. It was a three-hour flight to Taipei, and he expected to enjoy it.

At 0235 local time, PacEx 687 passed over the international reporting point called Ololo Teypa. After making the required radio call, the copilot noted the time, heading, fuel, altitude, airspeed, and outside temperature in the flight log. The Airbus was cruising at 33,000 feet and 520 knots. The skies were crystal clear, unusually so, with a deep Milky Way spreading overhead and Venus so bright, it looked more like an orb than a star. Visibility was thirty miles or better, but the night was very dark, for the half-moon had just set. There was no visible horizon between the sea and the sky, only a complete, sullen blackness between the stars and the water.

Inside the cockpit, the two crew members took turns "flying the aircraft," which consisted of nothing more than monitoring the instruments before them. Neither pilot had touched the controls since leveling at 33,000 feet. The autopilot held the course, altitude, and airspeed with precision. The copilot, who was "flying," stared into the night, glancing at the displays every sixty seconds or so.

The aircraft landed at Taiwan's international airport at 0258 local time.

The crate with the nuclear warhead was the first thing unloaded from the jet.

As the crate was extracted from the belly of the jet, a digital timer clicked on. The internal GPS searched, then locked onto the orbiting satellites, providing its position down to a few feet.

The crate was then loaded onto a Boeing 757 aircraft that would fly it to the States. Strapped to the side of the warhead, the internal computer and GPS receiver tracked its way across the Pacific. The tiny computer recognized the descent and landing at the three intermediate stops: Taiwan, Honolulu, L.A. Then it tracked the aircraft's course across the United States en route to Washington, D.C., recognizing the aircraft's descent and approach for landing at Ronald Reagan International Airport.

The coordinates of the target were already fed into the

machine. When the package carrier began its descent into Reagan National Airport in downtown Washington, D.C., the barometric trigger would kick in. Passing through 3,000 feet, the firing device would explode. The nuclear warhead would go into final two-minute countdown and then detonate.

Five hundred milliseconds later, most of Washington, D.C., would be gone.

"And all they who receive the oracles of God,
let them beware how they hold them lest they are
accounted as a light thing, and are brought under
condemnation thereby, and stumble and fall when
the storms descend, and the winds blow, and the
rains descend, and beat upon their house."
—Doctrine and Covenants 90:5

chapter thirty-six

WASHINGTON, D.C.

Sara Brighton got up at her usual hour, which was early, and walked down the old wooden stairs to the high-ceilinged kitchen. Her two sons were still sleeping, and she stood alone by the sink, staring at the huge oak trees that lined her backyard.

A sudden shiver ran through her and she snuggled against her own arms, wrapping them around her chest and holding them tight. She'd been anxious all night. She'd been anxious for days. She'd fought it and fought it, but it would not go away, this feeling of dread and oppression and anxiety in her heart. She had felt this feeling before. It was a warning, she knew. And it was as clear to her now as the morning sun on her face. It was as clear as the marble tile or the cup of juice in her hand.

She turned and picked up the telephone and dialed her husband's cell number. It rang only twice, then went to his voice mail. She didn't leave a message; it was at least the tenth time she'd called. She knew that the White House was jamming all incoming and outgoing cell phone signals—standard procedure when there was a national security crisis. It was irritating, but it was also the only way the White House could ensure communications security during a critical time.

She hung up the phone, sipping her orange juice again. She hadn't heard from Neil since the morning before, when he'd called very quickly just to see how she was. He couldn't talk long. He had sounded utterly drained—not merely stressed, and not tired. He was far beyond that. He sounded . . . used up. Worn out. Like a patch of thin cloth.

It had been four days since the nuclear bomb had gone off over Gaza, four days of continual world condemnation of Israel and her ally, the United States, four days of panic in the stock markets, a flat-out collapse, four days of $200-a-barrel oil, gas shortages, military posturing, and a continuous stream of vile invective and hatred directed against the U.S. It had come from all corners: Europe, Asia, Russia, China, South America, Africa, and, worst of all, of course, the Middle East. No one seemed willing to stand up and defend the Americans. They had no allies now—not even the United Kingdom, where the prime minister had already resigned, forced out of office, his personal relationship with the U.S. and Israel simply too much for his people to bear. And certainly not Germany and France, who declared their continued opposition to American and Israeli interests abroad. In Italy, the United States' second closest ally in Europe, the prime minister had not been seen for two days, after a nearly successful attempt on his life.

No, the U.S. stood alone now, completely isolated from the rest of the world.

Even within its own borders, there was an almost frenzied dissent. Two million protestors filled the streets of D.C.; anti-war vigils were held in every city, every night; calls for the immediate withdrawal of the military from the Middle East were issued from the Senate and House. Having learned they were unlikely to persuade enough of the people through public protests, the anti-war activists were ready to try something new. Turning to their federal courts, they sought emergency decrees. It wasn't hard to find willing judges. A federal court in California issued an order freezing all Israeli assets within the country as well as prohibiting international aid to Israel until the appropriate use of the money could be reviewed by the courts. Another federal judge in Massachusetts issued an emergency injunction opening the door for the federal courts to hold senior military commanders and even the Secretary of Defense as war criminals if it was determined they had colluded with Israel in the nuclear attack.

It had been four days of extreme crisis such as the world had never witnessed before. Not since . . . Sara didn't know, there was nothing in her experience she could compare it with. Pearl Harbor, perhaps, but this was far more dark. It was as if a suffocating blanket had been hanging and then suddenly dropped, draping the world in an uncertain cloud. This was a nuclear drama of a category beyond anything she had to compare.

She huffed in frustration, then dialed her husband's cell phone again. She got the same message and hung up the phone. Then she dialed his office number, but the White House switchboard picked up.

"White House," the operator said. "Is this an emergency?"

"No, no," Sara answered softly. "My husband works in the West Wing."

"Is this an emergency, Mrs. Brighton?"

Sara hesitated. "How do you know who I am?"

"Caller ID, Mrs. Brighton."

Sara knew it wasn't as simple as that. The White House communications office was a very powerful thing.

"I want to speak to my husband."

"All of the national security staff have been sequestered, Mrs. Brighton. I'm sure you know that is standard procedure during a time of crisis, ma'am. Now, if this was an emergency, we could pass a message to your husband, but otherwise, the president is asking for your patience. He and the national security staff are working through some very tough issues right now, and security is obviously the highest concern. Communications will probably be limited for just a few more days. Meanwhile, the president wishes to convey that he appreciates the sacrifices of all the families of the national security staff."

Sara huffed once again. "There is nothing I can do, then?"

"No, ma'am, there is not."

"Could I send him a message?"

"If it's an emergency, ma'am."

"You already know that it isn't."

"Then I'm sorry, Mrs. Brighton."

Sara started to say something, then simply gave up. "All right, then, thank you very much."

The phone line went dead.

Sara stared at the floor, the uneasiness building inside. She felt so alone, so helpless, so frustrated and scared. But she was no longer uncertain. She knew what she had to do.

Having finally made a decision, she started to relax now for the first time in days. Turning, she almost ran. The boys' bedroom was at the top of the stairs. She pushed their door open and pulled up the shades. Luke and Ammon groaned together.

"Hey!" Luke protested sleepily, his head shoved between his pillow and the wall.

Ammon lifted his head from his pillow and saw the look on her face. "What's wrong, Mom?" he asked as he rolled out of bed. Luke turned and looked at her, then swung his feet onto the floor.

"We've got to go," she told them, her voice trembling now.

"Go!" Ammon stuttered. "What do you mean?"

"I mean we are leaving. We're going to get out of the city!"

Ammon stood up and started pulling on his pants. Luke rubbed his eyes wearily, but he didn't move. He didn't understand yet, and his face was confused. "That's crazy talk, Mom. What are you planning to do!"

"We're getting out of the city—"

"Have you talked to Dad?" Ammon interrupted anxiously. "Did he tell us to leave?"

Sara shook her head. "They still won't let me through."

"Does he know what we're doing?"

"No, he does not."

Ammon hesitated. "Are you certain then, Mom?"

She stopped, her face pale as a gray paper. She took a step toward him and her shoulders slumped. Moving her hand to her mouth, she tried to stifle a sob, and Ammon walked toward her and pulled her into his arms. "It's all right, Mom. It's all right. I've been feeling the same way. I know we should do this, and I know that Dad would agree."

She rested her head on his shoulder, then suddenly pulled away. "Listen to me, boys, I don't think that we have a lot of time. We've got to leave right now. Every minute we stay here, I get a bigger knot in my chest.

"Ammon, take the Honda. It won't hold as much stuff, but it's much better on gas. Go down, fill it up. Take those red gas cans your dad has in the back of the garage and fill them too. If you can find something else to carry gas in, take it as well. Fill up the gas containers, then run to the grocery store and buy all the bottled water you can."

Ammon stared at her. He was simply amazed. Frightened and nervous, but amazed all the same. She was so together.

Sara turned to Luke. "Get the three-day emergency kit. You know where it is. Check everything. Then run downstairs and get some food, get everything that is in cans . . . and don't forget a can opener . . . and a knife, we might need that . . . "

Luke gritted his teeth in frustration. "Stupid, stupid, stupid!" he grabbed his hair as he cried. "Why is the White House so stupid! I want to talk to my dad! Why can't they let us talk to our father! I think it's important we talk to him before we do something dumb!"

"Listen," Sara said, her voice even and calm. "You've got to accept this, Luke, it's the way it has always been. The military, the White House staff, they live in a world of their own. They have a far greater weight and responsibility than you and I could *ever* imagine. The future of our country, the entire future of the world may be hanging in the balance right now. They don't do these things just to make it harder for us; this is the way they have to operate! You know that. You've seen it. You know how the military works. How many times have I had to do things without your father? How many times has he been forced to leave us? He was gone for a whole *year* during the second Gulf War. I know you might feel abandoned, but there's nothing we can do. And you know that your father would help us if there was any way that he could.

"Now get dressed and get the emergency kit. Come on! There's no time."

"No time, Mom! You're kidding. What are you talking about! Why do we need all that stuff, the emergency kit, all that water? Do you know some kind of secret? What's going on in your head!"

Sara took a patient step toward him. "Listen to me, son. I don't know what's going to happen. I have no idea. None at all. I haven't seen a vision. I had no revelation in the night. But the Spirit has been warning me that we have to leave. It's been telling me for days." She glanced quickly toward his brother. "Ammon feels it too. It is what it is, Luke, and that is all I can say. Now, are you going to trust me, or am I going to have to fight you? If I have to fight you, that's fine, I'll do what I have to do. But it sure would make it easier if you would trust me for now."

Luke stared at her, his face uncertain and grim. "You're going to pack up and leave. Just like that, bang! we're gone! This isn't ancient Jerusalem, Mother. You're not Lehi. I'm not Nephi."

Sara pressed her lips together. "If your father were here, would you listen to him?"

"If Dad was here, I don't think we'd be packing up to leave. I mean, come on, Mom, where are we going to go? What are we running from? What *is* your plan!"

Sara took a breath and looked directly into his eyes. "My *plan,*" she said simply, "is to follow the Spirit. I plan to follow where it leads us; that's all that I know. I can recognize the Spirit and I know what it is telling me now: *Get out of the city.* I am as certain of that as I am certain of anything. Now, if you can't trust me, I understand that. It's a pretty big leap, I know, but I'm telling you, Luke, this is what we're supposed to do."

Her youngest son stared at her. His face began to soften as a warmth filled the room. He felt it, a sudden burning from somewhere deep in his chest. "All right, Mom," he said. "Let's do it. Now, what do you want me to do?"

She embraced him, then held his shoulders. "Get us some food. I don't know if we'll need it, but it might come in handy somehow."

Luke nodded and got dressed quickly, then disappeared down the hall.

Sara turned for her bedroom. "I've got to get dressed," she said.

"Where are you going?" Ammon asked her.

"To the bank. I'll have to go down to Main. There's a branch that opens early. I'm going to go get some cash."

"How much?"

"I think ten thousand is the most they will give me at any one time. If they'll give me more, I'll take it. I'll get all that I can."

"How much do you have available?"

"We've got about forty thousand in our emergency fund."

"Get it all if they'll let you."

"Don't worry. I will."

"I'll get the fuel and some extra containers. Then I'm going to email Dad. I'll also leave him a note on the counter and tell him where we are."

Sara started walking but then stopped suddenly. "Where *are* we going?" she asked Ammon.

He stared straight ahead. "West. We should go west."

"All right, then . . . West Virginia."

"We could stay the night in Charleston," Ammon suggested. "Remember our old friends from Germany . . . what were their names, I think he retired out there."

Sara thought for a while. "No. Let's just get out of the city, then see how we feel. Maybe this whole thing will blow over. Who knows, in a couple of days we might feel like it's safe to come home."

"Yeah, Mom, okay. Now get down to the bank."

Sara hurried to her bedroom and threw on a pair of jeans and a sweatshirt. When she came out, Ammon was waiting. "I told Luke to pack us some clothes."

"Good," Sara said as she passed him in the hall. Ammon touched her shoulder and she stopped. "Mom, you know Dad has some gold coins hidden in the basement. I'm going to get them. And I'm going to bring his gun."

Sara hesitated, a shiver running through her. "Get them," she whispered, then turned and ran down the stairs.

chapter thirty-seven

THE WHITE HOUSE
WASHINGTON, D.C.

Major General Neil Brighton got the phone call while working at his desk. The White House operator buzzed his personal line. Her voice was low and professional, but Brighton could sense a slight strain.

"General Brighton," she said when he picked up the phone, "I've got King Abdullah al-Rahman from Saudi Arabia on the line."

Brighton almost gulped. "You're kidding!" he said.

"No, General Brighton. He is demanding to speak with you."

"Me! Are you certain?"

"Most certain, sir."

"Has he said what he wants?"

"He has said nothing, sir."

The general took a breath. "All right, get your voice recorders going. And call the NSA. Tell him who I'm talking to and get him in here."

"Yes, General Brighton. Are you ready for the king now, sir?"

"No, no, not yet. Where is the president? Where is he *right now?*"

"The president's caravan left the White House just a few moments ago. He's on his way to the State Department to meet with the NATO ministers."

The general's heart skipped a beat. "Get him on the other line," he commanded. "Tell him to stand by." The general didn't know why he had said it, there was no reason to, but something inside him was screaming. "And call the Secret Service," he continued. "Tell them to stand by."

The operator hesitated. "What exactly shall I tell them, sir?" she asked in an uncertain tone.

Brighton shook his head. He didn't know. He didn't know. "Okay, hold before you do that, let me talk with King Abdullah first. But get the National Security Advisor in here."

"Yes, sir, I will. Now are you ready for the king?"

"Put him on," Brighton answered.

The king's voice came through the phone, gruff and proud. "General Brighton, you remember me, I hope," the king of Saudi Arabia said.

"Of course, your Highness. My condolences regarding your father and your brother." Brighton could not resist.

"Yes, thank you. You are gracious. Now, General, as you will soon see, time is of critical essence at this moment, and I must get immediately to the point. You know, I hope, that my brother held you in such high regard. I would even say that he loved you, certainly respected you, which is why I'm calling you now."

The general only listened. "What can I do for you?" he replied. Undiplomatically, he didn't try to hide the disdain that he felt.

"What time is it there, General Brighton?" the king replied

sourly. He spoke English well enough that Brighton heard the bitterness in his voice.

Brighton hesitated while he looked at his watch. "Why do you ask, your Royal Highness?" He noted the time.

The king snorted, then said, "Isn't it 4:45?"

"Yes," the general answered.

"And I'm guessing that you have already asked to have your president put on the other line?"

"Yes," Brighton answered.

"That is fine," Abdullah said. "Now, I want you to tell him something for me. He has seven minutes. That is all. Seven minutes to live. I hope that is enough time, but it might not be. Still, I hope they are able to evacuate him in time, for I want him to see the death and destruction that he has caused. That is the only reason I am calling. I genuinely want him to live. I want him to see the downfall of his nation, the great whore of the earth. I want him to see his great city after it has been turned to black ash. I want him to see the fireball like those in Gaza did.

"Now, as for you, my good general, I'm sure it is already too late? They may have time to evacuate the president, but they will not evacuate you. So please, give my regards to my brother. And my father as well."

The telephone clicked. The dial tone sounded. The general stared straight ahead.

His hands started shaking. His mind filled with fear. He thought of Sara and his children. He thought of the president. He thought of the city and the nation he loved so much. He sensed a sudden trembling, as if the world shook. His heart started racing; his palms were sweaty, his vision blurred.

The NSA raced into his office. "What did the king want!" he cried.

The general thought again of Sara. He thought again of his sons.

He stared at the National Security Advisor, a single tear in his eye. The NSA glared at him, his face too turning white. "What *is* it!" he demanded in a high, piercing cry.

"FLASHDANCE!" the general breathed.

The NSA staggered back.

The general shook his head, then picked up a red phone on the corner of his desk.

Presidential Caravan
Downtown Washington, D.C.

The president was in his limousine with two other men, members of the national press who had been invited to join him for a quick interview as he was driven to an emergency meeting with NATO ministers at the Department of State. The presidential motorcade proceeded down E street and drove quickly west, then turned south on Virginia Avenue before pulling a U-turn into the parking area outside of State. The president's closest bodyguard, a senior Secret Service agent code-named Bull, was sitting in the seat opposite him. As always, a tiny receiver was stuffed in the Secret Service agent's ear. He was tense and alert, but intensely fatigued. Being assigned to the president's detail, he worked sixteen-hour days. Since the nuclear explosion over Gaza, he had literally not slept.

As the motorcade proceeded to the north side of the State building, the president was finishing his interview with the members of the press. Unexpectedly, he heard a sudden chime from the telephone in his armrest. At exactly that moment, a code sounded in Bull's ear. *"FLASHDANCE. FLASHDANCE. THIS IS NOT A DRILL!"*

For just a fraction of a second, the bodyguard didn't move.

He stared straight ahead, a terrified look in his eye. He leaned into his lapel. "Confirm FLASHDANCE!" he said.

"Roger that! FLASHDANCE. This is not a drill!"

Bull frowned. It couldn't be! "FLASHDANCE. SEVEN MINUTES!" his radio cried.

The Secret Service agent swallowed.

FLASHDANCE in seven minutes. That was not enough time. It took at least eleven minutes to get the president out of D.C. They had drilled it forever.

Seven minutes was not enough time.

PacEx 178
Five miles southeast of Ronald Reagan
International Airport
Washington, D.C.

The 757 package carrier descended out of five thousand feet. It was flying northwest toward the airport, having been diverted over the Chesapeake Bay. The runway at Washington's Reagan International Airport stretched roughly north and south at the ten o'clock position, and the aircraft was in a gentle turn to line up for its final approach. In the distance, the pilots could see the Mall, with the Capitol on the east side and the Lincoln Memorial on the west. Midway between them, the White House was hidden in a group of tall trees. The pilots knew that the airspace immediately around the White House was a strict No-fly Zone. Penetrate the airspace and they would be shot down.

The air traffic controller gave the PacEx carrier his final landing instructions. "PacEx 178, continue left, heading three-three-zero. Intercept the glideslope. Call the runway in sight."

"Left turn to three-three-zero. Tally on the runway," the freighter pilot replied.

"PacEx 178, you are number three to follow American

168 and Delta 352 on final. Descend to one thousand five hundred. Contact Tower now on 124.5."

"Tally on the Delta," the pilot said. "Descending to one point five and switching to Tower."

"Roger, PacEx 178. Good day."

The pilot pulled back his throttles, and the aircraft began to descend. With the flaps at 20 percent, the increase in drag brought the aircraft down very quickly.

The suburbs outside the Beltway passed underneath the aircraft's nose. To the pilot's right, the waters of the Chesapeake sparkled in the afternoon light, the slanting rays creating brilliant, flashing diamonds at the crest of each wave. The sun was low in the sky but bright, the skies clean and clear. The pilot passed over the 495 freeway, which was stop-and-go, as always, the fourteen lanes of traffic hardly seeming to move. Rush hour was just getting under way, and the city was packed from one end to the other. To their left, in the distance, the Pentagon parking lot was a madhouse of traffic; same for Bolling Air Force Base, across the Potomac River from the airport. Directly ahead now, Reagan's main runway, eight thousand feet of white concrete, shone brightly against the backdrop of downtown D.C. The copilot stared below his flight path, keeping the preceding aircraft in sight while the pilot adjusted his throttles, further decreasing his power. The aircraft continued to descend.

Inside the aircraft's cargo compartment, a series of valves opened up, allowing outside air to begin to cycle through.

The cabin pressure inside the aircraft was equal to the outside pressure now.

At 4:49 local time, PacEx Express Flight 178 passed through 3000 feet. Inside the crate with the warhead, the barometric sensor detected the appropriate altitude.

The final countdown began. Two minutes to go.

PRESIDENTIAL MOTORCADE
DOWNTOWN WASHINGTON, D.C.

Around the motorcade, more than two hundred protective agents slipped into gear.

The motorcade began to accelerate, moving past the entrance to the State Department's secure parking area. The chime continued from the speaker in the armrest, then fell suddenly mute. Three, then six police motorcycles moved in on the limousine, their sirens now blaring, their lights flashing bright. The bulletproof window separating the front seat from the presidential cabin rolled up.

The president frowned and looked over. "What's going on, Bull?"

The Secret Service agent didn't answer, for he was speaking into his lapel. But the president picked up the code word, and he knew what it meant.

FLASHDANCE. Code for an impending nuclear attack.

The limousine moved fifty feet down the road, then came to a sudden stop, its wheels screeching on the asphalt, nearly causing half a dozen collisions behind it. Bull opened a side door. "GET OUT!" he screamed to the two members of the press. The frazzled men were pushed out the door and onto the street. Three additional Secret Service agents then jumped into the automobile, their handguns drawn, their eyes wild and darting. They pushed the president into the center of the limo and held his head near the floor. Four other agents wielding Uzi machine guns with collapsible stocks jumped onto metal running boards that had been extended from the lower carriage of the black limousine. They gripped the handholds with one hand and held their machine guns with the other. The limousine moved forward onto 23rd Street, screeching through the intersection, surrounded now by more than a dozen police cars. Ahead of them, there was a sudden squeal of automobile tires, then a solid crunch as a D.C. police car intentionally rammed into the side of a Metro taxi that had proceeded into the intersection in front of the presidential limousine. Jamming his gas pedal, the policeman pushed the taxi out of the way, crunching it into the side of another car. Two Marine emergency choppers sounded from overhead, sweeping over the motorcade from their security perch. Higher up, an F-16 pilot hit his afterburner until he fell into position over the presidential caravan, his air-to-air missiles armed and ready to go.

Two and a half miles to the south, all airline traffic at Reagan National Airport was commanded to hold. Seconds before, a single Delta airliner had taken to the air, too far down the runway to abort without ending up in the Potomac River. The F-16 pilot saw the Delta climb as it tucked in its landing gear. He slammed his throttle forward and was pushed back in his seat. He lowered the fighter's nose and moved a small piper on his Head Up Display, targeting the Delta with two of his air-to-air missiles. The earpiece in his helmet growled. The airliner was locked up. The Delta continued flying north, taking a path that would place it less than two miles from the presidential motorcade. A small course correction and ten seconds were all it would take to turn the airliner into a missile targeting the president. The F-16 pilot tensed up, his gut in a knot. But he had his orders, and he would not hesitate. He switched his radio to guard frequency and cried, "Delta aircraft taking off from Reagan, break left RIGHT NOW! Turn left NOW, Delta, or I will fire!"

The airliner wobbled, then turned hard to the left, rocking up on one wing. The fighter pilot drew a deep breath and pulled his finger away from the fire button.

Below him, the presidential limousine screamed south on 23rd. Bull had a decision to make and only seconds to make it.

Keep the president on the ground and try to get back to the White House, or get him in the air?

"Ground or Air Evacuate?" the Secret Service controller demanded over his radio.

Bull turned to his watch. A little more than five minutes to go. Not enough time to get back to the underground command center at the White House. "Evacuate the Cowboy!" he cried in reply.

The senior agent looked at his men sitting on both sides of the president. "You copy that?" he asked. They all nodded their heads. "Twenty-third and Constitution!" Bull commanded into his microphone, telling the choppers where to land.

"Roger, 23 and C," the controller replied quickly.

The president remained quiet. He was nothing but baggage now. If he were to say anything, he would be told to shut up.

He sat back and placed a trembling hand over his face, then groaned once in anguish as his limousine screamed down the road. By now there were more than forty police and security vehicles in the caravan. More were joining by the second. The entire district seemed to wail, from the north and the south; flashing lights and police sirens could be heard everywhere. Fifteen miles to the southeast, a flight of two alert F-16s took off from Andrews Air Force Base and flew in afterburner to set up a combat patrol overhead. Below them, a single Air Force chopper took to the air, followed by four other emergency evacuation choppers, all of them heading toward the Mall. They would set down in the grass outside the Capitol Building to begin the evacuation of the senior congressional leadership.

The Marine presidential helicopters had moved into position. "Birdeyes are ready," the lead pilot said.

The limousine and its security escorts accelerated down the crowded city street to seventy miles an hour. At the corner of 23rd and Constitution, their brakes squealed and burned, hot smoke belching from their tires. The road had already been cleared by Secret Service SUVs, and the two choppers were sitting down in the middle of the street.

"GO!" Bull screamed before the limousine had even come to a stop.

The doors to the president's black sedan burst open. The agents pushed the president out, nearly knocking him down. A half-dozen men were waiting to surround him and they grouped together, forming a protective ring, before shoving him into the second helicopter. The president felt like a child, helpless and weak. A group of other agents propelled a presidential look-alike into a second limousine, and it squealed away. In seconds, it was over. Doors slammed, tires squealed, the choppers lifted into the air. The decoy presidential limousines drove away, heading east on Constitution Avenue for two blocks, then split up, each limousine heading in different directions toward the White House.

Inside the Marine helicopter, the president was surrounded by his men.

"Which way?" the pilot shouted.

Bull did not know. Where was the attack coming from? What was the safest direction to go?

"Give me a vector!" the pilot demanded again as the chopper lifted into the air.

Bull spoke into his radio. "We don't know, we don't know!" was all he heard in reply.

Bull looked north and then south. The chopper was at five hundred feet. Glancing out his window, he saw the line of airliners flying away from Reagan International. They had all been turned away when the FLASHDANCE had been called.

Could it be the weapon was loaded on one of the airliners? he wondered. It was only a guess, but it was all he had.

"Turn north!" he screamed to the pilot. "Get away from all the airports as quickly as you can!"

The chopper's nose dropped as it accelerated. The pilot let it fall, leveling to just above the trees. He steered toward the small canyon that wound its way on the west side of D.C., following the contours of the Potomac River, seeking cover from the cut-out terrain.

The Secret Service agent looked down at his watch.

Less than one minute.

He took a long gulp of air.

The control tower at Reagan International Airport was set in a panic. The senior air traffic controller's voice suddenly crackled over the radio. "All aircraft approaching Reagan International Airport, TURN AWAY FROM THE AIRPORT NOW! This is an emergency message. ALL AIRCRAFT *MUST* COMPLY! All inbound aircraft turn away. Proceed under VFR flight rules to your nearest holding point. All aircraft on the ground at Reagan, HOLD YOUR POSITION NOW! Delta aircraft on takeoff roll, *abort* if you can. This is a national emergency and this is not a drill. I say again, all aircraft approaching Reagan, CLEAR THIS AIRSPACE NOW!"

The PacEx pilots didn't hesitate. The aircraft banked up and started turning away. They were very low, only three hundred feet in the air. Their gear had been extended. They had been ready to land.

Inside their cargo compartment, the timer continued counting.

Thirty seconds to go.

The aircraft's wing dipped and the nose climbed as the jet turned away. The pilot shoved up the power and accelerated, then set a course for their hold point on the east side of the city. The aircraft's landing gear receded into its belly.

They were on the southeast side of the White House by now.

The Potomac River drifted under the aircraft's nose. To the west, the Pentagon was only half a mile away.

The aircraft continued turning, banking up on its wing.

Twenty seconds to go.

The White House fell in the distance behind it, little more than three miles away.

The aircraft leveled out and kept climbing.

Five seconds to go.

"All aircraft . . . " the controller started crying through the radio once again.

Then there was a bright light. An explosion.

And his world disappeared.

The presidential helicopter was four miles from the epicenter of the nuclear fire ball. It was low, seeking shelter among the wide canyons that had been carved by the Potomac Falls. The light flashed from behind it, causing the nuclear-hardened windows to turn instantly opaque. Then the wall of superheated air approached the helicopter at three times the speed of sound. The compressed air smashed the helicopter, sending it up on its side.

The Secret Service agent threw his body across the president to protect him, all the time crying in fear.

The energy released in a nuclear reaction is ten million times greater than in an equivalent chemical reaction. While a conventional bomb derives its power from the rapid decomposition of a burning compound, this reaction only releases the energy from the outermost electrons in the atom. An atomic bomb, on the other hand, reaches deep into the nuclei, destroying the very nucleus that holds it together.

The Pakistani nuclear physicists who designed and built their nuclear warheads didn't understand everything Einstein taught in his Special Theory of Relativity, but they understood the basics. The combined energy of mass and speed equaled a very big bang.

The Pakistani warhead hidden inside the PacEx aircraft was a medium-sized weapon, one of the newest the Pakistani government had produced. A simple device, similar to the Little Boy that was dropped over Hiroshima, Japan, it was small and yet extremely powerful.

The simple fact was, the shelter under the White House was not large enough to protect all of the staff. More than a thousand people worked in the White House, and the underground shelter could take no more than half of them.

General Brighton was on the access list to the shelter, but he remained at his desk for as long as he could. The other staff evacuated around him, but he remained on the phone. Once he knew that the president was onboard the evacuation chopper, he made one more frantic call to the Pentagon to tell them what was going on.

He looked down at his watch—4:50. Less than two minutes to go.

Standing, he turned and ran for the stairwell. He had drilled it many times, and he knew exactly where to go.

He ran down the hallway, turned right down another hallway and across the Portola porch. Down a flight of stairs, a short hallway. He came to the double doors. He glanced again at his watch as he ran. Fifty seconds to go.

He pushed on the door. But it didn't move. He pushed again, and started calling.

The door was locked.

Someone had panicked. They hadn't waited. The door was shut tight.

He banged the door with his fist, then turned and started running. Up the stairs, on the other side of the hallway, was another set of stairs, another access door.

He started up the stairs, reached the top, then saw the bright flash of light.

The stairwell collapsed in a fury of white heat and smoke.

But General Brighton felt nothing, for he was already dead.

Over the landscape of downtown Washington, D.C., the bright light flashed across the sky as the second sun appeared.

The initial destruction of heat was almost instantaneous. The fireball over Washington was a horrifying sight, a boiling mushroom cloud capped with a crescent of white from condensation and heat. The fireball was white in the center, with orange and red tints at the rim. Below the fireball was a thick column of fiery dust and smoke that reached down to the ground, a solid pillar of fire that seemed to support the fireball like a golf ball on a tee.

There was no time to react, no time even to look up.

The instant the weapon went off, a burst of supersonic pressure moved across the ground, demolishing everything below into cinder and smoke. A donut ring of debris rolled outward from the center of the explosion. The fireball illuminated the day from overhead, much brighter than the sun, creating black and devilish shadows that danced in front of the expanding ring of debris.

The first indication on the ground was a two-second blast of white light and heat. Then the fireball rolled upward through the sky, more than a thousand feet wide. Ten thousand degrees at the center, the thermal radiation burst outward at the speed of light, burning everything it touched almost instantly. Clothes, flesh, hair, wood, asphalt, paper, shingles, plastic, steel—everything turned to ash underneath the rolling cloud. Then, like thunder after lightning, a high-pressure blast wave followed the burst of radiation by a second or two. It moved across the ground, creating a ring of enormous overpressure at the front of the blast while tornado-force winds rushed in to fill the vacuum behind. Steel buildings blew apart as if they were made of paper and sticks; houses fell over and burst into flames; high-rise hotels blew to pieces as if they were nothing but mist. Oak trees snapped at ground level and vanished into ash, smoke, and heat. The sand on the beach along the river was instantly baked into glass, leaving human shadows etched in the glossy formations where innocent children had played. Water in the Chesapeake Bay boiled and rose in clouds of radiated steam, then fell almost instantly back to earth as contaminated rain. Ash, dust, and dirt were pulled thirty thousand feet into the air and sucked into the rolling fireball in the upper atmosphere. The fallout blew northeast, toward the city of Baltimore and the suburbs on the outskirts of D.C.

As the fireball rose, it grew dark, a horrible red and purplish hue. Below it, there was nothing but black ash and baked earth.

* * *

The fireball began to dissipate.

Below it, the devastation spread for miles in a near-perfect ring. Two miles under the detonation, there was nothing but blackness and smoke, a circle of smooth ash and nearly perfect level ground. Here and there, a steel rod or square of cement protruded from the smoothed-over debris. Four miles from the center, a few steel structures remained, the framework of once-mighty office buildings and grand hotels. Here, the sidewalks were baked into ash and the hulks of burned-out cars were tossed on their sides. Four miles from the epicenter, at

Bolling Air Force Base, the presidential fleet of helicopters were burned in their hangars, melted as if they were wax. Cars and buses had been lifted, blown into pieces, and scattered through the air. The devastation grew less intense with each passing mile, but it was seven miles out before there could be found a green blade of grass.

A few minutes after the explosion, the fireball rose into the atmosphere and normal daylight returned.

Then the sounds and smells of human suffering began to drift through the air.

chapter thirty-eight

BLADE 45
TWENTY-SIX MILES SOUTHWEST OF BASRA, IRAQ

Sergeant Samuel Brighton sat in the gunner's seat, looking out on the nighttime desert as it passed below. Lieutenant Joseph Calton sat opposite him. They were the only two men in the chopper, except for the pilots, who were sitting in the cockpit in front. The cabin doors of the HH-60 helicopter were pinned back, and the cool night wind gusted though the open cabin. The pilots were talking to each other, using the aircraft interphone. Sam and Bono rode in silence. They wore their combat fatigues, and underneath their seats were four tan-and-brown canvas bags. All of their gear had been stuffed inside them. They held their Kevlar helmets in their hands.

"Where we going?" Sam asked Bono. He had to yell above the roar of the engines and blades to be heard.

The lieutenant shrugged, then leaned to Sam's ear. "We're picking up a charter flight down in Basra. Someone's going to meet us. That's really all I know."

"Come on, come on, I think you know more than that."

Bono shook his head. "Really, that's all the colonel would tell me for now."

Sam sat back, satisfied. "We're going to be Cherokees, baby!" He slapped the lieutenant on the knee. "The best of the best. The razor tip of the spear!"

Bono leaned closer to him so he didn't have to yell quite so loud. "I thought that Deltas were the best?"

"Yeah, well, that's before we were invited to join the Cherokees."

"You realize, of course, that we're so good we won't even be able to tell anyone what we do. There'll be no pride or ego. We won't be able to say anything. The Cherokees are so highly classified, we can't even confirm our code word. We can't brag. We can't talk. And when we hear the cover story they provide us, I bet we'll see that the girls will not be impressed."

Sam deflated a little, then brightened up again. "When it's over, we can tell them."

Bono smiled and nodded.

Sam stared at the moonlight night passing by. Reflecting the stars, the desert looked like a huge, silver ocean, the dunes enormous waves that were frozen at their crest. "Why do you think they chose us?" Sam asked after a while.

Bono was sucking on a lollipop, and he pulled it from his mouth. "They chose me," he yelled, "because I'm fluent in Arabic. That, and I could pass for any of the locals, thanks to my mother, you know. They chose you because I said I wouldn't go without you."

Sam hesitated. "Really," he said.

"Yep," Bono answered. "You're the best sergeant in the unit. Since the day that I got here, that's how I've felt. After what you did for that girl . . ."

There was a sudden motion from the front of the cockpit, and both men looked forward. One of the pilots was shaking. The other one had lifted both arms to the sky. He seemed to cry out in anguish, and the chopper wobbled up on its side.

The two soldiers stared at the pilots, then looked at each other. "What's going on?" Sam asked.

Bono shook his head.

The helicopter suddenly dropped toward the desert, flared aggressively, then set down hard on the rocks and bounced until it came to a stop. The engines kept going, but both pilots stared ahead. One of them wiped his Nomex glove across his face. The other one bowed his head. They seemed to have completely forgotten about the two troops in the back.

Bono watched, shaking his head in confusion. "Might be engine trouble," he said.

Sam had been on helicopters when they'd had engine trouble before. This wasn't an engine problem. This was something else.

"Hey, what's going on!" he shouted to the pilot nearest him.

Both of them ignored him. Either that, or they didn't hear.

"I'll find out," Bono said. He undid his harness and crawled forward. "What's happening?" he asked.

Both of the pilots were crying. Bono's face showed confusion and fear. Sam watched him carefully, a sickness rising inside. The copilot rolled the throttles back so they could talk without yelling. Bono listened, then seemed to fold over as if someone had punched him in the gut.

He looked up to ask another question, but the pilot shook his head.

Bono hunched his shoulders, looked away, then pushed himself backward across the cabin floor. Even in the dim light, Sam could see that his face was pale. "What is it?" he demanded.

"Oh, geez," Bono muttered.

Sam felt a rising sense of dread. "Tell me!" he demanded.

Bono took his hand. "There was a nuclear detonation.

They said that D.C. is gone. They think a quarter of a million people are dead. The president, all his cabinet, the Congress, the Supreme Court . . . everyone . . . all the city . . . everything is gone."

Sam sat back. He didn't believe it. It was some kind of sick joke. He thought of his father in the White House. His mother and brothers lived not too far from there. "No," he muttered weakly. "Bono, you have to be wrong."

"Everything . . . " Bono stammered. He didn't look at Sam anymore. "Everything . . . everybody . . . our government gone . . . " Then he stopped suddenly. How could he be so stupid! How could he have forgotten!

He turned back to his friend. "I'm so sorry, Sam . . . your family . . . "

Sam angrily shook his head. "It can't be!" he almost shouted. Bono just stared at him.

Sam saw the anguish in his expression and it finally sunk in. He took a slow breath and held it, then unbuckled his lap belt and leaned over, falling onto the cool desert sand.

State Road 68
Southern West Virginia

Ammon drove, his eyes tearing, his hands trembling on the wheel. Luke was sitting in the back, holding his face on his palms. Sara stared straight ahead. She seemed not to react at all.

The radio announcer cut back and forth from one special report to another. Everyone knew precious little about the situation in D.C., and the reports from across the rest of the nation were incalculably bad.

There had been no communication with the president. Was he dead or alive? Congress had been in session at the time of the detonation, and most of them were certainly gone. The reports of destruction throughout the capital were simply unbelievable. There was little left inside the Beltway. Two hundred thousand . . . perhaps a million . . . who knew how many were dead?

Across America, there was panic in many city streets. The grocery stores had been raided within a few hours, leaving nothing on their shelves. The freeways were crammed with hordes of panicked masses fleeing all the major cities. Al Jezzera television was reporting that five American cities would be destroyed, one city hit with a nuclear bomb every day for the next five days. So far the U.S. government had no response to the report, but everyone seemed to believe that Washington would be the first, not the last American city to be hit. Fuel was being hoarded, the pipelines and underground fuel tanks that fed each service station running dry within hours. The cities still had electricity, but in order to conserve the suddenly limited reserve of energy resources, all the power plants had been ordered to cut back their output, leaving brownouts and blackouts across almost every state.

The reports went on and on: riots in New York, rumors of an impending nuclear attack on L.A., almost a hundred people trampled or run over in the streets as two million panicked people tried to flee.

In less than a day, in less than a few hours, order had been replaced by chaos. The sense of invincibility that had permeated the nation for more than two hundred years had been replaced by an utter sense of pandemonium and vulnerability.

All in one afternoon. After a single attack.

The reporters kept on talking. All of the airports had been closed. No civilian air traffic was allowed to take off, and all airliners already in the air had been diverted away from the major cities to alternate landing airports. The roads leading out of New York City were completely impassable now; more than four hundred accidents had been reported on the Jersey Turnpike alone. Hundreds of thousands could be seen walking . . . the same thing in Seattle . . . Chicago . . . Dallas . . . every major city . . . pandemonium . . . armed men stealing people's vehicles . . . siphoning the fuel right out of their tanks . . . shootings in Nashville . . . looting in Manhattan . . . fires reported in downtown Chicago . . . the Secretary of Interior was the highest ranking government official to be identified . . . he broadcast a desperate call for order from some unknown location, but he had not been seen on TV . . . false reports of foreign terrorists taking hostages in downtown Miami . . .

Ammon listened, shaking his head in despair.

The anchorman suddenly cut to another reporter: a military pilot had reported flying directly over the White House, or at least he thought it was the White House, or where the White House used to be . . .

Sara moaned in anguish as she listened to the reporter's voice. Ammon reached for her hand and held it painfully tight. "Remember, Mom, there's the underground Situation Room. He would be safe down there. He's all right, I promise . . . " He squeezed her hand again, trying to sound convincing.

But Sara knew it wasn't true.

She had lost her husband, the only man she had ever loved, the light of her life for the past twenty-five years, the man who had brought her more joy than any person had a right to ask. The father of her children, the north star in her life, the man who had held her and loved her and kissed the tears from her eyes.

He was gone now. And she knew that, because she felt him near. He was speaking to her as he always had. "I'm so sorry," he seemed to say. "I'm sorry that I wasn't there to be with you, but it was supposed to end this way. I have another work.

So do you now. Keep the faith. Carry on. I will be waiting for you, Sara, and I will always be near. You will feel my breath in the morning, in the soft warmth of the sun. I will look for you in the evenings. Then we'll be together again."

Sara brought her hand to her face to hide her quivering lip. "I love you, Neil," she muttered.

And his spirit was gone.

Ammon glanced over at his mother. "What did you say, Mom?" he asked.

She turned to him, her eyes red, her cheeks stained with tears. "I said I love . . . " she answered, then glanced back at Luke. "I love you both so much!" she repeated.

Ammon kept driving, but he had slowed to a crawl. He wiped his eyes and bit his lip and kept the car moving west.

Luke leaned forward from the backseat and put his arms around his mom. He leaned into her shoulder and wept like a five-year-old boy. "I want my dad. I want my dad. I want my dad," he cried.

Sara turned around and held him. "I love you, Luke," she said as she held his head. "Your father loves you. You know he loves you."

"I want my dad," he cried again.

epilogue

Mount Aatte
North of Peshawar, Pakistan

Omar carried the young boy on his shoulders as he made his way up the final crest on the trail. It was steep and dangerous, with a vertical drop on his left that fell almost three thousand feet. The mountain was rocky and bare, and the trail cut back and forth a dozen times as it wound its way up. Omar huffed as he toiled, his breath coming in gasps though his footsteps remained steady as he climbed up the trail.

A third of the way up the mountain the ridge suddenly dropped, revealing a hidden valley on the other side, a gentle canyon tucked neatly between the extended ridgeline and the mountain: rolling green hills, a small river, fruit trees, and long grass. It was wet, the ground spongy and soft from the previous night's storms. Above the river, against the mountain, the rising terrain had been leveled, a thousand years of backbreaking work turning the side of the mountain into ascending terraces, some less than ten or twelve feet across. Wheat and oats had been planted on each terrace, and the grain was full now, the heads plump, almost ripe. The growing season was short on the mountain, and the wheat would barely have time to turn golden before the first snowfalls came.

To call the cluster of small mud huts and thatch barns a village would have been an overly generous description. There was no road to the houses, no electricity, no water except what they drew from the river. Even the river valley below them was isolated, and the small village hidden behind the jutting ridge was even more remote.

Omar stood at the crest of the hill where the trail broke from a thick stand of pines. Looking down on the hidden valley, he finally smiled.

Remote. Isolated. The people who lived here were shepherds and farmers who worked the dirt with their hands. The outside world meant nothing to them. And the feeling was reciprocated—they meant nothing to the world.

Omar relaxed for the first time in days.

It was a very long way from home, a long way from Iran. Even further from Saudi Arabia. To another world he had come.

Here the prince would be safe.

He adjusted the boy on his shoulders, then started down the steep trail. The air grew warmer as he descended, but his burden was light.

The village leader was waiting. Omar paused at the door to his home, the finest mud hut in the village: three tiny rooms, an indoor cook stove, and the ultimate luxury, an ancient clay pipe that drew water from the river upstream and brought it right to his front door.

The leader was a young man, perhaps less than thirty, though his thick beard and sun-baked skin made it difficult for Omar to guess. He sat on the floor in the corner and listened to Omar while chewing brown leaves. His face was hard, but it softened as he studied the child.

"You take advantage of my generosity," the young shepherd said.

Omar shook his head. "I bring you a gift. A chance to serve Allah. I call upon the Pashtun law of sanctuary, and that is always good."

The leader stared and then nodded. Yes, that was true. And they were honor-bound, for Pashtun law required them to render aid to the homeless, the wounded, those who had no one else. Several times, the village leader had stood up to the Taliban, hiding young boys they had forced into service. On this matter the leader considered the Qur'an to be clear. He had a moral obligation to provide sanctuary and he would not disobey the holy word of God. And though the Taliban had threatened to destroy him and the village for defying them, they had not carried through with their promise, at least not yet.

The leader considered a moment, then walked toward the young boy. Kneeling, he smiled at him gently and held out his arms. Sensing the safety, the young prince walked into his embrace.

Omar watched, then reached into a deep pocket under his robe. "You will keep him," he said, pulling out a thick wad of cash.

The village leader glanced at the money, scowled, and looked away.

Omar extended his hand. "Not for you. For him. His expenses—"

"He will have no expenses that God will not provide. I don't do this for you, Omar. I do this for Allah. I do this for the law."

Omar nodded and begged forgiveness. Then he walked toward the young prince and knelt down by him. Reaching into another pocket, he pulled out a slender gold chain, thin and fine, with a single diamond attached at the end, a beautiful star radiating silver slivers of light. He unlatched the chain, placed it around the boy's neck, and kissed him on both cheeks. "I give you this to remind you of who you really are," he said. "You are the diamond of the future. You are worth every star."

The boy looked at the diamond, then at Omar, and he smiled wearily.

Does he really understand? Omar wondered. *Does he have any idea at all?*

He tucked the jewel under the young boy's clothes, placing it near his chest, then pulled back and held the prince by the shoulders. They stared at each other a long moment, as if they could communicate without saying words.

"What have I told you?" Omar finally asked him, breaking the heavy silence.

"You will come for me," the young prince said.

"That is my solemn promise."

The boy stared in silence at him.

"And until that day?" Omar asked.

"I am to prepare myself."

"Prepare yourself for what?"

The young boy lifted his chin and squared his shoulders, his eyes burning with a sudden light. "For the day that I will be king."

"You were born to be a king. You must prepare. You must be worthy. You will reclaim the kingdom. Now, I know that is difficult for you to understand, but you are wise, I can see that. Even now I can see there is wisdom and great strength in your eyes."

The young prince only nodded. Omar pointed at the shepherd. "You must listen to him."

"I will, Master."

Omar pressed his lips, then stood and touched the boy on his head.

He had no sons, only daughters, and he loved this young boy as if he were his own. He would have died to protect him. He would have done anything.

It was time to go. Omar drew a long breath. Looking around the room, he wished he could think of the right thing to say. Then he leaned toward the child and whispered in his ear:

Ye shall shine forth,
Ye shall be as the morning.
And ye shall be secure,
Because there is hope.

The ancient prophet Job had spoken those words such a long time ago. It wasn't much, but he meant it, and it was all he could think of to say. And the words were as true now as they had ever been.

"Hope. Always hope," he whispered to the young prince again.

East Side, Chicago

Azadeh stared at the tall building. The highway behind her was crowded and noisy, with honking taxis and the smell of burning fuel heavy in the air. The public housing was bland—not depressing, but close to it—a tall, tan-brick building covered with soot and small windows evenly spaced on all floors.

She stood alone at the front entrance to the building and stared.

Five steps up from the sidewalk. A metal, double door. A chrome bar for a handle. Thin panes of reinforced, covered glass.

She glanced at the small bag at her feet, which contained everything she owned. Lifting her eyes, she looked at the double doors again.

Inside, the woman was waiting.

A new life. A new home.

Her heart beat like a hammer, causing a rush through her head.

A new home. A new family. A new start in life. America was a strange place—generous, sometimes warm, sometimes cold, demanding, unforgiving, charitable always, but with certain expectations attached.

She took a deep breath, her dark hair covered in a simple blue scarf. Two young men, their dark skin ripped with muscles and barely covered with undersized body shirts, walked up the sidewalk toward her; she took a step back, embarrassed to see so much of their chests. They stared at her a moment, then walked into the building that would be her new home.

Azadeh followed them with her eyes, looking at the front door again.

The woman was in there waiting for her, on the other side of those doors. Her heart skipped a beat. She was terrified.

Then she heard it, in her mind. The words seemed to come out of nowhere, but they were crystal clear: the song that her father had sung to her since she was a child, before she was old enough to understand the meaning of the words that he sang:

The world that I give you
Is not always sunny and bright.
But knowing I love you
Will help make it right.
So when the dark settles,
And the storms fill the night,

Remember I'll be waiting
When it comes,
Morning Light.

Taking a breath, she walked up the steps and through the front door.

She stepped into a large foyer and looked around: brick walls, fluorescent lights, tile floor, cigarette machine and ashtrays, a couple of worn-out fabric sofas, a soda machine, and a chrome fountain that, judging from the rusted basin, no longer worked. The foyer smelled of stale cigarette smoke and appeared to be empty. Then Azadeh turned to her right.

The woman who had agreed to be her guardian was standing near the door that led into the stairwell. She looked shy, almost frightened. She was evidently new at this too. She was holding a package wrapped in white paper and tied with a bright bow. A small woman, she had the kindest smile Azadeh had ever seen.

The two women stared at each other: a proud black woman from the one of the poorest neighborhoods in the United States and a young girl from one of the poorest villages in Iran. Both were alone. Both were survivors. Both were hoping to find something more.

Azadeh took a step toward her. The woman held out the present, uncertainty in her eyes. "Welcome, Azadeh," she said cheerily, her voice was as warm as her smile.

Azadeh lowered her eyes, took the gift, and felt instantly at home.

Camp Smash
Eastern Iraq

Sam Brighton stared into the small fire. It was raining and, though his poncho kept him dry, he still felt chilled to the bone. There was a scattering of tents behind him, small, camouflaged units that sat low to the ground. There were a dozen or so men at Camp Smash, but Sam and Bono were the only ones around at the moment, almost three in the morning. Neither man was tired, though Sam was considering getting in a quick nap before the sun rose, if it ever would break through the clouds and light rain.

He glanced over at Bono, who had closed his eyes and tilted his head, as if he were listening to something in the night. Sam watched him a moment, then asked, "Bono, you served a mission, didn't you, buddy?"

Bono pressed his lips together and nodded, but his eyes remained closed.

"And you were . . . what do you call that, you know that president thing?"

"Elders quorum president."

"Yeah, that's it. You were one of those, right?"

"Yeah. In fact, I still am, or I used to be—I'm not sure about it now. I was the quorum president in our branch back at Camp Freedom, but we left so quickly I never even got a chance to talk to Major Bailey . . . "

"Okay, you know, whatever, you've got some experience. You could teach me, right?"

Bono tilted his head in the other direction, listening, keeping his eyes closed. "What do you want me to teach you?" he asked.

"I want to understand this church. I want to understand it all. I want to know what you know, what my mom knows, what my dad knew when he was alive. I've never really given it a chance, but I think I need to now."

Bono nodded slowly. "All right, I can do that. It would be a good thing."

Sam stared at him through the light of the flickering fire,

then, satisfied, lowered his head. The two men were silent while the fire simmered and popped. Sam relaxed, letting his chin drop until it hit his chest. He could sleep like that for hours.

He almost drifted off. But there was one more thing.

"Bono?" he asked.

"Yeah, buddy," the lieutenant answered.

"You know that King Abdullah ordered the nuclear attack on D.C."

Bono was silent a moment. "That's what we're hearing," he said.

"Then you know, once they confirm that, they're going to take him out. No way the U.S. isn't going to go after him. And if they do, they will use us. The Cherokees will go."

"Probably right."

Under his poncho, Sam folded his arms, holding them near his chest. "I guess I need to repent, then."

"Why's that, Sergeant Brighton?"

Sam shifted on his log. "He killed my dad, so many of our leaders, so many of our people, all of them innocent. How many women and children? The whole thing makes me sick—I mean, physically ill!

"Now I want to be the one who gets him. I want revenge. I want justice. I don't feel any mercy toward him. I know that's not right, and I've tried, but I can't bring myself to feel much of anything else."

Bono opened his eyes and looked at Sam, then shifted to stare into the dark. The fire popped and sizzled as the drizzle came down. The night was calm and heavy and the smoke seemed to linger, not lifting into the air.

But Bono didn't answer. Truth was, he felt the same way.

TWO BLOCKS SOUTH OF THE WASHINGTON D.C. LDS TEMPLE
KENSINGTON, MARYLAND

Sara stood at the crest of the hill. Around her, the leaves and bushes, generally full and green at this time of year, had turned brown and brittle. The sky was dark, with gray ash hanging in the air and a low bank of rain clouds forming on the western horizon.

For more than a week, she and her two sons had been wandering around the outskirts of the city, seeking information on her husband, trying to confirm his death, trying to get as close to the bomb site as they safely could. But after it all, they had ended up here, near the temple grounds, the primary reason being that there was a small hill just a few blocks to the east from which they could look south onto downtown D.C.

Sara stood on the hill. This was as close as she could get. Behind her, the temple spires jutted up from the trees, the glistening marble a glaring contrast to the brown leaves and dirty air. The temple had no exterior windows, so little damage had been done; some of the houses to the south had had their windows blown out.

Turning, Sara Brighton looked toward the district again. Farther south, the damage became more stark and terrible. If she squinted, she could make out bent metal girders and burned-out cement walls in the distance. The damage was eerie and irregular, for the aircraft that had been carrying the bomb had been lower than the Saudi scientist had hoped it would be, and so the blast from the heat wave had followed the contours of the ground, burning everything it touched directly but sparing those buildings that were protected behind any rising terrain. It was remarkable, almost unnatural, how some areas had been spared. Arlington National Cemetery—destroyed up to the crest of the hill, yet General's Lee's mansion and the graves on the western side of the hill had been spared. The White House and Mall—entirely destroyed, but some of the smaller buildings directly behind them had survived the attack. Most of the government offices housing the Congress had been destroyed, but the northern wing of the Capitol Hill building was still intact. The list went on and on, and a pattern began to emerge: areas west and south of the Potomac had been spared; east and north, turned to ash.

Sara squinted again, then lifted her hand to her shade her eyes. Luke and Ammon waited behind her, their heads bent, looking down. It was just too hard to look at, too painful, too bleak. Their mother stood without moving, then turned back to them. "I wish they would let us go down there . . . you know, just to see."

Ammon nodded, but inside he was very relieved. He had seen enough—more than enough. He knew his father was dead, killed in the blast, and he didn't feel a need to explore the place where he had died.

Luke shook his head. The last thing he wanted was to see any more.

It would be months, maybe much longer, before civilians would be allowed to go into any of the areas that had been affected by the blast. Out here in the suburbs, where the winds had kept the radiation at an acceptable level, refugee camps and tent cities had already sprung up, but downtown was deserted except for the special military units and emergency response teams, all of them protected in radiation suits. The teams were plodding through the wreckage, looking for survivors and chronicling the damage for the day when they might be able to rebuild, or at least go in and try to retrieve some of the documents, government records, and artifacts the government needed in order to exist.

But the truth was, there wasn't much left of the federal

government. It would take a long time and a lot of work to rebuild it completely.

Sara thought for a moment longer, then walked toward her sons. The great white temple rose behind them, a beautiful castle glistening against the gray sky. She nodded to it, and the two boys turned. "I'm so relieved it wasn't damaged," she said. "I love this place. I've always loved it. We were sealed as a family here."

Ammon studied the temple and then turned to his mother. "It's time now," he said. "We've really got to decide."

Sara shook her head. She knew that. She'd been avoiding the decision because she felt so unsure. "What do you think?" she asked Ammon.

"I don't know, Mom. I really don't . . . "

Luke pushed a dirty hand through his hair. "We should go west, to Salt Lake. That's what we should do."

Sara cocked her head toward him. "You really think so?" she asked.

"Yeah, Mom, I'm certain. There's nothing left here for us now."

"But Salt Lake . . . we have no family there . . . " Sara's forehead creased in doubt.

"We are the only Church members in our family. We have lots of friends in Utah, friends who believe the same way we do. We need their strength now. It will be safe if we can get there. I feel certain that is where we should go."

Sara listened, frowning.

"It will be nearly impossible to get there," Ammon quickly said. He glanced over at his brother. "We don't know if the roads will be open. Will we be able to buy gas? Food? Find a place to stay? There will be gangs and vigilantes. We've heard how dangerous it is now. I don't know . . . I don't know . . . " His voice trailed off. "But when I think of staying here," he continued, "when I consider any other option, then I think Luke is probably right. It will be hard, even dangerous, but I think it's the best choice we have."

Sara nodded slowly, lifting her gaze to the temple again. "I miss my husband," she whispered as her eyes filled with tears. Ammon held out his arms and moved toward her, but she took a step back, raising her hands to stop him, forcing herself to keep her emotions under control. "When I realized that your father had been taken, I only kept breathing because I knew God wanted me to live," she said.

Then she paused and sighed deeply, her face turning peaceful and calm. She lifted her eyes to the dark sky and thought for a while. "I love it here," she repeated quietly, as if she were talking to herself. "It is so peaceful, so still, even in the midst of the storm, so calming, so eternal. I mean, look around: We are in the midst of destruction, yet standing here, under these crystal-white spires, I can remember there is more. More in our lives. More in the eternities. More things we must do.

"It wasn't fair that your father died, but this life isn't fair. God never said that only the evil would die in these days. Even the good, sometimes *especially* the good, will be called on to sacrifice. It has always been that way. The pioneers lost some of their best on the trail leading away from Nauvoo—innocent women, sometimes children, all of them paid a price. Can we expect our days to be different? I don't think *that* would be fair."

A sudden wind blew through the trees, fresh and cold. It made her arms tingle, and she took a deep breath. "Do you understand what I'm saying?" she asked her sons.

Ammon and Luke met her eyes, but they didn't reply.

No, they didn't see it. But she knew that someday they would.

"There is much more to come," she continued. "Heartaches, I'm sure, but I think there will be many incredibly good things as well. There will be more opportunities to do the Lord's work than we've ever had before, more ways we can serve him, more people who need us than ever before."

She stopped a moment, looking hard at her sons. Her eyes bored into them, steely with her resolve. "You are the fulfillment of scripture," she whispered to them. *"You were sent to be a light unto the world, and to be the saviors of men."*

"But my father . . . " Ammon said, his voice choking and tight.

"Your father is busy on the other side of the veil. He had to be taken from us; that was part of the plan. God wasn't taken by surprise. *We* just didn't know it was coming, and so we were left unprepared. But that doesn't mean it wasn't supposed to happen."

Luke walked toward her. "What do we do, then?" he asked.

"We have hope. We have faith. That is all that we have left. We play our part. We keep walking. We do what God asks us to do."

Ammon's lower jaw trembled as he struggled inside. "I don't know if I can do that."

"Of course you can, son."

"I want to . . . I want to . . . but I don't know how."

"You wake up. You keep praying. You have patience and you wait." There was no more heartache or sadness wringing Sara's eyes. She looked strong, and it seemed as if a soft, unseen ember had been lit in her soul.

"You have been saved for these days," Sara said to her sons. "I was sent to be your mother, to prepare you for what will come. You each have a mission to fulfill. Our days are not yet finished; we have much work to do. I know that. I can feel it. The Spirit tells me it is true."

She paused, her face certain.

"We will go to Utah," she concluded. "We will find a place to live there, and we will make a new home. And once we are settled, we will ask God what he wants us to do. Then we will work to further his kingdom until his Son comes back to earth."

about the author

Chris Stewart is a *New York Times* bestselling author and world-record-setting Air Force pilot. His previous military techno-thrillers for the national market have been selected by the Book of the Month Club and published in twelve different countries. He has also been a guest editorialist for the *Detroit News,* commenting on matters of military readiness and national security. Chris is president and CEO of The Shipley Group, a nationally recognized consulting and training company. In addition to the highly acclaimed series *The Great and Terrible,* he is the coauthor of the bestselling book *Seven Miracles That Saved America.* Chris and his wife, Evie, are the parents of six children and live in Utah.